Sacred Dust

DAVID HILL

SACRED DUST

Published by
Delacorte Press
Bantam Doubleday Dell Publishing Group, Inc.
1540 Broadway
New York, New York 10036

ISBN 0-385-31534-1

Manufactured in the United States of America

To Lonnie

Heartfelt thanks to the following angels, living and departed:

Patty Mayer, Steve Malin, Marjorie Braman, Lea Queener, Linda Oates, Sunta Izicuppo, Michael Jeter, Muffin, Libby Boone, Michael Cherry, Marion Brayton, Bob and Betty Hill, John Pielmeier, Martha Holifield, Gary Cearlock, Kate Permenter, Jeanine Edmunds, and Ed Schmidt.

I am also grateful to: Phylicia Rashad, John Irving, Tennessee Williams, John Matoian, Sarah V. Clement, Virginia Woolf, The New Dramatists, Lisa Bankoff, Phil Rose, Linda Woolverton, and Jeanne Williams.

Say to those who are of a fearful
heart,
"Be strong! Fear not!
Behold, your God
will come with vengeance,
With the recompense of God,
He will come and save you."

Then the eyes of the blind shall
be opened,
And the ears of the deaf
unstopped;
Then shall the lame man leap
like a hart,
And the tongues of the dumb
sing for joy.

Isaiah 35, Verses 4–6

Sacred Dust

Before "the Trouble"

Old people down here still say "the Trouble." That house was built . . . or that family left town . . . or there hasn't been an ice storm like this since . . .

Before "the Trouble"

. . . means all that began with the universe and it was our cradle, our fresh clean toes tucked between sheets perfumed by the meadow sun as we slept in our houses across a dirt road from each other. . . .

Before "the Trouble" was only called time back then, our time to taste warm night air laced with the new leaves or the coming of autumn or fresh turned earth. It was our grassy eternity of childhood peeping through the sorghum jungle into the cemetery at black faces long tormented with lament and the singer was shrill as a jay and held us under her mournful spell and we were thrilled to know there was a dead man in that casket.

Even the morning of the day that snaked into the night when eternity split was before: warm wet earth sinking under racing bare feet. How deceptive, our snug, our final, four-cornered wild rose Saturday together.

Even so passing over late Saturday morning, without a sign, boding presence or premonition—no warning bell! The dust road coil-

ing through our woods was not, had never been, a road, rather the submerged spine of a three-clawed Sleeping Evil.

Nor did we imagine in our fast fading sublime then time the perfumed breeze warming our necks as we sang and waded in the stream was no breeze, rather the slow waking breath of the consuming Serpent.

We talked our favorite old different sides of the same coin litany.

"I'm eight and you're eight."

"I'm eight and you're eight; I like horses and you like horses."

"I'm eight and you're eight; I like horses and you like horses; my name's Miller and your name's Miller." Moena had added something I never knew.

"How'd we get the same name?"

"Your great-granddaddy give it to my great-granddaddy when he bought him."

All was in perfect, as ever and always, asymmetrical balance as we dried our blue tingling toes in the sun and Moena, a stalk of sweet straw wedged into the groove behind her singing tooth let slip that Beauty B. was making me a doll for my August birthday, a gypsy fortune teller from a magazine picture Mother showed her.

We were imperious to assume August, arrogant to proclaim dominion over pasture, creek and wood. We held each other our most sacred protectorate, hopelessly confusing ourselves with each other.

The straight up sun announced dinner which was what you called the big Saturday noon meal back then in Prince George in the country.

Half past noon and our white sprawling house creaked amiably. The meal was still drifting onto the table. Saturday dinner was Hattie and Florence's chore. Washed up, I sat down to await Hattie's rolls. I vamped and blinked repeatedly at Father's "Where'd you get to all morning, Eula?"

Flossy spoke, nervously obsessed about dangerous railroad tramps which Mother rightly guessed came of reading trash novels. Mother off on a sermon about mental putrefaction and the wages of disobedience. Now she cut her eyes at Hattie who had charged several yards of expensive silk to Daddy without his permission.

There was a distant booming like thunder. Fate was galloping towards us on horseback.

Fate was galloping towards us, but silently.

One o'clock. Dessert was peach cobbler. We lingered in the dining room, almost bilious and quite giddy and ignorant of the invisible threads of fate gathering and twisting and knotting up into a hard, thick noose.

In the dying light of the day under the night God forsook us, before the shining gold mist of first dusk leapt into darkness, I sat nervously in the dining room waiting with Hattie for the doctor because Wee Mama had turned badly again. I was all dread and thrill to watch her die and do the grown-up things I dreamt of, washing the corpse, setting the hair, seeing her laid out in the beautiful box. It was already a brooding Paradise, sitting alone with Hattie, listening for the doctor in the chair with cracked wooden seat that pinched you if you stood up too fast. There was a long low rumble like distant thunder. Hattie asked if it was sprinkling.

I went out on the front porch to see. It was a clear, windless night waiting for a moon. No, it wasn't sprinkling.

It was raining pure brimstone evil.

1
Hezekiah
(1941)

They had hung Seraphine by a rope around her neck from a bough of a cypress that snaked out over the river. She looked like a sacrifice to some oozing god of the waters. Her tight blond plaits had worked loose, probably in the struggle or while they were raping her. Her eyes had been plucked out. Her teeth were broken. The men had known that eventually the rope would rot. What the buzzards left of her would slip into the silt beneath the shallow water.

He had no time to bury her. He shinnied up the tree and crawled out to the rope. He drew his knife from his back pocket and sliced it. She dropped into the black river. He watched the shining circles widen until the surface was glassy again. Twice he quieted the voice that urged him to leap in after her. Then he ran.

He ran north through shallow cypress ponds, through red and black leafy sludge into thick, wet night, stopping only long enough to catch his breath or draw some swamp water to his parched lips and then spit it out again because there was fever in it. He kept his eyes darting over the endless places where men and alligators could hide while his ears searched around and above. Eventually he reached some solid ground and he kept to the grassy edge of a logging trail when there was enough wagon rut and moonlight to make it out.

Sometimes a shack sat too close to the road and its dogs threatened. He would cut a wide circle through low marsh and brush to pass it safely. He stumbled onto a rusted pair of iron rails and followed it to a creeping strand of open boxcars. But it was rolling east towards towns and certain death. By midnight the mosquitoes had drawn bleeding sores up and down his arms and at the back of his neck. Night vanished behind a second day. He crossed more swamp and the sky was dark and the rain came in sheets. By first dusk he scraped at more than a hundred bites on his face.

They said you died slow with the fever. They said you shivered and your eyes burned in their sockets and you choked on your own scorching spit. They said no one would come near you right on your last because your breath could flood their bodies with the same wretched agony. So far there was only the itching, the swirling head and the rattle in his chest. He'd have to travel north for a week before he could risk conversation with any man black or white. He might make it.

Once he saw a lantern light dipping down under leaves behind him and he adjusted his course to the right and back, circling behind the men. He climbed a tree and looked for their campfire. But there was only endless night and the fragile blur of a dying moon behind a starless sky. He crept through sinking blackness, pausing only long enough to feel the mud cover the top of his shoe, and then he lifted his foot and stepped and then the other, pausing again and lifting, stepping, hands seeking vainly for ballast, and finally he stumbled upward and waited on solid earth for the moon or daybreak or death or an angel of God.

His body begged for sleep. He knew if he accommodated his aching limbs and heavy eyelids he might slumber forever. He closed his burning left eye, measuring the relief by a count of five, and then the right, six-seven-eight-nine. . . . Now he opened the left before it stuck and now the right. He repeated the ritual until the blackness was dappled and scratched with dark purple that faded into infinite blue behind vine laced hulks of cypresses and oaks. A jagged thread of pink and orange broke and spread low on the horizon. A sudden fluttering overspread the twisted treetops. The virulent marsh echoed and trembled with the sawing screams and hacked-off moans of a billion birds of prey. An arc of red sun began to swell into a bloody orange sphere that floated up. The blighted velvet night withdrew behind a veil of blinding silver mist. He bore forward wading grassy pools of shining black, now ankle, now shoulder, now waist deep swamp.

The voice of every hunted creature's need of heaven sprang from the unyielding mire.

Cut your reason away from your pain and hold it out in front of you and follow it.

Now he was lost. Now he belonged to the swamp and the fever. His cracked lips were scabbed and bloody. Try as he would to outrun it, the inferno roared in his chest threatening to consume his shirt. When his boots grew too heavy, he dropped down and pulled them off. He filled them with mud and buried them in a wet sandbank. He went on, slowly now, his fingers pulling and pinching his stinging flesh. The ground beneath his bare feet was warm and soft. It tried to suck him home as he moved over it. He'd never make it.

His best option was to sink into sleep and let their dogs sniff him down cold and lifeless. If he was still alive, he prayed only that he would hear them coming, that he would manage to run a little and force them to shoot him in the back. Otherwise they would torture him. He went to his knees in the sand. Every burning cell clung to the earth. His torn and swollen lips pressed the moist dirt. He smacked endless clumps of leafy brown soil into his tormented flesh. Now a thousand itching craters of infected blood boiled. He wailed in excruciation, madly sanding his limbs against the razored bark of a tree until he was covered with a syrup of blood and dirt. Possessed by searing torture, he slammed his skull into the dense wooden trunk over and over until, mercifully, he plummeted into insensate oblivion.

When he came to midmorning sun drilled through his eyelids and he was blinded by glaring yellow mist. By sustained effort of trembling arms, he forced his throbbing head and torso up into a sitting position. When the mist was thinner he saw a grassy break in the woods, a fit enough place for dying. It was a quarter of a mile up a sandy knoll to the clearing. He managed to approximate a standing position by pressing his back into a tree trunk while clutching its lower limbs and coaxing his leaden legs into straightening. He listed with nausea. His legs couldn't hold him. He held himself at three fourths of a standing position until his bony hands and arms threatened to shatter. He dropped back to the ground, and gathering his dwindling breath, he crawled towards the clearing, taking long rests every ten or fifteen feet. First dusk had faded purple when he reached the edge of the clearing and noticed the building.

It was new. It looked to be a barn that had changed its mind and tried to become a house. There was no clear trace of whoever had built it and no sign of a reason why. It was full night before he leaned his shoulder into the wooden door and it swung inward. Hez crawled inside. It only had one room. The dry mud floor had been pounded smooth with a wooden mallet. The scent of the thin pine walls and tar paper roof reminded him of the turpentine farm, of South Carolina, of the life that was oozing out of him. The acrid stench of the newly milled pine kept the mosquitoes away.

The gates of hell were opening. A black winged bat with the face of a child was looking in a book for his name.

Hez moved in his sleep. He floated up out of sheltering oblivion. There was a pillow under the back of his head and a blanket covered his torso. Someone had removed his outer garments, bathed him and rubbed camphor all over his body. The nightmare itch was gone. The running sores had started to dry into scabs. A strong male tenor voice rang out.

> *"Say to him of fearful heart,*
> *Be strong. Fear not!"*

Hez was too weak to move. He couldn't draw enough wind to push his voice past the door. He faded back into sleep.

Joseph had returned from his supply trip four days after Hez crept into his building to die on its smooth earth floor. The boy's breathing was so slow that Joseph took him for a corpse. He rolled him over with the toe of his boot thinking to check his pockets. Hez coughed.

Yellow fever. Worse ways to go—especially for a wanted colored boy running circles in a white man's swamp.

Joseph pulled the comatose adolescent into a sitting position and beat his back until green spume covered his trousers and lay in a puddle on the floor. He squeezed a wet handkerchief over his mouth, repeatedly moistening his parched tongue and throat. Then he stripped him and laid him on a blanket in the sun to treat his jaundice. Later he balanced the boy's head on his chest and spoon-fed him broth and herbs. He repeated the ritual several times.

It was night when Hez woke again. It was pitch black inside the barn and the air was close. For a moment he thought he was dead in his grave. Then he pushed blankets and straw away from his face and there was a little light. He smelled smoke and meat. He sat up slowly. He had dreamed of flames, but that must have been the fire in his chest. There was only one way out of the barn and that was through the open door where the man leaned over the fire. Hez slowly pulled himself to his feet and the room swirled. He sat back down and when the spinning stopped, he stood up again. He moved warily towards the door frame.

Joseph was bent over, stoking the fire. He was a sinewy, long jawed man with enormous round blue eyes and long, wavy silver blond hair brushed back and tamed by a leather string at the nape of his neck. He was all angles. His wide shoulder span spread over an incongruously narrow frame. Joseph looked up over the fire at him. From full front Hez saw taut skin stretched into a handsome skull face. Obviously not one of those who hunted him. They wouldn't have stopped to build a fire. They would've dragged him out and hung him straight off.

"Welcome to the Ebenezer Tabernacle." His half smile revealed two abundantly supplied rows of perfect pearl enameled teeth. His slightly elongated incisors lent substance to his beautiful face.

Hez squinted at him. He coughed up some dried blood. It lodged like a handful of broken glass in his throat.

"Hezekiah, is it?"

The man knew his name. It didn't bode well. He had been drawn into consciousness by his hunger and his need to piss. Joseph was turning bacon in a new iron skillet which he had placed on a bed of rocks in the middle of the fire. He was young despite his gray hair. His boots were new and they had cost plenty. Hez had worked enough mercantile to know the price of things. The sweet scent of sizzling pork liberated a new wave of nausea. He lurched away to puke in the circling darkness.

When it was finished, he sat down in the tall grass. His breathing steadied. Bit by bit his nausea eased. He returned to the fire and sat down.

"Hungry?"

Hez nodded. He stepped into the shadows to piss. He came back and sat down and the man handed him a plate. The pair of them ate in silence.

There are eternal things that thump between opaque leaves and yellow blotches of sun when no men are there to disturb them. There are living rings of purple and pulsing swirls of red that float between the air and the eye and reveal themselves to the Chosen.

Hez figured it was the fever that spoke. He was certain it wasn't the man. Maybe it was the echo of one of Beauty B.'s sermons from the tall old days in South Carolina. She had often spoken of a sky choked with falling celestial beings. He pushed the obligatory words through the cinders in his chest.

"Mighty good, mister."

"Get you some more."

"Not just now, thank you."

"Where are you headed?"

"South Carolina. How far above the Everglades are we?"

"You're smack in the middle of the Everglades." Hez had been running in circles. Joseph's eyes weren't blue. They were gray. They looked as if some event or cataclysm or revelation had drawn all the hue out of them. They invited you in. They locked into Hez's again and a silent voice traveled out of them. Fever, madness or revelation—it was all the same to Hez as the firelight diminished and he pondered his stalking death.

"They won't be after you tonight. I seen them in Bellefleur twenty miles south of here this morning. They had left two back in the swamp with the fever. There were only four. They was ragged and hungry and wet to the bone. They wanted dry rooms and hot baths and whiskey. Bellefleur is nothing but a strip of whorehouses. They won't make it this far before midmorning."

How did he know? And why'd he shelter and heal him? Very possibly a stratagem. He could be fattening Hez up like a goose before killing-time. There was no measuring human perversity. Still, there was no sign of complication or deviousness about him. He seemed to be whatever he was right out in plain view.

"I best be on."

"Pick your dying tree and wait for them beneath it. There's a five thousand dollar price on your head."

This time when he heard the voice he was sure it was Beauty B. come down with the Angel of Death to bear him the last mile of the way.

"Follow me home."

It was her, clean and close.

"Hezekiah, the son of Ahaz, king of Judah." The man smiled. "I'm Joseph. Called up of God and sent into the wilderness to build His tabernacle."

Hez shook his hand. Joseph handed him a cup of warm chocolate.

"What evil possessed you to take up with a white woman?"

Hez stared into the fire.

Joseph was silent for about five minutes.

"If you was mine to judge, I'd judge you hard," he said. "But that's Jehovah's office."

When full darkness had fallen, they went into Joseph's citadel and lay down on opposite sides of the room on the packed dirt floor.

"You lie still when they come. I'll do the rest."

After the fire had died in the clearing and the moon was hidden behind the trees, Hez spoke to the darkness.

"Mister, what are you saving me for?"

"Lord God Jehovah ain't delivered you from swamp and fever to the Ebenezer Tabernacle so you can die at their hands, boy."

"But you're against what I done."

"What you done makes my flesh crawl. It blasphemously violates God's natural order. You'll suffer God's eternal judgment soon enough. But Jehovah sent you to test my heart. Do I willingly serve mankind? Can I overlook the most heinous sins and minister to one and all?"

It blasphemously violates God's natural order.

A burning sorrow dropped over him like a heavy iron chain. Joseph's Lord God Jehovah had abandoned Seraphine to a hideous death. It cut the faith out of Hez's heart and scattered it in the darkness. He listened for Beauty B., but no words came. Only death —Seraphine's and his. Hers was already carved into the past. His crept towards him through the woods while Joseph slept.

You'll suffer God's eternal judgment soon enough. . . .

Because dying is remembering all things experienced or told, his mind ran downhill through his short past and farther below his past to long before he was born. He remembered the thing they had all admonished him never to forget. Grandfather and Beauty B. and his mother, Moena, were tortured and then chased as human prey. For the vile offense of their dark skin they were driven out of Alabama in the night. Beauty B. had held him under the pump when he was five and sworn him to know that one thing above all others as if it contained the secret of life.

"Stoned, driven, ridden out, plucked like the eyes of a dead cow, cut out like an infected boil from our own farm and thrown to the winds." He had been too frightened and too cold with the water running down his naked back to ask why or how that cataclysmic event had come to pass. "No more inviolate ground where our dead might sleep undisturbed and dissolve with time into sacred dust—and that means you, nigger child, mean no more to this world than a mangy stray mongrel dog! Don't you never forget that you're cursed. Bend low. Trust no white man. Or find yourself hung by the throat and your flesh on fire! Do you hear me, boy?"

He had inherited that curse. It ransacked his dreams. It washed over him at unexpected moments. A sudden, boiling tide rose out of the void behind him and sucked him choking, facedown, farther and farther through foaming fetid liquid nothing before plunging him into the icy, airless black depths, and his bones screamed as a hundred million mounted demons swarmed over him on flaming hooves. Then the swirling water spiraled into a vortex and he was drawn by burning wind to the screaming surface and slapped back by a tide of blood to the dead sand shore.

He woke and wondered in the glistening blue black darkness how the platinum stars held fast to the sky, how the moon still glowed green through broad leaves and a dulcet thrush cried out for its mate, how he could be moved by such tender things and yet despised, *chased as human prey. . . .*

He would die in the night. He would die in the morning or on the following afternoon. Die and face damnation and torment for violating the natural order. . . .

He had planted the forbidden seed of his destruction deep within Seraphine. The men would pull his arms out of their sockets and break his feet. They would flatten his face and twist his lower legs around until his knees snapped. Only then would they lay the rope around his neck. Then as the rope clenched and the neck bones cracked, they would douse him with kerosene and hell would be a relief.

"Behold, your God will come with vengeance, with the recompense of God. He will come and save you."

Joseph of God had risen. He sat watch high in a magnolia. It was a clear night and the breeze had chased the damp. If by some miracle this wild hermit stood apart from them, he would pose no more obstacle than a drop of rain moving against a drought. If . . .

When they arrived, the zealot would ad-lib to save his own neck. He would say that he had captured Hez in his barn and he was holding him for the reward. It might well be the truth. It might be the man had no stomach, as many don't, for killing. It might be he wanted the sin on others' souls; he was leaving the actual torment and murder to the others.

Or he might mean what he said about protecting him.

Hez tried to squeeze a drop of light from the dry heap of facts the old people had told him about his birth. He couldn't specifically invoke when or how he understood that Moena, the shy, mumbling woman who visited from Charleston, was the vessel which had borne him from creation and deposited him like thieves' cargo on the indifferent banks of the great world. It was as given and true as the root of a tree or his obedience to the unuttered command that he neither address nor consider her as mother. The father seed had affixed itself like a blight within her deepness. She had come home swollen and, so he overheard the women who washed Beauty B. for burial whisper, ignorant of her condition. Hez still marveled that Grandfather hadn't beaten Moena to death for her pernicious humanity.

Moena had surrendered him to Beauty B. and Grandfather on the night of his birth. It was said that she left without a word the next morning for Charleston. Shortly thereafter God rescinded her eyesight. Her visits to the turpentine farm ceased. Only his most concerted mental effort would produce an approximated blur of Moena's physical shape. The impact of her abandonment, however, was an open wound the intervening years could only deepen.

Memory attempted to etch Beauty B.'s shining purple sorrow, her baleful almond eyes and her upright, sanctified visage in Moena's place. Yet she had never offered herself as a replacement for his mother. Beauty B. had already become sanctified, she was already three quarters out of her flesh.

She eschewed all routine and understood things. Nothing that could be described or experienced engaged her. She might sit entranced on a yard stump three days and nights gibbering. Or lay her fork on her supper plate to wipe her lip and remain frozen, the napkin between her fingers, until sunrise.

A gnarled limb of green oak had hissed pale blue smoke from its bed of embers since dusk. A sudden troupe of dancing yellow and white flames leapt across it. Its reflection shone in the tree branches overhead. What had been hovering darkness burst into a thousand shining fragments. Presently soft raindrops thumped and twittered the leaves.

He remembered about coming up a child on the little turpentine farm with Beauty B. and Grandfather. He remembered Beauty B.'s preaching, her gyrating, hypnotic orations and mystic visions on Sunday evenings in the woods. Her foaming lips were spewing fountains of increasingly incomprehensible oracle, divination and prophecy which dazzled and soothed ever growing numbers of the devout and the curious. Sometimes she would lift Hez naked before the assembly crying out that he was the bastard child of the bastard child of the Bastard Child of God. Once she placed him on a tree stump, offering him as a sacrificial oblation and igniting the base of the trunk, which she had soaked with kerosene. As the mortified child screamed inside the circle of rising flames, she ordered silent obeisance to Jehovah's will. If the stump and the child were consumed by her mad conflagration, then Jehovah had willed it His holy pyre. If the blaze went out or burned away from the stump, then the boy was anointed of God to deliver them from oppression. The fire had gone out quickly, but Hez still marveled that all those people would have sat there and watched him die. Not because they were bad or indifferent or deluded like Beauty B. It was her inexplicable power to charm and entrance.

Hez lay in the dark room waiting for death and trying to count the times Beauty B. had instructed him that a righteousness would wake in him one day. She fervently believed her own oracles. He had been sent like Christ to be raised in modest circumstance, an unlikely crown prince who would don the mantle of divine favor and show his people the way. He was her sacred charge. She compelled him to memorize tedious, ineluctable passages of Scripture.

She enforced three day fasts. She kept him separate from other children and worldly influence. She washed his feet. She dripped hot oils over his head. She beat him regularly to exorcise demons.

He remembered Grandfather's meanness and how the old man would drink moonshine of a night and go out and find a low down woman and bring her home. He would pull Beauty B. out of their bed by her hair and have the woman while Beauty B. and Hez sat on the porch reciting, "Genesis, Exodus, Leviticus, Numbers . . ." and on down. Beauty B. was never more serene than when they sat in the darkness while her husband and another woman set the iron headboard knocking on the other side of the wall. Grandfather beat his women after he had them. They always fought back, especially at first. Gradually the shrieking and slamming sounds would become a battery of muted thuds as he punched her unconscious. Sometimes the first blue haze of morning hung over the pine groves before the bruised, half-mutilated good time girl trudged across the front yard, her sporadic wails diminishing gradually as she moved up the road.

He intuited things he would never say to Beauty B. or Grandfather. For one, Beauty B. was a part of Grandfather's strange rituals with his sluts. The hapless tramps had no way of knowing it, but she was a means of communicating some private information that only Grandfather and Beauty B. understood. For another, Beauty B. was only about half as sanctified as she tried to be. Her holy priestess of the woods was for the most part an act. It dressed up her day to day despair and lent an exotic patina to her haunted existence. Part of what Grandfather did on those interminable, bleak nights when Hez and Beauty sat vigil wrapped in quilts on hard wooden porch benches or, looking back now, perhaps most of it, was an effort to effect behavior as bizarre and hurtful to his grandmother as hers was to him. Beauty's serenity on those occasions was because she understood Grandfather's intent. She found it touching that he still wanted and needed to converse with someone she had once been. If it wasn't an expression of affection, it at least acknowledged they had once owned a farm, shared a passion and conceived a daughter in a sane place and time now lost forever.

There was tacit, mutual awareness that each was only the true and logical result of the displacement and disillusionment born one evil Alabama night. It was no more or less than the madness of two people who shared an untenable loss.

The summer after his twelfth birthday, Beauty was struck dead by lightning as she ranted in tongues from the back of a wagon at an all day June singing. They had buried Beauty B. without his ever having gotten a clear understanding of why she and Grandfather and Moena had been ripped up and run out of Alabama.

Grandfather didn't run with women after that. He took Beauty's electrocution as a Sign that God would not long suffer her false righteousness. He was disconsolate and sat weeping on the front porch in the evenings calling out to the empty air in the vain hope of invoking her spirit. Eventually Grandfather got himself up like a bishop in his old starched Presbytery and his one decent pair of shoes, rubbed the ache out of his arthritic joints with pine pitch, and habitually walked three miles every Sunday morning and Wednesday evening to attend church service.

Joseph's breathing was long and heavy. Every moment of this interminable night was a discomfiting blanket of eternity and dread. Something pattered like distant hooves. Hez sat forward, straining to hear their voices as his executioners approached. Rain. It was only rain and the swamp would be impassable until it stopped. It fell steadily for half an hour.

South Carolina.

Hez got to thinking about Mercelle Scott, the ugliest girl in South Carolina—black or white. Mercelle had waked him to the little thrill of doing it when he was seventeen and she was fifteen. He thought she was doing him a big favor; he thought she knew worlds he didn't, so he went on down there to the woods with her a few dozen times and engaged in that rippling pleasure.

Eventually he grew tired of Mercelle and he wanted to expand his experience with other girls. Mercelle went crazy with rage when Hez quit her. She followed him to the turpentine groves and plagued him with tears and threats all day. When his indifference to her bleating finally sank in, Mercelle turned mean. She took to telling around the county that Hez was courting Rayetta Flowers, a white girl who lived up the road.

Rayetta Flowers was twice as common as Mercelle and her people were poorer than Grandfather. Mercelle did a big job of talking. When Rayetta's daddy, a Pentecost preacher, caught a tale that his daughter was screwing a nigger boy, he didn't wait for confirmation. Rayetta's daddy beat her unconscious and when she came to, he beat her until she was blind in her right eye.

That night a storm of white men came into Grandfather's yard demanding for Hez. Hez had hid under the porch and listened while Grandfather, who all the white men thought they knew and liked, stood on the porch with his rifle and told them he had beaten Hez and the evil boy had run off in mortal shame. Grandfather waxed his fiction for ten minutes, all about how he intended to be there when they strung up the low, bastard nigger. From his hiding place, Hez heard his grandfather beg the honor of laying the noose around his neck when they caught up with him. The men took off, noisily theorizing about where Hez had run and frantic with the need to find him before he got too far.

Grandfather gave Hez ten dollars and found him a ride on a pickup down into the Florida Everglades where he was to track down an uncle who worked in the produce fields. No one in south Florida had seen or heard of this uncle. Hez lost the tag end of his cash in a poker game. For a while he survived on piecework, mostly picking lettuce.

Lettuce season was already dwindling when Hez got to south Florida. Pretty soon he found himself out of work with less than a dollar in his pocket. He tried a sawmill, but all the workers were white. However, the supervisor, who lived in a rooming house close by, said Mrs. Jackson, his widow landlady, was half crazy with work and looking for some good, cheap help.

Mrs. Jackson had a sprawling white clapboard house with wide porches and green striped canvas awnings and tall dormers poking out the third floor. She kept it freshly painted against the damp. It was known as the cleanest rooming house between St. Petersburg and Miami. Directly behind it, a long dock reached out into the river.

He didn't know how it would sit, a dark stranger moving straight up the front steps and onto the porch. But he saw no other entrance except from the dock and that could only be accessed from the river, which was actually a swamp that narrowed and deepened into a proper channel a few miles downstream. She was a white lady and kept her priority, but Mrs. Seraphine Jackson was also young and friendly. She sat him down on the front porch and she had the kitchen girl bring him cool cider. She smelled nice. She was pretty and she had a directness that told you immediately she was a good woman. She inquired about his schooling and his habits. She explained that she needed general help. Hez would be expected to do the heavy household work. She was without a cook as well and would need him in the kitchen for preparation of the boarders' evening meal. She wanted someone who would learn fast and not wait to be told if wood needed gathering or the porch wanted sweeping. For his labor he would receive room and board and eighteen dollars a week.

Hez settled into an attic room and fell into a daily routine. "Miss Seraphine" Jackson was an excellent teacher, and once she saw that Hez was a boy of good sense and character, she began to invest him with the subtler duties of a large house. Hez, who had never earned so much for doing so little, quickly took on a hundred routine chores without reminder or remonstrance. The arrangement suited each of them beyond their expectations.

He quickly came to know the names and faces of the boarders, congenial white men who supervised various local trades in and near the swamps. He came to understand their willingness to pay Miss Seraphine Jackson's fifty cents more per week than other boardinghouses in the area. She sold them a modicum of civility, a pretense towards elegance that workingmen who raise themselves to low supervisory positions will immediately seek as proof of their exalted station.

Miss Seraphine didn't allow them to imbibe liquor or bring women on her premises, so the boarders were either in bed asleep or amusing themselves elsewhere in the evenings. Nights calmed down early and Hez slept deeper in his attic room than he had ever slept back in South Carolina.

Months slipped past in a haze of contentment and a few pleasant, decorous and necessary words between Hez and Seraphine. Gradually he came to feel that the Everglades was a world unto itself and the outside laws of light and dark people didn't apply as much here. He still gave the white men a wide berth and kept a small distance while he worked in the kitchen with the young widow. Yet these men weren't like the arrogant white people he had known in South Carolina. They didn't keep talking when Hez entered a room. They didn't act like he wasn't there. No one seemed to mind if, standing a little ways apart from the men on the porch, Hez smiled at one of their jokes or offered a passing salutation as he mopped the glistening white enameled planks. An older, more experienced man wouldn't have placed as much store in their seeming tolerance. An older, worldlier man would have carefully marked his route through each day and cautioned himself not to invoke their circumspection by deviating from it.

Eventually Seraphine took an interest in her young steward's education. Between working the turpentine groves and picking cotton, Hez had been to school off and on through the eighth grade. He could read and write pretty well. Miss Seraphine lent him the use of her deceased husband's books. He had been a literature student who eschewed poetry and prose and turned to farming. In the late evening, Hez would lie in his attic room with the window open and listen to the swamp and read about medieval warlords and Crusaders and battles and cities and lovers and lost kingdoms.

Miss Seraphine would drill him about the works he read as they set the evening dough to rise. In the beginning her zeal for his gradually increasing knowledge embarrassed Hez. He sometimes thought he could descry a frenetic loneliness in it. There were no other white women of her station for miles around. She had no friends. She almost seemed to lean on their kitchen time together for virtually all her social discourse. By supervising and guiding his education, she was attempting to create an intellectual peer. Even in the Everglades Hez had no illusions about that. His caste was less formalized here than it would have been back in South Carolina. But it was equally real. The men would have plenty to say if they knew she was plying him with Robert Browning and geography and math.

He was putting by about thirty dollars a month. He figured when it came to a thousand he'd head back towards the Carolinas and buy himself a little farm. It was a lonely existence, there in the swamp with no other people to talk to except the two Creole serving girls. They were older, homely virgin women who lived upriver with their mama, who took all their earnings. They had no interest in a seventeen-year-old kid. They seemed to hold some deep, unspeakable prejudice against any person or idea from the world beyond the Everglades. They were as a rule hard to please and always ready to condemn him to Seraphine, usually via some false infraction of the house rules on Hez's part. They frequently went to Seraphine to complain about him. His hands were dirty. He had spit on the kitchen floor. Seraphine invariably upbraided them for their lack of charity.

Aside from an occasional exchange with one of the white men on the porch, Hez's entire social life consisted of listening to Miss Seraphine while they prepared the evening meal. As the months passed she shared more and more of her story with him.

She was the daughter of a Baltimore Methodist minister. She had married Evan, a young would-be farmer who had brought her to south Florida five years earlier. Evan had designs on farming produce, pulling in two or three crops a year, and making a fortune. He put his young savings down on the house and the land and his first few lettuce crops. For a year or two, things went very well for the newlyweds. Seraphine loved her hardworking husband ferociously and labored to turn his house into a proper place in which to raise his children. She furnished and decorated their house with antiques inherited from an aunt up in Maryland. She had artistic eyes, a knack for organizing and a penchant for perfection that conspired to make theirs the most painted and polished house for miles around.

In April of their third year together, with no one but Evan to help her, Seraphine gave birth to a son. The young couple's rejoicing was short lived. One morning a month later, Seraphine leaned into the child's crib and found the infant stiff and lifeless.

Devastated, they buried their child and tried to comfort each other with the promise of more children. Evan took it in his head that this loss was God's judgment on them. He drowned his grief in hard whiskey and working doubly hard long hours in the produce fields. He left her alone with the loss while he took his solace with whores in town. He was afraid to sleep with her, afraid that she would conceive and the curse revisit them. Seraphine held no such view. It had been a dark accident of fate. She was young and strong and ready to bear more children. She tried to believe that her young husband, if left to his own devices, would eventually regain his faith and his better nature.

The following September brought a hurricane. Salt water ran forty miles inland from the ocean and the lettuce crop was destroyed. After that Evan sat on the porch and drank whiskey. Soon the bank took the land and he was unable to secure the loans he would need to start over. He was slapping Seraphine away by now. He abandoned all civility to his death wish, gambling in the swamps among lowlifes with money he didn't have to lose. Hez had played enough back eddy poker to know the rest of the tale. The lost man had got in over his head with some drifter who had taken his due with a Bowie knife and left him for the gators.

Young women with half Seraphine's griefs turned back up at their parents' doors and became brittle, gray ghosts slipping about behind drawn shades in upstairs rooms. Seraphine had summoned enough wit and strength to throw open her house to boarders and draw a living from it. She had buried both her husband and her child in the Everglades. She said that rendered it her native soil. The only hope of conquering it lay in embracing it.

About a year after Hez began working for Seraphine, he began to notice the changes in her. Her pale cheeks had begun to show color. She was taking pains with her platinum hair. Grief, she was beginning to understand, is eternal, an undiminishing burden which might, if squarely folded and stowed, lend a heavy ballast to her lonely existence. From time to time one of the men would invite her to the picture show in town. But she always refused them politely. Later in the kitchen she would gently deride the men to Hez, detailing their unfortunate, vulgar and wholly inferior natures, the roughness of their manners, the ignorance betrayed by their coarse speech. Often she would use the opportunity to draw comparisons between her boarders and Hez, pointing up his virtues and saying that he was destined for loftier ground. By this time Seraphine had taken an almost obsessive interest in Hez and not only his studies, but every other aspect of his existence as well. Seraphine insisted that he write to Grandfather, let him know how the wind was blowing. She located a colored church fifteen miles up the swamp and lent him her boat so he could attend on Sundays. She took Evan's blue serge suit out of mothballs and cut it down for Hez. Hez looked so fine when he showed up at church that the little congregation took him for a visiting preacher and begged him for a sermon on the spot.

These days she took a little whiskey in sugar water as she cooked. She always poured Hez a similar amount in a mason jar which he would slip back into the bottle when her back was turned. Now she wanted him on the stool by the stove, his eyes adoring her as she stirred soup and admonished him to get an education and move way up north where a colored man might have a chance. Now she wanted his opinion if she changed her hair or wore a different necklace. There was, if not a carelessness about her, then a widening of outlook. Hez assumed it meant that soon she would tire of these environs and, native soil or not, head north towards her civilized youth and the prospects of sharing her life with a man of her stature.

One afternoon she offered him a small piece of fresh salt rising bread and her finger lightly brushed his lip as he tasted the warm, moist dough. Another time, when she had taken a second glass of whiskey and sugar water as they cleaned the kitchen after dinner, she said that he was all that stood between her and a black swamp.

He thought he heard his heart break when she said that, and he prayed that heaven wouldn't let her hear it too.

Their first time was a Saturday night while the men were in town. He was in his room reading one of her books. She appeared in the door wearing a loose fitting dress of coarse white cloth that he had never seen. She was free and easy with him by now, so it didn't seem strange at first. Except that he didn't remember that perfume and her lips had been lightly traced with red. He struggled to supplant his increasing desire for her, but he knew she could sense it.

His ache for Seraphine had been a solemn secret between himself and God for the better part of a year. It was something fine and private, a recurring dream, an ecstatic agony he had vowed to stow deep in his breast and carry to his grave. The slightest indication on his part that he desired her would be all the justification the men would need to haul him into the swamp and hang him.

That Saturday night the power that latched his door behind her would not be silenced or stopped. What he had held within was only half of something and she held the other. That night when she crossed to his bed and kissed him, he decided that no consequence or eternity in hell was too great a price for the majesty and the wonder she brought him. After that night, it would have been pointless to live without knowing that the passing hours would bring her back to his room and they would lie tenderly together until dawn and breakfast duties threatened.

Months passed in quiet days, their love safely sequestered beneath their kitchen conversations and locked behind the door to the attic stair which could be bolted from the inside when it was closed. It was torment to sit by the dining room door and watch the men eyeing her as she laid out food on the sideboard. It was agony to overhear their crude assessments of the flesh she hid under her high collars. Yet these and so many other scenes out of their daily routine were tolerated because they led the lovers to their next secret rendezvous.

Twice in those months Hez had waked from dreams that the men had found them out. Both times he trembled in the darkened room, covered with icy sweat and vowing he would run at daybreak. Then daylight and the songs of a thousand birds reminded him of the enchantment of her moist eyes when, alone and nude, she kissed him and tickled his flesh with her long, thick platinum hair.

Long before he would admit it to himself, Hez sensed it. First it was a half-imagined tightening of the serving girls' attitude when he entered the kitchen and spoke to them. They no longer quite criticized him. Their scant conversation was light and vague. They knew. They knew and it was impossible not to see that they had gone upriver and spoken to their mother about it. She had sent the rumor back downriver, where a phrase in the ear of a mill supervisor soon became endless whispered diatribe and supposition. Now their former loose conversation took on an almost stilted tenor when he refilled their coffee cups. He tried to convince himself otherwise, but Hez could touch it in the silence that hung in the third floor corridor outside the door to the attic stair, which he kept locked. He kept his windows shut and the curtains drawn even on the hottest nights, vainly attempting to contain what had already spread and grown all around him.

Over and over he commanded himself to run. He planned every detail of his leaving, packing and then, unable to pull himself away from her, unpacking a hundred times. The fleeting months passed languorously now with day after day of unbearable surface calm.

Beauty B. had taught him long ago that his life would last only as long as his ability to maneuver past white men. He feared what they would do to him, but he shivered with near hysterical dread when he let himself wonder what terrible end Seraphine might face. A second year passed. Gradually the danger came to lie small and unspoken between them. Now and then he saw it in her eyes when she slipped from his bed in the late afternoon in order to be at work in the kitchen when the men returned from work.

It dried the end of his tongue and gnawed savagely at his gut as he swept the parlor carpet. Then he let the brass knocker tarnish because he was afraid to go out onto the porch because now their eyes searched him for a sign of the forbidden truth. At last he understood. The differences between these white men and those he had known in South Carolina were insignificant.

Now as he served cream and sugar for their breakfast coffee, there might be a half-heard snigger or the ominous scrape of a chair leg or an ominous pause in the table conversation.

They never spoke of it. The subject lay like a brooding body of forbidden water between them. There was a brittle edge to her laughter. He took pains not to speak directly to her when the men were about. He couldn't summon the will to envision his life without her close. Alone each routinely weighed the increasing danger against the emptiness of life without each other.

Three days before Hez found her hanging from an oak limb over the river Seraphine had come to his room as soon as the men had gone out for the day. One of the serving girls had come clean with her. Three men had come to their house the evening before and demanded information. The men had roughed them up and threatened their mother unless they imparted what they knew. The two serving girls, frightened for their lives, had shared their suspicions. The men had been drunk. After the women had shut themselves back up in the house, the men had lingered in the yard, laying their plans. A mob was gathering. Seraphine would be given the opportunity to prove that he had forced himself on her. If they were convinced, she would be allowed to leave. If not, she too must die. Hez looked out the window as she revealed her plan of escape.

There was no time to pack. He must leave at once. She gave him the keys to the pickup truck. She would prepare a story. She was certain, she said, that they wouldn't harm her if he was gone. She gave him the name of a minister in Baltimore who would shelter him. She would follow him after things were settled here. From Baltimore they would flee to Canada. It was the only time Hez ever knew she was lying. He tried to believe that she did it to protect him from the awful weight of saying good-bye.

Something darker stirred beneath it.

By noon he had driven due north a hundred miles, all the while dissecting their last encounter. Her words had vowed they would be together. A hundred miles was as far as he could ignore the unmistakable shame he had seen in her eyes and felt when they embraced before he left. She had entered forbidden country by loving him.

Her last gaze told him the inescapable truth. She had loved him as a means of destroying herself. Her losses had twisted her much as Beauty B.'s and Grandfather's had broken them forever. She lacked the courage to take her own life. The men would take it for her. They wouldn't believe any protestations of innocence on her part. If life had been her goal, she would have sent him and followed after him months ago.

He turned the truck around and drove into the encroaching night. Perhaps by some miracle he could save her. He was all action in that moment, all will. If he allowed himself to consider the situation fully, he knew he would head north again. A throbbing in his chest explained it to him. His life would be meaningless unless he risked for her all that she had been willing to sacrifice for him.

It was full dark when he drove up to the house. There were no lights. He walked through the downstairs rooms and called her name. Everything was blue and vapid from the moonlight off the river. Everything shimmered and seemed to be dissolving. He waited for angry white arms to grab him. But there was no one. No sound except his own footsteps as he walked out the back door. She hung stiff from the limb of the giant pin oak that reached out over the river. He cut her loose. Hearing or believing he heard angry voices, he ran north into the swamp.

He woke under a heap of blankets and straw. He opened his eyes. A cool wind had risen out of the swamp. It was daylight. Apparently his mind had stayed awake in his sleep. He took a slow, deep breath that promised to slice him in half. Then he heard their muffled truck doors slam. He should have run. Why didn't he run? Another eternity of silence. Then someone called out.

"Howdy."

There was muted talk. He caught a phrase.

"Hunting us a nigger boy . . ."

And then, ". . . seen him, had you?"

"Yup." That was Joseph.

"Whereabouts?"

"A mile in. Two gators fighting over what's left of him."

Then a closer, dubious, malcontent voice spoke.

"What's in there?"

Hez held his breath. The man was in the room, scuffling about. There were quick footsteps behind his.

"Yo!" That was Joseph. "I been accused of some low down things in my time, but nobody ever accused me of hiding a scummy coon boy who sins against God and man by fornicating with one of our women!"

Silence. Then the man spoke again. Hez recognized his voice. His name was Tyson. He'd asked Seraphine out a dozen times.

"No, man, it ain't like that. I'se just curious about your barn here."

"It's a consecrated barn."

There was low laughter. Joseph offered them breakfast. They said they wanted to check out this nigger boy's body in the swamp.

"Be careful. Apt as not the boy was fevered." Joseph gave them directions, warning them there might not be anything left to see. Then it got quiet. Joseph said in a voice that told him he wasn't looking directly inside the barn to stay put. Hours passed. Finally, he slept.

It was dusk when he woke. Joseph stood over him. He was wearing a white robe.

"They're long gone." He told Hez to kneel while he anointed the youth's forehead from a bottle of what was probably sunflower oil.

"Hearken to me, you who know righteousness, the people in whose heart is my law; fear not the reproach of men; and be not dismayed at their revilings. For the moth will eat them up like a garment, and the worm will eat them like wool; but my deliverance will be forever, and my salvation to all generations."

It was a rough, hilly logging road. Sometimes the rutted mud was so deep they had to wedge branches beneath the rear tires and push the truck forward. There were sudden bursts of blinding rain that forced them to wait on the narrow shoulder. It was almost morning before they hit paved road. It was noon when they reached the Orlando branch whistle-stop.

Joseph waited with him while a silver steam locomotive churned to a stop. He slipped the conductor two dollars.

Their parting was even less ceremonious than their meeting had been. Hez offered Joseph his hand. "Thank you."

Joseph's mind was already seeking his next mission. He barely acknowledged Hez before he turned and walked back towards his truck. Hez climbed the steps of the last car and found a seat.

He dozed off and on through the long afternoon. He bought an egg salad sandwich for supper. His mind wandered through the hours.

The evening sky was bleeding red behind the jagged edges of the pines. He sensed the familiar shape of the rolling South Carolina hills. He felt the sudden ballast of a place he knew. Beneath and through him two ends of something long and curved bent inexplicably into each other completing an unlikely ellipse.

He watched the hulking blackness of the trees moving south under a round sky that was crimson, then dark purple and finally blue black as it slipped above the stars.

2

Eula Pearl

(1989)

All of them think I'm crazy because I say such a little nowadays. What is there to talk about at my age but the past? They'd find that a whole lot less tolerable, my gumming on about things hated and beloved. I'm old now. I feel old. When I watch the world passing on the road in front of the yard, when I listen to how the world talks on the television, I know that I *think* old too.

I drift. Sometimes I'm sitting in church when Nadine drags me to service, and in between "For Thine is the kingdom" and "Amen," I'll swear I'm off someplace three forevers beyond the sunset. It's like I'm practicing dying or letting go of this world a little along. I don't know.

Now Searle, he didn't talk about such things if it was this way with him right on the last. Of course, Searle went sudden. Or so we was left to believe. He sat up in bed one Saturday night and his hands went to his chest and he was gone. If he had any idea he was going, say that Saturday morning, he never mentioned it at breakfast.

Funny. I remember thinking, "What am I going to do now?" at his funeral. It was a gray hot Monday morning with just enough wet dropping to dust down the cotton. It was May and the dirt on his mound felt warm when we went back to pull the cards off the flowers around suppertime. Rose of Sharon took me. I remember thinking she looked so pretty that day. The sadness become her. Or maybe I just looked at her good.

No, I remember so well wondering what I'd do without Searle. But you do pretty much the same. I sold off the cotton gin and paid what was owed against it. We must have pulled bank money out of that gin a dozen times in the forty-two years we owned it. I had a good deal of money left over and half of it went down on a good brick house for Rose of Sharon and Dashnell and little Carmen. It was one of those miniature *Gone With the Wind* places with baked white aluminum columns made of new brick that's supposed to look old. It was just this side of Birmingham. Rose of Sharon had two kitchens, one to set and drink coffee in, the other for putting up vegetables and ironing. I didn't see it but one time. I didn't much want to go. I don't sleep good in other people's houses. Besides, new houses stink of paint and carpet. But Carmen was graduating high school and I was the grandmother. I had no choice.

But if Searle had been having my away and back again experience before he died, he never mentioned it to me. He might have told Rose of Sharon. She never let on to me if he did. But she wouldn't. Not from meanness. Rose of Sharon don't have that capacity. If she did, I doubt she would've married Dashnell. But maybe she would have. So all I could conclude was Searle went or was took in a flash. I like my way better.

My way you outlive all your dreams. Then you outlive any regret over that. I used to think, if I had an old age, I wouldn't mind it because by then I'd know things that only time reveals. But I see the folly of that now.

I miss sleep, and by that I don't mean rest so much as laying my head on the pillow and dropping down into a deep and holy blackness that draws a clear line between the day past and the one to begin. Now I lie with my head propped against six pillows. That, I'm told, helps keep the fluids from filling up in my lungs and drowning me. I lie there and fixate on pieces of the past, pleasant or excruciating, but I never go all the way someplace. I can always hear the clock ticking or the trickle of water on the rusted streak in the bathroom sink. It's not that out of body stuff they talk about on the morning TV shows. But it has a kind of enchantment about it.

Rose of Sharon and Dashnell moved back up home after Carmen died. I probably should say, "after Carmen was killed." But that sounds like he was murdered. He went in a car wreck. I wouldn't say it to Rose of Sharon, but that boy was born with a shadow over him.

Rose of Sharon takes me to the doctor, but half the time I get there and I can't recall the original complaint. I invent one so as not to be embarrassed. No. Sleep is for people who got something to do tomorrow.

I got one strip of bacon and one egg to turn in its drippings all the tomorrow mornings I got left. I might not have any left. I can't buy a two-pound package of bacon without that in mind. But that's old age. Then, if I feel up to it, I got a cup and a half of my weak coffee to make. Searle used to threaten to leave me over that coffee. He walked all over France and Germany with his division swearing he'd joined up to get away from my coffee. His whole family was peculiar about their coffee. One of his uncles claimed to have moved from Mobile to Houston just to get away from Maxwell House coffee. There's a lot of foolishness with his people.

Tomorrow, if I live, I'll toast a slice of pound cake and spread some jelly on it. When I get the breakfast things rinsed up, I'll slip out onto the front porch before it gets too hot and pinch around my plants. Dashnell comes in the fall and puts them in the garage for me and he comes back in late March and hauls them out. He does it like he's doing me the world. It don't take but half an hour. I never liked Dashnell and he never liked me. I bit my tongue in half when Rose of Sharon told me she was going to marry him. I'll always believe her marrying him was my greatest failure. Or so I say. I have a few million to choose from. But who doesn't?

After I get my fill of tending plants, it'll be time to listen to my story on TV. I'll turn it over to Channel 2 and catch the news. I'll nap on the glider until the mailman wakes me. If he leaves a green check in a yellow brown envelope, that'll mean Nadine will be by to drop it into the bank for me. Rose of Sharon fusses that I could have it sent straight to the bank, but I like to feel it between my fingers first.

No, sir, here will come Nadine, talking loud because she confuses old people with deafness. She'll want to know can she hold enough back from the check to pay the boy for cutting the grass on Saturday? That always makes me tired because you'd think by now, she wouldn't feel the need to make like she has to ask. She sure don't have to ask, "Which account do you want it in?" But she will. Nadine knows to the penny what I got in checking, but she figures, if I got anything, it's in savings. If I was to tell her to put a check in savings, I'd have to give her my little passbook and she'd know. I won't have the talk. I could spit at Nadine for her nosiness, except you don't spit at a good neighbor. Nadine keeps me from having to lean on Rose of Sharon. God, take me two minutes before I become a burden to my child.

It burns me. But I just let Nadine have her petty thievery. See, the boy charges twelve dollars to cut the grass. Nadine always holds back fifteen. She's no tipper. She's keeping it for herself. Nadine would call herself too Christian to charge me for dropping my check by the bank. So she steals an average of six dollars a month from me instead. You have to overlook things in people if you want anything out of them. It has been told in these parts that all six of Nadine's kids grew up hating her. What really gets me is that awful perfumed perspiration odor of hers when it's too hot. God deliver me from my judgmental ways. I talk like I'm not a shrunk-up, shriveled sight, apt as not to frighten children away.

They used to say I could make piecrust blindfolded, and it must be true because I still keep a fresh pie on the table. I make six or eight crusts at a time and freeze them. I used to spend the entire afternoon cooking seven and eight dishes for supper. But all I ever wanted at mealtime was iced tea and a fresh slice of pie.

But I did, though I thought old age would bring me wondrous and terrible revelations. Foolish though it was, I actually believed it would come in some biblical fashion, like say a column of fire rolling down the hill over Moena's yard or a revelation from a talking sparrow or the world aflame. Moena's house has been gone seventy-five years. It's just pasture now. But I still say Moena's house like it could bring her back.

No, I wanted the Fabulous Conflagration of All Conflagrations to come when I was younger, sure and straight and Christian. But you get too old to trust your own religion specifically. You get too old to pretend you got some exclusive hold on Jesus—or that Jesus has any exclusive hold on you—that he'll be there for you, and you alone, when you know he's got to be there alone for a million others mailing their money into the TV like you done in a weak moment.

But here I have to say things that have been forbidden to my lips. I have no hesitation with saying them, but I tremble to realize that their utterance no longer frightens me. *That* frightens me because in my advanced years, I have let go of all fear except one—that I outlived my good sense.

I did, though. I mailed in the money to the television. It was not, as I wrote on the note, so the Lord would remove the cyst from my spine or send a healing to Mama or take my desire for cigarettes away. It was because Holly Trace copied my spelling, stole my boyfriend Earl and drove Cadillacs with impunity until she died suddenly in her sleep at age seventy-six. Her crook son-in-law put her in a marble mausoleum over there in the fancy old part of the cemetery. I'll be under a little flat piece of stone in the new part. I wanted that straightened out.

I sent that money into the television for all the times I looked at baby Rose of Sharon and wanted to grab a carving knife and spare her the torments of this life. I got so scared of that, one time I made myself stand over her crib and hold a knife in the air just to prove to myself that I wouldn't go through with it. I mailed in my check because one night, when she was asleep and Searle was away, I let a half-grown dictionary salesman in. I sat there like a lady in the parlor listening to him, getting hypnotized by his soft voice and his curly blond hair. Later I slipped down into the orchard under the stars with him. I smiled after he went because I could see he thought he'd took complete advantage of me. For a year after, I let myself watch out the window and beg God to send him back. What a pity you have to be old and useless before you can justify the warming sun on the rosebud, the dew fading, the leaves opening, offering water to the sky. I sent money to my television. But I never gave a single drop of water back to heaven.

I'm ninety-four or I'm ninety-seven. I forget. Nadine knows. Rose of Sharon pretends to. That young one who comes in the black panel truck and makes everything work, he might know. He's a grandchild of one of Searle's cousins. He wants something. Won't take a dime when he mends the screens or cleans out the gutters. Still his isn't Christian charity. Rose of Sharon was a change of life baby, a complete surprise. I had no idea how to mother her. I fought with everything in me to keep her from knowing I didn't want her.

I can't hold a thought in the present tense. My heart drops back into the woods and the silky dust on bare feet in the worn place in front of Moena's porch. I can't keep today straight because remembered voices never die and time, like space, runs in circles. I drew that much from school or maybe it was Daddy. I had thoughts of becoming a math teacher once. I had regrets that I didn't once. But it would all be the same now either way. Daddy's been dust for forty-three years. Moena's been gone ages longer than that. Daddy went away in a flower covered mahogany casket with a choir singing. My Moena left crouched up on a wagon with the end of the world in her eyes.

I lived out my life thinking she would be back. But I think I confused her returning with her memory never leaving this house. I can't get it straight in my mind what went with the doll she give me. I tried not to let Rose of Sharon play with it. But it may have gone the way of all things forbidden to the children in a house where there's no help except the wife. It used to gall me. I had plenty of money for help. But there was none to be found in these parts. These ignorant white women around here would let their kids starve before they'd earn a wage cleaning my house. They was all too damned good for that. Well, I wasn't. I've been cleaning it for eighty-five or eighty-eight years. Before that Mama had Beauty and her sister Dot in here six days a week. It's a big house. It took the pair of them to keep it right. The best I ever did was keep it decent. Mama raised me to be a lady like her. But the world had no use for such a thing by my time. I slipped into Searle's roughshod ways. Lightning strike me for saying it, but Rose of Sharon slipped down from there.

Beauty was Moena's mama. She made dolls for white girls like Mama wanted me to be, like Doctor McKutcheon's girls in White Oak. You thought you'd seen finer. Hers were cloth stuffed with tobacco, and their hair might be corn silk. But you couldn't resist the faces. They were painted on flat muslin heads and they'd rub off because Beauty didn't have any real paint.

Beauty B. was charmed. She said very little to me because I was a child, but Mama knew her well. Her dolls looked at you. It was like that portrait of Wee Mama's granddaddy in the parlor. It catches you when you walk in the room, and it holds you the whole time you stay in there. Beauty's dolls claimed you the second they looked at you on Christmas or birthday morning, before the tissue was off them; they promised a silent companionship that would outlast any lover or husband or vow you made never to speak to, never to do this or think that. Beauty B.'s dolls grabbed a little piece of your way-down deepness. They knew you before you knew yourself. I only know the whereabouts of three of those dolls today, and that's because they lie in the caskets of three dead Prince George County women who were buried with them. I say three, I mean four. Because I got one around here someplace. At least I did.

Moena was like my sister, but she was more like my reason. I had Hattie and Florence, but they was older. Moena was mine. We stood together. This I remember. This I know. This is not no in-law Birmingham boy cousin crawling around under the house in no December freeze and his fat girl wife making idle talk in the parlor and that black panel truck. This is not that awful tugging at my soul because I need the boy doing things here and he never knew Searle or how he loved Rose of Sharon and why the house goes to her if she never lifted a finger to help me out.

No. This is Moena. It breaks me to see that fat girl in the parlor with her basket of food. I'll say this. She can fry. She can throw half-boiled potatoes around a skillet and dump out a right good salad. But she can't think no longer than a passing car. Her skinny, hairless husband with his bass voice and his tool kit, flipping switches, wrapping frozen pipes, going into the shed and making Searle's Chevrolet crank, it's almost bewitching. But it don't obligate me.

Moena comes back so clear some nights I think she's going to swallow me. I think I'm dead and she's come to lead me home. But that's never it. It's just so I'll remember her. Or because I remember her so well. I did not love Mama or Hattie or Florence or Searle. I have a connection to Rose of Sharon that rivals love. But none of it is love next to Moena. Maybe that's because she was taken from me when I was a child and hadn't learned to hold back a little love for myself. Sometimes when Moena wraps me in her veils in the dark, I halfway let myself think she wants me to hold on to this life. See, now, I'm bawling because it's so hard to hold on. I hate it when I let a thought like that break through. It takes me half a morning to recover myself. Because I know Moena is gone and not just removed from my sight, but no longer living. I don't think she would visit me now if she were still living. Unless hearts can travel.

But this I'll say. This I'll tell you. I hold on to this life for one reason. There's a kingdom coming and I don't mean no kingdom that was ever told about in no Sunday school. It may have been rumored in Scriptures or hinted at in sermons, but I don't relate it to that. The best I can do to explain it is to tell you to look into the eyes of one of Beauty B.'s dolls. It's there and it was before I was old and crazy and outlived a husband, a grandson and all my religion. Beauty B. saw it and she put it there. I may not live to see it. But I'm inclined to try. It's as real as the demons I saw the night they told me Carmen was dead. I only heard Beauty B. tell of it once when I was a child. She said it would roll down that hill in a shining light. You'd best believe we're coming nigh onto the time. This is no tale of no monster in no lake. This is no Bible story or bony end of no world. This is the change of all changes, the circle completed. I drag myself up out of my bed and through this house praying I'll see it. I don't know that my Redeemer liveth. I don't know that I'll see it. But I was meant to. So was Rose of Sharon if she'll ever find the courage to open her damned eyes. Lord, my mind takes these fantastic turns and I believe these crazy things I'm saying and it's no use praying now, I've outlived all my good sense.

3

Rose of Sharon

I thought when Dashnell got on at KemCo and we bought the house on the lake, it would be better. I never saw his attraction for Birmingham. I don't mean Birmingham like it is today because Birmingham like it is today might as well be Bowling Green or Raleigh. It must be one strong town, though, when you think about it, because it was burned to the ground during the War Between the States in the 1860s and then bulldozed back into the dust by urban renewal a hundred years later in the 1960s. Now here it comes building itself back again. Maybe they'll do it right this time.

I thought the lake would give us back a little peace for our years and our efforts. I'm far from miserable here. It's a sweet house. It took three years of Dashnell and me roto-tilling roots out in back, but I have a real garden this year. My deep freeze is groaning and the corn isn't even in yet. Of course the major portion of the yard still needs sod. Dashnell has tried every grass seed known to man. Grass won't grow for Dashnell. I keep telling him sod is the answer.

At least I'm close here, I can run by and look in on Mother. I don't know her, old and thin and pale as rice paper and shuffling around on a walker. I never did know her very well. Now I have to get up close to her to understand half of what she's saying. I have to listen hard. She's in and out. Mostly out. Not that she'd dream of coming to live with us. She can't stand Dashnell. She never could. If you listen to Mother, all the world's evils begin and end with Dashnell.

It's all I can do to drag her by the beauty shop on her birthday and bring her out here to the house for a cake. I don't know what she knows. Mother held the biggest part of herself away from me even back when she might've told me things. I hate that. Sometimes I even resent it. My mother knows how to live. When I feel sorry for myself I say that life is one secret my mother kept from me.

Now Daddy, he'd talk to you. He'd come home from his cotton gin and sit down on the porch with me and run his mouth till midnight if Mother let him. I'm not saying Mother didn't teach me a lot of the things you need to know. She kept me crisp and clean and starched and combed. I came as a surprise at a time when Mother was past longing for motherhood. She had outlived the instinct.

I believe I missed something, but I can't deny that I'm a very strong woman. Looking at my declining years ahead, I'm thankful that I have the spine to face them. I don't mean to sound like I have one foot on a cake of soap. I'm only fifty-three. That's not old. But the die is cast. I'm past wondering if I'll ever leave Dashnell or start back to school or even see Rock City. I won't.

I wanted to fence the yard when we moved up here but Dashnell says it's not done at the lake. He was right. People wander on and off each other's porches all day and half the night. Dashnell thinks the world of it, but I'm not used to that. I like loneliness. I like to sit in the quiet and watch the sun on the lake and sip my iced tea and hold on to a thought till it branches out and it blooms and eventually dies away to make room for another one. I like to remember voices and faces and what was said to me and what I said back or what I heard people say to each other. I like to study back on a situation and think what I should have said. I rarely get life right the first time.

I have some peace in winter while Dashnell is at work. Most of the year there's always Marjean or Lucille or Jarvis calling to me through my back screen door. I'm not one to sit and hen with the women. They make a fine art of filling the air with pretty words that say less than nothing. They consider it next to sacrilege to express any idea they haven't heard their husbands say. Mother is right when she says I've done an excellent job of hiding my brains from the world. I often think I was meant to be somebody else. I don't know who she is exactly. I feel more like her when I'm alone. I've kept myself a secret from me all my life. I believe it's because Mother never taught me how to live. Mother would say it's because I'm mentally lazy. She has a reason for everything.

I put up vegetables and I sew and they all laugh at me, but my idea of a good day is to bleach and iron sheets. They've all gone to printed no-iron polyester blended linens. I like plain cotton. I like the smell of the starch and the scrunching sound the iron makes as it presses all of life's wrinkles away. I like to turn down the covers at the end of a day's work. I like the hiss of a top sheet as it sticks ever so lightly when I pull it back away from the bottom one. I have always imagined it would be that way in a good hotel.

When we buried our boy Carmen, I looked at Dashnell and I told him we had to go on. Period. I said now let's don't confound ourselves with the Lord's will or time healing things. I says the hurt has made a big hole in our lives and we got to jump in that hole and learn to live in it. Period. I said, if you don't, you'll turn to liquor or we'll turn on each other or away from life. I was making a brave, empty speech because Dashnell turned to liquor long ago and we both turned our backs on life the day we married each other.

What I meant by those words was I had no idea how or what to do. Carmen was my only brush with life, my only accomplishment. All my dreams were secondhand. Whatever Carmen wanted became my dreams. I suppose I was asking Dashnell to look inside himself and see if there was some courage or compassion he had overlooked. It was the only time I ever asked Dashnell for help. It might have been the only thing real that ever passed between us. All our lives together before and after that, he's played the stronger and I've played the fool. It terrified him.

He sold the house in North Birmingham and got on up here with KemCo. Dashnell won't talk about the why and how of things. They are simply the way they are. You don't pick at them.

We had no clear call to leave North Birmingham, and as much as I despised it, it was where we had made a life. Moving back up home to Prince George County on this lake was the wrong pill. I'm not inclined to work at making Dashnell see how foolish he was, not on top of the hurt he already feels about Carmen. Dashnell has hypnotized himself into believing Carmen's death was all to some eternal good. That's how he bears it. I have no alternative for him. I can't look at him and tell him at our age we'll have another boy. I can't turn back the years and start over. I can't manufacture the amount of love it would take to offset his anguish. So I leave him to it.

He's taken up with the men who live around here. They run around like they all did back in high school. They all drink too much and they gamble too much and to my way of thinking they don't have much tolerance for anything or anybody including each other. They're the kind who bear watching. Dashnell once planned to take an early retirement so we could travel. He wanted to go out west. He used to talk about San Diego, California, which he visited on a 4-H trip in the eighth grade. I spent a lot of years reading everything I could find about San Diego. I used to doodle a house plan. It was a little two story place built into the side of a hill. It was all screen porch across the front. That was so we could sit out there and watch the sun on the Pacific Ocean. The downstairs was all one room, a big dormitory for Carmen's children when they came for long summer visits. Carmen took one of my doodles to an architect and had it drawn up proper. He gave it to me the Christmas before he died.

Of course I don't hear a word about San Diego, California, anymore. Dashnell's major preoccupation is sitting around drinking beer with the men talking *nigger* this and *nigger* that and what all they'd like to do to the *niggers*. It's all for the want of sense, especially since there are no black people here in Prince George County and there haven't been since my ninety-six-year-old mother was a child.

I garden. I bake. I put up fruits and vegetables. I sip tea and visit with the women on the porches. I read books from that box I keep hid because they was Carmen's books and Dashnell doesn't want any reminders. My figure is not what it was, but I still rinse my hair brown and I pull a comb through it before I go to the grocery store. I own several tubes of lipstick. But I'm no fool neither. I know when the butcher teases me about running off to Vegas, I know he's teasing. It doesn't set my heart fluttering. I don't keep silly romance books hid in my dresser drawer. I don't invent a better tomorrow. I can always find something to do and I do a lot of things well.

Mother called Dashnell and his bunch Neanderthals when they were teenagers raising dust in their daddies' pickup trucks on the road past our house. She said she harked back to a day when Prince George County had young men of good sense. She said the decent people either moved or died off. Dashnell's crowd was all there was left. I thought Mother was just one more older person saying the youth had gone to the devil. But they aren't young now and they're still raising dust. I tried looking the other way as long as I could. You're going to hear things up here around this lake whether you want to or not. I've heard plenty to tell me those men are up to more than talking and drinking. They're organized and they're itching for trouble.

Now, I try going along, keeping shut, cleaning my oven and taking my walks around the lake in the late afternoon. I try to hold my place with the other women up here. I try to be tolerant, to take the long view and above all else to embrace the fact that everything always changes.

It may be vanity or pride, but I always suspected that there was a decided difference between me and the rest of the crowd living around this lake. Now an evil business has come to pass. Now my suspicions are confirmed.

It was supposed to be Marjean's all-day birthday party. The men came around eleven in the morning and they were drunk all over the backyard by two in the afternoon. The women laid out lunch, but none of them went near it. By suppertime, they were sitting in my kitchen with glassy eyes. Their loud talk had gotten low. There were eight or nine of them. Every few minutes one of them would rush off for another case of beer. It was just a matter of how much beer it would take to shut off the remaining decency in all of them. Men like that regard decency as an encumbrance.

Several of the women including Marjean stood back a little, goading them on. I'm talking about small minded, tight jawed women who pinch their lips and roll their eyes and say *"nigger"* with enough venom to kill every fish in the lake. There wasn't a soul in my kitchen who didn't know that something was fixing to happen.

I had food here. I had a honey-baked ham and grilled chicken and potato salad and Waldorf salad and pies. I had cold cuts and relishes and deviled eggs and baked beans and cheese corn casserole. I could see by the way the men just picked at it, that they didn't want it to get in their way. They were fueling their rage with alcohol. They wanted their insides to burn until the vapors from those fires rose over them, creating demons for them to conquer.

I tried three times to pull Dashnell out of the room and talk some sense into him. He wouldn't so much as look me in the eye. He'd just grunt the way men around here do at their women when other men are around. Then Jake says, "Let's go up to the house to play cards." We've all been with our men and their tomfoolery enough to know that Jake runs the show. Jake was giving them the high sign. Dashnell grabbed a fresh gallon of Jim Beam bourbon from over the stove and they were gone. No one thanked me for the meal they hadn't consumed or explained why not. I was given to understand they were mobilizing on official business.

We knew they weren't about to play poker or five card draw either. Not before they'd sneaked out and done whatever evil they had planned. Suddenly we were like women in wartime, cleaning up after a rally, women wrapping the bloody deeds of absent men under Saran Wrap and stowing them out of sight. Later we felt like a coven sipping coffee at the table, and Marjean, Jake's wife, started whimpering about how hard our men have it, how good our men are and all like that, like they were facing Hitler's storm troops. All agreed, all nodded and pursed their lips and the air went out of the room. We talked on. We made conversation avoiding the topic at all cost. We drifted through Jeanine Thompkins's new kitchen and what all was said at Sunday school and tried to act like they were really up at Jake's playing cards.

One by one we'd all say, "Marjean, we haven't lit your cake. It's still sitting in my deep freeze today. Every time I open that deep freeze and see that cake, oh, God. . . ."

See, I knew by Dashnell's denying about Carmen, I knew he'd be the one who'd feel the most entitled. From what Marjean told me later, I about had it right. They all went back to Jake's after they did the thing. Marjean had gone home by then. She told me later that they came in ravenous. Jake had her pulling the cupboards bare trying to fill that emptiness it left in them. Meanwhile my kitchen was groaning with a week's worth of cooking, half of which I wound up throwing away.

Marjean said after the men gorged themselves at her house, Dashnell sat on her porch and told the men about Carmen. He must have told it right because Marjean says Dashnell went off crying by himself to the lake. She said the men let him go alone. Marjean said the men felt privileged to know all about it. She said a religious and brotherly feeling came over all of them. That went through me like a plutonium razor.

What did my only son's senseless death have to do with the deliberate and malicious slaying of an innocent man sitting defenseless in his boat on open water in the moonlight? God help me, I pray I never make that connection!

Not that the men were talking about it outright. It was an understood thing among them that none would ever mention it. When Marjean came telling me about that night, she kept her actual words to what a good time they'd all had at my house. She pretended she wanted to know the secret to my potato salad. Anybody outside the window listening to all the things Marjean and I *didn't* say would know right off we had the whole story.

The sheriff understood that, too, when he come asking Dashnell if he'd seen or heard anything the day they found that black man slumped over dead, a bullet through the back of his head in the boat. The sheriff danced a pretty show, flipping his pad and writing down answers to questions that any fool could see were pointing farther and farther away from the truth. Of course he was one of them. The sheriff of these parts always is, at least in my memory. Our tall sheriff always pulls out of the group while he serves out his term of office. That's so he can better protect them. Mother rails sometimes that she can recall a day when a different caliber ran this county. Old people talk like that. But in Mother's case, I halfway believe her.

We have no black people around this lake, nor anyplace else in Prince George County, not in the living memory of anyone much younger than Mother. People in Prince George call that *a known thing* with such intensity you would swear, and no doubt some believe, it was once handed down from heaven on a stone tablet.

The trouble started last spring. Word got out that someone had seen a black man out there on the water fishing bass. Then it died down. We just naturally assumed it had all been a rumor. No black man who wanted to live would be that foolish. All that's left of black people in Prince George County turned to dust decades ago in a section of one of my daddy's fields that used to be a cemetery.

Gradually it became substantiated that this black man was out there on the lake most Saturdays fishing bass and catching bream and crappie for his trouble. Dashnell and I talked about it. I told Dashnell to get in his boat and go on out there and tell that man he was encroaching. I figured he might be from up north or someplace. It might be that he didn't know the lay of this land.

Dashnell had heard a rumor that he was from Yellow County, and Yellow County is close enough to know. Pretty soon you'd hear little clusters of men muttering about it, and women too. Every now and again you'd hear somebody say they didn't see the harm of one little black man fishing in an aluminum boat on a U.S. Government owned and operated reservoir. But the notion never took hold. It was drowned in a cloud of spittle about what somebody ought to do about it.

I can swear on the Bible I never put a black face and a name together in one spot until I was maybe seventeen. I'd be hard pressed to recollect a Jew, and if there was one, he or she probably changed their name and went to the Presbyterian or the Baptist church.

It wasn't so much a source of pride as a fact with us that the black people had all been run out of Prince George before anyone here had a telephone or a storm window. It was seventy-five years ago and I felt no connection to it. Mother remembered it. But she hated to talk about it. I think it still pains her in some way. All I ever knew was white and Christian people. I never knew any other kind while I was growing up here. I see no evil in myself because of that. I didn't find out how ignorant I was, until I'd lived in Birmingham for many years.

One Saturday morning early about a month before they shot him, I tried to warn the man myself. It was around six-thirty in the morning. The first thing I do after I start the coffee is grab some air on the porch. There was a strong mist on the lake. I wasn't sure right off that it was him. All I could make out was a silver line of boat and a blue shirt. By walking all the way to the end of our dock, I could see that white hat with the yellow band around it. It was him all right.

I must have been a sight trolling that water in Dashnell's boat in my nightgown with my life jacket around it. The water was flat and gray. The sky was moody. There wasn't another soul except him and me out there on that lake. I was thankful for that. If Dashnell held to his usual Saturday morning sleep pattern, I figured I had an hour, plenty of time to get back before he'd even know I'd been gone.

It took fifteen minutes of trolling through weeds to reach the other side of the lake. It took five more to make it up into the backwater where he'd tied his boat to a cypress stump. I killed the engine and made my way by pushing off the bottom with my oar. The man was standing up in his boat, fixing to cast off. It was a nice boat. It had padded yellow seats. He looked at me with that protective curiosity strangers feel encountering another in an otherwise deserted place.

"They bitin'?" I smiled.

"Just got here," he says.

I could see he had a tent still folded and a camp stove up on the shore. He meant to stay the night in the woods.

"Looked like rain earlier, but I believe it's going to burn off." I hadn't planned what to say.

"We had a cloudburst down in Yellow sometime in the night."

Yellow. So he really was from Yellow. He *knew.*

"Well, I'll say."

But say what? I'd headed across that lake so deep in my intent, it hadn't occurred to me how I'd put words to it.

"Water's awful cloudy," I tried. "You probably won't catch much in these parts—except trouble," I added with that stupid weak smile I use when I say things I know I shouldn't. He went about his business. "Appreciate it," he says. Nice looking man. Oxford style clothes, a little fancy for fishing. Starched cotton like Carmen wore. He'd order them with heavy starch from the laundry, then iron more starch into the collars himself before he went to the office. Dashnell liked to have had a fit.

"Mister," I tried, and I wasn't smiling now. I was scared for him. I was scared for me. I wanted to turn around and look at my house across the lake, but I was afraid I'd see Dashnell on the dock staring at me. Or maybe a neighbor who'd want an explanation for why I was across the lake in my nightgown talking to that fool black man.

"Mister, somebody is going to shoot you."

"Appreciate it," he says again.

Only his eyes were narrow now. I was the enemy, I was some damned fool white woman in a raggedy nightgown, hair in curlers, life jacket pinned around me representing things in his mind. At the very moment he was thinking that, I was feeling far away from all that I had ever known. It was more than I had ever done about anything outside my family in my entire life. I was weak from it and he had completely missed my point. I wanted to choke him.

"I have no personal truck with you, sir." Did he have any idea how my ears would burn if Dashnell heard me calling a black man "sir?"

"I have no personal truck with you either, ma'am."

"Mister, I truly hate to bother you like this, but these people around here, they're pretty set in their ways."

"Yes. I understand you. Thank you for your kindness. I'd like to fish now." He settled himself back down into his boat and the reeds blocked my view.

"Well," I called out, "I reckon fools come in all shapes and colors." I paddled back out to the open water and cut the engine on high. I fixed my eyes on the house, but my mind stayed back there with him. I was furious. I wanted to call him a derned fool. I wanted to turn that boat back around. I wanted to holler, "Man, you think you know so damned much." I could imagine his drift, I could just hear him telling me what year it was and what country it was and all about his inalienable rights, as if that would ever mean anything in Prince George County, Alabama. I cut the engine back and I turned back towards him. I didn't go all the way up into the reeds this time because I knew he could hear me all right.

"Look here," I shouted. "I don't care what constitutional things you think you're doing up here—"

"Appreciate it." His voice stabbed me in two. For a minute I wondered if he was like some kid saying the opposite of what he really meant. It just slayed me. To this day I don't know what people would say and do if they had any idea that I was out there on the lake engaging the man in conversation. The thought of it makes me tremble. But I did it.

The White Oak Reporter, our local paper, ran a story to the effect that an "as yet unidentified body" had been found in a boat on the lake. You'd have an easier time finding out who actually crucified Jesus Christ. At least Jesus Christ was charged with a crime before they murdered him. I don't want the details. If it was Dashnell who pulled the trigger, then he used somebody else's gun. His .38 was in the drawer and his .45 was in the glove compartment of his panel truck. I went and looked after the women left that night. Not that it makes any difference. One of them, meaning all of them, did it. Dashnell's as guilty as the next one.

The night it happened I sat on the porch after the women had all gone home. There wasn't much moon. It had dropped cool and there was mist off the water. Once I thought I heard a pinging sound. An hour later, I could hear the men laughing and talking down at Jake's and Marjean's. Sometime later, though I wouldn't look, I was pretty sure I could hear Dashnell out there blubbering drunk on Jake and Marjean's dock.

I try to comfort myself with the fact that I warned the poor man; but I feel a part of it. I was too scared in my kitchen that awful Saturday night to beg the men not to do it. I was too scared to call the sheriff and ask him to stop them. It wasn't that I thought they would kill me. It wasn't just that Dashnell would have never let me hear the end of it. Right or wrong, speaking out would have been setting myself apart from them. It would have forced me to declare the unspoken contempt I have for them. What they did was evil. But what I didn't do was worse.

I went to church the next morning and I prayed that this thing will pass over us. I actually asked God to let the evil stand! If I step forward now, if I open my mouth, if I tell the wrong people how I feel, I really will be in a mess. Somebody will run me off the road coming home from Mother's one evening; or I'll be found in the lake floating face up.

Meanwhile, everybody else around here goes on like it never happened. I'm weak enough to want it all to go away. But this thing is just a loop in a raveling evil. I get so afraid some mornings alone here in this house, I can't pull myself from my chair. There is something lurking in the cedars, something gathering like an invisible storm in the air. I try to tell myself it's just my guilt; but this feeling, this raveling evil, is turning. Or maybe I'm just losing my hold on things.

4
Hezekiah
(1943)

Hez returned home like a prodigal son. He held himself back from chasing women and he didn't touch liquor. He had been delivered from the swamp and he attempted to honor his deliverance with gratitude. He went to work six days a week beside Grandfather running sap in the turpentine grove. He tried to get holy. On Sundays, he stayed in church from morning till night. He spent six nights a week studying Scripture. Whenever he found a biblical passage he couldn't understand, he walked into town and waited in the alley for the old white Episcopal rector to call him up on the back porch. The old man would ramble on for half an hour with his interpretation, always admonishing Hez to build cathedrals in his heart to the One True God of the English kings.

Eventually he began preaching wherever they would let him. It was hard at first because the woods were full of preachers, most of them eager to holler and sweat and cast out demons. But Hez possessed an eloquence that set him apart from the local preachers. He considered it his legacy from Beauty B. He was soon being asked to orate at the smaller established churches in the area. These were in country towns, communities where ordained and educated ministers were a rare commodity. He did all this and a good deal more, hoping to feel called up or inspired or revealed unto. But that didn't come to pass. Nor did any righteousness steal over him, no matter how hard he sought it.

Instead Grandfather had his first stroke. The old man was bedridden after that, so there was no one to help Hez tap and boil the pine tar. It was hot, hard work for two men. But it was impossible for one. Hez soon grew to resent it. It had been to God's work and His will that Hez had returned out of the Everglades. Hez had tried to regard his daily labor as toiling in the vineyards of the Lord. Gradually it had come to feel more like a thankless curse. Now the nickels seared his palms when he dropped his turpentine kegs at the warehouse by the railroad track on Saturday afternoons. An inexplicable sadness, an angry longing, gradually stagnated his zealous efforts to repay God for lifting him out of the black waters of the Everglades. Try as he would, through prayer, meditation and positive thoughts, he could no longer accept his empty life as his place and his time in the overall scheme of things. Time ran through his nostrils in pointless drafts of sleepless summer night air. The Scripture he read in the evenings seemed a deliberate and unsolvable puzzle sent by an unjust heaven to mock his good sense. His life refused to take root or purpose. The walls of sanctity he had built around his soul grew thin and tired. Eventually he took greater solace from corn whiskey than all the Songs of Solomon.

Now Beauty B.'s Bible gathered dust on the shelf over his bed. Now he was walking out after dark to the shadowed places where transients and low men gathered to drink and gamble and easy women lurked. He pacified his nameless rage in the warm flesh of a hundred women whose names he forgot as quickly as he learned them. He regarded the daylight as a scourge to be endured until the night drew him out again and again. This went on almost a year. Then he came home just before dawn one steamy August morning and he found the old man dead.

He sent to Charleston for Moena, his mother, who was by that time blind and working as a seamstress. It was an awkward reunion. The two were strangers. Moena held herself in. It troubled Hez that his mother was so stiff and pulled-back with him. He had looked upon her coming as a last ditch hope to feel some connection to the rest of the world. She packed up two of Beauty B.'s quilts and a couple stuffed tobacco dolls for remembrance. She told him he could burn the rest. Hez busied himself building the coffin and digging the grave in the woods. He had a great desire to tell his mother what had happened in the Everglades. He had never shared Seraphine with anyone. But Moena's face was a mask of indifference and her manner reminded him of dry oak. His efforts at more than necessary conversation were answered with a measured sigh that silenced him.

He hid his troubled heart from her. She kept herself shut away from him. Her coming had been an enormous disappointment. He wanted to bury the old man quickly and send her away as soon as possible. With Grandfather gone and the Army recruiting for the Big War raging in Europe, he figured to enlist.

Hez recruited several young men to help haul the casket up to the graveyard and dig the hole. After it was lowered, he read a little Scripture while the men rubbed their dirty hands on their pants legs and Moena stood back slightly with rigid shoulders that seemed to defy anyone to give them further weight.

They were sitting in the yard waiting for one of the cousins to take Moena back to the train after the funeral.

"Boy, we some hard people."

It was like words left lying around in a dry old jar you might use to catch rainwater. Moena would swear Hez had spoken them. Hez would go to his grave believing the words had come from her. The truth is it was probably a thought felt simultaneously. It was a white, hot afternoon. Suddenly something had let in a little air.

"We got no other choice."

That was Moena. Hez thought she meant her blindness or Beauty B. taken by lightning from the back of a wagon and the hard edged, low down life they plodded through as if it made sense. Moena caught his drift.

"You don't know nothing."

The tears were streaming down her cheeks. She was three weeks shy of thirty-seven; but suddenly she looked like a tormented child. He felt an overwhelming desire to comfort this strange woman he called mother. But he sat back and waited for her to speak. Finally, when it was evident that she couldn't, he tried to patch the holes in the awkward silence.

"You want some water?"

"Yes."

But she was still crying when he came back from the house. She held the cup between her fingers as if it contained the rest of her life. When she was calm, she said, "You didn't know him."

"My daddy?"

"Grandfather. *My daddy*. Up in Alabama when we had a place. When he worked his own fields and Mama kept a tight little house and I played free in the woods."

"Beauty never talked about Alabama, except to say y'all was run out. Was it something Grandfather did?"

Moena smiled wistfully. "Hellfire would be a birthday candle next to Alabama. It wasn't nothing your grandfather did."

She told him, haltingly with tears. She spoke of a breathing, shadowed world out of which she had come. Her mask of wood, her iron facade, fell away. She told him the beauty of it. She talked about low mossy places where ferns grew waist high and the wind was like a choir in the trees overhead. As she spoke, she breathed clover and jumped in new hay and shared secrets with a girl her age from across the road. She told how she would lie on her feather bed in the loft and listen while Beauty B. and Grandfather, still young, still hopeful, still believers, rutted happily with warm rain singing outside and the dream of a son, a little brother, filling the darkness with sensation. She made him understand Grandfather when he was tall with a young heart. She made him know that Beauty B. had once been full and fleshy and happily of this earth.

Then she took him through that night when a hundred houses burned and a thousand black people gathered what they could carry and ran away. She made him understand trees quaking with fear and hope dying as she clung to her place on the back of the wagon. She put her long, cold fingers on his shoulders and bade him tremble hidden under a blanket as she had while the white men pulled Beauty B. down off the wagon and dragged her into the woods screaming. She forced him to stand as she had the next morning where Grandfather lay unconscious with both arms broken. She took him into the woods where Beauty B. was huddled, her hands drawn over her stomach to keep her insides from falling out. She made Hez wait with her, screaming for help by the side of the road as frightened friends and cousins passed too terrified to stop. For three days and nights they hid in tall grass before Beauty B. could stand up. Somehow the two of them got Grandfather, still unconscious, onto the wagon. Then they made torturous, slow progress in the wagon on the wet and rutted road for more than a month until they reached the turpentine woods of South Carolina.

Moena had finally revealed the secret. At last he understood what had turned Grandfather to stone and driven Beauty B. deep into that madness she had mixed with the remnants of her religion.

"It means a lot to know these things," he said.

But the truck had arrived to take her to the station. His eyes searched hers a moment. Her mask of wood was back.

5
Rose of Sharon

There was one man at my house that Saturday night who didn't go on up to Jake's with the rest of them. Glen was twenty years younger than the others. He's a nice looking man, tall and thin with a long face, deep green eyes and thick dark hair, probably in his early thirties. He has a four o'clock shadow and a broad, quick grin that comes and goes. He fidgets with his watchband even when the rest of him is as still as a tombstone. His voice is sonorous and deep, his manner polite; but there's a quiet enervation. You don't feel like you're getting the whole story with Glen. He slipped home early, disappearing down the three backyards and porches that separate his house from ours. It isn't that Glen doesn't fit in. It's more like he doesn't want to.

Glen Pembroke and his wife Lily moved up here about eight months ago with their two kids. I had to invite them to Marjean's birthday party. You don't invite one up here without inviting all. Lily didn't come. He said they couldn't find a sitter. But she called down here to talk to him twice and it was plain from the way he flushed and whispered into the phone that they were deep in troubles of their own.

Glen plays the outsider. He holds himself apart from the rest. He isn't a native of Prince George County. He can get away with that. At least for a while. Eventually they'll catch up with him and force him to declare allegiance. If he refuses, they'll run him off. I gave him credit that night. He managed to pry himself loose from that bunch without offending a single one of them. That's hard to do.

His wife, Lily, is an altogether different story. She's younger than him, bleached white hair, frosted lips and a pound heavier than those two-piece bathing suits she wears to sun on their dock in the afternoons. She's a beauty, too, but it doesn't sit easy with her. She keeps astrology books around and she's forever worrying Marjean to tell her fortune. Marjean claims to read tarot. I have nothing against her except that she talks too much and thinks too little beforehand.

She turns up on my porch around three-thirty most afternoons, a plastic glass of wine in her hand, a flimsy robe over one of her thousand two-piece bathing suits. She brags about what they paid for the house and her Neiman-Marcus furniture. She talks about Glen too. He's a whiz bang with computers, has a very impressive job at a big company just this side of Birmingham. Their house is twice the size of any other up here at the lake and the only one with marble bathrooms. She says the house is their last chance, as if any house on this earth could fix what's wrong between two people. Of course Dashnell and I got here under similar delusions, so I don't have too much to say about that.

Lily sat here one afternoon sipping wine and told four of us ladies all about Glen's carrying on with a secretary at his office like she was talking about homemade ice cream. She went into such detail that Marjean spoke up and asked how she could know so much without being there with them. Lily said it was because Glen felt so guilty about it that she could draw it all out of him in bed. The house, the beautiful lake house, was his way of making it up to her. They couldn't really afford it. He had borrowed half the down payment from his daddy. I never quite know how to take what Lily says. I have an instinct that she makes things up. Or turns them completely around.

The worst is when Lily catches me home alone. I will go to my grave puzzling over it, but I attract people like her. They trust me. Lily spares no detail of her misery. She relives every mild flirtation she ever experienced: a five-minute conversation with a gas station attendant in Galveston, Texas; a young Lutheran minister who kissed her at a christening when Glen left the room. When she gets near the bottom of that big long plastic glass of wine, she'll tell me how it was last night with her and him, exactly how it was until I'm beet red and asking her to please change the subject. It's like that poor child is absolutely starved for attention.

The peculiar thing about Lily is, if you can get her off soap operas and her hand embroidered silk sheets, that girl has a brain. She has an awareness of things that catches me off guard. For all her loose and foolish talk, Lily Pembroke is a college educated English major. She reads the newspaper front to back every morning. She has strong opinions about all kinds of things of which I've barely even heard. She can make me tired. But she can also make me think. I mean, she's read books about the Central Intelligence Agency and the American racial problem in economic terms and all like that. She's too smart for her husband, Glen, but not quite smart enough to figure out a life without him.

She was up at the house the day the sheriff came pretending to investigate that murder. He had to make some kind of an official display of a phony investigation. Dashnell and Lily and I were sitting at the picnic table on the porch. The sheriff explained he was investigating the dead black they found in a boat on the lake. Wanted to know did we know anything? That was a solid week after it happened. The sheriff hadn't exactly rushed up here to gather evidence.

All I could have sworn on the Bible to know was the dead man's name was George and he was from over in Yellow County. Those two things had become well known, so I saw no need in speaking. Dashnell claimed not to know anything. He give the sheriff a beer. The sheriff put his report book on the picnic table and begun asking Dashnell about his new boat. As usual Lily was about half dressed in one of her swimsuit and robe outfits. That sheriff wasted no time sliding in beside Lily and commenting on her perfume. I could see how that irritated Lily, but I didn't see her making any moves to cover herself either. She backed a little away from the sheriff and then spoke up real quick.

"Y'all don't seem to be in much of a hurry to find out who killed that poor black man."

"Accident," the sheriff says, turning the conversation back to Dashnell's boat.

"You really think the man was shot in the back of the head by accident?"

"It happens, sugar." That was Dashnell.

"To a black man in Prince George County?" She rolled her eyes. That kind of provocative talk was purely for the want of sense.

"Did you see what happened?" the sheriff asked Lily, none too amused by her conversation.

"No, I didn't." She sounded tense and maybe a little bit afraid.

"All right, then."

I'll say this for Lily. I don't think she knew Dashnell was in on it. I don't think she had any idea I could have told her exactly what happened. She was foolish and loose tongued and shameless, but she meant no harm. It was as obvious to her as it was to anyone else that a black man found shot in the back of the head in a boat in Prince George must have been done in by some locals who didn't want him there, who wanted to send a message to all blacks everywhere to keep out. What wasn't obvious and should have been was that it's not a thing to discuss out loud. When the sheriff snapped, "All right, then," at her, she hushed. Directly he and Dashnell went down to look at Dashnell's boat.

"How can he say it was an accident?" she asked, as soon as they were out of earshot.

I still thought then, I still believed, that I had to stand with Dashnell and the other men and their women. I honestly believed whatever pale good the truth might do, it would hurt more people than it would help. Besides, I had the dull comfort of having tried to warn him away. I had the factual relief of not having actually heard anyone plan the specifics or carry out the deed. Except for that ping in the dark I heard when I was sitting on my porch after the women left that night. What facts could I give and to whom?

"Lily, you're lucky you're a woman. If a man talked to the sheriff that way, he'd lock him up and swallow the key."

Lily was an Alabama girl. She knew better than to disrespect the law.

"Times have changed," she says. "Doesn't that sheriff know he can't sweep a thing like this under the rug anymore?"

"Not here, they haven't," I said a little too adamantly.

"You go along with it," she accused.

"Didn't say *that,*" I snapped from someplace outside myself.

"Well, I didn't hear *you* joining in when I asked the sheriff about it." She was genuinely offended. "Look. Either I read you wrong, or you think it's just as sick as I do." I didn't know what to say. The truth would hang us both.

"I think a lot of you," she offered.

"I think a lot of you too, Lily."

"No, you don't. You think I'm another stupid blond tart whose peroxide has seeped down into her brain."

"That's not true!"

"Cool your *dumb act.* I'm not no stupid *man.* You act any way you have to around your husband. I know all about that myself. But brains and ideas don't scare me. You have more of both than you're willing to let show."

I sat there blushing while Lily accused me of sputtering and whining and looking at the floor every time the conversation required an opinion deeper than what to fix for supper. She had me. Mother would've said it a whole other way. But basically it was what she had tried to get me to admit for years.

"I think it's pure terrible what happened to that man on the lake and I know durned good and well it wasn't an accident." I knew my face was red as fire. I could feel it flush. It troubled me that I'd spoken like that and it nearly made me sick that I couldn't somehow draw my words back. Because once a thing is told it keeps on telling itself. Of course Lily was thrilled to hear me admit how I felt. You never saw such a satisfied grin on man, woman or child.

"Thank you," she purred. She pecked my cheek. She was halfway back up the yards towards her place yelling for her kids to quit fighting. I was so shocked at myself I sat there and let the chicken burn and Dashnell didn't hush about it until bedtime.

6

Hezekiah

(1943)

With Grandfather in the ground and Moena back in Charleston hiding behind a wall of regret, Hez sank deeper into a vague and listless existence. He abandoned the turpentine farm and he drifted through a dozen swampy South Carolina towns picking up what day labor he could and doing his best to avoid the law, which meant white people. Once again he was little more than a vagrant, a bum, a pointless drifter, an animal whose existence was used up in the endless pursuit of food and shelter.

He kept to himself. If he worked a field or a railroad bed with other men, he made only as much conversation as was necessary. He was nineteen now, a tall, sinewy man. He was black and godforsaken because God was white and God had perpetrated evil and suffering on generations of his people. He held no hope that it would not always be so. He kept a knife inside his coat. When he couldn't find work, he robbed gardens and churches. Sometimes he would find a woman in a bar and take up with her for two or three days.

He told himself that his only friend was death. He felt it near and he felt it often. Sometimes he wanted it. Other times he merely regarded it close and inevitable. He was low and without purpose, a bad joke in a dead universe. He fell deeper into a melancholy that no combination of whiskey and woman could alleviate. He shut out all sensation except those base sensibilities on which he depended for survival.

One autumn afternoon when he had no place to stay and no immediate prospects for work or whiskey money, he walked into an enlistment office and joined the United States Army. The Army would feed and clothe and house him. The Army would dictate the course of his days, and with a war on in Europe, it might bring them to some meaningful conclusion. Hez had no will he could identify or own. His existence had worn his sensors through. He was numb. Life had picked him clean. He desired no sensation. The Army might change everything or nothing.

He stood in his socks and underwear in a line of skittish young black men waiting for his physical. It was done. His fate was sealed. At that moment in a Nazi boot camp, a German recruit already carried the bullet that would spare him the trouble of making his own end. Dying was the single human experience in which Hez had any interest.

It would happen on a sunny day, maybe in an orchard near a small stone church. Death would be a German farm boy with empty blue eyes creeping out of Gethsemane on all fours over fetid corpses of dead soldiers and excrement. He'd be long and sinuous and he'd hold his rifle up on one elbow as he slithered forward, his body writhing, his whole being aroused by that savage lust for human quarry, that holy homo sapiens ardor for stalking his own species. Once his hunted was locked to his sight, the fervent killer Hans Jesus would reveal his presence in order to savor the consummate split-second ecstasy of this unique sport, his target's total apprehension of his fate. He would be blond, his German executioner and savior, ash blond like the Lutheran Jesus. It would fall out from under his helmet and stick in dark sweaty wisps across his pink forehead. It would shine gold at the nape of his neck. His heart would leap with boundless joy when he realized that he had killed a nigger.

Whatever sensation dying was, it would be Hez's own. No one else could alter, pervert, denigrate, steal or destroy his death. Peace would descend to him or he would ascend to peace.

The physical was over. He sat with the others on metal chairs listening to a stout red-haired sergeant with bloodshot eyes lecture on the Value of the Negro to the U.S. Army while slides of black men working as waiters in officers' clubs, chauffeuring generals, or vacuuming the living rooms of deeply appreciative officers' wives lit the wall behind him. When it was over, the sergeant flipped on the lights.

"Y'all got any questions?"

Hez's hand shot up. "Does this mean you don't want to send us overseas?"

"Overseas? Some of you."

"How many of us?"

"How *many*? Keep bugging me with your lip, Mandingo, and I'll personally send you overseas—all the way back to goddamned Africa."

It wasn't the cracker sergeant's arrogant remark that kept his mind racing that night. It was the obeisant guffaws of several of his fellow recruits that kept him awake.

7
Heath

I robbed Frank Taylor's bowling alley and I got caught. I gave two hundred back right after they arrested me. Daddy came down to the jail and offered them the other forty-six dollars on the spot. That should have been the end of it; but I was too redneck to let it go. A redneck is a man who'll insist to his own detriment that a bold-faced lie is the truth. A redneck will demand his day in court. Most of all a redneck will turn a dented fender into a train wreck trying to manufacture something honorable out of an open and shut case of petty theft. I stood up in front of a judge and jury and tried to convince them that what appeared to be a robbery was in fact a deed of the highest honor and morality. I made a complete jackass out of myself with a high toned explanation that I had spotted a fire inside the bowling alley, broken in to extinguish it and then taken the money to prevent its being burned up in case the fire wasn't completely out.

Yes, that's stupid. I'm a redneck. A redneck is made of his need to lie to himself and the world about his ignorance. A redneck will cheerfully sit down on a bed of hot coals to duck the eye contact of a man who can see he's lying. We never see what the rest of the world sees when we look in a mirror. We're all the time talking about our *blood* and our *rights* and trying to pass off our ignorance and laziness and poverty as the simple virtues of the rich in spirit.

That judge was so disgusted he sentenced me to six months in the state pen. Of course I immediately jumped up, spouting off how I'd appeal and see him thrown off his bench, and I did it with such convincing morality and honor he immediately doubled my sentence. I won myself four all expense paid seasons in a stinking cubicle in the Folsom Prison, named for that fine old redneck who once governed this sorry state.

The law is a wall you must never ever try to scale without the proper equipment. That includes an advanced—say a college—education, money, property and at least two or three highly placed friends or relatives. Without those things, you are better off lying down in front of a steamroller. It is also a great advantage to be innocent when you plead innocent to a charge. I fully intend to be innocent the next time I'm charged with any crime.

I carried sixteen tons of attitude into Folsom Prison. I figured I needed it to get me through. All it got me was trouble and the contempt of my fellow inmates. I realized too late that my attitude cost me the opportunity to know some fine people. You couldn't know that about prisons unless you'd been in one. It's a sad, hard fact. Sure, you've got some hopeless, depraved, mean and dangerous people in there. However, the vast majority just did something dumb and got caught. Or maybe they stood in the wrong person's way. Shoot, the average Presbyterian minister has done something as bad or worse than what turned the average Folsom inmate into a convicted felon.

I alienated everybody. I was just as redneck inside Folsom as I was out here. I was infected with the plague of my inability to be honest with myself. I spouted off about my *rights* and the entitlement of my *blood* and nobody wanted much to do with me. We all need some companionship here on the outside. Without it in a place like that you have nothing but time in a smelly box. I soon felt like the unwanted runt of the litter stuck in a metal cage at the back of the pet shop. Eventually I got tired of my own voice. With no one else listening, I started to hear myself a little bit. I didn't sound too good to me, so I shut up.

That was the most amazing thing I ever did. If you find yourself locked up in a cage with no one to talk to and you keep still, a tremendous thing happens. You start to realize you have a brain. With nothing to react to, you're forced to experience deliberation. I'll stick by what I said about the virtual sameness of most people in and outside of prison. Yet I came to value my experience there. If the State of Alabama hadn't locked me up in a cage, I doubt if I ever would've shut up long enough to discover the reward of thinking things through.

The first thing I learned was the incredible fact that I didn't know everything. I didn't even have to know everything. Gradually I understood how little I actually knew. Then I went on to lists of things I'd like to know about. It was too long, so I whittled it down to things I ought to know. That was still big enough to weigh me down, so I narrowed it down to one category I called "How to Live." That's what I'd been stumbling over for twenty-two years. I didn't have a clue. I divided it into two parts, "Things I Already Have," and "Things I Need."

I had time. I had the present and the future. I began to consider my days on this earth as my basic fortune. I'd squandered a lot of it. I made up my mind not to waste any more of it starting right then and there. No, that's not *total* rehabilitation. But it's enough to let the world sleep safe or, if not the world, then any bowling alley owner who ever heard of me.

I offered myself back to the State of Alabama and the people of this earth as new and ransomed as a freshly baptized infant or a sprout of grass in the first warm March rain. I lay flat on my back on a bunk in a cold cell through a year of confinement in the Folsom Prison with nothing to warm me but the moist breath of the Living God. It was longer than forty years in the wilderness and deeper than death. I paid in full the debt I incurred.

At the beginning of my incarceration I clung to that nameless rage which had always defined me, but the shadows and the passing weeks eroded it. Time and darkness swallowed it. When it was gone I believed for a time I no longer existed. But the Breath of the Living God is a true and tender thing that sustains when there is nothing else.

I lived without dream or ambition or discernment of time in quiet dark forgetting the sound of my voice and my face and neither hoped nor feared and, as days crept, I remembered less and less. I passed through that silent, turning tunnel where everything and nothing merge. The State of Alabama erased me for a while. My mind dove headlong into blackness and swam, but there was no motion, no point of departure or place to arrive. Presently there was in that close, windowless room, a breath without source. I holed up inside it. It contained me. I gave it my rage. I hope that means I changed. It's hard to remember how I was before.

I came back home one year later. Daddy was lying back in the same Naugahyde chair with the taped arms in his stocking feet cussing at the news. Mama was still slamming the back door making runs to the garden or to feed the dogs or, sometimes, to pray because Daddy won't allow it in the house. I carry with me the memory of a breath in the dark. It changes nothing except me so deep within no one notices. I ponder its meaning. There was a breath without source when this Universe began. It enveloped me. I am begun. I go through my days hunting work. I mow Mama's grass when her arthritis flares and she's not up to it. I help a cousin paint his barn. I listen when Daddy gets onto his beer and his philosophizing of a Saturday night. Everything is precisely as it was before I went to prison.

Except me.

Now I'm searching for my time. I'm seeking an understanding of that Breath. I don't mean I can know or name or understand God. I leave that kind of talk for the Baptist ministers. I believe that there is a thing to be done. When I find it, I'll find myself and the rest of my life.

I wouldn't mind finding a woman to share it either.

8

Lily

I had tried to tell Glen that morning. I had tried to explain it. We just didn't work. I needed air or a psychiatrist or a change of scene. I had tried, but the words had slipped out sharp and hateful and he'd gone off to work with his back arched and his lips pursed in that way he has of letting me know that my lack of gratitude is killing him. When he goes off like that I feel like the lowest common denominator: thankless, unworthy, miserable and selfish. Sometimes I cry and sometimes I pray, but the only thing that helps is activity; so I generally clean house whether it needs it or not. It was worse than usual that morning. I tried to wax the kitchen floor, but I couldn't shake the feeling that I might kill him or myself or innocent people. I drove to the grocery store which was ridiculous because I'd been the night before. I tried every way I knew to pray. Over and over I kept begging God to make me thankful. Not even God could accomplish that.

It's not that simple anyway. I don't like to think about it because I'm alone with it, but Glen turns darker in certain moments than anyone else in the world will ever know. You'd have to be locked in our room in the pitch black dark between the sheets of our bed to know. He pretends he doesn't mean to hurt me. Sometimes I almost think he intends to kill me someday. I tell myself I'm exaggerating. I hope I am.

Finally I slipped into my bathing suit and headed on out to the dock to bake my troubled brains for a couple hours. I lay there and read and looked at the sky for an hour or so. I kept thinking how I must look to a stranger passing in a boat on the lake. Here's this woman sunbathing on her private dock behind this beautiful house with a landscaped yard. Inside her head sirens are blaring and cannons are firing. The stranger wouldn't know any of that. It would all be a picture to him. On the other hand I might see a stranger passing in a boat and not have a clue what he was thinking. His doctor might have just told him he's got six months to live. His girlfriend might be pregnant. Maybe he just lost his job. Maybe he's planning a bank robbery or thinking about running for the United States Senate. It all boiled down to the fact that there's a different reality playing itself out in living color inside every head on this earth. That brought me back around to the fact that if I live to be a hundred I'll never have a clue what the world looks like to Glen. He'll never see it through my eyes either. Then I wondered if someone was to make a movie of the two of us, and if Glen and I sat and watched it, would we finally get a clue as to what the other is trying to say?

I could see a man working out back up at Rosie's. He had his shirt off. He didn't appear to be much more than a kid. He was laying in squares of sod. He was going at his work like killing snakes in the midday sun, a nice looking boy.

In these parts, there's two kinds of boys, hell-raisers and born-agains. I tried to study which he was just to take my mind off things.

I was seriously depressed that afternoon. It's the same damned thing over and over—living with a man I don't trust and never will. The woman in the silly book I was reading was being made love to by a prince in between an eight course meal. She was torn with guilt because her husband was upstairs bed-ridden. That book was as stale and useless as a piece of white bread that's been in the sun all afternoon. I kept running my eyes up the other backyards to where the guy was sweating in the sun. Judging by the intensity with which he swung his pickax, I took him for saved. The saved romanticize their backbreaking work. No matter how menial their task, they tell themselves they're building God's kingdom on earth. Their comforts wait in the next world—blah, blah, blah.

Glen is a closet born-again, but he's too damned scared to admit it. Glen has an abiding fear that someone will call him a redneck. He's that enervating half-a-cut above, a two-damned-dollar millionaire with a college degree. There is an enormous distance between a degree and an education.

I took him for a dumb country boy and I pitied his wife. They all have wives. You see them out at Wal-Mart, their carts filled with hollow-eyed kids, their shoulders slumped, their faces pinched from wondering if they're pregnant again. I pity those women. The sight of them terrifies me because I can't shake the fear that God intended me for one of them.

Every now and again I'd catch him glancing down in my direction. No doubt he disapproved of my bathing suit. Or the sight of a woman at leisure in the middle of the day. That made me tired. I gathered up my book and my towel and started towards the house.

"Excuse me, ma'am. Do you have a grass rake I might borrow?"

He had a boy's face except for some little lines around his eyes when he squinted. He was freckled and good looking. There was nothing saved or judgmental about him. That meant he was a hell-raiser. Yet, there weren't any whiskey circles under his eyes. He stood at the edge of the yard awaiting permission to trespass.

His hair fell every which way. It was sun streaked almost white on the top. When his eyes found shade and he opened them good, I could see they ran deep, two pure gray almonds that had seen things and absorbed their meaning. He wasn't dumb.

"Where's Rose of Sharon today?" I asked.

"She took Miss Eula Pearl to the doctor."

"Do I know you?"

"Heath Lawler. I'm Dashnell's nephew . . ."

Dashnell's kin. That gave me pause.

". . . but don't hold that against me." He grinned. It was guileless. It washed through me. It made me feel easy. It made me feel all right. He was neither saved nor a hell-raiser. He was absolutely himself, whoever he was. That gave me permission to be myself.

"I wouldn't know a grass rake from a tractor tire, but let's look in the toolshed."

He followed me a few paces behind. We dug out a rake.

"Beautiful place you have here."

"It is that," I said. I was lightheaded. It was probably the sun or the fact that I hadn't eaten anything that morning.

"If y'all need any work done around here, I'm your man," he said somberly. "I can always use work." There wasn't a hint of arrogance or flirtation about him. Yet he was no innocent. I generally divide the men in this world into two categories, those who want me and those who don't. He appeared to be neither.

"I'm Lily Pembroke."

"Pleased to meet you."

His manner was so completely undecorated that it didn't dawn on me for the longest time just how handsome he was. He either didn't know it or he'd never used it against anyone.

"Thanks for the rake."

He went on back to his work. Every now and then he'd glance my way and I'd look his. I could feel the loneliness knotted in my stomach. I could see by the shadows it was around three o'clock. The kids would be home at four-thirty. Suppertime and Glen and the darkness would follow. He came back with the rake.

"Tell your husband if he doesn't put up a retaining wall at the edge of the lake, it's going to flood come spring."

"I've been telling him for six months. But nothing I say sticks with him."

"Well, if you do get it to stick, tell him I'm the man for the job," he mused. "Mind if I grab a drink from your hose?"

"Would you like a Coke?"

"I don't want to be trouble."

"I was about to get myself one. It's no trouble."

The wind was up when I came back. The thin May leaves were shimmering yellow-green in the late afternoon sun. The water was choppy and stippled. The sweat on his face had dried. His hair fluttered over his forehead. He had helped himself to the chair next to mine and pulled it into the shade.

"Peaceful up here on the lake."

"Quiet as a tomb," I brooded.

He drank his cola in two sips. He set it down with an air of finality. I felt a sudden panic as if he was about to abandon me. I wanted his company. I wanted to feel I deserved it.

"I'm having a bad day," I muttered more to myself than him.

"How's that?"

"Husband trouble," I went on, like he should care or show the slightest interest.

"I wouldn't know about that."

"I was just lying here feeling lonely and sorry for myself and I wouldn't mind if you passed a few more minutes with me."

That's what was crossing my mind. So I said it. It sounds so common to me now.

"Everyone is struggling in their own way." He was talking about me, but I could see he had weights of his own.

"If they'll only admit it." I finished the thought.

"Most conversation begins with talk about nothing and ends just the same. People are afraid to say what's on their minds."

All either of us wanted that afternoon was the close proximity of another person. We talked easily and freely. We were like strangers on a train harmlessly spilling our hearts to each other because we would never see each other again. I told him I lived with a man I don't love. He said he was trying to get his life started.

"Do you ever wonder if you'll pass through this life and never touch another living soul? Or change anything? Or matter?"

"It's my worst nightmare." It is. This was no empty sodbuster looking for a joyride. He was talking to me one person to another. It was thrilling. I felt alive. We passed an hour like that. Then the school bus pulled up out front and Heath went back across the yards to his work. I sat on the back porch and helped the kids with their math and watched him quilt squares of sod into a lawn in Rosie's yard. Later I gave Glen his supper. He fussed at me about a credit card bill. When it was dark, I walked down by the lake. I could hear Heath's voice low and polite among Rosie's and Dashnell's and the clink of silverware on china plates as they ate in the kitchen. Later when the lights came on I could see him silhouetted at the table opposite Dashnell while Rosie darted in the background cleaning up the kitchen.

I stood on the dock and waited. Finally he came down Rosie's back steps to gather up his tools for the day. I picked up a minnow bucket and dropped it hard on the wood planks to catch his attention. He stopped. He looked towards me. I motioned to him. He moved towards me.

"Hey."

He didn't answer. He just stood there and looked at me.

"Beautiful evening," I tried.

He just kept looking. Then he kissed me so hard I thought we were both going to fall into the lake.

I bathed the children and read to them before they slept. Glen worked at his bench in the garage until eight-thirty. He was asleep by nine. At nine-fifteen I slid down the back steps and moved through the dark backyards down the path through the woods beyond the last house. The air was a furry blue veil and there were scattered drops of rain. It was pure foolishness to compound my troubles by meeting a man I barely knew in a deserted place in the dark. For all I knew he'd kill me and throw me into the lake. Maybe word was out that I'd given the sheriff a hard time about that dead man and Heath was leading me into a setup. Or suppose Glen had followed me? I had given him plenty of reason to be suspicious in the past.

The moon was back by the time I reached the clearing. Heath sat so low and still I took him for a fallen limb until I was right on him.

He smelled like summer and I could see the trees overhead and the moon passing through the leaves. The blanket was soft and new and the stars drifted down in white rivers through the haze. His fingers were warm water flowing under my back. He was a slow and tender lover and his eyes were wet when he kissed me.

9
Heath

Lily and I were riding on the back of a dragonfly. Dozens of passing stars made yellow spinning pinwheel fountains. When I woke around four A.M., the warm dropping rain pelted the tin roof.

Now, walking dumbstruck through my days, a small voice reaches out to me. Common sense tells me I can't be in love with a woman I don't know. Fear reminds me I slept with another man's wife and ought to consider the consequences. But when I woke this morning, the world was new and when I let the hounds outside, I stayed in the yard and watched the pink-eyed sun float up over the woods.

Today I'll go out and search for work. I'll answer the blank looks of the indifferent world with smiling eyes. Tonight I'll wait in the woods. Tonight I'll roll her in my arms. I'll feel her breasts tingling against my chest. Every cell in my body will give her the boundless joy she draws out of me. If she asked me to fly, I would fly. She is my unending happiness, my hope and my prayer. Lily turns the universe inside out and shows its wonder to me.

Hers is the breath of God on my shoulder. Lily is the sense of all things. She liberates my heart and sets my life in motion. I'm begun at last. I'm risen up out of darkness. I'm set apart from chaos. I'm moving. My heart is dancing. I see everything now, the bursting privet bloom and the shadowed patterns on the porch post. I see the blue eternal sky through the brown and green pines. I rub my palms together and sense a soft, electric thrill. I brush the dry back of my hand across my cheek and get comfort because there is Lily. How can it be, this quick, burning happiness where for so long there was nothing? Lily is my mantra, my prayer and my song. She is the long awaited answer to all my supplication. Tonight in the shining grass I'll kneel before her and humbly thank God for sending the promised angel. I'll ask His guidance as I pledge my ceaseless vigilance and unqualified protection.

10
Rose of Sharon

People like me live their whole lives in fear. People like Lily dance with danger every day and never seem to know it. I've got a situation here. I told that girl. I says, "Lily, you do what you're going to do. But you keep it to yourself." Lord knows she's not the first married woman to carry on with somebody while her husband's at work. Some people do that. Some people don't. You'd have to walk a couple miles in their shoes before you could even offer an opinion. But she's pushing me here. So is Dashnell's nephew Heath.

Dashnell hired him to sod the backyard. But somehow he twisted Dashnell's head around and got him to say he could paint the house too. It was painted eighteen months ago. We had a mild winter. It doesn't need it. It's just an opportunity for Heath and Lily to get together. In *my* bed! I came in from the grocery this morning and the bedspread was on sideways. I had no choice but to tell Lily I wouldn't be taken advantage of that way. She tore off home in a huff.

That didn't stop Romeo and Juliet. He'll slap three strokes of paint on my house and then slip down to her place for an hour. I got tired of it. I don't want the boy hanging off a ladder outside my windows all summer. I don't want Glen pointing fingers at me if he catches on either. You can find more trouble trying to mind your own business than you can out looking for it. I went down to Lily's and knocked on the door and Heath answered it with his shirt in his hand, grinning ear to ear saying he'd be back up here in a few minutes. I said, "Well, all right. But I am *not* paying you by the hour!"

An hour later Lily was at my back door.

"I thought we were friends," she says, tapping her foot like a spoiled brat.

"Friends don't do each other the way you are me."

"I'm sorry."

"I don't think you are." I was making pickles. I didn't have time to listen to how she was starved for love.

"I took advantage of you, Rosie. I'm truly sorry."

I told her I wanted no part of it. I said I wasn't about to incur the wrath of her husband when he got wind of it. There's something touched about Glen Pembroke. I figured him for the very type to blame an innocent party. Apt as not he'd get Dashnell in on it. Lord knew what might happen then.

"You tell Heath I'll get somebody else to paint my house."

That's when she told me she was trying to cut it off.

"Well, I'm glad of it," I says, wondering how I'd get the pickle mess under control and make supper before Dashnell got home. I said that a little harder than I meant to. I'm twice her age and I wasn't half that pretty when I was young. I couldn't imagine having the chance to do what she had done. It never was an option. Lily's eyes narrowed.

"Well, aren't we sanctimonious?" she says, biting salty tears from her bottom lip.

"I'm sorry if I hurt your feelings, Lily. I've got twenty quarts of pickles going and supper to start."

"Rose, I'm scared," she said in a matter of fact tone that wasn't asking for sympathy. I thought she was telling me that Glen had figured it out.

"I wish I'd never met Heath Lawler." She was sobbing, shaking from head to toe. She looked about six years old.

"I know I'm an imposition, Rose. I know you'd like to see me out and latch the back door against me."

"I like you, Lily. It's just that your timing isn't always the best."

"Along about now I get a dull line of pain around my middle because I know he's on his way home."

So did I. It's a little panicked feeling. How many sheets to the wind will he be when he walks in the door? What will I do if he's bad? What's he going to say when I tell him I ran out of flour and with pickling I didn't have time to run to the store in White Oak? How would I feel if the phone rang and a highway patrol officer told me that Dashnell was dead? Would it be sorrow or relief or regret?

"Rose, I know how it is with the afternoon sun dropping and a husband's expectations to be met." She had successfully ducked around the subject of Heath. Or so I thought.

"Rose"—the irritation had crept into her voice—"I said something here; I told you something. Why haven't you responded?"

"I'm not in this world to mind your business, Lily."

"Rose, who else do you talk to?"

I said I knew all the women up here on the lake.

"Why do I never see them sitting on your porch?"

"The ones who don't work have small children. They're busy," I excused myself, from what I had no idea.

"I'm a peroxided piece of work, Rosie. I ought to be on my knees with gratitude to Glen Pembroke. If it wasn't for him, I'd probably be a call girl down in Atlanta, hooked on heroin or dying of AIDS or both."

"Is there no in-between?" I was dumbfounded that she knew herself so well and mortified that she realized I wasn't always thrilled to see her at my door. I thought I'd done a better job of disguising it.

"I never understood it," she said glumly. "Husband, mortgage, kids and recipes. I'm no good at it."

"Then you need a career," I said. I had told myself the same thing a thousand times. After it was too late.

"You mean typing all day?" she asked with disdain. "And then come home to husband, mortgage, kids and recipes."

"Plenty of women do," I said grandly.

"I'd sooner be a call girl."

She'd talked a complete circle around me and as usual I'd missed the point. Typing looked good to me. I didn't have her options. The best I ever did was a minimum wage an hour clerk's position at a Birmingham department store.

"Rose, are you stupid?"

"Smart enough to know I made my own bed and I have to lie in it."

"I made my own bed. . . ." She rolled her eyes in disgust.

I took umbrage at that. I told her as much.

"Every word out of your mouth is something you've heard others say."

Supper. I'd dice ham and melt cheddar cheese over it and serve it on sourdough bread. I went into the larder and pulled a quart of corn chowder out of the freezer.

"Well!?"

"Make your point, Lillian."

"You never make *your* point, Rose. You're terrified someone will notice and tell Dashnell that you have a brain."

"I try to avoid trouble."

"Trouble? You avoid human contact."

She was up from her chair, standing right behind me, my best French linen dish towel in her hand. She laid it down absentmindedly on the stove and before she noticed the burner was warming, it was scorched. I grabbed it up. It was the last of six Carmen gave me the Christmas before he died. Dashnell had used the others to wash his truck windows. I blew apart.

"When I want my brains pecked to pieces, I'll see a psychiatrist! Whatever human contact I miss out on, I'm still not so low and deceitful I'd entice a kid into my husband's bed while he's off earning us a living! Your kind has to either stay in trouble or start it for somebody else. Go on out that door and don't come back!"

She looked like she'd swallowed a gopher. I checked myself carefully to see if I felt any remorse. To my great relief, I didn't. Lily stood there, her eyes coolly seeking mine. I wouldn't give them to her directly. I busied myself about the kitchen and waited for her to make that long sigh she always gives out before she leaves a room.

"Evidently I read you wrong, Rose. I apologize," she said in the same flat tone she had used earlier to tell me that she was afraid. "You've been a lot more decent than most," she added as her hand reached for the screen door.

I suddenly wanted to tell her everything. You forget when you draw up into yourself and pass the days alone. Loneliness is a precarious state of being. The most immediate and inconsequential things take on false importance. Diced ham and dish towels override people.

She was almost to their dock by the time I reached my backyard. She was smiling. I needed her friendship. I wanted it. I took more pleasure in her company than I had ever admitted to myself. Following her home was an act of surrender.

"I apologize for what I said."

"Don't apologize, Rosie. Trouble travels with me. You didn't say a word I haven't already thought."

I explained why the French linen dish towel set me off.

"I ruined one. I was careless, but it was unintentional. You threw me out. Dashnell has used five of them to wash his truck? What did you do to him?"

She couldn't possibly understand Dashnell or what it takes to keep things calm and even between us. I didn't say anything.

"We don't talk about Dashnell?"

I allowed I preferred that we not. I knew she was going to push it. Whether her intuition took over or she had seen more than I realized, Lily plucked a forgotten string.

"Rosie, I have eyes and ears. I know what's going on. I know how afraid you are. Just remember, I'm here when you need me." I wasn't ready to pour it all out. But her kindness gave me a great deal of hope that some things were still possible even for me.

It was dark. We sat on the bench at the end of the pier and waited for the moon. A lovely, aching feeling washed over me. It was tenuous and familiar and humbling. We were taking in the tender lapping of the water on the wooden pilings, the sporadic puffs of warm evening wind, and the sudden balm of our newly found friendship.

"He's decent, Rosie. His eyes give more than they take." I stopped my mouth. I didn't let myself play dumb and ask, "Who?" That would have been a backhanded warning not to mix me up in it. I just listened. "He doesn't understand deception. He doesn't have anything to hide. He's all that he appears to be."

She was in love with him. I could tell it frightened her. Well, it frightened me too.

"Every other man I loved was either deluded or duplicitous. I always saw it right away. It never caught me off guard. I'd determine his fatal flaw and stow it deep in my mind. I'd have it to blame later when our cloud ran out of gas. I was fatalistic. I had to examine every exit, to know my way out before I'd let myself fall in love. Until I met Heath."

I was immediately engulfed by shame. The notion that there was anything beyond the physical indulgence of two pretty young people had never entered my mind. The possibility that Heath Lawler was remotely decent had completely eluded me. I was far too envious of their beauty to consider their hearts and minds. Mine had been an exalted existence in an unreachable tower of self-pity. I was the unsung, martyred and deeply poetic keeper of all emotional truths. Lily was loose, blind and common next to me. Heath was certified Prince George County trash who had by an outrageously generous creator been given a comely form to disguise the brutal emptiness which set the Lawlers apart from the rest of the species.

"Why so quiet, Rosie?"

"I'm just trying to see this from your point of view."

"I didn't expect his kindness. I thought he'd deflate the tension of one relentlessly boring afternoon. It was a game of chance. Could I seduce that handsome young boy? Could I extract a measure of admiration? If I managed to lure him into my bedroom, how long could I keep him there?"

So I hadn't been completely off base.

"Why does his kindness upset you?"

"No stored well of falsehoods to throw at him if he gets too close to me. I'm defenseless. If I'm not careful I'll wind up hopelessly in love with him. I'll be powerless to stop. I'll do something crazy like walk out on Glen. I'll lose my children. God knows what Glen might do."

Suddenly I saw it. Lily and I were the same trembling birds of prey.

"Rosie, I play the slattern with the razored tongue. It's not altogether by choice. Glen *likes* it. It enables him to play the deceived, hardworking and relentlessly good man. Rosie, I'm not some thankless, unappreciative wife who refuses to work. Glen doesn't want me to work. He wants me at home where there's less temptation. He won't admit this, not even to himself, Rosie, but sex is his way of punishing me. He hurts me. He takes me when I'm asleep. He makes it excruciating. He slaps me and calls me names and plays choking games. If I so much as whimper he punches me and that excites him more. Rosie, I don't mean to embarrass or humiliate you, but I see, Honey. I know what you endure. I know that panicked look you try to hide when you hear his truck engine."

It was as if a stone fortress in my breast had suddenly toppled. I couldn't lie to myself anymore. My initial, instantaneous distrust of Lily had had nothing to do with her character or lack of it. She knew what I had hoped to hide from the world by moving up to the lake. She didn't arch her brows and purse her judgmental lips and accuse me of staying because I was sick or had any desire to be beaten to death.

To the world around us, Lily and I were two entirely different breeds. Beneath the wrapping we were prisoners of men who we knew would hunt us down and kill us if we left them.

We held on to each other and cried for a long time. The sudden din of a billion cicadas woke death in the looming pines.

A broken silver-pink moon hung in the east. Lily and I could read it plainly in each other's eyes.

Someone was going to die before this was over.

11
Glen

I know she's up there at Rose Lawler's running her mouth about me, drawing tales to get sympathy from those women who sit out there on the porch when they ought to be doing any of a hundred things. I've lived with her nine years now. I know her. That doesn't mean I know what she's going to do next. Or that I want to.

I tell myself I stay because of the kids. But if that's all there was to it, common sense would dictate that I take the kids and go back to Augusta and live with Mama and Daddy. I point out the foolishness of loving a woman like her. I make lists at the office of all the reasons I should leave her. I've been to three ministers about her and one psychologist. The psychologist was a nice guy. He made it easy to talk about her. He told me flat out there's nothing wrong with me. It's the environment I'm in. Yeah, well, hell, I knew that when I went to see him.

I won the southeast regional Golden Gloves Middleweight Championship twice. I played tight end for the University of Alabama. Played baseball too. I had aspirations towards pitching professional ball, but my right eye is weak. I took a master's in computer programming from SMU down at Dallas. I was on a fellowship and Lily taught elementary school. Daddy sent us money and I worked part time.

I used to pride myself on the fact that I was a simple guy. Give me a pretty woman, a little money in the bank and a hard job to do. I'm nobody's walking brain trust, but I'm not a fool. I took the middle path. I don't mind a hard question as long as I know there's an answer someplace. But the older I get, the more I realize that no one is that simple. Anyone who thinks he is hasn't looked very hard at himself. There are definitely more questions than there are answers in life. Take love.

Love is the most destructive force on earth. It gets in a man's way. It clouds his reason. It thwarts his intent. It keeps him in debt. It forces him to work at a job he hates. It makes him look in the mirror and wonder who that idiot is looking back at him. Sometimes she'll be on her third glass of wine, talking nonstop about one of her subjects, and I'll just sit there wondering what's wrong with me. I'm a good man. Some would say a strong man. I'm loyal and levelheaded, and five years from now I'll be a corporate vice-president. Why do I waste myself on her?

You want to know the worst part? There's no good end coming. She'll up and leave (again) or walk in with a loaded .44 and blow me and the kids off the planet or wind up in jail or God knows what. You can bet she won't ever settle down into what we have and make the most of it. I try to hate her for that. Sometimes I do. I know she has no power over her discontent, and I know there's times when she feels bad about that. That's why she goes off telling awful things about me that aren't true. She wants them to be true to justify the way she shudders when I touch her.

There is no lie detector like the bedroom. I'm a man. Sometimes I just have to have it. She cooperates because sometimes she does too. But that's all it is—cooperation. She doesn't love me back. It's the way I'd imagine it with a paid woman. I feel worse when it's over. Lonely, selfish and abandoned by God.

My love for Lily is my terminal illness. I'm incurable. She uses that against me when she slips off with other men. It's the same pattern today that it was years ago in Dallas. I pretend not to see it. She pretends she doesn't know that I know. I swallow the anger. I bite my tongue in half to keep from accusing her because if I ever do, I'll lose her. This way I have some chance of holding on to her.

My love for her is my madness. It's contrary to everything my mind tells me to do. In that regard it's pure and holy and changeless. It's insanity; it's god-awful painful, but it's constant, endless and perfect pain. She can't touch or alter that in any way. It's my power over her.

12
Rose of Sharon

It got deep with Lily. I hid away trying not to get too deep with anyone. You weigh the loneliness against the things that can happen if the wrong person knows the wrong thing. When we're alone we tend to tell ourselves we can bear anything. We turn ourselves to stone trying to keep our fearful secrets. We learn a way of getting by and we go on and become habituated to our private sorrows, to keeping silent about the things that matter to us the most.

I was making supper. Lily says I'm always making supper or cleaning up after supper or running off to buy food for supper. She was here. Seems like she's always here. I tease her about it. She knows she's welcome.

There was one bleeding secret I hadn't shared with Lily. I barely acknowledged it to myself. She was onto it. Or close.

"Rosie, this isn't your ordinary bunch of pretty little houses on a lake."

I couldn't be sure how much she knew and how much she was trying to wheedle out of me.

"Well, no, we all live up here year round. We're mostly Prince George County folks. We don't get much of a weekend crowd."

"Oh, give me a break, Rosie, we're a little more organized than that."

It was like somebody was running through my house opening windows.

"You just won't admit it for fear you might have to do something about it."

That made it plain. See, Heath had to know all about the Order. His daddy could be part of it if he chose to because membership is inherited. She had taken Heath to her bed and satisfied him and then she had laid her head on his chest and drawn it all out of him.

She told me right then and there. She'd suspected it for a long time. She'd begun to put pieces of it together.

"Glen is the only homeowner on the lake who isn't part of the Order. Isn't he?"

"I don't know for certain."

I didn't want to. I tried very hard not to. It was easy to look around the lake and see sweet little houses and docks and pines and let it go. The truth is I hadn't known the full extent of it until we moved back up here. Dashnell's daddy had been part of the Klan. I knew Dashnell had some inherited right to belong. I didn't know this lake community was an official enclave. I thought Dashnell had brought us back up here to get away from things, to have some peace, to be close to nature. It was months before I realized he'd brought us up here so he could devote the rest of his life to the Order.

"Rosie, they all met at your house the night it happened."

I was speechless. Heath had told her more about it than even I knew. Lily Pembroke confirmed that it was Dashnell's hand that aimed the gun. It was Dashnell's finger that pulled the trigger that shot the man on the lake. It was like listening to the end of the world.

I tried to gather my wits. I tried to think where I could run. I was glued to her eyes, trembling, ashamed, afraid.

"How did Heath know?" Of course there were a hundred ways he could have found out. Heath's a Lawler and they're highly regarded among the Order, if no place else on earth.

"We have to *do something* about it, Rosie. We have to *tell* someone."

I wanted to turn the subject back to her and Heath, but I couldn't figure a way to do it.

"Lily, if we say a word, we'll lose everything we have."

"Neither one of us has a damned thing we value, Rosie. At least I don't—or I wouldn't have involved myself with Heath."

"Let me not say it so nice this time, Lily. They'll kill us. They have ways. It looks like an accident or a suicide or a person disappears."

She went as sallow as her hair. She started crying. I had no earthly comfort to give her. I was in the identical steel jawed trap.

"Rosie . . . I'm scared too."

I still couldn't look at her. In a minute she got up and I heard the porch screen slam. There had been cicadas earlier, but now the air was silent. A boat motor across the lake scratched the stillness. In a few minutes I heard Dashnell's truck grinding into second as he double-clutched up the driveway.

13

Eula Pearl

Sometimes while I lie there in the dark counting the cabbage roses on the wall over my bed, I feel those horses thundering up the road. I know I smell them. You live in one world, then a phone rings or a newspaper is dropped on your porch floor or horses come thundering out of the night and nothing will ever be the same.

The worst fight Searle and I ever had was about him plowing over where those people are buried at the edge of the pasture. I had to dig post and string the fence wire myself to keep him from going back on his word. (I know my thoughts are random and it displeases me most of all. I can only follow after them and bale them together as best I can.)

"Them bones been dust fifty years," he says. "Maybe more."

"They'll be back," I says, but I didn't get my own meaning. Just that way leads on to way, and circles turn, and all like that. I reckon it's so heavy on my heart this morning because all through last night I listened to the rain and came back over that night Death rode past on those horses and my childhood came to an end. It must have been a clap of thunder in the distance that set those horses running through my mind. I've been crying all morning. I'm back then. I'm here and now. I'm suspended between. Old people spook easily. Old people cry.

Rain fell hard in the night, pitching crab apples onto the roof.

The wind knocked my night-blooming cereus over, smashed the pot to bits. Nadine hauled me another pot out of the garage. She asked me what plans I had for Searle's hammock. She said it would ruin in the garage. I wouldn't say take it. I'll offer it to Searle's great-nephew and his fat wife if they turn up again. Though they might be getting the hint. Rain and the air's turned to steam and the sky is still purple and the way the crickets are hollering, I'd say there's more coming. Rain like that always undoes me. Takes me back where I don't want to go.

Everything was fine, you know, and then the Trouble came and they passed taking Moena with them and then you'd hear the grown-ups whispering about "the Trouble," and then they was all forgotten, sucked up by the years. But I wouldn't forget.

You wouldn't know that fine paved road as a river of mud, but I did. You never heard the wet clay sighing underneath that asphalt or envisioned the pavement cracking into bits, dissolving, the old wheel ruts returning, the electric light posts melting and darkness closing back in. You never saw a wolf in these woods or danced on a canvas stretched over tree stumps near the marsh that they flooded to make the lake so Birmingham would have enough water and power to mushroom into its sassy self.

It's like his voice swam out over the dry August air and then turned back around towards the yard here and curled itself up in the crab apple tree and waited, waited ten, twenty, thirty, eighty years and then suddenly, last night, Moena came back and found it and hurled it through that window as I lay here. "Nigger gal," Doctor McKutcheon's voice split the night behind us, "don't you go into town tonight."

Now I'll be confounded if I can stop crying. I had to hide my face from Nadine while she scooped dirt into that pot. I will be confounded because if Rose of Sharon swoops in here unannounced and catches me like this, she'll haul me up to the doctor's. It's not that I mind the doctor's. It's stealing the time from Rose of Sharon. Especially here lately because she has a torment on her soul. I don't mean Carmen.

She's under a cloud. I half expected her to tell me about it yesterday when she brought me new sheets. I wouldn't dare ask. She acted jolly. But her face was near about as gray as it was right after she'd got the news about Carmen. But, no, Rose of Sharon is over Carmen. She's a strong woman, I'll say that.

"Nigger gal, don't you go into town tonight," clear as spring water, swirling around and round in my bedroom. It comes back to me like that in disconnected pieces of back time before the Trouble. Wee Mother's bed in the parlor. Wee Mother old and yellow, her hands knotted and rooty, and Mother in the chair beside her day and night. Hattie and Florence were allowed to go up to her and whisper in her ear or stroke her forehead because they were older. I could only peer in from the hall when no one was looking. Her eyes would come right out of her skull at you but she didn't know you were there. Fifty years later Searle refinished that bed and the chest just before Carmen was born. Rose of Sharon was thrilled to get it for the boy. I was tickled to have it out of my house.

Pieces of it slamming up against each other in my mind like the wind slapping the garage doors back in the night. Pieces, and you shut them out because you know if you don't they'll find each other and make it whole and real again and it'll draw you back there again. Most of life passes and you don't fiddle with why. But not the night the Trouble came down like the sky collapsing. I run from these thoughts into the kitchen, reach for the radio, play with the dial, but it's useless. It's got me. I'm gone back there.

"Nigger gal . . ."

Doctor McKutcheon's Model-T Ford had been in front of this house twice that day. Once in the last dark of night when the starlings screamed out of the sunrise behind the woods. They were all down there in the parlor with Wee Mother. I could see them hovering over her. Everybody was crying except Daddy, who kept calling Doctor McKutcheon over into the corner and holding his head close while he asked questions. Mother saw me and shooed me back up to bed. Then it was full sunup. Everybody was kind of giggly with relief at breakfast because it had just been a spell and not the end.

The doctor's Model-T Ford was there again when we got back

from church. He had checked back by and he stayed to dinner. He fussed at Mother for not getting me piano lessons and he told funny stories and spilled gravy all down the front of his gray seersucker coat. After the cobbler and the boiled custard he drove away. The women had afternoon naps because they'd been up so early with Wee Mother and I ran across the road to Moena's.

We played "Scratch the Hen" in the yard and Mother came over to sit on the porch with Beauty B. after a while. Mother was half-way peeved because she said it was taking Beauty B. three forevers to finish my school dresses and here Moena looked like she walked off a bandbox, Beauty B. had made her so many new clothes that summer. Beauty B. explained that Moena had to have them because the white Methodist Church was starting a new school for colored girls and school was to start in July. That was so the colored girls could be let out for six weeks in October to pick cotton.

I was already mad about me setting in school on yellow October afternoons and Moena getting to be out in the fields with the butterflies. Rosa Lynn Brown passed in the road on foot sometime in there. Mother spoke, but Rosa Lynn wouldn't deign to send her dignified hello up onto Beauty B.'s porch. Moena said that was on account of Beauty B. had made Rosa Lynn a fur-lined cape at Christmastime. When Beauty B. went to deliver it Rosa Lynn tried to pretend she had paid Beauty B. in advance. Beauty B. had to send the colored bishop from Yellow County to see Mr. Brown about it.

The bishop, who looked whiter than me, had grown up on the Browns' place. Years later I would hear rumors that Mr. Brown was the bishop's father. In any event, he gave the bishop Beauty B.'s two dollars at once. Then he gave his daughter Rosa Lynn what for because he had given her the money to pay Beauty B. and she'd squandered it.

All the same, I eyed Rosa Lynn with silent fascination as she passed that afternoon because I had heard at Sunday school that Rosa Lynn was engaged and I'd never seen an engaged woman before.

Moena and I held secrets and the woods held us as we crept over the moss to the stream. We had saved a gourd full of watermelon seeds and scattered them in a sunny place on the bank where the roots would have plenty of water except maybe for a couple weeks in August when the creek was almost completely sand. Her granny had taught her about growing truck that way. It was early August that Sunday and the melons were small and green inside, but we found one the size of a coconut and we took it to the swamp oak that grew sideways out over the creek bed and we sat there, the green melon halves in our laps, fingering the least bitter bites out of the centers.

We had no aspirations or designs that afternoon. All we had was the sunlight filtering through the leaves and the silent, slow moving green water below. Could a child of eight lean her sweaty back hard into the bark of a swamp oak to scratch it and smell the sun and the summer grass off her best friend's arm and say, "This is perfection"? Or is that remembering? If that's remembrance then why does my heart hear Moena say, "I know"?

There's a fellow over in Yellow County, an old man who paints pictures of flowers and gardens and whatnot. They have one in the doctor's office, misty looking, magic pictures. Nadine says he must not see very well because everything looks hazy. Maybe. But I'll say he's not looking at the thing he paints. I'll say he's looking back at it through time, and he's trying to find God in it. That's how it feels to remember that afternoon by the stream.

I have to quit crying.

Rose of Sharon called to say she'd be by. I can wash my own hair, barely, but I like the feel of her fingers on my scalp. She doesn't normally come two days running. Maybe it's on account of how I looked to her yesterday. Or whatever it is that's troubling her. Her washing my hair is how we talk, me and her. It's how we touch each other.

14

Hezekiah

(1943)

He had been in the Army six weeks when he went to see the doctor about the swelling and the ache in his joints. The doctor gave him aspirin and sent him on a fifteen mile hike with his platoon. It was blistering hot, highly unusual for late November in North Carolina. The aspirin brought his fever down and he figured the sweat was good for him. When he woke that night in the barracks his legs were screaming with pain and he was trembling with the cold.

Blaylock, his sergeant, was a tight assed, light skinned black man who used his high yellow complexion to curry favor from the white officers. Blaylock pasted on a hollow sneer and ordered Hez back to his bunk. Hez pleaded with him. There were pointed daggers drilling and scraping his elbows and knees. Blaylock wasn't about to bother his white superiors at such an inconvenient hour.

By morning Hez was seeing demons with triangular shaped heads and giant ears and tails. His legs wouldn't move. He shook with chills. The pain in his chest was so sharp he thought someone had broken it while he slept. They put him on a stretcher and two enlisted men placed it in the open bed of a half-ton truck and drove him seventy miles to the army hospital near Durham.

Indian summer had vanished in the night. There was ice in the rain that soaked through the blanket as he lay on the cot in the freezing wind with fire in his joints. Far above in the white and gray marbled clouds, a dark winged figure followed. Hez tapped the rear window of the cab, asking them to let him ride up front. The driver didn't turn his head. The passenger, a pimpled farm boy with buckteeth and pale gray eyes, glanced around at him and grinned. Then he looked away and switched on the radio.

White Christian choirboys. He hunkered down pressing his back into the cab. Turning the cot on its side to use it as a windshield, he wrapped the wet blanket around him. What would their German blond Jesus say to them about this?

There was nothing to do but go way away inside himself. He went back, down into South Carolina and into Florida. Back through those well-worn scenes on the turpentine farm and Grandfather's temper and Beauty's sermons and back to pink twilights on the porch with Beauty when she'd had enough corn liquor to face Alabama and it had seemed even then as long ago as Noah's ark. It wasn't the idea of a home place as much as the sudden tenderness, the tranquility that steadied her as she inhabited a lost moment, her calloused hands crossed over the end of the hoe as she paused in the garden and her bottom lip brushed a dry patch on the back of her hand and she licked it once or twice and a sudden cool trickled down her spine because the sun had dropped behind the April woods.

Later in the dark, his ears sandwiched in the feather pillow Beauty had made for the old white lady in the giant bed in the parlor of the house across the road, he would secretly drift across Alabama and sleep for a while in the warm purple grass behind the garden by the path that led down to the creek and back up the opposite bank into town.

He knew every rabbit hole and root in that field. He knew it in March when damp patches of burnt-orange earth showed through the brittle ivory stubble and there were green patches of daffodils and onion grass. He knew it on dry November evenings when the air was warm and the leaves crunched underfoot.

He had never seen it in late August.

He stood transfixed by fluttering clouds of white butterflies that burst gold in the late afternoon sun over the tall, thick grasses. The woods on the far end of the field, he heard singing.

A little white girl was coming towards him. She had brown orange hair and orange freckles and pink eyelids over pale gray irises. "You seen Moena?"

This was Eula. Beauty B. had said Moena and Eula Pearl were halves of each other.

He told her he hadn't. He wondered if she knew he was Moena's grown up son visiting his mother's childhood. Eula Pearl seemed to understand a great deal. Beauty B. said a band of angels followed Eula Pearl everywhere she went. He could feel them. Did she see them? Yet Alabama before the Trouble wasn't a place where a little girl was to be detained and subjected to superfluous questions by an interloper.

"She's run off with my shoes and Mama's fit. If Mama tells Beauty B., she'll get a whipping for sure."

She asked if he'd seen any snakes. He pointed out that it wasn't likely in dry August this high above the creek. He knew where Moena would be. Beauty had taken him there to fetch her home many times. He had watched while Beauty rousted the sleeping child, placed her dolls into a cloth sack and hurried her home before the mosquitoes rose in the evening damp.

It was supposed to be Moena and Beauty's secret place. He respected that. Alabama in August in Beauty B.'s memory was exalted as a realm where children's secrets were held in regard.

Little Eula Pearl squinted into the ball of rust flame that sat on top of the trees at the bottom of the meadow.

"She'll be stretched out with her dolls by the creek and you can't come. It's our secret place. It's far and I have to get my shoes from Moena and be home before dark." She ran across the field, leaping over patches of thistle and cow pies.

"Eula? Why didn't she want me?"

His eyes burned with humiliation at his unwitting boldness. The question wasn't hers to answer, but it invited further conversation.

"Did you hear about Rosa Lynn Brown?

"Beg pardon?"

"They found her beat up, half dead and worse."

Under the yard pump with the water stinging his nose. Beauty B. shaking and drowning it into him. *Stoned, driven, ridden out . . . Rosa Lynn, Rosa Lynn, Rosa Lynn Brown* . . . So this dying afternoon would descend into that woeful night of madness. Except he was dreaming it. Better to wake in the freezing rain with the flames in his joints.

"Eula?"

"I'd best be on."

"Eula, wait. Wait. Eula, is this a dream? Am I dreaming?"

She tossed her head to one side and flipped her hair with the back of her hand and she laughed. Then she bolted into the woods.

It was pitch black and he couldn't find Beauty B. and sudden torrents of men on horses swept off the tops of hills and there was barely time to dive into the brush before the trees bristled in the savage orange light of their torches.

It was better to wake up, but he couldn't wake up; the dream held him prisoner. Wake me up, wake me up, he shouted, then he stepped back onto the road. But which way? Bats were swarming. Then a tide of humanity spilled out of hiding. A spuming sea of black faces, denatured, ghostly, fleeing men, women and children, some weeping, breathless, old people, gasping, dropping down and screaming, "Don't leave me! Don't leave me!" They foamed towards him, running barefoot, riding wagons and mules. Some had their possessions. Others carried what they could. Wake me, wake me, wake me. . . . A woman dropped a bundle into his arms. It was her infant. He eyed her, incredulous, unable to speak. Her face entreated him.

"If I take him with me, neither of us will survive."

"Don't you love your child?"

"I don't want to die, mister."

"You have to love your child."

"Everybody's not strong like you, mister."

She broke off into the undergrowth. The infant wailed as he ran with the crowd. There was a low fooming whoosh. They had been moving up a long grade. At the crest of the hill a giant cross flamed. They were surrounded by torch bearing horsemen.

Oh, God, wake me! This was dying, this dream; when they killed him with the others here, he would die back there. His tormented existence would finally pass. Let it. Let it. Their Nazi Christ had ordained it. He would be branded by their burning swastika and slaughtered with the other cattle and descend into celestial oblivion. It was futile to resist. There was no exit from his dream until it dissolved into silent blackness. He let fly one long cry of woe, a soaring, sorrowful and beatific echo of his being that split the ceiling of that fearful night. Then he was empty of all longing and regret.

He was calm. He had surrendered. He was easy all the way through as he embraced defeat. What folly it had been to rail against the immutable order of all things. The infant sensed that the madness and the torment had flown. It kneaded its head into his chest and closed its eyes and slept. A river of joy sprang from his heart, a broad, spreading compassion that blanketed the child. The men were setting fire to the trees all around them. Death, as senseless as all the years of his life, would soon choke the life out of them. His joy endured. He was flooded with gratitude and humbled by impossible, illogical peace. Then from above an ancient voice descended:

"Say to those who are of a fearful heart,
'Be strong. Fear not! Behold!
Your God will come and save you. . . .' "

The horsemen tried vainly to rein in their nervous steeds.

A glow appeared in the sky. Panicked, the captors spread in all directions and shouts of deliverance and triumph rang out. The light grew into a draped and folded whiteness. The voice continued.

"And the ransomed of the Lord shall return,
With singing and everlasting joy. . . .
And sorrow and sighing shall flee away. . . ."

He gazed into the serene white linen above him. He blinked with wonder. He closed his eyes and drifted a moment, then opened them again. She was an old nun. Her eyes were watery and her pink skin was creased and spotted. Her small hands clutched her rosary beads as they rested on the Bible in her lap. Her teeth were as white as her habit and she smiled with profound gratitude.

"God sent you back to us." She clapped her hands. Her Bible and her rosary fell to the floor. She threw back her head, delighted by her clumsiness. It was night. He was on a large ward. Instinctively he tried to lean forward to gather up her things. He could barely lift his head. The effort made him dizzy.

"Not hardly yet." She bent down, then stood up with a groan. "Rheumatic fever, child. The army hospital was full." She leaned forward and whispered into his ear. "We know that's a lie." Then she sat back and cracked her knuckles. "They gave you up to us for dead. It's been almost a month ago now."

Slowly her words began to sink in.

"God had other plans for you." Then she giggled. "I've read to you for weeks, all four Gospels and the Psalms, and you were a most unappreciative audience. Until Isaiah. Old Isaiah made you sit up and listen." She excused herself and went to ask the nurse to bring him some food. The dream of the evil night was still with him. One hand cradled a pure white pillow like an infant on his shoulder. The other moved with considerable effort to lift Sister's Bible off the bedside table. He opened the cover and read an inscription.

Given with love to Margaret Helen O'Brien
in recognition of her graduation with honors
from All Saints Academy, Dublin, Ireland,
16 June 1894.

He slowly lifted and dropped the weightless, opaque pages, taking strange comfort in the sudden familiarity of their arrangement . . . Genesis, Exodus, Leviticus, Numbers, Deuteronomy. . . . Pages irrefutably dusted by decades of the pious sister's scrutiny . . . Joshua, Judges, Ruth, 1 Samuel, 2 Samuel. . . . There was a worn green velvet bookmark nestled between Isaiah 34 and 36. Holding it close with both hands, he searched the page until he found it.

And the ransomed of the Lord shall return . . .
and sorrow and sighing shall flee away.

He closed the book. He stared at the ceiling. He listened to low, distant voices and echoing footsteps. He slept a dreamless half hour. He woke. He ate some stinging hot soup that made him cough. He rested. He picked up the Bible and turned to 2 Kings, where he found the story of his namesake King Hezekiah as bland and uninspiring as ever. He went back to the verse in Isaiah. Pretty words. If they contained some personal meaning, it eluded him. Still, they were pretty words and they had waked him from a deathly slumber. Had he not been ransomed and returned? He couldn't ask them to mean more than that. Ransomed, why? Returned, where? Surely these words had not lifted him from that well of darkness merely that he might addend his violent, surreal, happenstance existence. He touched something scratchy at his throat. He picked up a small hand mirror. He had grown a full beard. His eyes were clouded and sunken, his lips parched, swollen and ghastly gray. Yet death was nowhere about, and underneath something rooted, affixed itself, took hold and drew willingness out of darkness and time and it was bounty to breathe in and out, to hear low, distant voices and echoing footsteps, to believe that more meaning slept in those words, to enter the path of an honest and productive existence and follow it to its awakening.

The voices had all faded. Lamps had been switched off up and down the ward. Through a line of long, bleak windows over iron beds where afflicted, incurable men slept on the opposite side of the ward, the empty, shining enameled upper branches of ancient elms creaked and bristled blue over streetlights. At the far end of the room a dull and restive metallic knocking gave over to the hissing of a leaky radiator valve. Far off, he descried the faint and fleeting whistle of a southbound freight train; and sliding down into easy slumber he felt it might not be a train, but a shooting star sailing under the dark side of the moon, or the earth shifting on its axis, or the weary breath of time passing over the pink and gray marbled earth.

15

Lily

Mama says I'm thick to feel the way I do. That's because she'd be a duck in a swamp living in this beautiful house with a man who adored her the way Glen does me when we're out in public or in front of the kids watching television. Mama says I ought to get down on my knees and thank the Lord. She says I was born thankless. She's too thick to understand there's no love beneath his adoration, only some perverse need to make me grovel. I wonder, though. Is Glen a breed? Does Daddy hurt and humiliate my mama in the dark the way Glen does me? Does Mama sense that about Glen? Does she think it's just the way of the world? Or worse, does she like it? Has she been hiding bites and bruises all these years? She would. I certainly wouldn't put anything past my daddy.

I have to have love. I have to have love, physical love from a man. I mean warm and sweet. I need it. I want the other kind of love, the higher kind. But I need your garden variety, dime store, man going at a woman love too. That's what I wanted Heath to be, but that's the least of what it was. It shocked me. You'd think he was just a good time boy. He's built like Hoover Dam and pretty as a woman. You don't expect tenderness or consideration or vulnerability to show up in a package like that.

He looks straight into my eyes the whole time he loves me.

There's no hurry. He doesn't drift back into himself, hitch up his trousers and take off when it's over. It's hard to tell where the communication stops and the lovemaking begins. He calls here all day long. I keep telling him not to. He knows I don't mean it. I want him. I just can't drag a person as fine as Heath into my messes. He deserves so much more than me.

I know the exorbitant price of a passion like the one Heath Lawler and I could share. I learned firsthand down in Texas. When Glen and I were living in Dallas, I met this boy Randy at my yoga class. He was twenty and I was twenty-two. Randy had a shotgun Pentecostal wedding when he was nineteen. It turned out the gun wasn't loaded. The girl wasn't pregnant. She tricked him. Her father had a lot of money. Her mother spent ten hours a day in church. She and Randy lived in a trailer on their property. Randy was going to Bible college.

He had long, thick chestnut hair that fell over his shoulders. He played folk guitar and wrote songs. He made and sold silver and turquoise Indian style jewelry part time at a hippie store near downtown. I thought he was the end of the world.

It has often been rightfully said about me that I'll tell a lie when the truth works a whole lot better. I'm telling the truth about this. I went to that yoga class hoping something like that might happen.

I was bored witless with Glen six months after I married him. Glen has God and the Universe wadded up in his shirt pocket. Glen knows the reason for everything. If Glen doesn't understand, it's not to be pondered. I'm no intellectual. However, I'm curious about things. People like Glen won't live with unanswered questions. They race through this life like scared little rabbits. They have the world screwed on backwards and they worship their own worst fears.

On the first night of yoga class, Randy sat next to me. He knew a lot about yoga. He kept showing me how to take positions. We fell into talking after class. He took me to a coffeehouse. I had my first cup of espresso. We talked about life and philosophy. I made him laugh. It was strange. I was saying things that would set Glen off and he was amused by them. Of course Randy did most of the talking. I was too busy praying silently that he wouldn't say it was time to go. If I had been paying more attention, I would have asked myself why a married man in Bible college was sitting there talking to me about love and freedom and honesty. All I wanted that night was to roll myself up into a ball to crawl inside his chest and sleep.

I knew by eleven o'clock that Glen would be frantic. I didn't care. Sometime after midnight the place closed. It had started to rain. To this day I don't know where he took me in his van. I remember the sound of the rain. I remember when he kissed me I stopped hurting. It was a shock because until that nameless ache suddenly ceased, I had been unaware of it. He said he loved my boldness and my humor. I was completely captivated by his tenderness. I had never had a gentle lover. He called me a miracle. I cried with happiness. We laughed a lot. Then the sky was gray and pink in the east. I was certain Glen had the police out looking for me. It didn't matter. There was love in his eyes when he told me good-bye. All the way home I kept trying to make myself plan what I'd say to Glen. I wouldn't let those thoughts intrude upon my happiness. To this day I can't remember exactly what I told him. It was something about a girl in class needing a ride home. I think I said she lived way out in the country and that we'd had car trouble miles from the nearest phone. Whatever it was it relieved him. Glen was all over me, kissing me in that selfish, gnawing manner he confuses with passion. I let him take me to bed. I let him kiss me in that rough way he has of convincing himself he's all lover. It was all I could do to keep from laughing out loud when he told me I smelled nice. I was reeking of Randy's sweat and cologne. When it started to hurt, I pulled way back into my mind and pretended that Glen was Randy. Randy was making love to me the way Glen did as a joke. Then it really started hurting. I couldn't pretend anything anymore. All I could do was lie there and look at his thick, selfish face all scrunched up as he worked his way to the finish line and wonder who he thought he was loving.

I come from cold, hollow people who were raised up in Old Testament righteousness. We had the minister to Sunday dinner a lot. It was all Jesus, niggers, communists and Jews over deep-fat fried chicken at our house. I despised it from the day I was born. I could turn on the television and see it wasn't like that in other places. I made Glen promise we'd move out west or up north before I'd sleep with him. "Up north" was a bald-faced lie and "out west" turned into computer school in Dallas. I was thinking more like San Francisco or Seattle. Dallas is Alabama stretched out with a little more money.

Glen was the first halfway respectable boy who asked me out. He was solid and surefooted and I thought he'd keep me out of mischief. I've been in one kind of trouble or another most of my life. I was very grateful when Glen started paying attention to me.

The problem is you can suffocate on gratitude. There's only so long you can whisper "I love you" between the sheets and sigh and moan when the truth is he's hurting you because he comes at you all at once and he's done and asleep in a minute and you're lying there with a throbbing headache wondering how much more you can take.

Randy was Lord Byron in a denim jacket. Randy would always read to me first. Sometimes it was a poem he'd written. Sometimes it was from one of the little books I brought him. He would give me a glass of wine and lay my head on his chest and stroke my hair. His voice and all those beautiful words were better than wine. Sometimes our talking would get so deep and involved that we'd forget making love altogether. Randy let me love him back. I fell one thousand and ten percent in love with Randy.

Glen has all kind of names for what was taking place between Randy and me. To Glen a thing like we had is sordid, trashy and soap operatic. It's common, immoral, dirty and beneath contempt. How Glen loves to grit his teeth and say, "Beneath contempt."

Glen's ego wouldn't allow him to embrace what was going on right under his nose, in his bed. Glen could suspect, but he couldn't really imagine Randy drinking his wine, laying his head on his pillow, using his razor, his rubbers, his deodorant and once, because Randy had a class, his shirt.

I didn't do it to hurt Glen. I had nothing specific against Glen. It would have been a whole lot easier on me if I had. I felt tremendous guilt about it, but not enough to stop me. To this good day Glen Pembroke will go into a mood and demand that I tell him all about Randy and me in detail. He likes to beat himself up with it. I honestly think if I'd take a rubber hose and beat Glen silly he'd be the happiest man on earth.

Six months after Randy and I were together for the first time, his wife saw his car at my house. We had to start using motels, which was complicated because I had to explain my absences and motels get expensive. That little Pentecost woman was determined. She hired a detective. He followed us. He got pictures, license plate numbers, the whole sordid mess.

One Saturday Glen was sitting in the den watching a football game. A deputy sheriff rang the doorbell and handed him a subpoena. She was suing Randy for a divorce and me for something called alienation of affection. I was scared to death. I think we were both just too tense to talk. I packed and got out of there as quickly as I could. I found a little house up on Lake Grapevine which I could rent by the week. I drained Glen's checking account and hauled all his credit cards to cash machines for the money to get Randy and me through. I told myself it was the price of love.

Randy left his wife and moved in with me; but it was already different between us. I was costing him more than he had to spend. He tried not to resent me for that. But he did. Randy still looked me in the eye, but I could see a wall building back there in his head. He was trying to hold back a gathering storm he didn't want to share with me.

I knew the court date was coming up, and I kept saying that we should get out of Texas while we had the money to do it, and he kept putting me off. One day I came home from the grocery store and Randy and his things were gone. I rode by her mama and daddy's place, and I saw his car in the driveway.

It took me a few weeks of torment, but I finally put it all together. It ended that way because it had never really existed. I invented Randy that first night at yoga class. I turned an ordinary kid with no direction into a prince out of a fable. I lifted his station. I imbued him with a hundred kinds of poetry he would never possess. When

Randy looked into my eyes he saw that fantastic creature of my invention. I gave him a part he loved to play. What man with a grain of honesty doesn't want to think of himself as a shining warrior? For Randy that was a hundred times more pleasant than being himself, an unsure kid married to a woman he didn't love, attending a school he despised—all in the name of inheriting her father's money. Playing my prince was an illusion Randy couldn't sustain. That same core of decency that attracted me to him made it impossible for him to lie to himself or me forever. He had to get back to who and where he really was. He had to move up or down from there.

I called Mama and begged a plane ticket. I went home to Alabama and put up with her condemnations for a few weeks. All I needed was a place to lay my head until I could find a job and a place of my own. At least I was away from Glen Pembroke. I knew I'd be all right. Then I realized that I was pregnant. I hadn't slept with Glen in three months by that time, so I knew it was Randy's. Mama said I couldn't stay there. She wasn't about to help me raise a baby when Glen had all he had and he was crazy about me. She isn't about to help anybody if she can possibly avoid it. Mama is the sanctimonious, cold, smiling Sunday school type who gives Christians everywhere their bad reputation.

Today I'd beg, borrow or steal the money and have an abortion if I was in a mess like that. I wouldn't create unwanted children. I wouldn't bring helpless little burdens into a situation like mine and Glen's. I don't want them and their father doesn't know what they are. It gives them too much to overcome. I feel so guilty for believing that I bend double to spoil my children with kindness when a loving parent would give them guidance and parameters. How much better it would have been to save their souls for a sane mother who wanted them. Kids get shafted in this world. It warps them. They grow into adults who turn around and shaft their kids.

I suppose it was guilt. I had hurt myself and Glen. I hurt Randy too. Mama was tossing me out. I didn't have the guts to be pregnant and divorced and trying to make it in this world. I went back to Dallas, to Glen, to hell. The only relief I've known since then was a few hours with Heath Lawler. I won't do to Heath Lawler what I did to Randy. I won't create in him someone we both know he'll never be. Better to hurt him and myself now. Let him think I'm shallow and fickle. Let him blame me now and get over it. I'm accustomed to the strangeness in this house.

I won't stretch it any farther. I won't test the bounds of Glen's sanity. It's a twisted game with us. He deliberately chose a woman like me. He wants me to provide him an excuse to act out the cruel, perverse agenda he guards from public view. He's on a mission. As dark as it gets for me sometimes, as much as I long for a different path, I know Glen's unarticulated torments lead him alone into sulphurous pits of despair I can't even imagine.

There's no place in all this for Heath. He's worth more than that. I've told him everything. I've explained it. Heath says I'm just afraid of an honest love. He's right, of course. He's not twisted like Glen or weak like Randy. He's too decent for me. I'm afraid of a man I can't hold at arm's length. There's only so vulnerable I'll allow myself to be. I'm terrified of giving myself completely. If I wasn't careful, Heath could swallow me up. He'd absorb me. I'd dissolve and disappear into him.

16
Hezekiah
(1945)

It was burning hot in the sun, but the air was laced with damp. A chill seeped out of the ground and permeated the iron chair where he had been sketching most of the afternoon. His mind kept drifting away, his heart listening.

There are eternal things that thump between opaque leaves and yellow blotches of sun when no men are there to disturb them. There are living rings of purple and pulsing swirls of red that float between the air and the eye and reveal themselves to the Chosen. These are the harbingers of change, the revelations of the deepest truths, the answers that will not and yet suddenly and finally come. That was Beauty B. as clear as the dying sunlight that shone through the roses as he sat in the garden that separated the convent from the infirmary.

It had been a slow recovery with many setbacks. The fever would disappear for a day, then the aching and the sore eyes would greet him when he woke the next morning. It had taken weeks to collect the strength to walk from his room to the little sun porch where the nurses, most of them starched white nuns like Sister Margaret Helen, ate their egg salad sandwiches and sipped tea.

The U.S. Army, a typewritten letter informed him, placed no value whatsoever on a colored boy with a rheumatic heart. He was honorably discharged. Sister Margaret Helen was enraptured when he informed her he had read the Dickens and the Defoe she borrowed for him from the school library. She treated as a divine gift the discovery that he was for the most part fairly well educated. She considered the completion of his education her solemn duty, enlisting the aid of the principal, Brother Willamen, a corpulent monk who spoke with a thick German accent. He brought Hez an algebra workbook and another containing grammar exercises. When he had successfully completed them, he was rewarded with a Latin primer and a biology text. Brother Willamen and Sister Margaret Helen became determined to heal him, mind, body and soul. Their investment in him was thorough and for the most part genuine. All they wanted in return was to render one faithful Catholic to Rome.

However, church history, hierarchy and, most of all, dogma, seemed a million miles away from the basic ideas for living to which they bore exemplary witness. They lent far too much credence to church rules and the ever changing orders handed down from Rome. Stained glass houses of worship and alabaster statues of the saints were superfluous. Beauty B.'s pulpit had been a stump in the woods, her cathedral a clump of dry cedars that pointed towards heaven. Sister Margaret was as wrong about his suitability for membership in the Holy Church of Rome as she was right when she said that God had brought him back because he had things for Hez to do in this world.

They were dauntlessly devoted to serving God through service to other human beings. For all their vows of chastity and poverty and their blind obeisance to papal dictates, they were witty, articulate and generous people who worked tirelessly at loving others. Their unwillingness to question the efficacy of their toil in the face of a brutal, unjust world, inspired him.

He had luxuriated in their kindness and the ordered sanity of their world for six months when Sister Margaret decided that, after a few months of preparation, Hez could be given a test that would result in a high school diploma. After that she was unshakably convinced Hez would do himself and the world the most good by enrolling at Notre Dame University.

He listened politely as Sister Margaret's plans for the rest of his life evolved. He trusted her judgment and wanted more than anything to please this inordinately good woman who had been his saving grace. Yet the passing weeks showed him with increasing clarity that he must remain in the South. From the intractable distance of their safe harbor, he looked back with clean eyes on his life. For all the wrong turns and misery and injustices, he descried a rude majesty in, an undeniable desire to remain connected to, the malevolent, lovely people and landscapes of his youth.

Unlike half the people he knew, he saw no value in running away up north for sanctuary. The South was his home and he belonged in the South. He would embrace it. He would find the life for which God had saved him. He would do what intuition and not reason implied. He would grab hold of it the way a beaten child will bury his head in his abusive mother's skirts.

On a rainy Monday morning in June, Hez scratched a note of farewell and affectionate gratitude. He rolled up his tiny estate and stuffed it into a canvas U.S. Army release bag which he could hang by straps over his shoulder. He slipped into the garden and cut a small yellow rose. He placed it and the note, now neatly folded in the place on the table in the dining room where Sister Margaret Helen ate breakfast with the other nuns. He crossed the purple shadowed garden at sunrise. He took pains not to let the garden gate slam behind him. He walked sixteen blocks to the bus station and purchased a one-way ticket. "Charleston," he told the exhausted woman behind the marble counter. It was boarding. There was no time for regret or misapprehension.

Charleston meant Moena. Hez believed that his unwilling mother and he should be able to unlock dozens of mysteries for each other. He hoped that his pulsing gratitude would endure the long, slow process of forging some kind of rapport with her. He believed that the willing extension of his arm across the inexplicable gulf between himself and the woman who would or couldn't be his mother was both act of faith and prayer of confession.

It was right to submit himself. He was offering love and support to a woman he had used to explain and justify every weak, dishonest, self-destructive thing he had ever done.

17
Rose of Sharon

I learned how to deal with losing Carmen a little along. It was indiscriminate and constant hurt at first. It was every minute of every day. But gradually I'd pass an hour or two without hurting over it. Then an afternoon. Eventually he crept back into my conversation and memory, and I could think of him as he was in this life and not just how he died. Gradually I learned to separate my thoughts, to set aside time for the hurtful part.

But I've had no such luck with the man on the lake. I don't mean in dreams or night visions like I had with Carmen. I mean sometimes in the broad daylight, sitting on my porch, I look off across the lake and I see that silver line of his boat. There's a good fishing spot up in those reeds, so I probably really do see a boat. But my mind makes it his.

With Dashnell, it's just a thing that happened like that awful rainstorm last week. Now and again somebody will refer to it in passing, and I can make no discernible difference in Dashnell's demeanor when the subject comes up. That's how right he thinks it was. I'd like to crack his head open and yell way down in there where he hides that I know the straight of it. It wasn't really because the man was black. Race has very little to do with race hatred or pride. The issue of race is the outer wrapping. Some of those men did it because it made them feel a man. Some believed their victim was trying to take something away from them. Those would be the ones who feel less secure with all they have than Dashnell. Dashnell did it because Carmen, his sunshine and his joy, was taken away from him. Dashnell went off trying to balance the scale by helping to take another. But it's like peeling an onion, because there's a layer under that. Dashnell Lawler was no kind of father to Carmen. He never took him places. He barely showed up for his Little League or high school basketball games. The only reason he attended his high school graduation was because Mama had come and he was afraid of her disapproval. Alive, Carmen was little more than proof of Dashnell's manhood. But after he died, he became his sunshine and his joy.

I couldn't say that to Dashnell and spend another night with him. Thirty-four years of marriage wouldn't hold against that. I really can't visualize hauling my sewing machine and my doll collection back home to Mama's at this late stage. I often wish that I could.

It's been a month. All that's come of it, as far as I've heard anyway, is that a black minister from down at Birmingham called the sheriff demanding a thorough investigation. He says he wrote the governor about it. I stopped myself twice this week from getting in the car and riding over to Yellow County and finding that man's widow to see what her situation is. Think what that could start. If she had a brain, she'd know I knew something. If she had a spine, she'd pry it out of me, and then what? It's 105 degrees out here on this porch. But I shiver to the core when I consider it.

Lily came by yesterday afternoon. She looked real pretty. She was wearing linen pants and a white silk blouse and a silver Indian necklace. She says that she's quit drinking wine altogether. She's going to a little meditation and discussion group at the alternative school up in White Oak. She cut her hair and toned it down a couple shades. There was none of that hateful talk about her kids driving her up the walls and not a word about Glen. It was the first time I ever heard her comment on how pretty the lake is. I really enjoyed her company. I told Marjean about the change in Lily. Marjean says, "It don't mean a thing but that Lily must want something from you." Then she laughed that awful throaty rattle of hers that winds up in her cigarette cough. What in thunder do I have to offer Lily?

Fact is, I want something from her. One of Carmen's books was called *A Comparative Study of World Religions*. I really didn't get all of it, but I got the general idea. You boil them down and all religions say the same thing. If you're a selfish person, then you're an unhappy person. Lily says this young fellow Michael England who runs the school and conducts the discussion group, he leads them through all kinds of ideas like that. I'd really like to go once and hear them all talk. I couldn't do anything like that by myself, but I'd tag along with Lily if she invited me. It wouldn't be that hard to suck an invite out of Lily. The hard part would be keeping Dashnell from hearing about it. If he even dreamed I attended a discussion group at that alternative school, they'd have to place him in six-point restraint.

18
Eula Pearl

Mother gave Moena and me what-for because we had run off into the woods. We couldn't play together after supper, so we were standing across the road from each other hollering back and forth when Mr. Brown rode up asking if we had seen Rosa Lynn. She'd been expected at Dinah Tillingham's house that afternoon, but she hadn't shown up. Mother came out and talked to Mr. Brown a minute and then Hattie and Florence drifted out, curious to hear what was going on. As soon as Mr. Brown rode off, Hattie bet Florence a cookie that Rosa Lynn had eloped with her fiancé to get back at her mother for making such a circus out of their upcoming wedding. I remember that because when they all went back inside, I asked Moena what *eloped* meant and she said making a baby. Beauty B. had come out on the porch by then and she heard what Moena said, and she cackled so loud it set the starlings rustling in the cedars.

I was crawling into bed on the upstairs sleeping porch when the men came and Daddy went to help them look for Rosa Lynn. I could hear Hattie telling Florence in the next room that Mr. Brown had caught up with Rosa Lynn's fiancé and slugged him several times before he believed the boy when he told him he didn't know where she was.

I heard the stairs creak when Mother got up in the deep dark and went down to check Wee Mother's breathing. There were wagons up and down the road all night and men hollering across the pastures and searching the woods with lanterns. I heard them, but it was from faraway sleep.

I woke to thunder rolling long and getting closer. Hattie yelled, "Tornado," and Mother was swooping me up, carrying me down to the storm cellar. Soon we could hear the men's voices. It wasn't thunder or a tornado. It was hooves on the road, horses and wagons and men shouting, and we went out on the porch to watch them fly past. Daddy dropped out at the rear and rode into the yard. Daddy was a long-fused, soft-spoken man who read Scripture most Sundays at church. But a meanness had overtaken him, and it scared me so bad I ran back into the house and upstairs without being told. I crawled back into bed. I could hear them flying around, slamming doors and windows shut. For the second time that night, a big person swooped me up. It was Daddy, and he laid me in his and Mother's bed. His shotgun was propped by the window. Hattie and Florence got into bed with me. Mother was down in the parlor with Wee Mother and another gun. Daddy rode off towards town.

Mother had told them not to tell me, so it took a lot of whimpering and pleading. I think Hattie finally broke down so she could get some sleep. She told me they'd found Rosa Lynn lying facedown by the creek in the woods with a gash in her forehead. She said they found her unconscious and her clothes were torn. I had never heard the word *raped,* but I knew it was too terrible to inquire about, so I didn't. Hattie whispered that the slayer was still out there someplace loose, apt as not very close by. I grabbed hold of Hattie's hand and I started to fall asleep, but then I remembered Moena and I wanted to go tell her, but I was too sleepy and Florence told me that Moena already knew because her daddy was one of the men out there helping them look for Rosa Lynn. Florence got up once in the night. I could hear her crying. That was because she'd bet Hattie a cookie that Rosa Lynn had eloped.

Wee Mother ate a bowl of oats the next morning and we all felt happy about that. Daddy didn't come back until around midday dinner. He told us that Rosa Lynn was dead. He walked up the stairs, leaning on the banister. He caught a nap.

Mother and Hattie and Florence went to be with Mrs. Brown in her tribulation. Beauty B. came over to sit with Wee Mother. She let Moena and me play on the porch, but we weren't much for play. We kept looking up at the clouds and seeing Rosa Lynn there. I don't know what time Mr. Carter Crowley come driving up in his truck. He asked for Daddy, and Beauty B. took him into the dining room since Wee Mother was bedded in the parlor. The dining room is right inside the porch and Beauty B. cracked the windows to draw some air across Wee Mother. We could hear them talking.

"We got him." That was Carter as Daddy came into the room. Beauty B. was serving them both iced tea.

"Who did it?"

"Henry Gill. He's up at the jail." Henry Gill was a midget retarded colored man you'd see on the square on Saturdays.

"How did they catch him?"

"He had one of her rings in his pocket."

"Well, he'll hang, and good riddance."

"Some say he won't."

"Nigger rapes and murders a white woman?"

"Some think his being retarded could factor in."

Daddy said he was sure it wouldn't. He said he was certain the law would deal swiftly and justly with Henry Gill. Years later I realized that was because my daddy didn't have much stomach for what he knew they were going to do. Mr. Carter Crowley reminded Daddy that this was the second time a white woman had been raped by a nigger in Prince George County in a year. The one they got for the first one was a vagrant from nobody knew where. He'd sawed his way out of jail and fled to avoid lynching. He was never found.

I have often wondered about that first man. Maude Langdon, his alleged victim, was a skinny, hysterical woman who sang in the Baptist church choir. Hattie said she had copied off her test papers all through school. You'd see Maude Langdon everywhere running her mouth about everybody in town. They said what she didn't know, she made up and told as the truth. It may have been like she said. This vagrant broke into her house and raped her one evening when she came home from choir practice. In my mind, it could just as easily be the man knocked on her back door and asked for a drink of water. No one around here was likely to wait around for the truth to come out. I thought it was pure genius of him to saw his way out of that jail and run off.

I'll always wonder where he ended up, if he or his luck changed. It might have been he found decent work and settled down someplace with a woman. It could be he discovered peace of mind, turned a trade and lived to become a grandfather. In all fairness, it could also be he moved on to his next victim. Maude Langdon lived to become a great-grandmother. A few years after she was raped, the bank president's wife caught him in bed with her. It wasn't long after that Maude Langdon had herself a bank president and a new Lincoln every other year. I mean back when a Lincoln was a Lincoln. Searle drove up in a brand new Lincoln one time. It was a beautiful thing. I made him take it right back, though. I was terrified somebody might follow us home and see where we lived.

Whether Maude Langdon was a liar or not, Mr. Carter Crowley said Rosa Lynn Brown was the second white woman and more savage attacks could be expected unless they got the message out to the niggers right away. When he said it like that, I think Daddy agreed. He and Mr. Carter Crowley got into his truck and left in a few minutes. Just before he did, Daddy told me I couldn't have Moena up on the porch, that it might not look right to people passing. So I asked could we play in my room instead. Mother let us sometimes. But he said, "No."

Quick as Daddy was gone and we knew Beauty B. was busy giving Wee Mother a sponge bath, Moena and I slipped off down into the woods to the place where we'd been told they found Rosa Lynn, but it looked the same as ever. We played in the creek awhile, and then when it was starting to get dark, we headed back up through the woods towards the house, Rosa Lynn's ghost following us all the way.

Hattie was back. Beauty B. was standing at the edge of the yard and she just jerked Moena off the ground by her arm and moved across the road with giant, stiff strides. Jake, Moena's daddy, stood in the door of their house and I called out, "Hey," like always. But it was like he was deaf and staring straight through me at the end of the world. Hattie started fussing at me for running off.

Hattie said Mother and Florence were spending the night with Mrs. Brown on account of they had kin coming from six places and Rosa Lynn's wedding presents were still laid out all over the dining room and the upstairs rooms had to be made ready and you couldn't get a colored maid to step outside her door that day. Or if you could, she wouldn't go near Mr. Brown's house. I asked her where Daddy was, but she wouldn't say. Wee Mother woke with a breathing spell while Hattie and I were eating supper and for once I was allowed to rinse and replace the cool rags on her forehead until she drifted back to sleep, because Hattie was all nerves that night.

I was back in the kitchen washing up the supper dishes. Hattie had gone to peek in on Wee Mother. I heard her running up the hall, I heard the screen door slam behind her. I went into the parlor and Wee Mother was breathing hard, a foamy substance sliding down one side of her mouth. I wiped at it and then Hattie was back with Beauty B. who had brought Moena with her because Jake had been sent for Doctor McKutcheon and she wouldn't leave Moena alone, not that night. Hattie said it was Providence that Doctor McKutcheon lived in the country and that for the most part Jake could keep to the woods. Beauty B. said if Doctor McKutcheon lived in town, Jake wouldn't have gone for him if one of his own was at death's door.

Hattie and Beauty B. kept dabbing at the foam on Wee Mother's chin. Moena whispered to me that her mama was fit because her daddy had gone out on the road alone, a nigger by himself in the dark on the devil's night. Wee Mother was jerking in the bed now and we all had to hold her. Her eyes were wide and rolled back into her head and there was a terrible smell. Hattie commenced to crying that she had to get Mother. Beauty B. kept telling her she had to stay put. But Hattie was all in pieces and she ran off. Wee Mother quit jerking and her breath was steady and the foam reduced down to a trickle. Beauty B. kept going out onto the porch to watch for the doctor or Mother, she said, but we knew she was looking out for Jake. We knew for sure by then it was a bad night for a dark man to be out on the road alone. Beauty B. was all trembly and having a hard time holding back her tears. Her temper was gone. Moena said, "What's wrong?" Beauty B. sank down onto the steps sobbing, "They're going to kill every one of us tonight." I don't know how much time passed with no one coming and things moving from bad to worse and then finally Doctor McKutcheon drove up.

Beauty B. stood straight up all at once.

"Where's Jake?"

The doctor said Jake had been by his house maybe an hour before. That meant Jake had been missing at least half an hour. Doctor McKutcheon told Beauty B. that she needn't worry. Jake was no part of what was happening on court square. He was known, trusted and liked. The doctor was no part of it either. He was a class apart from it. So he really didn't know who was safe. Beauty B. told Moena she was going to run up the hill to her uncle's to see what should be done. She glared at me hard and said, "I don't care what your daddy says, you take her inside and you keep her safe till I get back, or they'll be hell to pay."

Moena and I went back into the parlor, and Doctor McKutcheon was giving Wee Mother a shot. When I asked him what for, he said so she'd go easy.

"Go where?" Moena asked. That made me so tired I kicked her.

I knew what I had to do, and I knew Doctor McKutcheon wouldn't let me, so I says, "Beauty B. just ran across the road a minute. We're going to fetch Beauty B. . . ." I leaned into Moena's ear and whispered, "Follow me," and I was out the door. Doctor McKutcheon could smell that I was lying. He flew out onto the porch behind us. We were already in the road by then, hidden by the darkness, disappearing up the hill.

"Where are you going?" he shouted.

"To get Daddy," I says.

That's when his voice slapped the darkness.

"Nigger gal, don't you go near that town tonight."

You have to wonder where words go when they're not heeded, because his words got stuck in this house like a bird in the attic that hides by day and beats itself half crazy trying to bust through the window at night. Those words caught up under the porch eaves and sometimes rest a few seasons between cracks in the wood, but they eventually work themselves loose.

"Nigger gal, don't you go near that town tonight."

I can be cooling fresh canned beans in ice water late on a Saturday night and they'll slide through my ears and swirl above me and disappear another five or seven years, but they'll come back.

"Nigger gal . . ."

But we were off the road by then, rolling over ourselves through the Delanys' pasture, stepping right on account of cow pies and left because of nonexistent snakes. The moon was bright and heavy in the east over town. I could just make out a line of black clouds, but they were still low and a long way off. We found a narrow spot in the creek and jumped the trickle, and then we were in thick woods sure enough. Rosa Lynn and murder were all around us then, but we kept shut and we kept to the path because even at this distance, you could hear the rumble. We thought it was thunder. Wee Mother was no part of it. Wee Mother was a departed angel and that at least felt right.

We had to cross the creek again where it curved back around by the railroad trestle, and this time it had to be done gingerly because there was quicksand, and a drunk tramp had drowned trying to pull another one out some years before. Hattie said passing railroad engineers had seen his ghost. I was past the change of life before Hattie told me that was all a lie. Directly on now, the path was surer passing through thick cedars and past a pond. Then we were back on the farm lane that took you to the main road all the way to the edge of White Oak.

We hid in the Johnsongrass and watched the wagons and automobiles and trucks. Men were piled ten and twenty on truck beds, shooting rifles into the air and shouting and blowing horns as if a war had ended or broken out in Prince George County. Moena crouched low and started whimpering about heading back. I had to find Daddy and tell him about Wee Mother, so I told her how people thought the moon and stars of her mama and daddy, and she was all right because she was with me. She kept on whimpering. I knew she was right to crawl back into the cedars and run home. I knew she wouldn't be safe that night in Prince George County, not even in the bosom of Jesus. I just said that she would because I was getting the picture and I was afraid and didn't want to go on alone, but I was glad when she ran away.

Three blocks from the courthouse, the traffic stopped in a logjam. Men were abandoning cars, trucks and wagons and carrying their rifles on foot. The crowd on the courthouse lawn was already backed down all the side streets running off the square. I was sidling past thick legs of men who reeked of whiskey and tobacco, and I was covered with sweat. Some were saying the U.S. Army was expected and that they were ready to fight. Some were laughing like, standing around out front in church. All had their eyes glued to Henry Gill's corpse hanging like a voodoo doll from the tree. Someone ran up out of the crowd and swung it back and forth and everyone laughed. Then a boy doused it in kerosene and set it aflame. That's when I knew it was still alive because it jerked and screamed, only the sound wasn't human. It was like the pigs when the barn burned. You couldn't hear it too good because of all the laughing and shouting and rifle shots. A pair of hands grabbed me, and I was looking straight into my daddy's eyes, and what I saw scared me more than all the rest because his eyes looked dead and he wouldn't speak.

Daddy didn't talk on the way out of town. That was highly unusual. Daddy was a talker. You could smell smoke through the trees and groups of men were breaking off in all directions with torches and kerosene. He didn't say a word and when we got a mile out, he told me to get down in the back and hold tight, and he pushed the horses like fire. I kept shut and he wasn't talking until I looked up when he was yelling, and we were up in Moena's yard. Jake was back, and Beauty B. too. Moena got into their wagon with the baby and we helped them haul things out of the house and throw them on Jake's wagon. Daddy was yelling at Jake, telling him not to try the roads that night. They had a powerful argument. Beauty B. finally joined in and convinced Jake that Daddy was right. In the first place, it would be daylight and easier to travel. In the second, it would be Sunday, and a good many of these riled-up, drunken men would be under the sedative of church and Sunday suits. Jake was wild and saying no church or sunrise would abate their blood lust. It took a lot of persuasion, but finally he and Beauty B. and Moena drove behind our house into the barn. Daddy sent me to fetch them blankets.

I thought the house would be brimming like the night my grandfather passed, but nobody came. I slept in my own bed, the same as now on the front over the porch, except nobody slept that night with so many men and horses and wagons and an occasional automobile running up and down the road, and Wee Mother a corpse, and Hattie and Florence and Mother still up at the Browns'. I was awake when the men came all in a cluster and I saw them in a circle around Moena's house. I heard them shout for Jake. I saw my daddy out there, shouting with them, making like he thought Jake and Beauty B. and Moena were still inside. I had never seen my daddy afraid enough to act out a lie like that. Then I saw three men, including my daddy, run up on Moena's porch and kick in the door. I heard my daddy holler, "Gone!" That house burned in a minute.

The men didn't linger to see it. Daddy rode off with them because they would have suspected him if he hadn't. They would have lynched him like they hanged Henry Gill if they'd had any idea he was hiding Jake and Moena and Beauty B. in the barn.

I watched Moena's house until I saw the flames spread across the yard into the brush and burn itself out as the rain started. But I was ragged by then and, merciful God, I slept. When I woke up I could hear the crowd downstairs. A neighbor lady helped me dress. *The sky was a deep gray veil through the front door glass. Underneath there was a green copper cast that held the seeds of an inferno.* Wee Mother was in the coffin. It looked a lot better than that awful bed. So did she. The dying smell had been covered over with the scent of perfume and tuber roses. As soon as Hattie and Florence and Mother got home from the Browns', we started for the church.

I wanted to run out to the barn to see about Moena, but I remembered I promised I wouldn't tell anybody where they was hiding. We passed displaced families on the road to the church, their belongings piled on wagons, their heads low, their mules moving as fast as they could pulling such heavy loads. I heard someone say in the churchyard while we were waiting on the coffin that, as bad as it had been, at least there wouldn't be any more *Trouble* in Prince George. The minister spoke and Mother and Florence cried, but I was holed-up down someplace in my mind trying to absorb all the sudden strangeness.

It was on the way back home on the road that we encountered Jake and Beauty B. and Moena and the baby. Moena was at the very back of the wagon.

"Where y'all going?" I asked Moena while Daddy talked to Jake.

"Off from Alabama," she says.

"For how long?" I says.

"Till it's better," Moena says, and she was crying, and I jumped up into the wagon and grabbed her and begged Mother and Daddy to let her stay. Mother and Hattie and Florence yelled at me to get back in our wagon before somebody saw. Daddy and Jake pulled us apart. I craned my neck watching that wagon disappear over the hill. When we got back home, I sat on the front porch and stared up the road in the direction they had gone and I cried. It was as if they had piled all mankind's hope onto that wagon and carried it away. Even then I didn't understand why my daddy let them.

19
Rose of Sharon

I didn't have to ask Lily to take me to that little discussion group. As it turned out, she invited me. Here's where I completely want common sense, because I got on my high horse just as if I expected him to change on the spot and tell me it was all right with him.

"It's a little philosophical discussion group that meets once a week up at the alternative school," I says. Then he says if I want a little religious discussion there's Baptist Church Circle and Sunday school galore. I says, "Dashnell, it's just a little something different to do of a weeknight." I didn't dare tell him Lily had invited me.

Well, he wouldn't hear of it. He said it was bad enough that "homo hippie" from California was allowed to open his filthy school in Prince George, and he'd let me have no part of it.

That was the first I'd heard about any homo hippie. I didn't know much about the school or its founder, only that it sounded like there was something more than gossip and pound cake recipes going on there. Dashnell doesn't take a position, he welds himself to it without examining why. He has a rich cousin in the wall-to-wall carpet business. The man donated the money to air-condition his church a few years back. Dashnell, who has always been insanely jealous of him, tormented him for half an hour at his family reunion about the immorality of cool sanctuaries in the summertime. No, when Dashnell stands against a thing, I step aside and evaluate how badly I want it. I determine how I'll move around him to get it. Or I let go of the notion.

When Lily honked for me late the next afternoon, I told her I wasn't much for going after all. Of course I was dying to go and I let it show all over the place that Dashnell was keeping me from it. I thought I'd at least extract a little sympathy. But I didn't.

"Get in this car, Rose," she commanded, screwing up her face.

"Dashnell won't let me." I smiled that pitiful smile which Mother has always said she wants to slap.

"Dashnell Lawler isn't the problem," she said, letting all the air out of me. She let the car roll backwards.

"If he's not, then who is?" I asked. How many times had I heard her blaming her husband for all the world's evils. She just pasted a Miss America smile on her face and kept backing out. That stung me. "Walk a mile in my shoes, missy!" I hollered as she wheeled around, shifting gears to pull down the road. "You're not mad at *me,* Rose," she said with such self-assurance I wanted to strangle her. I turned around to go back inside and saw Dashnell in the screen door behind me.

"What's she want?"

"Move," I says, swinging the door wide open. He did. He stepped back and let me through. But it wasn't real acquiescence. He had taken my tone of voice as a red flag.

"Come on back here in this bedroom and let me fix what's wrong with you, woman." He was just drunk enough. Another beer and the notion would pass.

"Not now, I got things to do," I says, moving towards the kitchen trying to invent something to pass the evening. He reached from behind me and pinched my breasts. It hurts when he does that.

"You refusing me?"

"I have to run by and see about Mother. I'll be back early," I says, breaking away and grabbing my car keys off the kitchen table. But he was right up on me.

"Are you refusing me?" he says.

"Dashnell, hush!" I says, hoping he'd drain his beer and grab another. But he grabbed me instead.

"Turn me loose!" I knew better. He wanted a fight, especially with me because I'm no match for him.

"I'll break that will," he snarled, slapping me across the face.

"It's broken," I whimpered, despising myself for not making more of a fight.

"Come on back here in this bedroom." I still don't know what came over me. It's so much easier to let it happen. But I shoved him a step backwards and told him I wasn't a dog.

"That's just what you are," he says, "a fat bitch dog, and you ought to thank God I'm desperate enough to bring my need to you."

"I want a say in the matter," I hissed, because my cheeks were still burning from the slap. He grinned. He took me by the shoulders and shoved me against the kitchen counter. His hands were running up my dress. He pinched my breasts again. He kissed me hard and mean. A voice kept telling me not to resist him, but I couldn't stop myself, I bit his lower lip.

This time his fist went into my face. My first thought was that no bones or teeth were broken and if I got some ice on it immediately, I wouldn't have any more bruise than my base makeup would cover. He hit me again, this time in the stomach, and the wind went out of me. I dropped to the floor and he started pulling my hair out in clumps.

I was afraid to whimper. I was afraid to move. I knew he'd keep at me until I blacked out, so I pretended to. He kicked me once after that, hard on my spine, and I thought I felt it crack, but it didn't. I lay there on the floor and listened. I heard him take a beer out of the refrigerator and snap the top. I heard him swoop up his truck key. I listened until I heard the front door slap shut behind him, then his truck engine started, then the tires spit gravel and the motor died away as he pushed down the road.

I got up and walked over to the sink and made a wet rag. I sat at the kitchen table and thought how it was good to have it over. It wouldn't happen again for months. He'd be a little nicer for the next while. It really hadn't been too bad that time. There was no blood and nothing broken. I always go through that. Then I generally go completely off in another direction, thinking about other things and walling it out of my mind.

This time was different. This time I couldn't shake it off no matter what. I made a pie; I took a shower; I trimmed my hair and set it to where you couldn't see any clumps were missing. I watched some TV; but it stayed with me. It wouldn't bury itself this time. Over and over I kept thinking I should have gotten into Lily's car and gone to that meeting with her. It wouldn't have happened. He would have been passed out in bed when I got home. I got stir crazy and I walked down by the lake. I studied the flat, murky water a long time. I could feel that poor man out there someplace in the mist. I thought how Dashnell had shot him out of some nameless evil he couldn't control. The dead man seemed luckier than me. He had died all at once from a bullet in the back of his head. Dashnell was killing me slowly. There was no escaping that. What had happened that night was going to happen again and again until I was dead on my kitchen floor. The jolt of that realization shut me down. I went back into the house, crawled into bed and fell into merciful and dreamless sleep. My back was killing me when I woke the next morning.

The bruise was bad. I stayed in bed the next three or four days claiming a terrible cold. A week later it was still tender to the touch. Lily was mad at me over not going to the meeting, so luckily she stayed away. Dashnell continued his usual routine as if nothing had happened. He always does. I expect Mother enjoyed her respite from my concern.

20
Hezekiah
(1946)

Moena tried to claim she rented the little shack on a pitiful street in the worst section of Charleston. Hez never saw any landlord come around. He figured that she had just squatted there. He slept on a pallet in an alcove she called the sewing room. He found night work baking bricks at a local plant. A minister Moena had known helped get him enrolled in the divinity college.

It was rougher going than he'd anticipated. He'd sit in the furnace room at the plant reading Latin and Greek and Hebrew all night. At dawn he'd go home and bathe. Then he'd head for class. On Sundays he'd go out with one or two other students and preach at poor country churches.

The others invariably kept their sermons strictly to expansions on Scripture. Hez always wrapped the meaning of the Scriptures around the plight of the poor and downtrodden. On one occasion he made the Book of Isaiah sound as though it prophesied the long awaited uprising of black Americans.

More than one member of the congregation was heard to whisper after the service that if the wrong white man ever heard one of Hez's sermons, they'd lynch him for sure. He woke fear in them. But he stirred hope in them as well.

Moena took no pride whatsoever in her son's sermons. She considered them loose and dangerous. She believed his free interpretations of the Scriptures were reckless slaps at heaven. Like many others she also feared the day when the wrong white man got wind of Hez's inflammatory words. It confounded her. The longer Hez studied at the Bible college the less true religion he seemed to possess.

Moena worshipped in a tiny storefront church called the Sanctuary of the Descending Spirit located down by the docks. The preachers there talked in tongues, inviting the most devout to share their own rhythmical, syllabic revelations.

Many in the congregation would soon feel their own raptures and fall gratefully onto the floor with holiness. They would rock and pray and bathe themselves in the divine tingling until a spirit whirled around them, cutting off their circulation, and they fainted. Sometimes in the hard swelter of late summer, even Moena admitted it was less divine inspiration than the effects of a relatively short supply of oxygen in conjunction with the humidity.

Twice Hez accompanied Moena to this spiritual orgy, long enough to see it as vestigial old time rural high jinks and hysteria. He told Moena she was blind in more ways than one. But Moena's blindness was the precise reason she attended Descending Spirit. Healings and the Casting Out of Demons were commonplace there. Charleston was overrun with stories of the lame who had walked and the deaf who had heard after attending a service at the Sanctuary of the Descending Spirit. She herself had watched while a visiting minister shrunk a goiter in the neck of a neighbor woman. Moena still clung to a thread of hope. When she had demonstrated complete obedience to heaven, her sight would be miraculously restored.

Hez had no patience with that and even less with the illiterate preachers who filled his mother with false hope in exchange for the hard won dollar bill she placed in their collection plate each week. She would come in on Sunday evenings drenched in sweat and ashen, wearing an annoying, beatific smile. Hez was usually at the kitchen table trying to cram for Latin or Greek or Philosophy. Moena invariably seized the moment when he was trying his hardest to concentrate to recount the day's miracle for him. His usual tack was to gather his books and go into the sewing area until he heard her body fall dead asleep onto her bed in the next room.

One rainy Sunday in March she came in and found Hez in his usual place over his books at the kitchen table. He had a toothache. He had gone out before dawn in order to hitch a ride to a little town fifteen miles south where he was supposed to preach. Traffic was light that morning. The cold rain had swollen his aching jaw into a ball of fire. He had all but forsworn alcohol in those days, but he purchased a fifty cent bottle of corn whiskey after he got back to Charleston hoping it would numb the pain.

"I been called up for a healing," she beamed, waking the pain in his jaw.

"What?"

"Sometime in the next forty days and nights." She was ecstatic, souped.

"Who's got you hypnotized now?" he asked, pressing his hand into the side of his face.

"The Lord my God." She chopped, chastising him for his sacrilegiousness.

"Hell," he muttered, gathering up his studies and shuffling in near stupor towards the sewing room.

"Hell is exactly where a nasty child like you are bound," Moena sang, her words lodging like darts between his shoulders.

"Hell is where I am right now," he yelled louder than he meant to.

Beauty B. had beaten her one true religion into Moena. Now Moena felt the call to make one final effort to do the same to her full grown son.

"You're a false prophet," she hissed. "You're a moneylender in the temple."

"You're a hateful fool!" he shot back.

"You caused my blindness!"

Hez had always known she believed that. But she had never said it aloud. Now he understood the full measure of her contempt. It was the force against which he had pushed his tired shoulders, the fathomless cauldron of fear that boiled endlessly like pine tar deep within. The tears were gushing down his cheeks before he could feel them coming. The pain and sorrow raced through his entire body and brought him to his knees. He was struggling for breath.

"You best be sorry," she muttered.

"Sorry I was born to an ignorant and hateful woman like you," he replied, rubbing his jaw.

"God is going to bring a mighty army down on you!" But that was barely a whisper. Moena had shocked herself by telling Hez the unbearable secret. She could feel her skin steaming under her wet clothes. She wanted to go back into her room, dry herself up and crawl into the bed. This wasn't a thing that a night's sleep under a tin roof would fix. This was the end of something.

"So that's what I am," Hez muttered because he couldn't find his voice, "—a curse on this world and the mama who brought me into it."

"Devil take you for making me say it," Moena said, trying to throw something back at the burning colors swirling in front of her.

"You're worse than a devil, Mama. You're worse than all hell's evil. You brought me unwanted onto this earth and let me fend for myself."

Moena was shaking. Her eyes blazed with tears. Terrible stinging threads of color seared her skull.

"Heaven called you to care for me and you turned your back. Satan whispered into your ear and you believed him. You believed I was a curse and a punishment and that's what your hatred made me!"

She understood this. She had prayed a wall against it. She had carved images of insurmountable oppression into it. Lit candles to it. Worshipped it.

"God has not blinded you! You burrowed into the darkness rather than see that you and not heaven have created so much suffering and grief. I was your child, new and helpless, and you condemned me by your indifference. You dumped me like a puppy in a hop sack on two old people gone strange with sorrow. You turned away from your own mother and father. You abandoned them to their bewilderment and loss. Your blindness is your selfishness. Your contempt for your own flesh is your curse! If I could, I would believe like you in the sulphurous burning lake. It would be my deepest hope to think of you there, eternally bound in molten chains. What kind of demon will love neither mother nor father nor child?"

He couldn't talk anymore. It hurt him too. It tormented him to let go of these things, to know them as true, to be powerless against the pointless invective they drew out of him. Then the fire of hell erupted inside his jaw as the sack of poison burst. He was gripped by torment. "O God, take me." He begged for the bliss of oblivion. Then almost as quickly as the torture exploded and spread, it diminished. He sank back into his chair, feeling the pain slowly ebb. He didn't notice right away that Moena was kneeling. He didn't see her shoulders heaving. Something cleansing spun between them. Something tilted, righted itself—settled. Neither spoke for a long time.

He had to apologize. He had to tell her it had been his physical torture castigating and condemning her. Hez had very little knowledge of the bleak and lonely path she had stumbled over the passing years. She was a lost, lonely blind woman clinging to her superstitions because she had nothing else to hold. Surely he could love his mother enough to allow her that much.

The wind was howling. A fresh, driving rain pelted the windows. The stove had gone out. He could hear her in the corner, praying.

"Mother, forgive me," and tears of remorse sliced his cheeks. "Mother, I'm as blind as you are. I'm fearful and lonely and I know you did the best you could. I'm sorry, Mother." When she turned towards him, her Moena's eyes looked straight into his. A terrible quiet descended. When he could stand it no longer, he spoke.

"You kind of almost seem like you're looking at me, Mother."

"You have Beauty B.'s eyes," she answered.

Her chicanery annoyed him. He retreated into himself.

"Son, you got a spot on your collar there. What is it? Egg?"

She reached up and scraped it with her nail. It was just like a thing a mother would do.

"You can see!?"

"Because you saw me."

"You can see?"

"Yes. And I see you're a healing angel."

Later he walked into sheets of soft, warm rain that washed the shabby faces of boardinghouses and liquor stores and ran in rivers that overspread the curb. It fell thick and steady as the daylight slipped into darkness. He stood on the seawall looking into the white hissing, black shining tide.

The storm was rolling out of the South. It carried that peculiar veil of moist feathered silk he hadn't experienced since the Everglades. It was good to stand on the high stone wall and reflect on the vast distance his heart had come through the intervening years. He wondered at his deliverance from that hopeless swamp. It seemed as miraculous as Moena's eyesight. Even more miraculous was the peace he felt looking back. He couldn't regret a single step of the journey that had brought him here. Soon he would move forward in the solid stride of an educated man of God. That was deliverance beyond comprehension.

The rain was thinner now. Dense fog hung over the streets as he walked home. He had taken a wrong turn, and then another. He sat on a crumbling stoop and waited for the inevitable light of first dawn.

He heard a voice from far away and though it was dim, it was clear and irrefutable.

"Say to those who are of a fearful heart,
'Be strong. Fear not!'"

Moena slept fitfully, waking herself now and again to reassure herself that the light hadn't fled. She felt easier after Hez came in. She drifted deep and slept through the rest of the night as if under a tender spell.

Hez slid back into his chair at the kitchen table. His dry robe was a great luxury against the evening chill. Outside a wind had risen and sharper raindrops slapped the roof. Beauty's Bible lay on the table. It was still open to the page where Moena had looked while he was out. He read the verse Beauty had underlined in black ink long before he was born.

Say to those who are of a fearful heart,
"Be strong. Fear not! Behold!
Your God will come and save you. . . ."

She had underscored the next line as well. The tissue thin page was slightly wrinkled and he had to hold the book closer to the lamp to make it out.

"Then the eyes of the blind shall be opened. . . ."

A tiny cry pierced the drumming roar of an ocean falling from the heavens. He moved to the door and opened it just wide enough to admit the cat. He dried it with a cloth Moena kept for dishes. He sat back down at the table. He worked another hour. Then he slept.

21
Rose of Sharon

I came in from the grocery around two-thirty and Heath was sitting on my back porch. His eyes were as red as fire. At first I thought it was whiskey, but it was from crying over Lily. My sweet tooth was humming a little. I was sucking three aspirin. I had groceries to put away and supper to cook. I felt sorry for him. He was a mess.

It took me half an hour to draw three consecutive words out of him. He finally said he'd come to apologize for doing such a piecework job of painting the house. He had a right to apologize for that, but I knew that wasn't what was on his mind.

"It doesn't hurt forever, Heath," I said, trying to pry open the subject. "It just feels like it will."

He said he was lost and hurting and he didn't understand. He said he didn't know another living soul he could talk to about it. I've heard it all at one time or another on my back porch. I poured us some iced tea and we sat down. It was one of those hazy silver blue afternoons. You couldn't tell the far end of the lake from the sky. He tried to go on, but he kept choking up.

I was hoping to pull some of it out of him with a light approach.

"What's a fine, strapping young man like you doing in tears over an old married woman like her?" I regretted it immediately. He took umbrage, defending Lily, her beauty, her mind, her complicated situation with Glen.

"I love her and I know she loves me. She thinks she's doing the right thing."

"Well, if you love her, then you want her to do the right thing." If a boy ever needed a long swallow of whiskey, it was him. I poured him a double shot, but that only loosed his tears. He must have cried and sputtered a solid hour. Nothing I said made the slightest difference. It was first dusk by this time and my sweet tooth was beginning to throb again. I had exhausted every comfort I knew to offer. The truth is there's just so much feeling sorry for yourself out loud that another person can take. I was nearing my limit.

"Aunt Rose, I don't think anybody on this earth knows the sorrow in my heart."

"You got a nerve." I sounded put out and I meant to. "You have strong, young life flowing through your veins; you have whatever you make of it. You're blessed and your real problem isn't Lily Pembroke. It's your lack of gratitude."

"You don't know how this hurts," he spit back.

"You are talking to a mother who buried her one and only son at age twenty. I know how *that* hurts and I pray you never do." It just sprang from me. I thought I was through it. All the hurt resurrected as if I'd just gotten the news. It seared me all over again. My head started pounding. I couldn't stop trembling. If possible it hurt worse than the first time. Everywhere I put my eyes I saw endless despair.

"What you had with Lily Pembroke was common and deceitful and you had no moral right to do it! You're paying a slim price, all things considered! My sorrow is everlasting and it came without warning or explanation. There's no comfort in this world! None!" I know I ran on a good bit more. I couldn't tell you what I said, only that Heath looked like he was watching a train wreck.

It was dark by then. Heath fetched me some Kleenex and a glass of water and he held me and rocked me and stroked my hair and apologized and cried with me all at once.

"He took whatever shred of decency there was left in Dashnell with him." I couldn't hold it back. "He took all the hope I had, all the reason to look forward to tomorrow." He held my cheeks between his fingers and stared at me and those wide black eyes of his drew the sorrow out of me.

"I wind myself up like a stupid clock and I go on doing all the things that have to be done because I don't know what else to do. But I would gladly surrender every breath in me, I'd happily lay down and die, to put my child back on this earth."

It was the kindest pair of arms I ever felt. When the dark was full, he helped me back to the bedroom and sat on the edge of my bed and rubbed my shoulders until the tears subsided. I could see through the window that the mist had lifted. There was a slice of moon resting on top of the cedars at the far edge of the lake. I laid back. I was almost asleep. He got up and walked to the doorway. He stopped and turned around and he said, "Thank you."

I slept soft and deep through the night. It was quiet when I woke. I could see by the towels on the bathroom floor and the empty Jack Daniel's bottle on the kitchen counter that Dashnell had come in the night and slept beside me and gotten himself off to work. The sky was clear when I walked out onto the back porch. There was a light wind. The water was choppy. I turned to go back into the kitchen and make myself a cup of coffee. I glanced at the clock. It was noon. It may have been the fog in my head, but everything looked different. Then it came to me that I had told Heath what I had been unable to tell anyone else. I had entrusted that boy with the deepest part of myself and he hadn't abused it. That endeared him to me. That put him among a handful of special people I've known. I gave Heath Lawler my sorrow and he replaced it with a measure of unexpected comfort. Until then I told myself that I held on to my grief because it was all I had left of Carmen. I finally realized that wasn't it at all. I held on to that grief because I was afraid if I let it go, there wouldn't be anything left that was real. I suppose I thought I would dissolve into thin air if I moved past it. I began that morning. I stepped forward. I woke to the possibility that I could go on, that there might somehow be a better way to live. It wasn't as solid as a fact, but it was more real than a day-dream: I might not cower in the shadows of that house for the rest of my life.

22
Lily

I look at the suffering in the world and wonder how I can agonize the way I do. But I do. I suppose that's because if I were in danger of being gunned down in a war zone, if I were terminally ill, if I had my legs amputated as the result of some horrible accident, then people would have an automatic sympathy for me. They wouldn't bother with who I voted for, what kind of mother and wife I was, or if and where I went to church. They wouldn't give a holy hell who I slept with. But I have none of that to pull up over me and snuggle beneath like kids running a quilt up to their chins on a fall night after ghost stories.

I have this madness (love), this need to love flesh and be loved by flesh and to feel all right about it. I burn, I hunger, I get starved for love, and by love I mean a mingling of flesh and spirit, a window to understanding the universe that only two can open, two perfectly tuned violins that play each other. Or something. I live in feelings, not words. People have always laughed at my poems. Sometimes when I read over them, I laugh at myself. I try to laugh off these feelings. I try not to succumb to such medieval ideas. Michael, he taught us that. He said that romance as a cure to mankind's ills was first embraced in the Dark Ages.

Michael talks about love as the light of the world, and I know he doesn't mean romantic love, but I wish he did sometimes. Because I feel foolish and ashamed and alone and I am trying to see it all the way he sees it. Energy and light and one race, the human race, in tune with the tides and all that.

Michael is beatific. He has a completely nonjudgmental way of looking at people. He's not making a dime running that school. He used the little his father left him to build it. He believes what he teaches. He puts it into action. He looks up at the stars at night and sees breathing patterns. I look up; I see gases glowing in the cold. We talk about Buddha, Mahatma Gandhi, Martin Luther King, Mother Teresa and dozens of people who made a difference in this world.

Michael remembers Bobby Kennedy holding a starving Mississippi Delta baby, its tummy swollen, saying this shouldn't happen in America. When I remember Bobby Kennedy, I think of Marilyn Monroe. I say that at discussion group and Michael responds that I have morality turned inside out. He says morality doesn't include how many movie stars you slept with. He says morality is how many people you loved. By loved, he means cared about, tried to help, leapt over yourself to reach. Looking back on my time with Randy, I realize now that I had him confused with a man like Michael England.

I get a tremendous feeling at discussion group. I start to feel the connection between all people and times. I try to keep it when I come home to Glen and my children.

I make them dinner and I try to do something special for each one —you know—Glen's favorite homemade salad dressing, Sarah's pop-up biscuits, Travis's Mickey Mouse napkins or Chicken McNuggets. Nobody makes a sound except chewing and slurping up iced tea. Nobody thanks me. It's probably because they know they aren't welcome. After supper we all get away from the table as fast as we can because we have so little to say to each other. I've tried fresh flowers and a candle. I've starched and ironed their sheets. They like starched sheets. It has some impact, but, dear God, do I have to wash and iron their sheets every day for the rest of my life just so they won't hate me?

The private time, the lights out, between the sheets time with

Glen, I try to make it the way I think he'll like it. I try to be open and willing with my shoulders perfumed and the creams rubbed into my skin. I try to open things up with a little conversation.

This is where our sicknesses hold hands. There's no genuine desire on my part to create physical communion. I'm playing a part, acting the decent, loving wife who's trying everything *Cosmopolitan* suggests to rekindle faded love. I do those things to protect myself, like a rape victim cooperating with her attacker. I do them from fear and I resent them. I resent the hairy backs of his bony hands. I despise the way he sands my nipples making little jolts of static electricity that burn clear through me. If I wince or ask him not pinch me or be so rough, his pleasure intensifies and he grins like a maniac, biting my lower lip or slapping me with throaty little sniggers, slamming himself so far up in me I think I'm going to break apart, scalding and burning my insides, insane with the thrill of his total dominion, his brutal power over me, and the smallest whimper or trembling on my part lifts him into a realm of sublime madness he can sustain for hours before he finally shakes violently, and clenching my throat with his fists to cut off my air supply, he takes his demon time, wailing as his evil seed spreads through me.

Then, where any normal man would roll away and drift into self-satisfied fantasies, he stays on top of me. He burrows his head into my pillow and sobs, lamenting that his love for me is slowly draining the life out of him.

When Michael hugs you, his fingers knead your back, his fingers tell you he's there with you and you're there with him, and his hair brushes your cheek and his eyes unite with yours and he lets your breasts linger against his chest. He knows you feel his hardness down there and it doesn't scare him to be a little excited or exciting. It's harmless. It's natural. He trusts you and assumes you trust him. He could hug a man the way he hugs a woman and enjoy the tenderness of it without turning it perverse. Why isn't that considered manhood?

I can go on biting my tongue in half when Glen is babbling his thick paranoia and Sarah is ten minutes into a tantrum. I can starch his pillowcases and ignore the insult when the only thing he compliments is the extra coat of wax on the kitchen floor or a hundred other things I do in an effort to deserve him and the children, to appreciate them, to be grateful for them and my health and my house and the sun on the lake. What I cannot do is love them.

Do my children know when I tell them stories at bedtime or hold them shivering after nightmares that my arms invent kindness my heart doesn't contain? Do they understand that I don't hit them because one slap would reveal my disdain? Will they ever realize that when I sit with them at the kitchen table and patiently tend to their homework or lend their sputtering stories my full attention I'm silently clocking the minutes until their bedtime?

We look wonderful in Christmas card photos, sitting on the front steps of our dream house. We draw comments, walking into church two minutes late: Sarah in the ruffled cotton dresses that take me an hour to iron; Travis, the little monarch in his burgundy blazer. Glen knows how to dress himself in olive and khaki suits, how to seem completely self-effacing as he steps back to let us into the pew; how to lay his hand benignly behind my back, showing off his familial devotion and his Rolex watch to the congregation of the righteous.

Sarah is Glen all over again; but someone smart and loving might be able to save Travis. I want him around Michael. I want him to know what a real hug is, what the stars might be, what a man can be if he lets himself or he can't help it. I pulled Travis out of that aluminum Piss-on-Jesus private Bible elementary school where Glen was sending him. Now I have to tell Glen.

I hosed down and waxed his garage and organized his tools this afternoon. I stood over a pot of boiling grease, making his grandmother's doughnut recipe. I made up our bed with five hundred dollar polished cotton sheets, turned his side down and laid my oyster pink negligee on my pillow. I'm wearing the perfume he gave me for Mother's Day. I went to the beauty shop and had my hair cut and curled into that baby doll look he adores.

When I told Rose what I was up to, she insisted on taking the kids for the night. I told her I couldn't impose like that, but she insisted so strongly I took advantage of her offer. She pulled down a pasteboard box of meticulously painted model cars and set up an old electric train all over the living room. She pulled dolls out of a trunk that made my teeth drop and an old fashioned, handmade dollhouse with miniature French furniture that belonged to her grandmother. She must have some fine ancestors back there someplace.

Sometimes I list my faults in one column, Glen's in the other. Mine runs off the page. His amounts to six or eight habits that get on my nerves. I wish he'd run after women or find Jesus or join the Air Force. I told Rosie one time I think Glen is a madman. It's just that he has the uncanny ability to make it come off normal. I told her I'd rather have a crazy old warthog like Dashnell. It doesn't take any scrutiny to see what he is. It's all right there in front of you. Glen hides his sickness.

She brought up Dashnell.

"Afraid to leave them up here with Dashnell about?"

I admitted I was.

"Children are his exception—his blind spot. You'll never see Dashnell Lawler abuse them or anyone near them."

You think you know people.

I used to get frustrated with Glen because I took him at face value. I thought he was just average, switched off, knee jerk New South Republican normal. It's uncanny how he manages to look and sound like everyone else. That's his mask, the intricately woven cloak of illusion behind which he operates. There's a demon coiling inside that man's brain, a crafty little monster, drawing itself up tighter and tighter. It lurks there, waiting for me to make a false move. Sometimes I feel it peering at me from behind his eyes. Every impulse I own says to flee, but I dare not. My only course is to remain here, its prisoner and its cornered prey, vainly hoping some miraculous distraction will deflect its hypnotic spell long enough for me to run. Even then, I'm doomed—unless Heath was right.

The last time we saw each other I explained my predicament. He said surrender and defeat were my only hope. He said they unbind secret wings hidden in our souls that bear us across our sorrows.

Pretty words spoken from a tender heart while the night breeze bristles the pines and makes the moonlight dance on the water—useless in the airless dark when his fingers rip my hair and my insides scream and he whispers, "Baby, I love you."

23
Rose of Sharon

I can't go back to that discussion group. Once a thing is told, it's told; it seeps out in the best, most confidential circumstances. The boy, I'll say the young man, Michael, has a way about him of drawing you out of yourself. He's tender. He reminds me of Carmen a little. Carmen wasn't that dark headed and he was a nice looking boy, too, but this one up there at that school, he's possessed of a charm that neither I nor Dashnell could ever have taught Carmen. He reminds me of a wizard or a magician.

At first I thought it was his brown cow eyes and the thick, curly lashes. He uses his long, pretty hands when he talks. At first, I was halfway annoyed with the softness of his voice, the way I had to strain to hear him, but then I realized that's because most people I've been around all my life practically yell at each other. Initially I took him to be very effeminate, but then I gradually realized it was only that he lacked that tension that makes most men a little stiff and bulky. I'll have to say to Dashnell's everlasting sorrow that I didn't detect one communist tinge unless you call looking for threads that bind people together communist.

Still and all, I don't get an overriding good feeling about the group. It's loose talk, and by that I mean ideas your average person might not accept. It's good to see the common thread, but common thread makes out into all different kinds of designs and those differences can't be ignored. At some point people are made and finished and not likely to change. I suppose that's why one generation leaves its messes to the next. Old dogs, new tricks. It doesn't work. It scares me. Change scares me. I've been contemplating all kinds of changes without letting myself admit it. I learned that tonight.

A lot of the group aren't native Prince George. Most of them moved up this way from the Birmingham area. One woman asked why there aren't any black people in Prince George County. That opened a deep discussion about Prince George and its history and how the black people were burned and driven out. Most of the group had never heard it in much detail. I grew up with the story, so I told it. I had never stopped to make a connection between "the Trouble," as Mother and Daddy always called it, and present-day life. The past was always something frozen and finished to me.

I no sooner had it told than one of them said we ought to do something to let the world know that the people here in Prince George aren't that way anymore. I had to bite my tongue in half to keep from saying, "But they *are* just that way!" Of course I was thinking about poor McCarthy Smith being shot on that lake a few months back, most likely *by my husband.*

Lily must have read my mind, because she immediately started talking about that poor murdered man in the boat on the lake and how it wasn't ever investigated. To her that was no less than a continuation of what happened on that evil night of the Trouble.

Something went off in my head, some Scripture we used to hear in church about sinners in the congregation of the righteous. *They sat on my back porch and sucked beer and planned it. I waited with the women while they did it.* Lily jumped off from there to say that she had read a piece in *The Birmingham News* that a minister had tried to get the governor to make something of it. She said that she had called that minister and told him everything she knew about it. I was trying not to let my face show.

Then I asked a question. How come, if that man knew the ways of Prince George, if he knew that he might be killed, how come he came here alone and unprotected despite both warnings and threats? Lily jumped back with "Well, maybe he sacrificed himself so we'd have this discussion, so I'd call that minister in Birmingham, so that minister would trouble the governor about it, so that change would take place."

They all agreed except an old banty hen named Esther, who kept trying to steer the early part of the discussion back to the likeness between all Protestant denominations. She got up and left without a word. As afraid as I was, as badly as I wanted to follow Esther out that door and back to Baptist prayer meeting, I have to say, in that moment, I thought Esther looked, well, maybe tawdry or ignorant or shut down, and to follow her would be like following Dashnell. Now that's a change in my way of thinking, and I don't like it.

They were all talking loud by then, different ones cutting in on the other with wilder and wilder ideas about what needs to be done to change Prince George. I didn't want to go against the grain, but when somebody said we ought to have a little demonstration to show that all people are welcome in Prince George, I couldn't hold back.

"You'll start a war," I said. "There aren't enough who think like you to make the kind of change you're talking. The hatred here is the kind that has to die with time." Lily flew down my throat. "Hell, it hasn't died in a hundred, maybe two hundred, years, it's time we killed it outright."

Michael looked confused. "You mean a little peaceful demonstration to the effect that Prince George County is part of the rest of the world would actually start a war?" That's when the words flew off my tongue before I could arrange or arrest them. "Yes, a war people like my husband Dashnell have waited their whole lives for the opportunity to fight!" The rest of them looked at me like I must be out of my mind to have a husband like Dashnell, as if almost every woman in Prince George County doesn't have a husband exactly like him.

"I don't know where you people think you live," I says.

Michael reminded us of the hour and said we should all think about this hard and talk some more next week. I brooded in the car while Lily went back to Michael's office with him and borrowed a book on Mahatma Gandhi. Suppose this evening's talk got out?

Suppose Dashnell heard what I said about him fighting a war? Suppose they became more serious about this brotherhood demonstration? I had to back away from these people fast. They were striking wooden matches on dry sticks of dynamite.

24
Hezekiah
(1960)

His church had been vandalized again. Windows had been smashed, books ripped into shreds, chairs and tables chopped up with an ax. Hez had spent the morning trying to explain to the Birmingham police commissioner that this was no ordinary robbery. It was an exhausting argument made all the more difficult by the fact that the man simply wouldn't admit that it was an act of terrorism meant as direct retaliation for the bus boycott. The commissioner didn't waste time trying to convince Hez that it was neighborhood kids. He didn't take Hez for that big a fool. Instead he tried to convince Hez that he himself fervently believed it had been neighborhood kids. Or so he tried to posture. The bald truth was clearly hidden in plain sight between the commissioner's words. He knew Hez was heavily involved with the boycott. He knew planning sessions had been held in Hez's home and his church. He knew that Hez was in direct contact with Martin Luther King, Jr., the real source of the trouble, and that Hez could expect much worse than a few broken windows unless he denounced the boycott and Martin Luther King, Jr., from his pulpit.

Meanwhile, Cheryl was at home packing up the baby. She was going to stay with her mother up in Memphis. She had left him periodically during their five year marriage, tucked tail and run home. Cheryl's father owned three large funeral homes in Memphis. She wasn't cut out to be a minister's wife. She had no tolerance for drafty parsonages, no experience doing without and no patience for the endless stream of suffering humanity she found at her door around the clock.

She had married Hez believing she would lure him away from his chosen profession. Hez had married her hoping the same thing. He despised the ministry. Cheryl's father was still more than willing to pay for a legal education or take him on in the funeral business. It was too late now. Hez was hopelessly chained to his calling. He was a man of God, a servant of his people, a community voice. Never mind that he despised it almost as much as his wife did. He had come to faith and through it to a sense of mission, a divinely intended purpose he couldn't shake. He tried to explain to Cheryl that he had no choice. She refused to accept that. She might have left him altogether, but then the baby came. It wasn't that she thought the child should have a mother and father. It was her hope that somehow she could use it and its needs for security to goad him into giving up the ministry. Of course that only galvanized Hez's stance. More than any luxury, his son would need a shining moral example of what a man could be. If anything the birth of their son served as a confirmation in Hez's mind that he must not waver from his divine work in this world.

Cheryl made what peace she could with that, using large sums of her own money to furnish and renovate the modest house provided by the church. A monthly check sent by her mother paid the full time housekeeper and the nursemaid. It also kept her in fashion and supplied her annually with a new Chrysler convertible. This did little to win her the trust and admiration of his congregation.

It did, however, ameliorate much of her immediate dissatisfaction. For the most part she and Hez got along extremely well. Cheryl was, for all her pampering, a wonderful companion. She was undeniably beautiful, a fiery, fun loving woman with a razor sharp wit. She was a voracious reader of books and newspapers and had a fondness for arguing philosophy. When Hez was home for the evening, an event of increasing rarity of late, Cheryl could keep him at the supper table for hours discussing any one of a hundred topics that captivated them both.

Cheryl loved and appreciated Hez as a leader and a man who touched others' lives, but she despised sharing him with so many others. Like the shabby parsonage her money had rendered decent, people presumed that Hez, being a minister, was their property. They called or appeared at the front door at all hours of the day or night. If it was mealtime, they expected to be comfortably seated and well fed. If their business kept them late, they expected beds and baths and breakfast in the morning. They made no distinction between the minister and his wife. They expected selfless and servile devotion to their church and its causes. They considered it no less than her divine calling to hover in the steaming church kitchen at spaghetti suppers, to teach Sunday school, to cheerfully attend and support the monthly ladies' circle meetings.

She avoided these expected sacrifices by holding herself completely oblivious of them. This sparked increasingly strident conversations. Finally, the wives of several board members demanded that their husbands formally address the matter at their next meeting. The chairman, a doddering elder, reluctantly asked Hez if Cheryl might be imposed upon for her attendance.

Hez was of two minds. He completely supported Cheryl's position that he and not she was obligated to serve the needs of the church. He also believed that Cheryl's absences from certain key events, like the Christmas Eve Candlelight Cantata, was part of her quiet effort to encourage him to abandon the ministry.

"The board wants to know if you'll meet with them."

"Why?"

Any response on his part would stir the embers of the irresolvable debate that threatened to undermine their otherwise amicable existence. He eyed her sadly. Her astonishing beauty and deeply rooted calm arrested his rising irritation. He stood there powerless to stem the river of love that poured out of every cell.

"If I had loved you just a little more, I wouldn't have married you," he choked.

He could've been more. He should have reached higher. His

thirst for knowledge and his capacity for learning might have led him untold places—places where Cheryl had already been. He might have studied law or obtained his doctorate. She had no peers. It was their ignorance that regarded her sophisticated demeanor as haughty affect.

"Is it your fault God grabbed you first?"

"I'll tell that board to take a hike."

"Kiss your baby son good-night. I'll be happy to talk to the board."

The men were nervous. For once they arrived on time. They eyed the soiled oak table and otherwise avoided eye contact as Cheryl approached them. She had a large, beautifully lettered chart on poster board. On it she had meticulously produced a rendering of the current budget—including staff salaries.

"Gentlemen," she started in that relentless calm of hers, "thank you for the opportunity to communicate with you."

Before any of them could pose a single question or fire off a sanctimonious and passive aggressive assault on her character, she was leading them through the dull, meager finances of their struggling institution.

"Has any staff position been omitted?" None that they saw.

She let them ponder the silence a moment.

"There is spreading concern that I have been remiss in my duties to my church."

Here the youngest, most recent board member, a strained shoe salesman, rose and presented a proposed list of usual, customary and expected duties for the minister's wife which his own spouse and several others had drawn up at his kitchen table that afternoon. The board members nodded and cleared their throats and murmured their unofficial concurrence, then eyed her as one, waiting for her response.

"So you propose to elevate me to an official church position?" Several men found the courage to speak, adamantly arguing that the minister's wife had traditionally been an official position.

"What is the salary?"

Silence.

"Since these duties include attendance at events away from the premises, is there a transportation allowance as well? What provisions have you made for the care of my children while I'm apart from them on church business?"

More silence. La Grange, an emaciated high school principal with a sonorous bass voice, cleared his throat. "Your expenses and whatnot would, quite naturally, come out of the reverend's earnings."

She flipped her chart over revealing two itemized lists of expenses. The first detailed Hez's average monthly expenditures on church-related business. The second showed dollar amounts a minister's wife would need in order to carry out customary duties.

"If that's true," she smiled, "you will have to triple the reverend's current salary."

Finally the chairman spoke in his tremulous stage whisper. "The matter is not appropriate for discussion by this board at this time."

She thanked him. Hez watched her slowly remove her poster and calmly leave the room. He didn't deserve her, but he would be eternally grateful that she was his wife.

Her actions created a ballast between them. She could now accept his vocation without succumbing to it. Even those who disapproved of her stance were forced to do so quietly lest they publicly admit they expected her duty and effort without remuneration. Or, as Hez chortled, relaying the incident on an overnight visit to Moena, "What black man in Alabama is going to publicly declare his support for slavery?"

Things grew easier at home. Things were understood. Minus the pressure of conscripted duty, Cheryl voluntarily expanded her participation in church activities. Hez was grateful for her effort and considerably increased his own to create more time for his family. They got along well. Cheryl was less inclined to visit her family in Memphis every chance she got. When unexpected callers appeared, they were asked to wait in the church office next door. Life was good. She presented Hez two more children, both daughters. The congregation grew.

Then the integrationist talk began.

Cheryl was a firm believer that the mingling of the races was a historical eventuality. She saw racial equality as the logical outcome of social evolution. Hez viewed it as his immediate duty—regardless of personal cost. This, along with a litany of cries for freedom and justice, had become the mainstay of his more recent sermons. Cheryl had tried to challenge him on philosophical grounds at first. If people rebelled openly, there would be trouble, perhaps bloodshed. That would advance no one. The path to freedom lay through education and time. Hez was inviting Armageddon.

Now plans were being laid for the Birmingham bus boycott at committee meetings held in their living room. Hez had joined the nucleus of a resistance that every white leader in Birmingham had taken an oath to squelch at any price. Birmingham was a small city and there were plenty of poor black men and women who could be pressured into telling what they knew. It was widely rumored that a list of black instigators was being circulated among law enforcement officials. Hez's name was certain to be near the top of that list. Cheryl was frightened. She begged Hez to find some less public way to support his cause. Then the church was ransacked. Cheryl was leaving town. In his heart, Hez was glad she was going. Like her he dreaded the violence which was almost certain to come. Unlike her, he regarded it as his ministerial duty to face it.

Three nights after Cheryl and the baby and the nursemaid left for her family in Memphis, Hez woke to what sounded like water dripping. It was followed by a thud and the rapid scuffling of feet. Then he smelled oil smoke. He leapt through the open bedroom window into the side yard. Within seconds the entire house and the church next door were engulfed by flames. Armageddon had come.

25
Rose of Sharon

After the meeting I sat in my car and all I could think was I'd rather die than have anybody local pass by there and see me as part of that group. Lily was quiet on the ride home, but when I let her out, she leaned over and pecked my cheek and said, "We'll talk."

I didn't tell Dashnell where I'd been. He was halfway down his second six-pack and asleep in front of the television when I got in. At least that part was easy.

My head was packed with swarming things. I hid away in sleep. It was fitful. I kept waking up. Finally, I got out of bed figuring I'd throw a jam cake together while it was still cool. You could just make out a glow under the night sky in the east. I walked out on the porch. The night was clear. The water was still. The lake was deserted. The air was silver. The reeds on the far side of the lake were white against the cypresses. I couldn't see the boat or the man. My heart knew he was there. I turned to go back into the house. When I looked back at the lake, the water was red. Then the sun was above the trees and the birds burst out all at once. I stood there in my backyard running my eyes up and down the neighborhood. I had this sudden, suffocating feeling. Because up one side of this lake and down the other you will find one common bond—ignorance.

I went by to see Mother after Dashnell left for work. She kept looking at me funny, almost as if she'd never seen me before. I almost told her about Dashnell and the man on the lake and the discussion group. We walked the yard, hunting blooms among the weeds, her telling what was planted here once and what was under Johnsongrass there and all like that. I was intent on the house, eyeing the foundation and looking where paint is needed and where siding should be replaced. I counted up fireplaces and lifted a corner of linoleum in her room to examine the wood underneath. I had forgotten that the attic walls are dark stained tongue and groove wood. I found a set of double doors in the basement that used to hang between the parlor and the dining room when I was a child, mahogany with curly gargoyles carved around etched glass. There's even brass fleur de lys design picture molding in all the downstairs rooms. Somebody could have a field day with that house.

I don't know why I was so taken with it. I kept thinking how it's a lot finer than most of the houses around here. It's one of those big Victorian ones built after the War Between the States. Daddy kept threatening to tear it down and build a new brick house. Mother wouldn't hear of that. She said it wasn't the house, but the ghosts and the memories it held. It wasn't that Daddy didn't appreciate the old place for what it was. He said the house kept Mother looking back into the past. I always hated it when I was growing up. Mother said that was because I'd never seen it right. Daddy and I used to beg Mother to fix it up. She just wouldn't.

Mother seemed a little nervous. I realized she probably thought I was making plans, trying to shove her out of the way and off this earth—which I'm not. I have no plan to leave Dashnell, no intention of going back to that discussion group. I'm going to die in that lake house and they'll bury me beside Dashnell or him beside me after, and we'll both lie there next to Carmen and Elisa. Elisa was stillborn. Carmen came two years later and took all the grief I had over that.

No, I'm going to latch my porch door to keep Lily out and take Marjean up on her offer to help me get on at Wal-Mart.

Except.

When I got home from Mother's, I sat down and I wrote on a little pad I keep over the stove. *Change is hard.* I crossed out *hard* and wrote *necessary*. Then I crossed out *necessary* and wrote *inevitable.* Then I crossed all that out and wrote, *Change is coming.* Then I dropped to the floor and asked God to show me what to do. The moving world outside my locked screen door keeps stopping here for me. One of these days I'm going to have to pick up and go with it.

26

Lily

I told Glen about putting Travis in Michael's alternative school and he said, "Fine." He didn't say, "No son of his . . ." He trusted my judgment. He even got a little excited when I told him Michael is a black belt karate instructor and requires all the students to study with him. That's the hard thing about Glen. Just when you predict his thickheaded response to a thing, he fools you. He demonstrates a little sense and some genuine possibility of sensitivity which makes it all the harder the next time you approach him about something and he ducks back behind his general cloudiness.

Rose took a job up at Wal-Mart. I expect they've got money troubles. Everything is nice and clean up at Rosie's, but there aren't any extras.

I thought I'd go out of my mind up here on this lake, and going to Rosie's in the afternoon had become how I stood it. When she went to work at Wal-Mart, I thought I'd die of loneliness. But then I had this idea. Sending Travis to the alternative school is costing us a fortune. Right? Well, Michael has this computer in the office he doesn't know how to use. He runs the school finances out of his personal checking account.

So I went in to see him after school the other day and I says, "Michael, let's us make a deal. I'm a crackerjack office manager and you need some help here. Suppose I keep your books, pay your bills, answer the phone twenty hours a week and you give me a break on Travis's tuition?" He went crazy for it.

Glen did too. He said he thought it was just what I needed. He told me I could get someone in to clean here at home three days a week, loves the idea that I'm involved with Travis's education, blah, blah, blah. . . . It's a lot more responsibility than you might think. Michael lives on a spiritual plane, and you have to be grounded in reality if you're trying to keep a small private school running in the black.

Michael grins at me like I'm talking Sanskrit half the time. Health insurance for the teachers and physicals for the students and private school accreditation aren't where he lives. There's also the plain dull organization of files and putting together a newsletter and substituting when teachers are sick. It's work I do well. It keeps my mind off me and the insatiable desires that lead me into trouble.

Tuesday after school Travis went home with his new friend Bobby. I stayed late to finish up the newsletter. Michael was in his room behind the office. He lives at the school. He goes back there between four and six to rest up for his evening karate classes three nights a week. I'd never been back there in his room. I'd watched him disappear behind that door a hundred times. I was curious to see it. I wondered if he had an altar to some of those Eastern gods he talks about. Or love letters from an old girlfriend or any other relics from the life he had before he came here. I have infinite curiosity about Michael England. It went against my nature, but I never so much as peeked behind the door to his room.

Michael is many things, but he's not much of a writer. He wanted me to put a long article in the newsletter I was working on that afternoon explaining a little bit about this observance he had planned for Martin Luther King, Jr.'s, birthday. I had changed his original sketch so much that I wanted him to read it before I printed it up. At last I had a legitimate excuse to knock on the door of the holy of holies.

Everything in Michael's room is white. He has this theory about white and energy that he'd have to explain. Not that there was much inventory—the rollaway bed where he was lying down, a little dresser, a lamp, a few books and a couple straw mats. The window was covered with a sheet and it was getting on towards dusk, so I couldn't immediately tell if he had his clothes off under the sheets. If you know Michael, you don't make much of a thing like that. Michael has no chicanery or guile about him. I never heard him condemn anyone, and I suppose, in exchange for that, he expects the right to live as he pleases.

He sat up on the bed, revealing his bare upper torso as he took the newsletter out of my hand and started to read it. I stood by the edge of the bed in that white room and condemned myself for what I was feeling. I was flooded with the sudden, stupid hope that he'd take me into his arms and make love to me. Maybe if I touched him, he'd guide me away gently and give me a lecture on spirituality. I wanted to test him, I guess. I don't know. I wanted him. Period. I had for weeks. He must have been able to hear my heart racing.

I felt lower than Glen had ever made me feel despite his best efforts. I told myself that having him this way—just having him close, just helping him achieve his goals—was better than all my dark thoughts.

"This is great," he said, and handed me the paper.

His voice broke my heart because it expressed a kind of appreciation that Glen never could, that Sarah would never intend, that I might be lucky enough to experience from Travis only if I lived long enough. His voice spoke an admiration for parts of me that no one else ever saw, or maybe I just didn't have the guts to show them. It made me cry.

"Is something wrong?"

It was the most terrible moment I ever experienced. Glen tried to make me feel low and common. But it only angered me, it only goaded me on. Michael tried to make me his equal and I wanted to slip between the cracks in the floorboards. Of course I wanted him, but more than anything, I wanted to hold on to his approval.

There is no terror like an unspoken love, particularly when you haven't even admitted it to yourself. Until that moment, Michael had been my one true thought. His teachings were my hope for a new and bearable existence.

"I think I'm in love with you."

My words splattered out, clanked around the almost empty room and landed in a silent heap in a corner. If I could have run, I would have cheerfully run, fled, driven home, starched and ironed sheets gratefully until midnight. But then I heard the same words again.

"I think I'm in love with you."

Only this time, they didn't clank and they didn't heap, they swirled around and around on a trail of little stars illumining that room, because this time Michael had spoken them. He was crying too. We let our eyes talk, we let our arms dream, we let those little stars that swirled over us become endless sky. The world let us off for an hour. We made each other one—fast—and we made each other one—slow. We let our hearts lead our limbs deeper and deeper into each other, mingling and swirling, exploding and drinking in sensation, wonder, each other, love beguiling—shameless, awe-inspiring, prince-and-princess-hidden-in-a-secret-tower-room-against-a-storm—love spilling over, washing away all doubt or disbelief, waking enchantment, hard and fast and furious and resurrecting love!

I went home. Glen was on the phone with a client. He had a migraine. Sarah wouldn't touch her butter beans. Her teacher had sent a note home about her not wearing shorts to third grade. Travis spilled Krazy Glue all over his brand new solid mahogany bedroom furniture. I stood in the kitchen after they were all in bed. I starched and ironed and ironed and starched sheets until after midnight. I walked out onto the porch. It was windy. The water was choppy. There were thin puffy clouds moving over the trees. Behind the moon, brilliant and fine, the stars were still swirling.

27
Rose of Sharon

I had been avoiding Lily. I knew she'd be all over me wanting me to come back to the discussion group. She caught me pulling turnips in the garden on Saturday morning. At first I tried to act busier than I was. It surprised me how glad I was to see her. I'd put in two weeks out at Wal-Mart by that time and I didn't know how much more I could take. Mr. Dumas, the manager, starts the new ones out as greeters. You stand at the door and welcome every mangy shred of humanity to Wal-Mart eight hours a day. "Welcome to Wal-Mart," like it was a step up, like they had arrived from some lower level in life. It doesn't have the effect that the management intends. It puts people off. Most ignore you completely and the ones who respond look at you like you're pitiful and walk away thinking you must be the most desperate soul on earth to stand there doing that all day. One lady with two kids in her shopping cart stopped dead in her tracks. "Welcome to *Wal-Mart*?" She hissed back at me, "Woman, people don't *come* to Wal-Mart. People *end up* here."

Other things. The employees' bathroom is filthy. I don't care for that crowd I have to eat my lunch with, and that includes Marjean. Marjean manages linens—if you call what they sell linens—and she feels entitled to say anything to or about me because she helped to get me on out there. I want so badly to tell her that I worked for

Pizitz in Birmingham. Pizitz of Birmingham was decidedly a place to go rather than end up.

Dashnell acts like I filed for divorce. My job is an insult to his twenty-seven thousand a year. I can't serve a leftover without his complaining I abandoned my real job at home. Suddenly he wants his bowling shirt ironed. He says I promised him, if he'd buy me the lake house, I'd make it a showplace. I'd love to know when I said that. I've only had two paychecks so far, and I haven't even opened them. They're hardly worth taking to the bank.

I had to admit Lily was a tonic against all of that when she caught me in the garden. She's taken down some weight, and you can really see how delicate her face is. She looks like an alabaster angel. I took her up on the porch and made us some iced tea. She was jollier than I've ever seen her, like she really appreciated me taking the time with her.

Of course she teased me mercilessly about my not coming back to the discussion group. She was serious, but somehow her manner didn't offend me. I gave her an earful about Marjean and Wal-Mart. She had plenty to say that made me laugh about Marjean. She went on about how she looks like a banty hen with straw hair and how Jake must have done that caps job on her upper teeth with his power saw and on like that until my sides hurt from laughing.

Dashnell came in with a stringer of crappie for me to clean. He was proud of his catch, so he brought it on the porch and set it on an ice chest where we could see it. Lily looked like she was going to vomit.

"Dashnell, do you really expect this poor woman to clean those nasty things? Where did you grow up? In a cave?"

Dashnell laughed, but I could see he didn't like it. He told me to call Jake and Marjean. He said I was fixing to fry fish and hush puppies and to chop slaw.

"I'd like to see the day Glen commands me to clean fish and then stand over a hot kettle and fry them for a woman who runs her mouth about me all day at work."

Dashnell flashes hot all at once. He either blows or walks away. He flashed. He didn't walk away either. I had to say something.

"Go on and get your shower. What time are they coming?"

"I hadn't asked them yet," Dashnell says. "I couldn't say."

Lily had to keep her presence and her disapproval known. "Couldn't *say*. Well, *I'll say*!"

"Run on home, honey. . . ." That was me to Lily with her arms crossed and her foot tapping and her own set of fireworks about to explode. Dashnell's look scared her. She cooled down some.

"Run on home, now."

"What makes you think she wants to clean and fry fish?"

"It's what she's good at," Dashnell says. "Now a woman like you, she might not be so good at frying fish. She might have other talents. . . ." He was drunk, of course.

"Like what?" Lily knew from his tone what he meant.

"Like yours."

"Just what would mine be?"

"Precious, I really think you ought to run on. Dashnell, get your shower."

I stepped towards the fish which he'd dropped on the porch floor by my feet.

"Not before this big, grizzly redneck explains his insult."

"Probably touching your toes together over my head and squealing like a pig," he says.

"Is that so?" She was on fire. All in one jerk, she had the stringer of fish, and she pitched them way off into the yard behind the woodpile. He hollered for her to get off his property, and threatened to fetch his gun.

"It's Rose's property too."

I said I wasn't concerned about whose house it was, I didn't care for the way things were going and I wanted them both to go on about their business.

"You *want* to clean those fish?" Her look flattened me. I didn't want to clean and fry fish for Marjean. She knew it. I knew it. Dashnell knew it too. Dashnell said he was going down to Lily's to fetch Glen, who he called a "squirmy worm."

"Dashnell Lawler, you're a disgrace to the buzzards!" That was me. "Now you reach way down deep inside yourself and you find that last tiny shred of decency you keep hidden there and you apologize to Lily right now!" I was giving the fool an out. I was publicly pretending I believed underneath all his fire he was semihuman.

"Get that slattern off my property."

Lily rose to leave. Something told me if I didn't make a genuine effort to take up for her I'd never see her again. In that moment I realized that Lily was the only real friend that I had made since I came home to Prince George County. Suddenly that mattered to me more than anything else.

"Lily Pembroke is nobody's slattern. Lily Pembroke is my very good friend. You're a damned fool and you're stinking drunk and you are not fit for human companionship."

It was his mindless response to everything. It didn't hurt near as much as it looked like it did when it started to swell. The blood on my teeth didn't help. Quick as he seen what he'd done, he walked into the kitchen. Lily grabbed some ice from a glass of tea there on the table and pressed it against my lip. I told her to go on home. I said I'd be fine.

"Sit down," she says, ignoring me, "and don't talk till you quit bleeding." I wanted to get indoors as quick as I could, because I knew Marjean and Jake could hear us from their place. It wouldn't matter to Marjean if we had a DOA on the back porch. If she had wind that I was going to cook fish, she'd be over in a New York minute.

"I'm all right now," I says. "Go on." How many times did I ask her to leave? A hundred maybe. I started to get up and she sat me back down, then she rubbed on my sore shoulder and finally she went into the kitchen and poured me a finger or two of rum into a Coca-Cola. I'm not a drinker, but that settled me. Through the screen I could see Dashnell inside the house, wet from the shower, digging through the hall closet for a shirt. The temperature had dropped considerably. There was mist on the lake. I was limp by now. The crickets were screeching madness in the trees. You could smell rain.

"Dashnell?" She called into the kitchen like nothing had happened. "Do you want to know how you made her feel?" Lily was standing opposite him in the kitchen now. Her voice was as calm as if she'd been the one sipping on the rum and Coke, soaking up the shoulder rub and the attention.

"I lost myself," Dashnell said in a voice I hadn't heard since he and the minister made arrangements for Carmen. I figured there was a trick underneath it. But how to warn Lily?

"But do you know how you made her feel?" He said he didn't.

"Well, I'll just show you," she says, and her fist was at his jaw before I could turn around to see. I heard his tooth crack. A sudden light came all around her as she stood there, preventing me with an upraised arm from moving to see if he was all right. A light swirled over her and it lit something in me that I would have to describe as a hurtful joy like the memory of childbirth or Daddy. Dashnell stood silent in the door with his hand over his mouth. The light must have come into my eyes by then, because Dashnell Lawler had the saddest look I ever saw on his face. After Carmen, sorrow was all he could feel. Sometimes that sorrow burst into anger like it had a little while before. Sometimes it exploded and diminished, but it would always grow in him again.

It was just beginning to rain lightly, the slow kind that builds through the night and pours its heart out all the next day.

Lily and I walked down to her house and she got her car keys and we drove down to the Catfish Hotel. We sat on the deck at an umbrella table and watched the rain on the lake and we talked till all hours. The things I said to Lily were true things and real things like memories of horse hooves in wet fields and funny people I'd known and little girl things like my dolls and waking in the dead of night and feeling cold and useless. My words felt sticky and odd because they'd lain unspoken inside me all my adult life. I had always been afraid to utter them.

I told her how I married Dashnell because I was twenty-five and afraid he might be my last chance. How I was always a little afraid of Mother and yet I admired her above all other women. How I have always been ashamed because I hate Christmas. How helpless I felt about Dashnell's misery and other things like how hard Dashnell was on Carmen and how the only other time I could remember things crossing lines with me and Dashnell was the time he took after Carmen with a board and I told him if he beat the boy, he'd never see either one of us again.

Mostly it was just that close feeling, a friend in the rain, a chain of heartfelt words building a shelter around us against the night.

When we were getting into Lily's car to come home, I said I'd never seen a woman slug a man like that. I'd seen plenty fight back, trying to protect themselves, but never one to haul off and swing of her own accord. I said it made me feel good and it made me feel worth something, but that it also made me feel weak. She said it was all right to be weak in this world. She said the difference between the humans and the animals was the human obligation of the strong to protect the weak. She said strength had no other purpose. She said weakness was human too. She said that it takes the greatest strength to admit weakness. She dropped me at home. We had a good, steady rain by then. I went out on the porch and I sat and looked through the fog at the lake. A few yards up I could hear Dashnell and Jake on Marjean's porch, their drunk and swollen voices muffled by the downpour. I grabbed Dashnell's slicker. I didn't care if they heard me; but I didn't start the motor because I didn't want to disturb others who might be sleeping. I rowed into the fog. I heard Marjean's screen door fly open and Dashnell pounding the steps and I saw him approach their dock about a hundred yards away from me.

"What the hell are you doing?" he snarled.

"I'm going fishing," I says.

"What? Are you drunk?"

"Might be, I wouldn't know."

"You get back here, or else!"

"I'm going fishing," I says.

"I'm not having this," he says.

"Well, sir," I says, "you'll just have to shoot me too." I switched the motor on, shoved it up on high, and I sailed through that fog like a kid on a magic carpet.

28
Heath

I thought maybe since KemCo is actually in the next county and it's owned by some Yankees, that they might at least let me fill out the application form before they tossed me out on my ear. I was hoping they wouldn't know about me or my time in the state pen for robbing that bowling alley. I heard they were adding a night shift. I got through the interview part just fine. In fact, the lady who talked to me was from over in Yellow County. She had never heard of me.

The company nurse listened to my chest and took my blood pressure and pronounced me fit to pull a plow.

I was getting fairly hopeful by this time. Daddy and I had a substantial set-to that morning about my not bringing in money. I was hoping I could waltz home with a good paying KemCo job and benefits. The nurse told me to see a supervisor named Mr. Kelly. His department was adding a shift.

She said he was in the lunch area at the back of the plant. Of course half of Prince George County was sitting in the lunch area rolling their eyes at me when I walked in. I'd rather dive into a pond filled with water moccasins than walk past those people. Still, an opportunity waited on the other side of them. I was thinking I could get myself hired and be turning in a super job performance before some of these Prince George monkeys got this Mr. Kelly's ear about my criminal past.

I knew him the minute I saw him. Mr. Kelly was not only from Prince George, but he was somebody I'd known all my life. He's Jake Kelly and he lives up on Lake Evelyn four houses down from my uncle Dashnell. It wouldn't have made any difference with Jake Kelly if I'd never been in prison. He and my daddy have been mortal enemies since before I was born. Jake is heavily involved with the Klan. Almost all of the men who live up on Lake Evelyn are. Ninety percent of them work at KemCo.

My daddy and Jake grew up near that lake back before people had fancy houses all around it. Lake Evelyn took its name from my great-grandmother. There's a story about her and a divining rod during a drought when she was a little girl. Apparently she went into the woods blindfolded and located a spring buried by rocks. The spring was opened and a pond that was formed took her name. The U.S. Army Corps of Engineers dammed it into a lake proper when my daddy was a kid.

Anyway, Jake took it personal when Daddy declined his invitation to join the Klan some years back. Then last year Daddy sold off what was left of his home place to Glen Pembroke. Glen was the first outsider to own property on the lake. Jake Kelly and his bunch regard the land around that lake as their sacred dust. I walked over to where Jake was sitting at a lunch table with several other familiar faces from up around Lake Evelyn. I tried to sound as respectful as I could.

"They told me to give you this." I handed him the yellow slip they had given me up front. Jake grinned from ear to ear. Uncle Dashnell was sitting beside him.

"Hey, Uncle Dash," I says. I wasn't exactly leaning on blood here. Mother hasn't spoken to Dashnell in a hundred years. Daddy makes a point of avoiding him at funerals and weddings and family reunions. But I had done a bang-up job sodding his yard a few weeks back and he had seriously underpaid me. I figured he owed me one. Besides, blood is everything to a red faced half-dog, half-man like Uncle Dash. At least that's what I told myself to slow my racing heart.

He leaned right over and snatched the paper out of Jake's hand and pretended he was looking it over. I sucked in some air and tried to keep my eyes on the prize. The man held the rest of my life in his hand.

"I sure appreciate the opportunity," I says. "You know how rough it is out there." Jake kept grinning. Several men and women had closed in around behind him and Dashnell by this time. Jake pursed his lips.

"Boy," he says in that deceptively low manner he has that hides how mean he really is, "I'm going to give you an *opportunity* to make it from here to the parking lot without getting your brains knocked out."

That's when Dashnell took the job slip out of Jake's hand and pretended he was blowing his nose into it.

"You can thank your scum faced, turncoat daddy for this." Dashnell is pure, ugly arrogance and stupidity mixed with confidence. He can't hide what he is. You can see right off what you're dealing with. Jake Kelly on the other hand is refried ignorance in a starched blue shirt. He's a halfway nice looking man who affects a phony cracker accent. I could feel the veins in my forehead bulging and I knew my face must be red as a Coca-Cola can. Something was testing me. Something wanted to know if I had the fortitude to walk away without busting Jake Kelly's pretty little nose.

"Jake, I'm an excellent worker," I said. "Uncle Dashnell can tell you. I just sodded his yard and painted his house a little while back."

"Yeah, he sure did," Dashnell allowed. "He took his pay out in trade on Glen Pembroke's skinny harlot wife." Nobody has any secrets in Prince George County, at least not for long. I could hear several of them sniggering as I walked out of the lunchroom. I got into my truck and I pounded the dashboard until my palms were numb and I begged God to let me live long enough to watch those sons of bitches choke on their ignorance. I started wondering. If Dashnell knew about Lily and me, then maybe Glen knew.

I went home and chopped nearly a cord of wood trying to cool myself down. Man, I wanted that job. I had stopped off to call Lily on the way home, but she wouldn't even hear me out. She just asked me to please not call her again.

I guess she feels she has to make a go of it with that thick-lipped, weak-eyed excuse of a husband.

I could have chopped a train rail in half with my bare hand. I spun around wasting invisible evils in the yard for more than an hour. I sat on the woodpile and watched the sun go down. There's something spellbinding and sad about the daylight fading. I could see Mother through the kitchen window making supper and Daddy washing his hands. I was watching their life. I didn't have one. It didn't all fit in my head. I had to let go of something. So I cried. It's no big thing. I cry at the end of TV movies when the lady is always safe and she has her cute little tykes back in her arms. I cried about Lily and I cried about the sorry state of the world. I thought about Glen and I cried for him too, because if Lily told me straight, he's probably the only other man in the world who knows what it is to love her in vain. I know, if no one including Lily does, the torment he endures.

Mostly I cried because to that point, despite all my best efforts, I couldn't get a job with a gun. I couldn't make my life start. Why did so many others put it all together and not me? I had a brain and willing hands and I had made a serious effort to turn things around. What was lacking? That evening on the log pile, I gave up. I quit. I let go. I surrendered. I said it right out loud, "I surrender." I didn't know what I meant. But I knew that I meant it. I was sincerely finished with grabbing for things I was never going to get. I told myself, "Fine, you may never be anything, you may never have anything, you'll just get on one way or the other until you die and that's all, that's it, there isn't any more than that anyway."

I started along that line mad as a swarm of angry bees. But it calmed me more than anything I ever experienced. I smashed into rock bottom. It was awful. But it was also the first time I can remember being awake and not feeling like I was falling, like I had to swing my arms and legs hopelessly trying to fight that constant downward sensation. I felt the earth under my feet. It was solid. I saw the sky above me. It was vapor and the setting sun was fire. I was small and powerless in a time and a place. It was real and I was real. I was a part of it. I was there. I was in it. It wasn't, as I had always believed without thinking about it, mine to own, to conquer or rise above. I was with it. I thought back to my time in Folsom Prison when I was certain I had felt the Breath of God. I felt it for the second time that evening on the log pile. I made a solemn promise to remember it this time. I didn't expect that to change anything in the world around me. I didn't fall on my knees and ask God to find me a job or bring Lily back to me. I did, however, head into the house for supper convinced firsthand that there's wisdom in acceptance.

29
Hezekiah
(1987)

He had nothing to offer them but his words. His sermon was true and inspired by God. These people needed money. These people called him throughout the week looking for help with the landlord or rat control or burying a family member inexpensively. No matter how much religiosity Hezekiah rubbed into his sermons, they seemed dusty and archaic next to the living needs of his congregation. They just didn't apply. The Living Word was dead as far as most of his congregation was concerned.

He tried the joke about the black man from Birmingham standing at the gates to hell. The devil says, "Mister, go on up to heaven. If you're from Birmingham, you already done your time in hell." That woke a couple of them for a minute. Most of them had heard it. Heard it, hell; they were living it.

Now and again, a passing cloud would send a shadow over the sanctuary or a dry leaf would scrape an open window or a bubble of hope would catch at the back of an otherwise dry throat before bursting. Now and again a loyal remnant from the glory days of the sixties would echo an empty "Amen," or a woman intent on a mole by her right eye in her compact mirror would send up an obligatory "That's right." But his sermon about the black man's journey to freedom and God's hand in it lay as flat as a Jell-O mold salad in the noonday sun.

" 'Arise, men of the Almighty!' the ancient Prophet wails, 'Arise and glorify Him by your shining witness!'

"But my people sit meekly in the shadow and refuse the helping hand of the Lord their God. My people hang around on street corners with their cold backs turned to His grace. My people lie in loveless fornication, blinded by their all consuming rage, their wonder at His majesty dulled by cheap wine, their bodies enslaved by debilitating drugs. My people have surrendered their ambition and their dignity and their hope to an all consuming despair born in the deepest under-regions of hell and spreading like a cancer among us.

"How can a man who will not believe in himself look faithfully to heaven? You have not been forsaken, my people. You have forsaken your God and, by doing so, you forsake yourselves and your children's children. Wake, my people, wake to the light in you, to the God in you, rise up and be a beacon to your children and a revelation unto yourselves."

There was no point in bringing up hell or damnation. This old raggle-dee corner of uptown Birmingham in the August heat *was* hell and damnation. The Coca-Cola thermometer on the drugstore across the busy avenue had reached ninety-nine by eleven A.M. Church bulletins and cardboard funeral home fans and handkerchiefs swayed listlessly in every face. Now and then a vagrant wasp would drift languidly down from its nest in the ceiling beams and hover over an old woman's head. Now and then diesel fumes wafted up from the bus stop under the open windows and the agonizing grind of a tired city bus eclipsed Hezekiah's words.

Half a block away, three cops held a dozen winos at gunpoint, their hands and faces pressed into the brick wall of a graffiti-covered school. The mayor was cracking down on the homeless by putting on this show for the Sunday morning set en route to the baseball stadium in the next block. The sun flew straight overhead, a furry white ball seen through thick wet air that threatened to burst. Hez had to wonder why Birmingham didn't sink and disappear from sheer disgrace deep into the earth.

Some unwanted and unloved kid out there had dropped a condom in the collection plate and the old deacon who laid the offering on the altar table either hadn't seen it or, more likely, didn't know what it was. It was sealed in a cellophane package that was decorated with a rebel flag. One of the pale yellow silk flowers in the milk glass bowl on the altar table under the portrait of Doctor King fell dryly to the floor. Hezekiah talked on.

His congregation wanted something more tangible than mighty arched words and phrases dipped in Old Testament righteousness. He knew that they had been born into despair and that most of them would die in deeper despair. The holy beacon of that great movement which had flooded them with hope twenty years before had been snuffed out. His people had tasted hope and smelled change and felt freedom in the air. They had stood arm-in-arm, an undefeated, holy power against fire hoses and dogs and the private armies of the demagogues who had held them in chains. They had sung of the ancient promises and become, for a moment, a pure and shining light. Then, one by one, they had watched in horror as the forces of darkness conspired to rob them of their leaders.

They had witnessed the assassinations of their dreams in Dallas and Memphis and Los Angeles and New York. Now they foundered in the returning dark.

There was a cry from the street followed by a disturbing series of small shrieks and then what sounded like several gunshots.

"Rise up, my people!" He was sweating profusely. His voice rang out. It was a true and living witness to the faith it embodied. But it failed to move them. He could fight with the city utilities people for single mothers. He could argue with the biased conservatism of the local press. He could do ceaseless battle; he could stand bruised and dumbstruck and unvanquished against police brutality. But his words were powerless to resurrect the spirit of his congregation.

"And the light shineth in darkness, and the darkness comprehends it not!"

A siren in the street drowned out the benediction. A bobbing sea of mostly gray heads slid into the aisles. Someone broke through the back doors of the church and spread the news. By the time Hezekiah reached the front steps of the church, the boy's mother, still in her choir robe, was wailing over his bloody corpse in the street. There was sixty-three cents in the red plastic purse they had to pry from his already stiff fingers. The old woman, his victim, was sitting on a car hood up the block holding her head. Someone had loosened her collar. Someone else had handed her a melting Coca-Cola. In a minute she stood up, declared herself all right and, leaning on her cane, hobbled quickly up the block before the cops took her name. On the corner a truck driver asked a passerby what happened, and he said, "A white man shot a nigger trying to steal an old nigger woman's purse." They put the boy's body in the back of an ambulance and the crowd thinned down immediately. They had been in Sunday school and church all morning. Their clothes itched and they were hungry. Hezekiah ran to get his car so the boy's mother wouldn't have to ride home on the bus.

Fifteen minutes later some junked down kid took a monkey wrench and loosed the fire hydrant. You could see the boy's blood mixing with the water as the puddle grew by the church. A couple kids got into the spray. But the same cops came back and the kids ran. They cut off the hydrant. When the street dried where the water had run into the sewer, it dried clean and new and the blood had washed away.

30
Dashnell

Well, hell, you know, you work to have a life. You sweat in some windowless factory, eating dust, taking gump, listening to threats, and all you want is maybe a couple acres someplace quiet, a little piece of a boat to go fishing in, a few friends, and in between, the thrill of decent whiskey rolling down your throat. You spend a third of your life sleeping, another third working and you want some recreation in between.

You do the marriage bit, you get a kid, you listen to your wife complain, you try to go on believing in life as long as you can, but then somewhere around fifty, you see the crest behind you and think, Christ, that was it? Maybe it was a trip down to Orlando to Disney World. Maybe it's watching the boy you never had the time to know graduate from college. Then it's back to work fifteen more years, if the plant don't close on you, if your back don't go out or lung or prostate cancer doesn't get you or maybe it's just the weariness. Weariness is a bigger problem than most pointy-headed politicians know. You'd think they would. Since according to most of them, they never sleep. Hell, no, they never sleep, they're all out chasing call girls and movie stars all night and spending yours and my money on it, which is what went with the once proud military of this country. The niggers took the schools. Well, Kennedy give our schools to the niggers in between diddling Marilyn Monroe and handing the Caribbean over to Castro and Miami, Florida, to his greasy Cuban convicts. If you could stand on a mountain and regard this once proud nation in total, you'd see nothing but Republican drug runners and Democratic nigger-lovers from sea to shining sea.

It's not but a handful of us left who even cares to notice. But it's like I tell Jake, it don't take but a handful of the right minds, shoulder to shoulder, standing up and refusing to take it no more. Take what, you say?

I worked down in Birmingham twelve years. We had our first house. It was a good, square brick house and we had plenty of yard for a bird dog run and a garden. She had her kitchen. The kid had his room. I had my woodworking table in the garage. Sunday afternoons she'd let me grab ahold of her and take what I needed. We didn't bother nobody and nobody bothered us.

One day I come home from work, and I'm turning up the main street alongside our subdivision, and I see a great big old nigger lamp in a picture window. All the goddamned room in this world, and these niggers got to take a piece of mine. Well, I'm no fool, I seen what was coming. We was five blocks away. I had a little time, enough to sell the house and find another a little farther out from the city before it hit most of the neighbors what was happening. Because one nigger lamp in a picture window brings more nigger lamps in more picture windows, and if you don't believe me, then you go on over there and have a look today. Go have a look at what happened to some decent, hardworking people's American dream. Torn screens, rusted cars in the yards, rutted driveways, nigger babies all over the place, crack cocaine, AIDS, and it's all being funded by that one third of your paycheck the U.S. Government steals from you.

Like I say, we got another house, a bigger one. She had the living room all blue and fancy. I never did sit on that couch she bought with her discount at Pizitz. She went crazy when we got that house. The kid's room had two beds and red carpet and bookcases crammed with TV, stereo and VCR and then a goddamned computer for college. We had a guest bedroom that was only used twice—once by her mama when the boy graduated high school, and once by a cousin of mine from Joliet, Illinois, who was on his way to Florida. She wouldn't put no vegetable garden in the backyard on account of the neighbors.

Well, that was some time after Kennedy handed the schools to the niggers, so it wasn't long before we had this nigger superintendent of schools moving in down the block. We just barely did get Carmen, our boy, all the way graduated before it became essential to send white kids to private school. I tried to talk it up in the neighborhood that we should band together and go down to that school and run those niggers out of it, because it gnaws at my fundamental American beliefs when I think of hardworking people having to come up with private school tuition. But they had all gone Reagan crazy, Reagan blind. It was like that son of a bitch laid a blinder on all the guts and the decency left in white America. People actually talked like they believed in a minute or two they was all going to be rich enough to move away from the niggers forever and ever.

She was nuts over that house, kept little cans of paint and touched up the walls twice a month, waxed down the paneling in the den every other minute, and everybody who come to the door had to endure a walking tour of every square inch of it. She dug in against me about selling out. She said that nigger superintendent made her no never mind. She was Reagan blind too. She didn't want to see he was the first wave.

Hell, I let her think that for a few months. In that day and time, you could sit on a house in Birmingham fifteen minutes and the value would go up a thousand dollars. I figured it being such a decent neighborhood, we had a little more time before the niggers run it over. Right before my boy was killed, I heard tell some niggers had been seen looking at a house three blocks over.

That was when I decided there was nothing to do but go back up home to the one true white haven left in this great state, and that's what we done. You can drive every road in this county and you won't find one nigger shack, beer drinking dive, beat-up Cadillac or coon pusher. If you find a Jew, you can bet your ass he's for Jesus. It's no official NIGGERS KEEP OUT sign on the county line. But it's known for miles. So when that woolhead showed up on the lake a while back, we took it for the sacrilege it was. Any nigger who has ever read his Bible knows it says quite clearly the birds of the air do not mix. Abel Thompkins knows how to take a person's license number and run it through a computer at his job. He's the one who got us his phone number. I called that coon's house sixteen times warning him to keep out of Prince George. When that didn't work, being Christian men, we thought to make the message a little stronger by shooting a hole in his boat. When he failed to grasp that, we let the air out of his tires.

I wrote him a note telling him clear what he could expect if he showed up again, and I left it on his dashboard. That seemed to work for a week or two, but a nigger brain can only hold on to an idea for so long, or maybe it's that mule's tenacity built into them. He was back. This time, as always with niggers, he had multiplied. There were three in his boat. One of them used the rest room in Wiley's bait shop. Wiley was gone and his wife was there alone, and in fear of rape, she didn't say nothing to them. A week later, he's back, alone this time with a tent, planning to camp on the ground on the opposite side of the lake. We had no personal truck with that nigger, and we regret any sorrow or hardship that was caused, but sometimes a thing has to be done for the greater good, to send out a message to all the blacks and to be a beacon of hope to a downtrodden white race. It was as easy as taking a sleeping duck on still water. We played one hand of five card stud for the honor, and I won. In order that we could all feel a part of the mission, I used Jake's pistol, and we loaded it with Wiley's bullets. We took Billy's truck, and Mickey drove. It was done quick and clean. Ping.

That's not to say even a mission as pure and necessary as ours can ever be completed without regret or second thought. That's not to wonder if we couldn't have used some other persuasive means. Hindsight is built into any great act. But we have our brotherhood to bind and hold us up and carry us through whatever difficult acts are required. Our task is a holy task and we are knotted together and welded to it. We have that oneness of spirit and purpose. We're united up and down this lake, except for that harlot's husband.

He has yet to make his position clear. Our bond has been offered, and he has declined to respond. He has been told that his wife's mouth is unwelcome here and we have given him the opportunity to silence it. He has been made to understand that whatever must be done will be done. He has been told to think it over fast and sign on or get out. It's a pretty place, and I'd hate to see it burn.

31
Rose of Sharon

Dashnell slept late, and that was bad, because sometimes after a drunk night, he'll get up early, still under the effects of the alcohol, and he's not feeling his hangover yet. That makes him a little easier to deal with. I heard him back there in the kitchen opening a beer. I waited. He showered. He came back into the kitchen and drank another and then opened a third. He filled the doorway. I couldn't see him, but I knew he was there by that awful sweat and soap and alcohol smell he has sometimes.

"I believe I've figured it out," he says. He swung the door open and stepped out onto the porch. I never knew Dashnell to have a problem that I wasn't the direct cause of, so I wasn't surprised at what he said. "You've lost what little mind you once had."

You'd have to know Dashnell as well as I do to know that was his notion of making an amend. He wanted to erase the slate.

"No, Dashnell, I haven't lost my mind. I haven't forgotten one bit of last night either."

I don't know how a person can forget something as important as this, but one thing that came back to me while I was sitting out there in the boat in the night mist was the fact that right before Carmen died, I'd had several long talks with Carmen about leaving Dashnell. Carmen agreed that I'd be better off in some ways, but he cautioned me not to wind up with nothing. Carmen had a love of material things. No, I'll say that right. Carmen was educated and had expectations for himself. His goals included many things a person like me might only consider dreams. Even that's not the whole truth, because I descended to that way of thinking as I lived with Dashnell year after year. If Dashnell Lawler ever made an effort to communicate with me, he did that morning. He came and sat down opposite me at the table, something he generally tries to avoid, and said, "Rosie, you've lost yourself completely. Nothing you do or say here lately is you."

Well, he had a point. I was different. I'd been unconscious most of my adult life. I gave up and I switched off. But somehow I had switched back on. It scared me because I already knew I could never go back and be the other way anymore. Dashnell was trying to say that it was on account of Carmen. It was more on account of Lily. The thing that had sealed it for me was the man in the boat. I had come around to the untenable conclusion that my willful ignorance had murdered him in absentia. I had to change as part of my atonement for that.

"Dashnell," I said, "I can't live with you anymore—not knowing what you and the others did to that man." I have to experience a thing before I can put it to words and mean it. A lot of people can take an idea from a book or another person and grab hold of the logic of it and use it straight off. But I have to do it to learn it. I have to look back over my shoulder at a thing I did or said or thought and hear myself talk about it before I know I mean it. Most of what I say to other people is just expressing it for myself. I was saying it and meaning it.

"What the hell are you talking about?"

"Murder," I said sadly.

"You have completely lost yourself."

He was white as a sheet. He swallowed his beer whole and went in for another one.

"Dashnell," I started, "Dashnell, you ought to leave off that beer and see what the world looks like. You're afraid of what the world looks like. It scares you, so you try to hide from it up here on this lake."

"This lake is all the decent left in the world, fool."

One other thing we learned in discussion group was that if you want to make a point with someone, then choose your most important point and say it simple.

"I'm leaving. Tomorrow."

"Why?"

I wanted so badly to say because I'm not wasting another precious second of my life with an ape. But how do you make that point with an ape? All I knew was that I'd been out on that lake in the boat. I don't mean a revelation came shimmering down from the stars. I mean I did it, alone, after midnight, despite how it looked, not knowing what I was doing or why, only that I was doing something. *Doing* something!

"Murder." He was back. I was pretty sure he'd poured some bourbon into that can of beer in his hand.

"Murder," I repeated, "the murder of the white race and the American dream and life as any decent person once knew it."

I don't know when he became so obsessed with it.

"Did you shoot him?

He give a little half grunt, half laugh.

"Yeah."

"I think you ought to do the right thing."

Lily said later I was courageous to talk to him like that. I never worry too much about expressing an opposite opinion to Dashnell. He puts no store in what I have to say about anything.

"What right thing?"

"I think you ought to go down there to the sheriff's office and turn yourself in."

He was watching me, trying to figure out how far I was going to go with this thing.

"Why don't you go down there and tell him for me?"

"Because I have no facts." That wasn't why. I knew the sheriff would laugh in my face, pat me on the shoulder, tell me I was out of my mind and say what a good man Dashnell was.

"Well, then, what are you going to do about it?"

"I guess I'm going to leave."

"It all went wrong when Carmen was took," he started.

I wouldn't listen to it anymore. "You don't want it to go right, Dashnell."

He was staring through me as if I were his executioner.

"If you wanted it to go right, Dashnell, you would have admitted a long time ago how little Carmen meant to you."

He chugged his beer and went back inside for another.

"I didn't see you coaching his Little League or taking him to Boy Scouts. You never once tried to help him with his homework or took him camping or ball games or the movies. You shoved him aside years and years before he was taken." I had always imagined I'd rail when I finally got those words out. I didn't. I just said them.

"This ain't you," he said.

"It's what I've come down to," I answered.

Dashnell walked back into the kitchen, opened the refrigerator, took out another beer, walked out the door and got into his truck. I was already on the phone telling Mother to expect me by the time he started the engine.

32

Eula Pearl

Rose of Sharon didn't give me but a few hours' notice. I couldn't work wonders. Nadine knew a woman and her daughter who clean and such. They're not cheap but they come on short notice. They got Rose of Sharon's bedroom emptied out inside half an hour. I'd been storing things in it for twenty or thirty years. They polished it up and we all held our breath when they pulled the curtains out of the washer, but the thread held. The lace shone. It's the best bedroom suite in the house. They call it Empire. It came from France. It drank lemon oil until it shone. It shamed me to have one corner of the house looking that nice. It showed me how far I'd let the rest go.

I have been hoping Rose of Sharon would leave Dashnell since the day she married him. In many ways I have always considered it an inevitability. I never dreamed that she'd leave him to come home. She didn't ever say why she left Dashnell or if it's for good. I have an idea that it is for good. It was one thing to marry him hoping he'd pull himself up. It would be quite another to go back to him now that she sees how far he's gone down. I knew he would. I take no pleasure in that fact. He had nothing to work with, no education or land or family money. He was bound to turn out low and to be proud of it like almost all the rest of the Lawlers.

I'm glad to have Rose of Sharon's company, but I try not to let on too much because I don't want her to have any mixed feelings about leaving if that's her intent. Meanwhile, it's a wonderful thing to be able to go to bed and lock the doors. I had taken the habit of leaving a door unlocked in case I die in the night. It would be an awful thing for her or Nadine to have to get someone to break the door to haul me out.

Rose of Sharon has a touch, a way of cleaning yet leaving things the way they were. She stays up to all hours running rags over everything. She says it relaxes her. It relaxes me to fall asleep in a house where someone else is awake, someone still part of the world.

Nadine is over here every morning exactly two minutes after Rose of Sharon leaves for Wal-Mart, trying to find out if she's shared anything. Like I'd tell Nadine if she had. I didn't realize how possessive of the place Nadine had become until Rose of Sharon came home. That's because she has no stake anyplace else.

Rose of Sharon has never complained to me about Dashnell. She wouldn't dare. I would have taken the opportunity to tell her all over again how stupid she was to marry him in the first place. At least I would have until a few years ago. I finally realized a thing like that is far more complicated than my addled brain could ever grasp. I'm stronger than I am smart. Rose is exactly the opposite. My guess would be that Rose has regretted marrying Dashnell almost from the beginning. Her torment now isn't the fact that she's finally left him. Her torture is knowing it took her three decades to find the gumption. Like I say, this is all guesswork.

I judged her very harshly for putting up with Dashnell all those years. I said very little. I didn't have to say much. It stood between Rose of Sharon and me. Lawler men are renowned for beating their wives. There's not a doubt in my mind that he beat her. Lawlers are low people. Dashnell is the lowest. I was very selfish. I considered her marriage to Dashnell a direct insult to me and all that I had tried to teach her. Searle chastised me for that until the very end. He said that her marriage to Dashnell was proof positive of our failure to provide her with other options.

I could have made a difference. I could have gone to her a hundred times and begged her to leave him. I could have insisted that she go to college and paid her way through any school in this country. She was a straight-A student. We might have sent her to Europe. I could have opened a hundred other doors than the one she took for fear of winding up old and alone at home. I didn't do anything except put on a fine wedding so that Dashnell's people would be embarrassed and uncomfortable. I guess as her mother I figured I had the right to expect her to go off and do all the things I never had the guts to do myself. I took it personally when she didn't. That's a whole lot worse than what she did trying to tough it out with Dashnell all those years.

She seems to like it here. She talks a lot about restoring the house. She sits for hours and listens as I go on about how everything looked when I was a girl. I told her she can do anything she likes with the place. I warned her, though, if she's not careful, she'll wake the dead.

33

Glen

I had begun to think Lily had finally come to appreciate what we have. Her attitude lightened up. She left off the wine. She made good dinners and helped the kids with their homework. We started having what I thought were some pretty good times in the bedroom. I thought building the house up here on the lake had finally begun to work.

How in God's name could I have been that stupid—twice? I can't confront her with it, not even indirectly, because underneath all my rage is the fear of driving her away, a woman who has given me two doses of the worst pain I ever experienced in my life. A woman who consumed my youth and put me in horrible debt. A woman who preyed on what was once my normal insecurity until it snaked into out and out madness.

The day I closed on this house Lily and I brought the kids up here and we had a picnic on the porch. I looked over the yard at that water and I thought there was more peace per square yard up here than anyplace I'd ever seen. It's not pretty to me anymore. It's evil. It's cursed. If I believed in ghosts, I'd say it was haunted.

I don't mean one pure, unholy evil spread by the Antichrist. I mean layers of evil, each one giving rise to the next, mounting up until you have to run or join in. Mine started with weakness. I shoved that whole Dallas mess under the rug as quickly as I could.

Out of weakness and fear came a whole storm of lies—all amounting to my choice to believe that Lily had come home to stay. Her lies like where we got our boy Travis. That led me to lie to myself and say I didn't care as long as I had a fine, healthy son. The more I think of him as mine, the more it torments me that Lily and I never had that conversation. There can't be any truth between Lily and me. Facts would disintegrate the little we have left.

That's just the beginning. I lied to myself about this house and the peace it would bring us. The truth is I went into twice as much hock as I could afford because I thought up here, off the beaten path, there wouldn't be much to tempt her.

She's powerless over men, especially halfway decent looking young men. She can't help but throw herself at them. She's sick with discontentment. She has a burning need for whatever she doesn't have.

You tell yourself you love her out of some spiritual goodness. You do it for her; you're making some kind of noble sacrifice, you're building your Christian character. Here's where the anger gets mixed into the weakness and the fear. A man who seeks out a woman he knows isn't trustworthy is buying himself a ready-made right to hate her. Justified hate entitles a man to feel moral about doing evil things. Sometimes evil things cross my mind.

I went what you'd call the regular way a long time ago. That meant ignoring my curious side. People say things. True things. Other people like me don't want to hear them because we don't want to tamper with the status quo. I'll say right here and now that it was Lily who made me acutely aware of that about myself.

I was so dead set on removing Lily from all temptation that I didn't think. I jumped at the chance to move up here without looking the local environs over carefully. This is no ordinary neighborhood. People are far more interested in what you think than what you have. You're in or you're out up here. You're with the others or you're on their hit list. They're organized. They're working evil at night. They know I've got them figured out. They're waiting to see if I'll join. I may have to eventually. If I don't, we may burn in our beds.

I can feel the evil beginning to add up: mine, Lily's, theirs, those broken men who kill in the night.

I was out in the yard sawing firewood. The sun was weak behind the clouds. The sky was spitting ice. I had just worked up a sweat when Dashnell Lawler came stumbling down his back steps.

"Hey," he says, smiling with menace.

"How's it going?" I said, trying to figure some way to get rid of him without offending him. He was stinking drunk.

"Smells like rain."

It was drizzling, but I don't argue the inconsequential with a drunkard who stands there running a penknife under his fingernails.

"The wife left me." He grinned like it had nothing to do with that fact he was stinking drunk at one o'clock on a Saturday afternoon as always.

"I'm sorry."

"It don't make me no never mind." He used the phrase in a self-satisfied way like he'd invented it.

"Oh, go on. A thing like that is never easy."

"I'd a hell of a lot rather have my wife leave me plain than slip around on me in plain sight."

"I would too." I forced a grin figuring the best defense was to pretend ignorance.

Dashnell jumped straight to his point. "So then, how is it with you? I mean, which way is the wind blowing? Are you for or against?"

"I'm sorry?" I had his drift but I didn't want it. I offered him a glass of iced tea. He asked for whiskey. I got him a shot and sat him down on a lawn chair.

"You got a note on this place?"

I said, who didn't have a note on their place? He made some statement about the interest on the note going to pay nigger welfare. I didn't follow. But I pursed my lips to give him the impression I did.

"Your wife don't care for me," he said.

"She doesn't take care of me either." Lousy joke.

"I reckon she told you she popped me in the jaw?" That grin again.

"Oh, yeah." I tried to sound nonchalant. "I'm sorry about that." I had no idea what he was talking about. However, I pretended that I'd sent her back to his house the next day to apologize, that I thought she had already done so. I said I would grab her by the hair and haul her up to his house to make full amends as soon as she got home. None of which he bought for a minute. I felt no immediate physical fear of the man, but I could sense he was holding something back, something I didn't want to acknowledge, because whatever it was, it scared the hell out of me.

"Well, no, she never apologized." He played along.

This is where I went too far. I lied that when she told me about the incident, she'd said that Dashnell had thrown a pass at her. I said I knew Dashnell was a man of enough character and substance to mean no harm by such a gesture. I said that Lily has a tendency to overreact when a man has a little joke with her. I said I'd speak to her about it. That wasn't a complete lie. I intended to find out what the hell he was talking about as soon as Lily got home.

He had that drunk's paranoid radar. He knew that I was afraid. I'd lived on the lake long enough to know that Dashnell and Jake and the others considered it their personal domain. They had asked me to go fishing or play cards or hunt with them a dozen times, and I'd always made my excuses.

"I wouldn't throw no 'pass' at a woman like her," he says. "I'd throw her down and have my way with her and then I'd pitch her on the trash where she belonged."

He was pathetic. I intimated he was too much of a gentleman to say a vulgar thing like that to a man about his wife unless he'd had a couple too many.

"You mean I wouldn't have the guts?"

"I mean you'd have better sense. You go sober up and we'll continue this conversation some other time." I got up and walked towards the house.

"Defend her. Defend that slut to me, nigger lover!" He slapped at the back of my head. I wheeled around and my punch put him on the ground.

"You know where she is right now?" He was trying to right himself. She was up at the school printing the newsletter. But I didn't see where that was his business.

"Man, you get off my property while you're still able to walk."

"She's up there at that schoolhouse, and that homo fairy's ridin' her like a goddamn Brahma bull."

It took at least two dozen punches before I had him back on the ground and he quit trying to get up. I turned and walked towards the house.

"Nothing goes down in Prince George County that we don't know about." He was laughing. He was on his back with blood oozing out of his nostrils and the son of a bitch was laughing. He got up and turned toward his yard. Then he stopped and turned around.

"She humped my nephew a dozen times yonder in the woods too."

Some invisible string that had held me upright broke apart. Dashnell Lawler had said to me what I had dreaded to say to myself. It was excruciating information all by itself. Coming as it did by way of him, the ice that fell from the sky had turned to glass. I stood there and let the frozen drizzle pierce my cheeks until I imagined my face was bloody and I was about to be nailed to a tree. All I had left was the time it would take to lose her. A few yards away the mist had thinned over the water and there were rippled sheets of shining black ice. I dropped to my knees and begged God to tell me that it wasn't so. I might have managed some way to deal with it if I had learned it on my own. This was an altogether different situation because, if Dashnell Lawler knew it, then everyone knew it. How could she be so careless? It was a question I didn't want answered. She was careless because she wanted me to find out. She knew my pride would do the rest.

34
Heath

Michael England's alternative school sits on a ridge at the edge of town. It's a plain, modern white painted concrete block building with long windows and a wooden shingle roof. I never knew or cared too much about it. The foundation was laid about the time I went away to Folsom Prison. There was a new building sitting there when I came home a year later. I pass it going to and from town and home. It sits at the back of a graded gravel parking lot. For several months I had noticed Lily's car among several others in the lot there on Tuesday evenings. I figured her boy Travis was taking karate lessons.

One night I pulled into the driveway at home and I suddenly remembered Mama had asked me to bring home a gallon of milk. I did a U-turn across the yard and headed back towards town. When I passed Michael's school, I noticed that Lily's was the only car left on the lot. I drove on down to the 7-Eleven and bought the milk. For fun I filled out a job application while I was there. Lily's Rover was still sitting in front of the school when I passed heading home.

I drove the long grade up past Miss Eula Pearl's place and headed into the open country. I switched on the radio and listened to the Braves stomp the Dodgers for about five minutes. The next cross road I came to, I swung back around and headed towards town.

Her car was still sitting there. There were no lights on inside the school.

The back of the school sits high on a clay bank. A little gravel road runs beneath it. I pulled up on the shoulder there as best I could. The clay is soft in winter and it's easy to get stuck. I pulled myself up the bank, grabbing onto the roots of trees that hung there. In less than three minutes I was standing outside the window of the room at the back where Michael has some kind of apartment. The curtains were thin and white. I was close enough to smell that they had been recently starched and bleached. I could make out a burning candle in a wine bottle resting on a dresser on the far wall.

I stood there for about five minutes and let the light fade outside. I could see them on the bed. They were naked and twisted up into each other. My first sensation was a deep, searing pain, a fluttering that threatened to burst my chest. I let that settle a minute. Then I was smitten by how pretty they looked. They were amber and they shone in the candlelight. Her hair was brilliant copper, his was shining dark rust. Their limbs were gold. The shadowed curves of their backs and shoulders, the wrinkled white sheets that half covered them, conspired to make a picture you might see in a magazine. It was as if I was some ancient artist and they were posing for me. Lily blew out the candle and I sneaked away.

I slipped back down the hill and got into my truck. I let it roll forward, pushing it as best I could with one foot out the open door so I wouldn't have to start the engine and disturb them. It wasn't that it didn't hurt to see Lily in his arms. It wasn't that I could be happy for Michael England. It was as if some power or purpose had arranged them for my eyes so that I would see that she belonged with him. They looked like lovers the way poets describe them. He was princely and smooth. She was soft and willing. He was as far above her in this world as she was above me. When I saw that, I saw why I couldn't have her. I understood what she needed. It helped. It was painful, but it was right. It made sense. I wouldn't know how to be a man like Michael England. I'd be a damned fool to try.

In a minute I was back on the blacktop moving out from town.

The sky had dropped in deep purple behind the shining silver trees. There was a churning swirl of gray, white and gold on the horizon where the sun had set. To the east a yellow moon had risen thin like a lemon peel. It was only the end of another dull, wet winter day; but it was the first one I ever completely saw and felt.

35
Lily

My daddy is a high school principal. My mama teaches third grade. They were licensed by the state of Alabama to impose and enforce their ignorance on young minds. Mama has a fearful nature that manifests itself in saccharine enervation. Surviving Daddy's temper exacerbates it to the point of lunacy. Daddy drives. Mama goes along. She takes fewer bruises that way.

I tried to tell her once. It was while I was home from Dallas right after Randy went back to his wife. Daddy and I had gotten into it at the supper table. I don't remember what about. I do remember that I had disagreed with something he said, probably about Ronald Reagan, who he reverently called "Mr. Reegun." The point is you don't disagree with him. He doesn't talk. He preaches, literally. Every other word is a quotation of Scripture. Mama loves to tell people she married him because he knew more Bible than any man she'd ever met before or since. Never mind the fact that my daddy believes the Bible was written to prove that he's right about everything. The high school kids used to call him Moses behind his back.

Daddy makes his pronouncements and Mama nods with her eyes pushed wide at you, instructing you to nod right along so he won't get upset. It's a habit he beat into her years ago. Or maybe it was beaten into her by my grandparents. Maybe she was ripe for the back of his hand by the time she married him. She never resists or complains about it.

No, it wasn't Mr. Reagan that time at the table. It was Doctor Martin Luther King, Jr. They had just unveiled a statue of him down at Birmingham and Daddy was livid because the school board had voted to bus his students down for the ceremony. Daddy was claiming to possess proof that Martin Luther King, Jr., was a carefully disguised Russian communist, a Satanic instrument of destruction whose activities were financed by the sale of Cuban marijuana. I couldn't *say* anything. I knew it would bring down the wrath of God. I looked at the floor. I counted the peas on my plate. I held my breath and tried to think about every dark, awful, sad thing I could.

Daddy was getting wound up. Mama was nodding along so fast with every word she looked palsied. I couldn't help it. I had to giggle. That hushed Daddy instantly. Mama eyed me like I had just committed the one unforgivable sin. I tried to collect myself, but the two of them looked so ridiculous that all I could do was throw back my head and laugh. Mama slapped the table in front of me, her eyes threatening perdition. Dad turned raspberry, then gray. I guffawed another minute, knowing all the while it would cost me dearly. Finally, I got my laughter under control. A dread silence fell.

"What's funny, Lilyun-yun?" Officially my name is Lillian Anne. He came up with it and he can't even pronounce it. Mama said that I was laughing about an altogether different subject. I hate her when she's gutless like that. I hate Daddy even worse for making her that way. Without delivering the Sermon on the Mount, I hate him for all the hell he put me through trying to make *me* that way.

"What's funny, Lilyun-yun?" he repeated.

"Nothing."

"I agree." He snorted.

Mama sighed with relief and her color came back. Apparently he was going to let this one go. I was trying to. He graduated to his next topic. Now a Russian backed Cuban army was planning to invade Miami Beach! I was gone. I was pounding the table. I spit tea on the floor. I hollered. Mama leapt back up from her chair.

Daddy didn't say a word. He just reached across the table and slapped me across the face.

I suddenly realized that I had married Glen to get away from that slap. I decided in that moment I'd go back to him to get away from it again.

"Honor your father and your mother, that your days may be long in the land which the Lord your God gives you."

That was Mama tiptoeing back into the room, looking at Daddy in hopes that she'd said the right thing. She had. He pointed at his plate, meaning that she could take it away and bring him his pie. She did so gratefully. I hadn't said a word. I hadn't made a move. He continued to eat his supper as if nothing had happened.

You can do anything you want to with Scripture. I went to Sunday school a few thousand times. I had it force-fed to me from birth. Some of it's perfectly beautiful. A lot of it's just old and not applicable. Daddy is one of those who love to say that there is only one perfect book and that's the Bible, especially if he's using it to make a point.

Every ounce of common sense I possessed told me to excuse myself, pack my suitcase and get out of there. I guess I wanted a parting shot. I put head between my hands and leaned towards Daddy:

"When a man sells his daughter as a slave, she shall not go out as the male slaves do."

I had run across that in a hotel room in Phoenix. Glen was at a computer convention and I had nothing to read but the Bible and the Phoenix Yellow Pages. It didn't take too much mental manipulation for me to apply it to my situation. Mama and Daddy had seen Glen as a miracle handed down from heaven to get me off their backs and put me forever on the right path.

You have to understand that Dad considers the Bible his personal Book of Revelations. He has the exclusive rights to pervert it to whatever end he deigns. Scripture out of anyone else this side of Billy Graham and maybe one or two mealy-mouthed Baptist preachers he's admired over the years is nothing less than blasphemy.

"What was that, Lilyun-yun?"

"I just told you that if your hand touches my flesh again, I'll bite it off."

He turned to Mom and said very quietly that I wouldn't be there when he returned from his school board meeting.

Mama wasted no time attacking my lack of gratitude towards a man who had fed, clothed and educated me. She said she'd ask Aunt Nina if I could stay with her until Daddy cooled off and I apologized enough times for it to take.

"I'm going back to Texas," I said. She went immediately beatific. "I don't want to go back to Texas, but I won't stay here and I can't think where else to go." I told her I wouldn't be back, not even to visit, that this was good-bye. Period. That produced no discernible effect. She was transfixed by the imminent possibility that I was out of her hair for good.

I figured it was time to set the record straight. I told her what she already knew. I told her the thing she had silently forbidden me to utter aloud a million times. On fifty occasions between the ages of thirteen and seventeen, when it stopped because I threatened to go to the police, my daddy climbed into my bed while Mama was out of the house and screwed me and called me his little Whore of Babylon and Ninevah until he shuddered and left me terrified that I had a monster growing inside me.

"You remember my senior year of high school when we moved to Whitville?"

Her look of betrayal was priceless.

"Didn't you think it was odd, Daddy up and deciding to move in late summer to a podunk school that offered a salary that amounted to half of what he'd been making?"

"The Lord took us to Whitville. I loved Whitville."

"The Lord got his ass to Whitville because I had already told three of my friends what he was doing to me and I was about to go to the police."

"Who?"

"Daddy."

"Doing what?"

"What do you think?"

She knew I was telling the truth. Of course she said it was just another one of my desperate lies. She clucked and shook her head and tried to act like I was nine again, telling another whopper and she just didn't know where she got such a bad little girl.

"Look, Mama, I'm out of it. You just tell yourself whatever you have to in order to keep from killing yourself or him." Then I packed my bag and I left without another word.

I haven't called or written or spoken to them since. I know every defiant thing I do and say has my daddy in it. I know that when I hauled off and slugged Dashnell Lawler in the mouth, I was hitting back at my daddy. Daddy dresses a little better than Dashnell. Daddy cuts his fingernails. He's got just enough education to articuate his ignorance a little more clearly than Dashnell. That makes him infinitely more dangerous.

My daddy made me the Whore of Babylon. My mama stamped his atrocities with her silent seal of approval. Some mornings I try to understand the evils that perverted my parents. I try to find the largesse to forgive them. If I could, then I might be able to change, to endure this flesh that's eternally threatening to split in two.

Then I'll hear Glen's power saw scream from the garage and it's hopeless. I told Michael about it. He likened me to Mary Magdalene. That likens him to Christ. It's true. I look to the men in my life for my salvation. The men in my life look to me for a certain elevation of stature.

Except Heath.

All other considerations aside, I knew I wasn't worthy of his innocent affection. Heath isn't looking for Mary Magdalene or the Whore of Babylon. I wouldn't know how to be what Heath Lawler deserves. I told him over and over that I didn't deserve a man like him. It was the truest thing I ever said to a man. He didn't understand. He didn't believe me. He's too good to understand something like that. It was the best thing I had to offer him. He fell in love with the woman I could have been. She deserves him. I never will. The only way I know to be with a man is to serve him. Heath would never accept that. He deserves a woman who'll walk tall and straight beside him. Glen is all for being served, but it's mindless slavery. Michael understands that I'm less than him. Yet serving him is helping him facilitate the good he does in this world. That's as close to a meaningful existence as I'll ever come. Unless I start believing in miracles.

36

Moena

They hang like invisible starched sheets about me as the darkness falls. I don't get them much during full daylight. Only sometimes. Now and again as I straighten up to rest a minute in the garden with the night settling, a dry whisper, a broken laugh or an odd idea hovers. Apt as not it's a gathered awareness. I'm feeling how it felt if, for example, they were sitting on the porch in the evening and I was just out of sight in the side yard and I'll think, "Thee great guns, it's them."

They left me aches and a hard way to go. I want to think they come back to comfort and guide me, but, no; it's not like that. There was never much love in their kindnesses to me.

I lived way longer than I had right or expectation or intent to. I become mostly old when I was still a child. This last seventy years is just hanging around after the fact. Some trudge up life's hill and attain a comfortable view of where they've been. That summit is the wherefore and why of every weary step that come before it. Hezekiah is that way. His life added up to a sum greater than all its parts. I never could figure mine. Though now abouts it's fairly tolerable. There's no discernible backwards or forwards, very little difference between my best and worst days, I don't get the extremes. I just trudge and some days I'll wake up and curse heaven for making me endure one more day. Some I can't pull my dress on quick enough so I can run out to my garden.

Hezekiah says life passes through me while others pass through life. I'm a born stranger. Even when they were young and hopeful my mama and daddy never really thought much of me. Their feelings were obligatory. Long before the Trouble I overheard Daddy asking Mama what made me so strange. All I ever loved was Eula because she didn't mind my strangeness. She took to me and maybe that was only because I was the only other child close by. She loved me endlessly. I put Mama and Daddy behind Eula and my singing heart was full. Eula was my connection to this earth. When she was taken from me, that was taken from me.

They come more often now. I listen, I wait for a summation, directive, pronouncement or sign of some sort.

Nothing.

They don't rile or scare me. It's them except he can't knock the wind out of me with his slaps and she can't screech fearsome nonsense till my ears hurt. It's no torment to me when they're close by. It don't seem to mean much of nothing. Except right on the last here, Beauty B.'s whispered "Git home," in a voice that a person would take for rustling leaves unless they stopped to realize there was no wind, nor leaves close about to rustle.

Cheryl had drove all the way down here from Birmingham by herself determined to haul me back up there to live with her and Hezekiah. She's a fine woman and better in my opinion than he'll ever deserve. Cheryl won't ponder a thing into a puddle fretting over whether she feels like doing it. If she thinks it needs doing, she's already halfway through it.

She pulls big money out of them funeral homes up at Memphis. Hez and them lives high. I'd be up there in more style than I ever knew. It might be nice to have some twilight with my grandchildren. Hezekiah and I probably wouldn't butt heads too badly. She's even told me I could have all the garden I required in their backyard.

Pity it's Alabama.

Alabama is evil ground. I will not go back to Alabama unless I'm carried there in a box. If it were in my power I would sew salt over every square inch of that wretched, godforsaken place. Hezekiah warned Cheryl I wouldn't go back with her. She came on to Charleston, though, because it wasn't no other way to show me her invitation was genuine.

Once she saw I was set on Charleston, she hushed about it. Cheryl has regard for other people. She stayed a day or two, long enough to have my back screens replaced and a new square of linoleum laid in the bathroom. She went by and talked to my doctor and got my medication sorted out. She took me to the beauty parlor and had me an extra pair of eyeglasses made.

Just before she was about to start home she remembered we hadn't turned my mattress. She saw the holes in my sheets and that led her to investigate the linens. She found a sale on sheets and towels in the newspaper and she drove off. I went out back to the garden to grab up some winter greens before it rained. That's when I heard that damned ruffled scratch whisper say, "Moena, git home."

Mother died regretting Alabama. South Carolina turned her foolish and loud. She tried to do what had to be done to keep things up. But her talk was one-way, crazy and cold. You'd tell her something and she'd look right through you. Some of the old people around the turpentine farms got to saying she conversed with spirits. The devil would be more like it. They say she got on some with Hezekiah. I wasn't around. I was in Charleston sewing drapes and slipcovers for cheap women who wore too much perfume and bathed twice a day. I don't know what passed between them.

I had a hundred inclinations to leave Charleston and do what I could for my mother and father and Hezekiah down on that farm. I made more than one trip there believing I was going to stay. Mother was talking in tongues by then, suffering visions and spells. Losing Alabama had broken my father. It had left him alone in a strange place where he had no more than he could earn draining sap from a white man's pine trees. He turned to meanness and whiskey and whatever low, whore trash tramp he could drag home. It was fearful and unbearably sad.

Mother wasn't completely sure who I was. Father addressed me as "Strange." He'd say, "Strange, you can chop some damned garden weed and set some dough to rise." What Hezekiah understood of Mother's madness and Father's decline I don't know.

I didn't know I could get a baby. I didn't know I had one coming. God help me, I thought I was dying with a tumor. I wasn't but fourteen.

I've seen hell in Charleston too. I buried a husband and watched my girls grow up into three kinds of fools. They had no example but mine to follow. I meant to love them and do better. I lived my life thinking *next year for durned sure.* Next year I'd be past my troubles, my endless, despised travail, and climb back up onto the world and walk with my head up. It ain't no next year. It's just more *now* and more.

I did the best by accepting life. I keep Alabama before the evil. I had a warm quilt on soft grass by the creek and Eula and when that was taken, I turned and remained old for the next seventy-five years. I won't be angry about it. I'd split in two if I let myself get angry. I try hardest not to mind about anything. If Dereesa moves back in on me for the fiftieth time, I don't mind. If she's working a job and has money, I don't mind. If she brings the kids, I don't mind. If she's stretched out on the sofa looking at stories all morning and wanting my money, I don't mind. If she comes in with a sackful of groceries and we have a big supper, I don't mind. If we do without, I don't mind. I stay half-dead to keep from minding. Dying is only the other half. Lord knows I don't mind dying.

What's this cursed "Moena, git home"? Why do I turn it over and over, examining it? Is old Beauty B.'s ghost any less crazy than she was?

I could see Cheryl felt bad leaving me. She did me the great kindness of not telling me so or squeaking up into some funny voice and cocking her head to one said and asking me one more time, "Miss Moena, we'd so love to have you; won't you please just come for a week?" None of that hooey. She pulled new cotton sheets over my bed, laid a stack of towels on the hamper and that Cadillac was crossing Carolina, thank you, ma'am.

I mind about that whispering in my garden, though. What would old Beauty B. want to trip me up like that for? Do the dead forget or is she still too crazy to know how it stands with me and Alabama?

Oh, that other Alabama!

She loved those paper white cherry blossoms, Eula. If I went back it would only be to visit her grave and plant that particular cherry tree. If she stayed and died in Prince George. Otherwise I'd have no idea where she's buried. I did used to regularly wonder who Eula married. What went with the farm? Did her sisters get all the money? Mama laid claim that Eula and her sisters would part ways over money. But I doubt it. Eula had an uncommon understanding of money, for a child or anyone else. Money stuck to Eula.

No, they won't never let me back in Prince George even if I lost my mind and went to Alabama and begged them.

Eula, git home?

To Alabama, state of utter disgrace, birthplace of evil, forsaken by ghosts and angels!?

Thee great guns. And, Dear God, please come for your pitiful world!

37
Rose of Sharon

Lily told me about Michael. I can't tell her what to do. But I can see what she's doing. She's balled religious love and romantic love up together. She worships him. Michael is not all he tries to be or he wouldn't take advantage of a confused woman like that. I tried to point that out to her, but she said I never had the courage to go after that kind of love. She's right. I never went after anything except a job at Pizitz Department Store and Dashnell Lawler.

To Lily that schoolhouse is a temple and Michael is the god on the altar. I don't mean to pass judgment. I don't know how much Lily and Michael are to each other. I have no opinion of Glen. I can't tell her to leave him or go back to him. I can't tell her with anything like conviction that her children need her at home. It's next to impossible to know what life is like inside other people's houses. I have been to enough discussion groups to see that Michael likes to be worshipped. It's also clear that something in Lily needs to grovel.

We had an unsettling discussion group last night. They all hugged me when I walked in ten minutes late. Lily had apparently told them about my leaving Dashnell. They wanted to show their support. It was very sweet. It made me tired to think that they had all been talking my business. We all sat in our accustomed circle and Michael asked me to say all the things I want from life while the rest of the group closed their eyes and tried to see it for me in their minds. I said I'd like to get Mama's place fixed back right and learn a skill, cosmetology or word processing or maybe even a little college work. I had two years of junior college. In the back of my mind, I always wanted to try to build that up into a teaching degree. I think the group was hoping I'd say something more spiritual.

Lily steered the discussion back to the man on the lake. She told them I had left Dashnell over his part in it. I immediately spoke out saying I knew no such thing about Dashnell and neither did Lily. She hushed, but she gave me betrayed looks for the rest of the evening. The rest of them looked at me as if I protested too much.

Michael took hold of the discussion and I was relieved to hear him say that we had neither proof nor the means to obtain evidence. Our primary purpose wasn't to solve crimes. He turned the topic to what we could do to demonstrate changing attitudes in Prince George County. He suggested we put together that Harmony Festival they've been talking about. He said it should be simple and symbolic, nothing to rile people, just a quiet walk around court square followed by a potluck supper. He was planning to do that with his schoolchildren anyway. Why didn't we become part of that?

When did anything ever stay quiet and simple? Somebody said we could do it in observance of Doctor Martin Luther King, Jr.'s, birthday. Another started talking about publicity. That's when we saw the two men outside the window.

It was a warm early January night. We always get a spell of false spring right after the New Year to keep us holding on through the coming winter. Dark was falling. It was the first hint of lengthening days. There's cedar woods on that side of the school. Someone stepped over to raise the window a little higher and he said he saw two figures crouching in the brush. We thought maybe it was kids. Michael went for a better look. He said it was two men and they had obviously been hiding under the sill listening to us.

Several of the men went out back behind the school. Lily went with them. When she came back inside, she said she had seen Dashnell and another man who looked like Jake getting into Dashnell's truck. She wasn't sure it was Jake. The truck was unmistakably Dashnell's.

Michael said that he had been followed and spied on for weeks. He didn't see that it was much cause for alarm. He said he figured his long hair was enough to raise a certain suspicion among some of the locals. There were always several local teenage boys in Prince George County with long hair by that time. Even in Prince George County long hair had lost its subversive implications. Something at the back of Michael's eyes told an altogether different story. Michael was scared to the bone. His school and his ideas were under clandestine investigation by the invisible empire, as Dashnell romantically refers to that bunch. He sat back, nervously glancing out the window throughout the rest of the meeting.

Dashnell had made a connection between my attendance at those meetings and my decision to leave him. It was beyond him to conceive that I had taken such an action wholly of my own volition. He assumed I had done it under group influence or duress. He can't help it. Everything he does and says is for the direct effect it has on his bunch. He has no concept of independent thought. He was outside that window trying to understand the source of their power over me. His next step would be to try to conquer it. I had an instinct that the group would never understand that; so I kept quiet.

Lily took over the meeting, assigning duties for the Harmony Festival, a mighty big term for a little walk around courthouse square. She acted like it was the Rapture, assigning one to call the radio stations and another to put ads in area newspapers. Later we had a good discussion about similarities between Buddhism and Christianity. We broke up about ten-thirty. Lily volunteered to follow me home in her car. I let her.

I kept running it over and over in my mind. What if Dashnell had heard Lily telling the group that I knew he was involved in killing that black man? That pack of dogs he calls friends would kill us both and bury us so deep we'd never be found. The mess was getting messier and I had no idea what to do about it. Surely some law enforcement official in the state would be willing to listen to my story. They couldn't all be in sympathy with the Order. Maybe that preacher down in Birmingham who was calling for an investigation could help me. Maybe he couldn't. There wasn't anything to do except keep silent. There had to be something, but what? It flew around and around in my head like that all the way home.

Lily pulled into Mother's driveway behind me. I walked up to her car to thank her for escorting me. I was about to ask her what to do, when she took my hand. "I left Glen today." She smiled. "I'm living with Michael now."

My first thought was completely selfish. Maybe that's what Dashnell and Jake were investigating. My attendance at the discussion group was bound to be second fiddle to a piece of news like that. Maybe I was worried about nothing.

"Is that what you want?" I asked her.

"With all my heart." She beamed. It was a convincing smile. I didn't believe it. I don't understand her. I don't understand much of anything anymore.

Mother was turning a pineapple upside-down cake from a skillet when I walked inside the house. That took me back a long, long way.

38

Heath

I noticed everything that afternoon. Everything seemed of one giant accord or purpose. The weather had been mild for almost two weeks, the surest sign I know of a coming blizzard. The January sun felt warm on my face. It turned the dust on the dashboard gold. The puddles on the blacktop were still edged with ice. I hadn't felt this kind of newborn sun since before I went to prison. My foot went to the floor as I crested the hill. On either side, the naked limbs were silky, wet and blue. There was low mist in the encircling woods.

I had heard that Lily and Michael England were making plans to leave town. I wanted to see them before they left.

Somewhere a long way off in the woods I could hear a chainsaw. The wet pavement turned to clay as I crossed the railroad tracks. Suddenly I was slipping half sideways up a long stretch of rust clay road that cut between tall banks where the roots of trees and dead kudzu hung like a million sci-fi snakes.

My dog, James Edward, rode in the truck bed. He's a toothless old pit bull I won in a poker game back in the dark ages of my drinking days before I went to prison. I was dead drunk when I accepted James Edward in payment of twenty-six dollars owed me. I was figuring to breed her. When I sobered up the next morning, I could see she was way past that. She also turned out to be a he.

Just this side of White Oak, I noticed the Miller farm was being painted, house, barn and fence. I thought maybe Miss Eula Pearl had died and the place had been sold. I figured Miss Eula must be a hundred by now. There hadn't been a drop of paint on the place since before I was born. Painted up, it was a lot bigger and fancier than I remembered it. Somebody had cleared about fifteen tons of brush away from around the front. It had turned into a big old wedding cake of a Victorian house. It had a side porch and an upstairs balcony I had never even seen. About half the picket in the fence was new. Aunt Rose and a hired man were slapping paint on it. I didn't know whether to consider her Aunt Rose or not now that she and Uncle Dashnell were divorcing.

Miss Eula Pearl was alive indeed. She sat in her accustomed place on the front porch wrapped in a coat and a scarf, her hands resting on an aluminum walker. She waved at me. It was that old time country wave that doesn't ask who you are or what your business is.

In a minute I passed the White Oak city limits sign. I'd begun my job at the 7-Eleven a couple months before. In fact, I was about to be made night manager. I had an hour until my shift started.

I had two reasons for going on this mission. I figured it might be the last time I ever saw Lily. I wanted to make some kind of a decent parting between us. We hadn't spoken to each other in months. I also wanted to talk to this guy Michael. I wanted to ask him how a man who held a karate black belt could let himself be so intimidated by a pack of ignorant rednecks that he'd allow them to close down his school. I could smell Dashnell and Jake behind his troubles. I was willing to stand with him against them. Though the truth is I wanted to make an impression on Lily. I still had some tender hurting need to demonstrate my loyalty. I was hoping to talk Michael into fighting back.

The trouble had started a week before with an ad in the *White Oak Reporter*. It invited those interested to join a group at the Michael England School for a "harmony walk" and a picnic on the school grounds on Saturday, January 22. It didn't specifically mention Martin Luther King, Jr.'s, birthday. It might just as well have announced a convention of international terrorists for all the local reaction it stirred.

People went nuts. Parents pulled their kids out of Michael's school. Every bearded redneck in the county left a threatening message on the school answering machine. His discussion group and karate classes were disbanded. Those who weren't diametrically opposed to a walk and a picnic on Doctor King's birthday were afraid to continue their public association with Michael or his school.

Glen Pembroke had been on local radio that morning denying all association with Lily, Michael England or their unpatriotic ideas. Glen was pressured into that. He was trying to protect his children and his property from the Order.

I didn't know when or how Lily had moved into the school building with Michael. I had seen Aunt Rose in the post office a week before. She told me Lily and Michael were planning to leave town together after school let out. The Order had apparently moved their plans forward.

Michael stood in the front door of the school and watched as I pulled into the parking lot. Lily's Range Rover looked ridiculous next to his old Chevy II Nova. I couldn't help but note the irony that Glen Pembroke was probably still making payments on it.

Michael was giving me the twice-over. I understood that. I was Prince George born and bred. He had good reason to doubt my earlier insistence on the phone that, unlike 98.6 percent of the rest of the people in Prince George County, I intended him no harm. I was a little hurt all the same. I thought surely Lily would have told him I was okay.

I shook his hand. It felt clammy. The back of it was covered with dark hair. He wore a silver ring, a snake that coiled up his finger into a ruby red eye. "Can I help you?" He didn't bother with hello.

"How are y'all doing?" I felt stupid. "Look here, Michael, I don't know what kind of support you're looking for, but you have whatever I can give you."

His eyes kept searching the thick scrub at the edge of the parking lot. He probably figured my visit for some kind of setup.

We started talking a little. He told me it had taken all the cash he could raise to build his schoolhouse. He'd been operating close to the bone to keep up the mortgage, sometimes supplementing the budget with his dwindling savings account. He lost a third of his students the day after the ad about the festival went into the local paper. The rest of the kids were whisked away by their frightened parents over the next week. It had taken four days to destroy the dream he had worked fifteen years to create. I felt sorry for the man, but nowhere near as sorry as he seemed to feel for himself.

Several of the parents told him they were personally in support of Michael and his school, but they feared for their children and their local businesses. They had to publicly distance themselves. Most of the kids just didn't show up. By that point, Michael could no longer vouch for their safety, as the phone threats were coming in two or three times an hour. Someone had also dumped a keg of nails on the parking lot.

His tone was almost whiny and his eyes never met mine for more than a second. Lily appeared in the door. I felt my heart flutter the old way a second. I smiled and she smiled back and it felt all right.

"Hey."

"Hey."

"Y'all leaving these parts," I said.

"Yes. Hallelujah," she said.

"Good luck to you," I said.

"The same to you," she said before she muttered something about the cold and walked back into the schoolhouse. If Michael minded any of it, he didn't let on.

Michael England and I stayed outside in the parking lot while the day began to fade. I reiterated my offer of support.

"I appreciate that"—Michael smiled and I read it as genuine—"but you're a little late."

"Too late for your school, maybe, but I don't see why the festival can't go as planned." It was definitely a case of figuring things out for yourself as you talk. I'm nobody's joiner and people around Prince George County know I've been in prison. I have extra reason to avoid courting their displeasure. Still, there it was rolling off my tongue in the evening chill just as if it made sense.

"I have a lot of teaching left to do in my life." Michael smiled again. This time, it made me uneasy. It was more pose than smile. It was cold. "I can't do much teaching with a bullet through my head."

"I thought you were supposed to be a black belt."

Michael said he'd take on any man with his hands in the broad daylight. His black belt wouldn't offer much protection if a bullet came through a window after dark.

"You mean on account of your Harmony Festival, or are you referring to Lily's husband?" I had my nerve to ask such a personal question. As far as I knew Michael and Lily had never admitted the nature of their relationship to anyone.

"She came to me after the trouble started. She had nowhere else to go." He was telling the truth and covering up a lie at the same time.

Michael eyed the horizon warily. He pointed out that it would be dark soon. Another night of sitting by the window with the gun, he said. Lily had to see a lawyer on Thursday. She wanted to file for custody of her children. They were planning to leave town immediately after that.

"They sneak around in the night because they're cowards. They're more afraid of what you're teaching than you ought to be of them."

I've heard of people seizing a moment, but it was like that moment was seizing me. I didn't know what Michael England had taught in his school.

"If you run away, their ignorance wins."

That set him off on a personal defense. He rambled on about how I hadn't been threatened fifty times day and night for the last several weeks. I had no idea how long he had saved the money to build his school. I was so much a part of the fabric of the place I couldn't understand.

"Heath, it's kind of cold out here and I've got some packing to do." Not even a thank-you for stopping by.

"Don't call off your festival, please."

Michael shook his head. That riled me. The man was either too ignorant or too scared to appreciate what I had just offered. There I was stepping over some ancient and forbidden line, pulling away from my own people on blind faith, and here he was wiggling his toes and wishing I'd go away and leave him to cower inside that schoolhouse with Lily.

It had been an inspired thing to come into this ignorant little town and shine a little light on things. Michael's lack of courage in the face of adversity made me wonder just how much he believed what he taught. I suppose you won't ever get an even opinion of Michael England from me. He was taking Lily away. I had the sinking feeling as I stood there watching him walk back towards that school that Lily would live to regret the day she met him. There was nothing I could do but climb back into my truck and move on.

If I think back on it, I half caught a figure crouching in the undergrowth at the side of the parking lot as I circled around towards the road. They must have run back through the woods and down the hill behind the school and gotten into the truck. There were three of them sitting in it at the crossroads by Miss Eula Pearl's peanut stand when I stopped for the intersection. It was full dark by now. I could see them in the rearview mirror, their heads covered in those damned white hoods. I had about a mile stretch of open fields on either side before I'd reach the next house. I slammed the pedal to the floor, but my truck is twenty-six years old and it wasn't built for speed. Theirs was small and new.

They got up beside me in less than a minute. One of them leaned out the side window and aimed at my left front wheel. I felt the tire explode and then a bullet sailed past my face and shattered the window on the passenger side. Just before they pulled ahead of me, one of them hollered, "You keep away from that faggot communistic nigger lover and his whore concubine or the next bullet will land between your eyes!" Dashnell. I was fighting a skid on a long wet curve. The back of the truck was swinging towards the shoulder and bits of broken glass were flying in my face. I was trying to straighten her out in order to miss a concrete bridge rail up ahead. I was looking at death at that moment, but I was seeing red, swirling, boiling, burning red. The wheel slid through my fingers and the truck spun slowly around and the tailgate slammed into the side of the bridge.

I took several shards of glass in my right arm. My forehead banged into the dashboard, but I was unconscious of anything except the rage that had turned pure white and hissed in little comet tailed circles all around me. Looking in the back of the truck, I saw James Edward sitting there like nothing had happened.

I climbed out of the truck and I moved forward into the darkness with the first clean taste of God's intent for me that I have ever known. Suddenly I knew why that crazy black man had turned himself into a bull's-eye out there on the lake. Those three men in that truck had scared me. They had turned a full grown man like me into their terrified prey. They had ruled my corner of this world with fear longer than I had memory. That fellow out there on the lake had made a clear choice. He had decided against fear. He had somehow summed up his life and chosen a brief but full existence over a lifetime of cowering. He went up there and pitched his tent knowing full they'd come after him. He would rather die than suffer the empty existence of a man who bows before evil. They took that poor man's life, but he kept his soul. I was walking up the hill on the road in the dark and the rain had begun. It was a road I had traveled a thousand times. But that night I knew for the first time it was going to lead me to places I had never allowed myself to imagine. That night I felt the sure, warm breath of the Living God on my back.

39
Rose of Sharon

Try as I would, I couldn't get his widow out of my mind. I thought about her all through the Christmas season. I wondered how it was for his children, if they cried trimming their trees. I thought I'd lose my mind my first Christmas after Carmen died.

I came to know his widow despite the fact that I had yet to lay eyes on the woman. She became part of every day. She was with me when I prayed in the morning and she was there when I switched out my bedroom light in the evening.

As time went on, I began to see the wrinkles of sorrow etched into her face. I'd drop my shoulders and feel hers slump. I'd see prime rib on sale and catch myself thinking, "I'll have to be sure and tell her about that."

She became something mystic and sanctified, as pure as a candlelight. I had a dream about her: All my family for generations back sat at the dining room table waiting for her to be seated in the place of honor. She refused to be seated. We followed her into the back pasture. Suddenly she rose into the heavens. The abandoned graves opened up and the long sleeping souls followed her into the air.

I put the man's obituary in my Bible. "Smith, McCarthy, Jr., 58, an apparent suicide. Survived by his wife. . . ." I am not spooky, but there was something to that. "Two sons, McCarthy III, 21, and

Nicholas, 24. . . ." It gave the address as 111 Foxglove Road, Yellow, Alabama.

I had pictured the house wrong. I had fixed it about as nice as our second house in Birmingham. That was from how Mr. Smith was dressed in his boat. I had taken him for a dentist or a college professor, but not after I saw his place. It was a little one story bungalow, thirties style, with a rusted screened porch and shrubs as big as the ones I've been hauling away from the front of Mother's house. It wasn't shabby, but the paint was faded and the chairs on the porch were those old metal round-backs they sell at the dime store. There were three black ladies sitting behind a four-foot-tall mother-in-law's tongue, which was probably bought at the same dime store where she got the chairs and long about the same time. It was sad and a little shadowy. The place had the feeling that a life had been lived there and then it had passed on out of it.

I could see her, Mrs. Smith, the dreaded woman from my dream. She had the same slightly sanctimonious air I had picked up from her husband that morning on the lake. She was tall and too thin with long grayish white hair that she kept a little blue with a rinse. She wore large round glasses and she kept folding and refolding her long hands at her side as I drove past. She had the air of a high school music teacher.

At the end of the driveway, I could see Mr. Smith's boat leaning against the side of the house. It had several bullet holes in the side clean as glass. I drove past other, better kept houses. I turned around and headed back towards Mrs. Smith's.

I was shaking like a leaf as I stood outside the screen door. I could see how badly it was rusted. One of the three ladies, a plump, pleasant-faced woman with a Bible in her lap, spoke.

"Can we help you?"

She must have thought I was selling something. I tried the screen, but it was latched. None of the three stood up to let me in.

"Mrs. Smith? I'm from over in Prince George County." I told her my name and that I was sorry to hear about her husband and wondered if she needed anything.

"Money," she said in a voice that could have easily been taken mean until the other two women giggled.

"You're mighty sweet," she said by way of showing me that she was teasing a little. Still no one got up to let me in. "I don't need a thing, honey."

"May I sit with you ladies a minute?" I could feel the perspiration rising up under my collar. I hadn't slept much the night before. At first I was restless and then a thunderstorm had waked me deep in the night. I hoped that they couldn't see I was shaking. My eyes weren't quite used to the shade and there was a giant purple spot turning in one corner of the porch. It gave me the willies. Mrs. Smith rose and unlatched the screen door.

"Sit here, ma'am." The third lady shoved a chair at me a little quickly. She was heavier and a little older than Mrs. Smith but she bore her a strong likeness. I felt like the preacher turning up uninvited in the middle of a family fight. Could I say I needed her to forgive me for being there the night Dashnell and the others plotted and carried out Mr. Smith's murder?

The heavyset lady was Grace. The other was Hoagie, Mrs. Smith's sister. Hoagie had moved back home to live with Mrs. Smith after Mr. Smith was killed. She'd lived up north someplace. So we talked about that. How down here at home in Alabama at least you could have a garden and you could afford a decent piece of beef more than once a week and on like that.

"I'm so very sorry about Mr. Smith," I said pouring heavy molasses onto the polite talk. The three women looked at me, obviously waiting for me to say something else.

"I've never been in a dark person's house before," I said. It sounded so pitiful and stupid that all three women giggled and I had to laugh right along with them. That eased me some.

"You come out of a church?" That was Grace. Maybe she thought some church up in Prince George had taken up a collection, guilt money. But it must have looked odd to them, this strange white woman making a condolence call and nothing in her hand for the bereaved.

"No. I just came."

Mrs. Smith went and got me a glass of iced tea.

"I just feel so terrible. It was such a waste, such a stupid, terrible waste." The ladies nodded. But then Grace said, "It was all his foolishness," and the other two nodded at that as well.

"You don't mean Mr. Smith's?" I couldn't help but say. All three nodded. "The man was murdered in cold blood."

"He was warned," says Hoagie.

"Told over and over again," Mrs. Smith said. "You go off up into Prince George and stay after dark, you won't come out alive. It's a known thing."

"I must have heard them say it fifty times." Grace came back in.

"Heard who?"

"His boys, Carty junior and Nicky, I don't know who all else."

"But he had the civil right to be there!" I was getting mad. This wasn't what I'd expected.

"There's no civil right in this world to replace Mr. John Common Sense." Grace again.

Wasn't that the kind of talk that had driven me to leave Dashnell? Here were these three ladies talking like it was meant to be. Then I realized they were shining me on a little. I noticed them eyeing me, watching to see what I'd say, watching me because they had no earthly reason to trust me or think anything of me except that I was a part of Prince George and to them Prince George was in accord, one united finger pulling the trigger that killed Mr. Smith. I studied Mrs. Smith. She was quiet. But going deeper her look seemed to say, "Lady, you took my husband; you ain't getting nothing else from me."

Or maybe I imagined that.

Maybe, like me, for the most part these women had other things to do besides change the world. Maybe like me they tried to kill off that part that *sees,* to silence that voice that *knows,* to concentrate on the other, almost bearable portion of life that carries the days with it.

"The boys feel the most bad." That was Mrs. Smith. "They gave him the boat a year ago last Father's Day." They liked to have had a fit when he told them he'd been fishing up in Prince George."

Grace and Hoagie let go a litany to each other, but meant for me. You only get one life. It's best to go along with what you have to and go around the rest, have a few things you want in between, and pray it's better for the next generation.

Was it at Sunday school down in Birmingham that I heard someone say that? Or was it Daddy? Whoever said it, they left out one part. You can get swallowed up by a thing trying to go around it.

"What of his killers?" I regretted that immediately. How would I know it was more than one unless I knew who had done it?

"They have their God and their King to reckon with." That was Grace. I didn't like Grace. Beyond her soft features she had beady eyes. She reeked of perfume and her hosiery and her underwear rustled when they crossed her legs. She kept running her pudgy fingers down her sides as if trying to contain herself. She looked at me and smiled and said, "You see, we're not prejudiced." That flew in my face.

Grace looked at her watch. It was a Lucien-Piccard and it was covered with diamonds. "Let me get on down the road," she said. In a minute she was gone. That left Mrs. Smith and Hoagie and me—feeling like a bigger fool every minute and trying to find some halfway decent way to make my own excuses and go. Hoagie said she'd better start supper and I was face-to-face alone with Mrs. Smith. Obviously the two women had excused themselves hoping I'd do the same. I had the distinct impression that if I left and drove back by in twenty minutes, the three of them would be sitting there on that porch.

"You're not the first from Prince George to feel bad about it."

At last we were getting down to whatever we were going to get down to. "I sure hope not," I said.

"I had cards, dozens of them, and more than twenty-five hundred dollars inside them. Two people from Prince volunteered to pay for the funeral. I won't eat all the food that came over from Prince George in the rest of my life."

There I sat empty handed.

"Well, then, why wasn't the thing properly investigated if so many people feel bad about it?" I asked.

She said they had tried to get something going out of Birmingham. A minister down there had written the governor, but she wasn't at liberty to go over to Prince George and see about it. She might not get back alive. She had to accept what she couldn't change.

"When is it going to change?"

"I ask the Lord my God," she said.

"What if I knew who done it?"

She laughed. She said if I knew who'd done it, then I'd be like a thousand other people up at Prince George. She said that half the cards she got weren't even signed. She said food appeared on her front steps in the night with no name on the bottom of the plate.

"People are scared," she said. "People are ruled by fear."

"How much longer?" I says. She said she didn't know. She could see I was afraid. She could tell that by the way I jerked my head around every time a car passed to see who it was. Was it some white person who'd tell it out in Prince George that they'd seen me down here on this porch in the broad daylight? That set my mind racing after a horde of dark possibilities which she interrupted with a slight clearing of her throat.

"What did you really come to tell me?"

"My husband did it," I said softly.

"I see," she said.

"I don't know what to do about it," I said.

"I don't either," she said.

Hoagie hollered from the kitchen asking which muffin tin to use. I muttered something about it looking like rain.

"My soon to be ex-husband," I said, grasping the full reality of that for the first time. "Everything I know about it is secondhand. If you know more, if you have any idea where I can get some proof, then I'll do the right thing."

She stared at me for a long time. Then she pursed her lips and said softly, "It might just be best if you go now, honey."

40

Heath

I leashed James Edward up and we made it to work on foot. I was half an hour late. I tied the dog out back. I had a knot on my forehead and my arm was bleeding. The boss gave me holy hell, but I could see it was an act. They like me down at the 7-Eleven. I give them a day and a half's work for a day's pay. I worked my shift and caught James Edward and me a ride home in the morning.

I had rented a little trailer and built a pen for James Edward. I had nearly saved enough money to lease the field behind it. I was planning to raise pumpkins and melons for a cash crop. I have always wanted to try to pull a cash crop out of the land.

That morning after I came in from work, I picked up the telephone and called the local radio station. I asked them to please announce that the Harmony Festival had been rescheduled for next Saturday. I asked them to broadcast my phone number. I knew a lot of people would say that I was trying to start something. The fact is I was determined to finish something.

I have tried to tell a thousand people since then that the things I did had nothing to do with race. I'm not here to champion one race or right the wrongs of another. The stand I took was a private choice not to be ruled by fear. That's what rules men like my uncle Dashnell and Jake Kelly and to a large extent my own father. That's what holds the world back. That's what stands between us and our purpose on this earth. You cannot live in fear and feel the breath of the Living God on the back of your neck. You cannot be afraid and change yourself, because the fear is a paralysis, a weight on your arms. Yes, I know awful things may happen to me because of what I've done. No, I don't like that. I don't want that. Fear is not just the unpleasant emotion we think it is. Fear is the failure to act.

That morning I didn't care. I knew if I didn't pick up that telephone and call the radio station, I would be condemned to a living death. It was Sunday. I made the call and then I crawled into bed and I slept as I have never slept. I slept as if I had been to the New Jerusalem. I would almost swear as my head hit the pillow and I glanced out the window, I saw it rolling over the treetops just above the pink-eyed sun.

I rolled out of sleep about noon. I sat up trying to remember the thing I'd done that I shouldn't have. It was a natural reaction left over from my drinking days. The quiet slapped the stubble on my jaw and the loneliness swallowed me for a minute. I still had no idea how to make coffee and a shower seemed pointless. I tossed yesterday's tuna salad to James Edward. The phone rang, probably Mama wanting to yell at me for missing church.

"Hello?"

"You're going to die."

"Who isn't?"

"You go through with your nigger walk, and you'll see." I tried to place the voice. I'd heard it a thousand times. But its owner wouldn't register.

"Excuse me, mister. But why are you calling it 'a nigger walk' when there are no known black people for miles around here?"

Click. Dial tone. Nigger walk? There it was. The whole beautiful thing that needed to be done. I had to find some black people to walk with me. Because that's their fear. They live in blind terror of the black race. All their bully tactics and their killing, all their threats and menace, add up to an unspoken paranoia that they might not be the only ones made in God's image. I had to find some black people. But I didn't know any except some fellows I'd met down in Folsom.

The phone rang again. This time the voice was old.

"I got a bullet with your name wrote on it."

I was too busy struggling to write up my press release to answer the phone the third time it rang. By the fifth call, I had it right enough to drop off at the local paper. It told people where to gather and when and it welcomed all races, creeds and religions. Then I broke for the shower. I was singing by then. I'd stumbled onto it. I'd found that *something,* that bigger reason or purpose or calling. I had to do this thing. I had to be the one to smash that wall of fear that people in Prince George had lived behind since I don't know when. I was hearing voices. I was dancing around naked and foolish. For the first time in my life I understood what it meant to be a whole and all the way living person.

I found a quarter sticking out of the floor mat on the passenger side of my truck, so I called Belinda Hodgkins after I dropped my announcement by the local paper the next morning. Belinda is the local correspondent for *The Birmingham News* and since I'm a longtime believer in wasting all found money on the spot, I told her answering machine the whos, whats and wheres of the Harmony Festival and I left my number, but she never called me back.

Then I set myself to the task of drumming up some local support. I tried preachers and schoolteachers and people I felt would see things my way. Some of them actually did. One or two said they'd think it over. No one actually said they'd walk with me. Scared little rabbits.

41

Glen

Examining myself or the events of my immediate past with Lily I can find no answers. I search the car radio for country songs about good men loving bad women. I try to tell myself that Lily is bad, that a terrible mistake has come to an end. It's all just my way of waiting for her to come home.

I sometimes think I'd be better off if she were dead. That way I could grieve and get on with living. I know now when she left me that time in Texas I had some unspoken hope or faith that she would come back. I know that's what kept me going.

I know I'm a fool possessed. I understand her more, I love her better, than any man could. I sit on the front steps and watch the road like I don't know every minute takes her farther away. I envision her pulling into the driveway and getting out of the car and kneeling down in front of me, telling me that she's sorry, she's seen the light for true this time. I have to believe that sooner or later she will.

I had the lawn seeded and bought those shrubs she wanted. I had a service out to triple-clean the place, and I spent several evenings painting the trim. I took up jogging and doing sit-ups and I'm letting my hair grow just a little. This time when she comes back, I'm going to make it perfection for her. I bought a book, *How a*

Woman Wants to Be Loved, and I look forward to sharing the things it's taught me with Lily.

I know she ran off with that guru because I was loving her wrong. His love could never match mine. I won't misuse the chance when she comes back.

The kids are down at Mama's for the time being. See, my Lily, she's smart. She knew I'd do that. She knew I wouldn't keep them here with a sitter while I went off to work all day. She knew. She called down there this morning. She gave Mama the address. They're at some leftover hippie-type commune or something near Galveston, Texas. She talked to the kids, told them she loved them. It's all just her way of keeping in contact with me, of feeling me out, of telling me not to despair, that she's easing her way back home.

The way I see it, Lily and I need this separation. It's to end the old way and allow a little space for the new one to begin. I see it so clearly.

Except when I wake in the night and see snakes crawling around the room, and my heart is like a two thousand pound dumbbell and I lose all hope. I don't feel that way long. Mostly I feel like, if it's ever written, ours will be the greatest love story ever told. I just wish she'd call me or send me a card or something, anything to hang my heart around till she comes home.

Oh, God, send her home!

42
Rose of Sharon

I found the little train set Lily described. It was my first trip to Wal-Mart since I quit, and they all hugged my neck and told me they missed me. Except Marjean. She stood back and wrinkled her lips into that electrified grimace she applies when she feels for some reason she has to be nice. It gave me pause to think of the hours that woman spent on my porch up at the lake. When did I ever have time for her?

I had the train set wrapped in Superman birthday paper and six different Wal-Mart clerks took turns nosing over to gift wrap to ask me who it was for.

Glen was out on the front lawn with the hose watering light green squares of new sod like it doesn't rain every other day in this part of Alabama in January or that sod had any intention of growing before the middle of March. I was in luck. I could pull into the drive and hand him the present and be on my way.

He came at me like a crazy man or a demon possessed, opening the door for me and kissing my cheek and taking my arm like I was his long lost mama or best friend. It chilled me, because I saw right off that he was holding on to me because he believed somehow it was holding on to her. He insisted on showing me all through the house. He'd had stereo speakers wired from the den to the bedroom and put a fully stocked wine rack in what used to be a broom closet. He wanted to know what color carpet I thought Lily would want him to order. It was like visiting people so bereaved that they have to convince you their dead are alive by keeping everything just like or a little better than the deceased ever had.

I saw I had little comfort to offer him and made a half dozen excuses for leaving, but his loneliness grabbed at me. He said the kids were down at his mother's. I told him he'd be a lot better off with them home and their needs to meet. I took the tour and we had made our way back to the kitchen. By then he'd showed me how he'd had all of Lily's clothes cleaned and wrapped in plastic and sorted summer and winter in the closets, the insides of which he pointed out he had just painted with three coats of enamel. I'd seen the newly mirrored wall in her dressing area and the extra phone over her commode and looked at his plans to convert the attic into an exercise area.

It put a hard spot on my stomach to see the monument he was creating, because I'd talked to Lily a few hours earlier and she sounded nervous as a cat and tired and scared, but she wasn't even dreaming about going back home to Glen. He pushed me down into a kitchen chair and poured us both a glass of wine. He acted like Lily had done something that was perfectly all right with him, like maybe she was at the PTA and he expected her home directly. It went downhill from there. All that sadness in him started mixing into his happy act. The anger and the regret began to boil up. He seemed to have no concept of where he ended and she began. He had himself confused with Lily. He had no self at all without her. I hurt with him, but I also saw his was a very selfish hurt that took none of Lily's needs into account. Without saying as much, he was telling me that God had created Lily to ensure his existence. It smothered me as I sat there, and I couldn't help but begin to feel how smothered she must have been trying to exist under the same roof with him.

Still, I wanted to leave him some straw to grab.

"I wouldn't know how to ask a person to live with me if they didn't want to," I said, and I didn't sugarcoat my tone of voice. I hoped that would pierce his delusion a little, but all he did was smile at me with condescension and explain that I had no concept of a love like theirs.

"You were miserable the whole time and so was she." He said it probably seemed that way. He said that Lily probably gave me that idea because she had a hard time admitting to herself that down deep she would never love anyone the way she loved him. I said that he'd never get over this thing until he faced facts. Lily had her share of faults, but like any other human being she deserved a chance at happiness. He was gulping wine and talking fast and sometimes he'd smile. Mostly he was angry at me, and I tried to tell myself that was because I was right there to receive his anger. The one he despised was in Texas with that dark and distant young man. I tried to leave, but he was raving, and I actually feared what he'd do next.

I needn't have. All his ferocity dwindled into heavy sobbing. I figured that it was good for him to cry. At the very least, it would help him sleep or wear him out, but I was weary of him. He obviously thought he was in some exalted state, some divine suffering that entitled him to all the world's comfort and condolence.

"She doesn't want you," I says. "She had to reach past all the guilt and shame she feels about that and try to live. Let her live. Figure out how to let her go and draw new strength from it." I sounded like something I probably read in one of those magazines I peruse on the checkout line.

Somehow he took me to mean that I compared him to Dashnell and myself to Lily. Before I could refute that, he was raving again. At that point, I didn't care how low it looked, I grabbed my purse and I stood up and walked out the door with him following, drunk and raving about how I wouldn't know nothing, I was the ignorant brunt of Dashnell Lawler's wrath. I was a dry old bag who'd given up on life and love long ago, and on and on like that until I finally managed to get my car doors locked against him and the motor started.

He chased me into the road yelling how sorry he was as I pulled away. I don't care what guilt Lily asks me to alleviate by running something by his house. From now on, the answer is "No."

I did have one thought on the way home. It came to me that

whatever you want to say about Dashnell, he's no mystery. He wears who he is consistently on his sleeve and it never varies. Glen's sickness is made of a closer woven and, in my opinion, a good deal more deceptive cloth. I try not to judge, but here lately I've quit upbraiding myself when I do. I knew from very early on where I stood with Dashnell. You couldn't ever really know that with a man like Glen. I don't think Lily ever came out and said she was afraid of him. I would've been. I don't think it's just because I'm afraid of everything. That man bears watching.

43
Dashnell

I seen Rose's car down at his house. I had to laugh out loud over that. Wouldn't that just be her? His tart takes out for Texas with that fairy, and Rose is up there throwing her homely self at him? No, I had to laugh and laugh myself sick and drink a boiler-maker over that one. I seen that car down there just before dark. I waited till the sun was down and then I stood outside his kitchen window watching the two of them. I couldn't hear what was said. But he was ranting and raving. Rose looked as if she was fixing to cry. They had some kind of fight with him following her to the car later on. She had obviously thrown herself at him. He'd rejected her. I did hear him say something about she's a dry old bag. She scratched off, and I come back up here to the house gasping for air, I was laughing so damned hard.

Jake and Marjean have stood by me through this, and that's a fine thing. They got an open door policy where I'm concerned. I can run down there for supper without invitation. Let me tell you, Marjean can cook, which Rose cannot. You know, in their way, all the boys has asked me was I doing all right, you know, since she left, and I've had a lot of good laughs over that. Am I all right? Hell, Rose is the one who's gone off her nut.

Some of them has tried to suggest to me that there's a connection between Rose losing her mind and me quitting KemCo. Well, they ain't met that skinny bastard supervisor I had up there. He always had something to say about me: I smelled like a box of wet puppies. I looked like I'd tied one on the night before. My work was sloppy. I insulted the women in the lunchroom. You name it. He had it in for me since day one. Hell, I knew him back in school. He'd wear the same clothes two weeks running and his teeth was black. But not no more. No, hell, prettiest white pearly teeth you ever seen. Pressed pants, slicked back hair, and I hear tell always running his hands up the skirt of a different secretary up in the front offices. Not that he don't sing in church choir every Sunday. Oh, hell, yeah, he's cleaner than Jesus Christ nowadays and all the time saying I smell like a box of wet puppies. As if I'm ashamed to sweat.

Well, it was one morning last week, the morning after Lily's dishrag sucker husband and I had some fun in his yard. You know, I kind of think that slick mama's boy has the idea he whipped me. I've had a lot of laughs with that too. I told Jake about it and he says, "Hell, you should have rolled him over while you had him down and made him understand your point!"

I laughed my ass off and says, "Hell, I would've, Jake, but I was scared to death he'd like it." We have a lot of fun up here on this lake.

Anyhow, I come into work ten minutes late that morning and Jerry, the supervisor, he's on me in a flake of a second. I says, "Jerry, a man has a damned point and you're pushing me to it." He commences to tear down my appearance and tamper with my manhood and I says, "You got a factory full of sheep to butt-fuck, you get off my ass." That's when he tried to tell me I was fired. Hell, I rolled my eyes and went over to my stand and started soldering per usual. I never did notice where he walked off to, but he was back directly with the manager. The manager told me I was fired again. I just made like I didn't hear him, so he blows a whistle and sends the whole line off for break twenty minutes early and then he has four security men eyeballing me. Was I going to go peaceably or was they going to have to haul me out of there? I laughed my head off at that and then I says, "You got no call to fire me. I quit." I walked out of there with my head so damned high it almost wouldn't fit through the goddamned door.

I hated to have to put that jig in nigger heaven. I have nothing personal against any nigger, no truck or grudge or unpaid debt with their race. This world is overrun with white hypocrites. Because the fact is, there's not a white person on this earth who wants to live around niggers. Truly decent niggers want to be with their own kind. It's just that half of one percent of troublemakers in between who see a way to get themselves some attention by stirring the waters. The men who framed the United States Constitution was slaveholders. They had no intentions of handing God's Promised Land over to the niggers.

My granddaddy could show you chapter and verse where it was wrote in the Good Book that niggers was meant as a servant race. I have searched and searched the Scriptures looking for that, but with our modern publishing companies controlled by Jew atheists, it was probably stricken right out, Holy Writ or not. Our Founding Fathers understood that. The great pyramids of Egypt, the Colosseum of Rome and the mighty Confederate nation here was built by the sweat of niggers who accepted that simple fact. I learned a very little in school, but in the peanut fields beside my daddy, I was privy to the wisdom of the ages. He wasn't what you'd call an educated man, but he understood the foundations of freedom and he showed them to me. In his time, if a nigger jumped off the path, you hunted the son of a bitch down like a fox and you brought him into town and you strung him up and burned him as an emblem for all the world black and white to see. It wasn't a pleasant task. It required stamina and courage and inner strength and vision. A lot of people would have you believe that those cherished characteristics have been lost by the white race.

Now, what got me to thinking about this is earlier this evening, I seen a Alabama Bureau of Investigation car parked up at Jake's house. I hung around on the porch waiting until it left. I just knew Jake would come down here like a bullet. But after twenty minutes passed and he wasn't, I walked on up there. I was barely into their backyard when I heard Marjean yelling that he'd better talk to the others and get a straight story worked out. That was just some of her stupidity, because from time unmeasured, men of good will have operated off the code of silence. You don't know nothing, and you don't know nobody who does. I went on up the back steps and walked into the kitchen.

Jake was already out the front door, and when Marjean come into the kitchen, she looked at me like I was fixing to rape her and says, "We got a cherished custom in this country called knocking at a person's door before you waltz on in." I grinned thinking how much hell Jake would give her when I told him about that.

"I see y'all had company."

"Jake did. I know nothing about it."

"Don't nobody know nothing about it." I grinned, opening the refrigerator and helping myself to a beer. Jake is a brother to me and welcome to do the same in my house anytime. "What was they asking Jake?"

"I didn't listen."

"Where is Jake?"

"I don't know."

"I'll just wait around here on the porch for Jake."

"I'd rather you not."

"What's crawling up your butt?"

She'd been plenty hospitable to me when I spent six Saturdays running helping Jake get a new roof on their place.

"It don't look nice. Me alone here with a man."

Even Jake said he had to black out the bedroom and close his eyes before he could touch her. Snaggle toothed bitch.

"Go on home, Dashnell."

Jake would be the first to tell you how mean she was. It never made sense to me, a good looking, square shouldered, tell it like it is fellow like Jake putting up with a bony mule like Marjean. If ever a man had a license to run around on his wife, she was it.

"What are you trying to hide, Marjean?" That scared her. She picked up her purse off the kitchen table and moved through the house out the front door, and I heard that Chrysler of hers cough and wheeze and then it spit gravel. How many times had my head been under the hood of that old Newport adjusting the carburetor and changing the filter? I set there and drank three or four beers waiting on Jake. Around midnight I heard Marjean's Chrysler hit the driveway. She came on into the house and walked directly into the kitchen.

"What are you doing in my house at this hour?"

She looked like she had just hopped off her broom and I told her as much.

"You get out and you keep out."

I just smiled pretty as you please and got up from my chair and walked over to the door.

"You thank your Christian God that your husband is a brother to me, horse face," I says. I get a lot of laughs. I swear to Buddha I do.

44

Rose of Sharon

Why does trouble always come in the night? Mother and I had our coats on. We were standing on the front porch admiring the azaleas and Burford holly I had planted that afternoon. She had told me a hundred times they had Burford holly along the porch when she was a girl, but it had died the summer Granny passed away, and she never had the heart to replace it. I'm not much for Burford. It won't grow much in a shady place like by the porch. It's scraggly and it doesn't trim up very neat. Mother was thrilled.

Next thing we knew, Marjean's old Newport was squealing into the driveway. She thundered up the porch steps like a ball of fire and says, "I need to talk to you."

She'd been on my back porch up at the lake a thousand times with exactly the same attitude. It was generally some witless piece of gossip she'd heard about herself, and half the time she'd come to accuse me of starting it.

"Let's go on inside," she says, cocking her head towards Mother as if she was blind or a child. Mother smiled sweetly at her, but underneath she was burning. Mother relegates Marjean to a group she refers to as that other class.

"How's Jake?" I asked, hoping to get her directly onto the subject. Marjean will moan and lament generally for an hour before she zeroes in on the specific offense. I didn't get up and go inside. I motioned for her to sit. I don't like Marjean, and at my age, I've completely give up hiding things from Mother. She figures it out anyway.

"It's private," she says. Mother was already insulted because Marjean didn't so much as speak to her, and she was getting cold out there anyhow. She stood up. She looked Marjean in the eye and made an effort at a smile.

"How are you, Marjean?"

"Hey"—that with Marjean's fists all knotted against her stomach and her tongue trying to dislodge something from between one of her teeth. Mother went on inside.

"How's Jake?" I repeated as she sat on the edge of a metal chair as if she wanted to be able to take flight at a moment's notice.

"It's Dashnell you ought to be asking about."

"Why?"

"He's in trouble. Bad trouble. He's going to need you."

Marjean talked like that. I learned a long time ago not to panic when she slaps you with one of her dramatic openings.

"I heard he lost his job," I said.

"That's the least of it."

I have no regret for leaving Dashnell except that I waited so long. But a change like I made comes at a price. It sharpens your edges a little. Marjean had bet my patience a hundred times before and my patience had always won. Not this time.

"I have no desire to sit out here in the cold and waltz with you, Marjean. What *kind* of trouble is Dashnell in?"

"Alabama Bureau of Investigation kind."

The man on the lake. Some black preacher down in Birmingham had hounded the Alabama Bureau of Investigation about it. They'd been up and down the lake asking questions. They had computer records of three gun owners up there whose weapons could have been used. One of them was deceased. The other only used their house in the summertime and could prove they were in Savannah, Georgia, the night it happened. The third was Jake. They had taken his gun with them. What they could prove by that no one knew.

"But Jake isn't going to set back and take blame for something he didn't do," I says. "Because you have six men ready to testify it was Dashnell who pulled the trigger."

"It was Dashnell's idea," she minced.

It was all of their idea. It was Dashnell they were planning to sacrifice. None of them amount to much. But all of them hold themselves out to be more than Dashnell. It was always as plain as mud to me that they sipped their liquor slow while he gulped his until he was fired up enough to do whatever they told him to do. It's not that I hold Dashnell innocent. It's just that I consider all of them guilty.

"What do you want me to do?" I asked.

"Don't he have people in Oklahoma?"

He does, a sister.

"Might be best if he went to see them for a while."

I'll own a certain amount of ignorance, but I won't accept that kind of stupidity. The Alabama Bureau of Investigation comes around asking questions, and Dashnell hightails it for Oklahoma. Oklahoma isn't Hong Kong, China. They could bring him back if they wanted him.

"How would that look to the authorities, him running off?" I says.

"They wouldn't have to know," she says.

"Oh, they'd know," I says. "It wouldn't take much to get any one of y'all to tell them."

That bothered her. She wasn't sitting on Mother's porch to put me wise. She was trying to figure out what I knew and where I stood and what I might have to say to the authorities. She had one concern, and that was how much I valued her skinny red neck. Was I going to tell the ABI who all had sat around my porch planning it that night? How much did I actually know? What proof did I have?

"The law doesn't make much difference between a killer and his accomplices when punishments are handed out," I said for the pleasure of watching her retch.

"Dashnell acted entirely on his own," she shot back.

It wasn't funny. But I had to laugh. I'm hypocrite enough to know another one when I see her.

"We were all there that night," I said. "We all knew what was going to happen. None of us did a damned thing to stop it. If the law doesn't burn us, the devil will," I said. I was actually enjoying it a little.

"You and Dashnell may have known," she says. "You and Dashnell may have planned it. More power to you." She muttered something about the sanctity of the white race like I was a pure fool. I had to hold back from saying any more. I'd said too much. I'd give her too much information if I kept on.

"Marjean," I says, "there's not but one thing to do and that's keep our lips pressed together and let it blow over. They won't ever prove a thing unless one of us spills our guts."

She asked me what I'd say if they came asking me about it. I said absolutely nothing, and she went off relieved. She went off thinking she and Jake could nail Dashnell to a burning cross, and if Dashnell's neck didn't satisfy the law, she figured on offering them mine. That was exactly what I wanted her to think. You don't tell a declared enemy what you're planning to do next.

I don't care for Marjean. But I despise Jake. In the first place, I don't like his looks. He's kind of regular looking, red faced and dishwater blond, and starves himself thin, though he'd never admit it. He wears those shiny cotton khaki pants like the fraternity boys and the landowners wear. He's always got them pinched in to show off his waist and they're always a half size too small. Jake has a white toothed smile that fools people. He makes an effort not to sound like a redneck when he talks, which isn't much. He doesn't want to get caught expressing his ignorance or taking responsibility for it. He also beats the fire out of Marjean.

Another thing. When he does talk around me, it's usually to say something ugly about Dashnell. I quit defending Dashnell to myself a long time ago. But a man like Jake will tolerate a man like Dashnell because it gives him somebody to look down on. If Jake hasn't come out and told the ABI that Dashnell got drunk and shot that man, it's because he's out getting the others to corroborate it first.

I have no doubt that preacher down at Birmingham is the one who pressed the ABI for an investigation. But there's only one person up there on that lake who could have put them on track. That's Glen. Glen was up at my house feeling like a duck out of water with all of them talking about what they was going to do. He's the only one who didn't go with them up to Jake's. It sickened him and he went home. I'll bet you next week's supper Glen Pembroke had a chat with the ABI.

After Marjean left, I went on in the house and called Glen to tell him to watch his back. He didn't answer. Mother was already asleep. I went on up to my room and I wrote down everything I could remember about that night they shot the man on the lake. In the morning I picked up the phone and got information for Yellow, Alabama. I reached Mrs. Smith as she was on her way out to the market. She remembered me right off. I didn't waste words. I told her about the investigation. Then I begged her, if she had any information or knew where it might be found, to please let me know. She said that she would, but I didn't much believe she meant it.

45

Glen

I couldn't wait to tell Lily what I'd done. I knew she'd see that I had truly changed. I had taken an action directly counter to the ball of fear in my gut. It would make all the difference. Mama had the number down there in Galveston where she's staying. I had to worm it out of her. Mama and Daddy have their minister praying that I'll put Lily behind me. They hope if Lily stays gone long enough, I'll turn my affections elsewhere. I lied and said that I needed to talk to her about the divorce. I made up some bull about having seen an attorney who told me, if Lily cooperated, we could do it on the courthouse steps.

Lily was real sweet at first. She sounded genuinely concerned about me and the kids. I told her what all I've done to the house, and I could tell she was really impressed. She asked me if I was planning to let her see the kids, and I told her anytime she liked. She said money was tight and she didn't know when that might be possible, and I said there would be a first-class ticket waiting for her at the nearest airport whenever she wanted to come home. She said she appreciated it, but she wouldn't take advantage that way. I told her the advantage was all mine, and then I couldn't help myself. I begged her to come home, broke down and cried like a two-year-old.

"Baby, come home."

Silence. I could hear her breathing, choosing her words. "Glen, I won't ever be home." Man, that went through me like a fistful of railroad spikes.

I told her about what Dashnell had said about her that afternoon in my yard, the names he'd called her and how I punched him out. It had no effect on her whatsoever.

"Glen, it's broken, and nothing will ever fix it."

That stopped me a minute.

"I can change, Lily."

"It's not *you,* Glen, it's me, and I don't want to change. It's messy, but I can already see that no matter what happens, I can't come back and torment you or myself ever again."

Rain of tears, rivers, I begged like the hardest prayer I ever uttered.

"Stop it."

I tried, but I couldn't.

"I'm going to hang up now, Glen."

"Wait!" I got myself a glass of water and drank it down slowly. It helped.

"Lily, are you sitting down? I called Montgomery and told the chief of the Alabama Bureau of Investigation about Dashnell and Jake and the others planning to kill that black man."

She said that I was wonderful. She said she never in ten million years would have thought I'd do something that magnificent. She said she loved me for doing that.

"Now, will you just get on home here, baby?"

Dead silence. I couldn't even hear her breathing. It seemed like she was considering her answer. When she finally spoke, she sounded sad and far away. She said she had to hang up. I kept begging her not to. She said that she wished me all the happiness in the world. One day when I met the right person, I'd have it. I still kept pleading with her not to hang up. She gave back the most terrible words I ever heard.

"Glen, I never loved you. Glen, I can't manufacture the desire for you. I wasted years trying. Glen, please, let go of me. Maybe someday you'll forgive me." Then she hung up.

That night, for the first time since I found out about her and Michael, I let myself imagine her in his arms, her lying beside him, underneath and on top of him, him saying, "I love you" and her saying it back. I'm ashamed to admit it, but I imagined him inside her too. I imagined him pleasing her and her sighing and squealing and rolling away satisfied. I imagined it so clearly I began to see him through her eyes. I could almost worship those dark eyes and his hairy arms and feel his thick hair. I could almost know how she felt when he entered her and I could feel his pleasure when she took him in her mouth and ran her tongue all around him and he had no shame about it like I did. She sat down on him and he lay there, a sultan who claimed all her pleasures as his due. He turned her on her tummy and entered her from the back and she cried out her adoration of him, and it made me cry, and it flooded me with the desire to climb up in between them and feel their adoration, and it was awful for me when I came. It was cold and dark and empty. When I stopped breathing heavy, I could hear a stray mutt barking from the other side of the lake, miserable, alone, and cold. It hurt me, that imagined coupling of theirs, because I know it's not imagined, and I see nothing but darkness ahead, and I hate them.

Later I heard footsteps on the gravel outside the bedroom window and Dashnell Lawler flashed into my mind. Sooner than later, those apes are going to figure it out. I looked out the window. It wasn't footsteps. It was a miserable hard rain and it had ice in it.

There was only one way to make her understand that I couldn't live apart from her. I had to go to her. I had to bring my Lily home. I dove into the shower. I packed a bag and I hit the road. It was rough going. The wipers froze up twice. I saw a couple rigs on their sides. But I made it twenty miles this side of Jackson, Mississippi, before I pulled into a little motel and slept. It wasn't too bad. I did wake once from dreaming that they were naked and in the room and laughing and pushing me away. Mostly I slept. There was four inches of snow on the ground when I woke in the morning.

46

Hezekiah

His half-sister Dereesa called at six o'clock on Sunday morning knowing full well Hez had his Saturday night whiskey to sleep off and that the phone wakes Cheryl and she only has Sundays to sleep until eight. She wasn't on any of her high horses, begging money or moaning about her kids. She was plain spoken and to the point. Moena was down and bad. She'd had no feeling on her left side all Saturday and refused the doctor and wouldn't let anyone call the hospital.

They were all used to Moena's little bitty strokes. She might come in from the garden and sit at the kitchen table. A neighbor woman crying the blues to her wouldn't even know she'd had one unless she saw her coffee cup tremble en route from the table to her lips. Pretty soon she'd steady herself and her cup and wipe that touch of hair under her nostrils and ask the lady to go out there to the garden and fetch her straw hat before the starlings pecked it to pieces. Afterwards, Moena might sit quiet for an hour or two on the porch, but she'd be back doing around the stove by suppertime.

She said they were wee mites of tremblings, and her time was nowhere close, and she said that's what the angel had told her a hundred times. Hez was the only educated one in the family *and* religious in that deepest of the deep old way—that went more with

Haggar and Abraham and less with the historical Jesus—Hezekiah believed his mother when she spoke of angels.

So, when the call came, Hez left off his usual grumbling about the phone so damned early on Sunday. He gave up his weekly opportunity to wax his elocutionist, electric way for the bored old people down at Third Street CME Church. He called in a substitute preacher and he hopped the next plane for Charleston.

He went straight to the hospital and he held Moena's hand. She wouldn't talk above a whisper or take anything but water. While he was in the room with her, there were several old people in the waiting area who said that, if God intended a healing for Moena, then Hez would be the instrument. They still remembered how decades before as a divinity student, Hez had lifted his mother's blindness.

The younger ones had an altogether different fascination for Hezekiah. His Birmingham church was still widely regarded as the cradle of the Civil Rights Movement. The aged Eleanor Roosevelt had delivered one of her last public speeches there. Presidential hopeful John F. Kennedy, Doctor Martin Luther King, and dozens of other champions of freedom and equality had shared his pulpit. Like so many of his fellow clergymen, Hez had helped to lead and organize marches, demonstrations, boycotts and pickets from Louisiana to Washington, D.C.

"Mama? You know me?"

Moena nodded very slowly, so slowly he asked her again and she did the same thing before he would allow himself to accept that there was communication between them.

"Are you ready to go?" She drew a long, deep breath and her color was better for a minute. "Can you give me an answer?"

She opened her eyes. "I know my God and King."

Hez pulled out his Bible and started to read to her passages Beauty B. had read to him when he was a boy down on Phelps Pine.

". . . The Angel of the Lord found her by a spring in the wilderness. . . ."

But while he read, she started turning her head side to side and he took that to mean "Stop." In a minute she could talk a little and she was saying that she came out of it best by moving her head back and forth that way. By four in the afternoon, she was fussing about the food, the itchy sheets and the poor television reception.

Hez tracked down the doctor on the golf course. It was much too cold and windy. But the doctor was the kind to stand out there on the fairway until he was frostbitten and then call his brother up north to brag about the mythological temperate southern winter. The annoyed man told Hez there was no scientific reason that Moena was alive, so he couldn't guess on how long she'd be around or why.

Someone had smuggled in a roast beef sandwich and Moena had polished off the better portion of it by the time Hez got back to her room.

"What'd the doctor say?"

"You're too mean to die."

Moena spit roast beef. "You'll get me to laughing at my funeral."

"To hear your doctor tell it, you'll be preaching mine."

The banter went on. Hez couldn't sustain it too long. He was hoping to make the last flight out of Charleston and they had some arrangements to discuss.

"You can't stay here by yourself no more, Mama."

She might just as well have left the room.

"Cheryl can come get you and you can try it up in Birmingham with us or we're going to have to make some other kind of arrangements."

"I'll get one of them nurses to stay a few nights. Go on about your business."

It was futile. She was entitled to live her last days as she saw fit. Why not pay someone to look in on her and keep her place decent and let it go?

"Okay, if you're afraid of Alabama, then you're afraid of Alabama."

She chewed and swallowed and took another bite and then a sip of milk. She asked him to be sure the cat was fed before he left. Then she said a movie was coming on television. He asked which one and she said she didn't remember. He'd hit the nail strong and square.

"Am I right?"

"I don't give my cat milk."

"Am I?"

She wouldn't look at him.

"Are you afraid of Alabama?"

"Not the place."

"Of what happened."

"Hush!"

Her face twisted. Her mouth pressed flat and trembled. Gigantic tears sprang from her eyes. She looked like a heartbroken child.

"I've tormented you. I'm sorry." He cleared his throat and withdrew an envelope with a check in it from his inside coat pocket. He tapped it and placed it in the drawer of the bedside table. Then he took her hand in both of his and held it while she cried. She closed her eyes and when her breathing was steady, he gently slipped her tiny arm under the cover and crossed towards the door.

"Of the feeling." Her voice was low and thick and strong. He turned around. She was calm. The child had vanished. He paused. Her voice neither invited nor forbade him to stay. He waited. She made no sign that she saw him. She appeared to be hypnotized or in a trance.

"Not everything burning or hiding in the barn, not what the men did to us, not the known world shattering or the dead fleeing the now forsaken ground. . . ."

She didn't see him. Her eyes were firmly fixed on the memory that possessed her.

"Get on out of here, Mother! Begone, Beauty!" She swung at the air. "Hush! Hush that! No! I will NOT go there!" Her voice faded, but her lips moved.

She was delirious. It was probably another stroke. He stepped forward to call the nurse. Something stopped him cold. For a split second the room burst bright purple. Whatever the illusion, it woke the untenable sense that Beauty B. was near.

Moena's hands leapt to cover her ears.

"Not fear, not fleeing or the dead man swinging or dying. . . ." It was a child speaking, a little girl begging to be heard. He had to stop this, but nothing would move—hand, foot, lips—nothing.

"That ripping apart, that tearing off, me from me, that pulling away of me that couldn't leave from me that had to go. Riding away, riding away and most of me left back in the road screaming for Eula and the little bit of the rest too weak to fight them, just a broke off piece of me, jagged and torn and the rest of me left back in the road screaming for Eula, but her daddy wouldn't stop. He wouldn't stop and they wouldn't let me go back. Even when that other most of me turned back around and I saw we were topping the hill and cried, 'Wait! Wait!' But we were too far. It was too steep. I couldn't run. I was too weak."

Moena wasn't remembering now. She was looking straight into Hez's eyes. She had taken his hand. Her voice had lost most of its timbre. She was telling him now, quickly and quietly, her former passion spent.

"I looked at me looking at me from the wagon. Then looked back from the wagon and saw me die in the road. Then we passed the hilltop. Mother was slapping me, telling me to hush or we'd all be killed. I knew, even if we got to safety, most of me was already dead."

She was finished. She rooted around the pocket of her bed coat and took out a package of Life Savers. She offered him one. It was yellow. He declined. She pulled at it. It was stuck. She pried it off with her teeth and placed it on the bedside table. The next one was green and it came right off. She put it in her mouth and stuck the remainder of the roll back into her pocket. Then she switched on the television.

He sighed and rose. He kissed her forehead. He turned and walked out of the room, pausing at the doorway just long enough to decrease the overhead light with the dimmer switch.

The plane was an hour late taking off. He leaned into the leather seat and drew the bourbon slowly. It was his second. There was only one other person in first class, a hard faced, leather skinned white woman with severely coiffed yellow hair. She sat directly across the aisle from him putting the stewardess through hoops. She flashed her perfect white grimace at him when he sat down. It was that peculiar I-don't-hate-niggers-but-you-keep-away-from-me flash of teeth. He pitied her for it. He pitied her because he could imagine her hovering over some poor gardener, lamenting the bugs and criticizing his work between increasingly candid quips about her indifferent grown children and her loveless marriage. She wanted iced tea. The stewardess couldn't make a pot until the plane took off. All right, then, she'd have seltzer now, but get right on the tea as soon as we're airborne. He had an inexplicable urge to cry for her, to go over and sit next to her and take her hands in his and offer to pray with her. He wanted to say, "Miss, why don't you just come on out and ask me what the hell I'm doing up here in First Class?" He wanted to shake her till her coiffure went flat. He wanted to argue all the ice off her shoulders, let her rage and scream until she melted all the way back down into something human and recognizable.

He wasn't a preacher bent on bringing humanity en masse into the baby powdered arms of Jesus. It was more like he wanted to drive and corral the chilly hordes into one beloved and loving, embraced and embracing, and profusely sweating throng of believers in a breathing universe.

His mind danced lightly back over Moena's revelations. He finally understood her. It wasn't what she remembered, but how she experienced the memory that illumined her. Intellectually, he had long assumed a connection between his mother's emotional detachment and the terrible event that drove her and his grandparents out of Prince George County. He had placed it among thousands of other hideous facts of racial oppression. Now he had visceral knowledge of her private torment. To this point he had developed and maintained an irascible affection for Moena, a generous tolerance for what he had always believed was her unmitigated egocentricity. That was based on his pugnacious belief that she willfully withheld affection. The hard won truth was kinder than his mean supposition. Moena was inextricably bound to that woeful night in 1908 and was immutably herself in light of it.

What had been decades of resentful affection for his mother had become something finer in the space of an evening. More than anything, he longed for the elusive means to lend some measure of peace to her rapidly dwindling days on this earth.

He had to bring her back to Alabama.

Hezekiah was not a man to reason a thing like this through. You could get stuck on the thing and lose sight of the rightness of it. The rightness of a thing came from God on high.

For one fantastic heartbeat he saw Moena standing on that remembered road. He saw a piece of her restored. He was flooded with the unquestionable rightness of it. He smiled at the notion and his eyes met the white lady's. He saw undecorated mortification in them. She looked quickly away, nervously blotting a drop of tea from her silk blouse.

No power on earth would ever bring Moena back to Alabama. Not if she was conscious.

His fingers fumbled for the seat lever. The plane hit an air pocket and his almost empty plastic glass slid off the tray table, spilling ice on his shoes. So be it. He drew the seat as far back as it would go. He closed his eyes, shutting out his mother and the nervous white woman slapping herself with a napkin. He was still snoring when the stewardess rolled back the exit door in Birmingham.

47

Moena

You tell me. Apt as I can figure it's as Eula's mama used to tell her about don't never say never unless you understand you mean the opposite. I woke up Monday morning in the hospital. Not dead. Tuesday morning, not dead. Wednesday morning, one little stroke froze me up to where I couldn't eat. Nurse commenced fussing when she jerked the tray from me, but paid no heed to the fingers stuck around the fork. I was half the morning prizing it aloose. It was just lucky them forgetting my bath.

Dereesa had me a ride home Friday morning, but she got called up on some cooking job ten miles somewhere out behind the country and forgot me. I fibbed and said my daughter went for the car. They wheeled me out, but the wind was blowing. I used my nice "Honey, it's too cold. Warm yourself. Here she comes." It worked.

Don't bet what I paid a taxicab. Junked down white boy with a tattoo and half his teeth missing. Sweet though. Wife left him and took his religion. I said if she could do that, then his religion wasn't worth keeping. That made him grin and say, "Neither was she."

Hezekiah took a load off of me last Sunday evening. He relieved a parcel. Lightened up this dry old Raisinet. That's part of it. That and it turning off too cold to think about my garden. I don't set up by a stove warming myself well for more than two days. I take no pleasure viewing my scratch pea mess of a yard when it's too windy to walk on it. I get hungry. I cook it and then I don't want it. Then the mess. Hez had some fat girl sent. Worse than useless except to eat what I cooked and didn't want. I got shed of her.

It may only be I was trained that you can change your mind but one time about something. Once it's changed, you go on. Not that anything I ever did made the news and this won't either. So you'd best tell me how I went from I won't to I'll try it. Cold, bored and lonesome comprise my strongest guess.

I packed right. I never went no place except down on the turpentine farm, but in my working years I packed off plenty of white ladies and their husbands and children. I know how. I washed, ironed and folded and bagged up my things in paper sacks. I mended and hemmed and took in a waist or two. I found that little suitcase one of Dereesa's kids used to carry her typewriter in. It done perfect.

Then I cleaned the house top to bottom. One of the neighbor women came by with some hot mush because she can't keep me straight with her toothless mother-in-law. I made like I was just too feeble to feed the cat and she took it home to keep until I get to feeling better.

I got a better taxicab driver and it wasn't nearly as much money. I found the ticket counter with ease. This cross eyed white witch with foot long fire engine nails and three sticks of Doublemint working.

"Where to, Granny?"

"I ain't your granny, *Miss Alabama.*"

"Where you going?"

"Birmingham."

She went crazy with a hole puncher and piece of printed paper. She took my money and handed me an envelope.

"Know why?"

"What, Granny?"

"Know why I'm going to Alabama?"

"Why?"

" 'Cause my mama done tole me to."

It was true, but that's not hardly the same as telling the truth. I was no more than barely settled into my seat before I finally got the picture. So obvious I giggled out loud at my own stupidity. I was near the front and I caught the driver's glance in the mirror over his head. The little sign underneath it says, YOUR DRIVER MARK WILLIAM DUNN, FRIENDLY, RELIABLE, COURTEOUS. That look he shot me wasn't none of that. He shot me several more narrow stares. Made me feel like I'd robbed a bank.

Be that as it may. I had this little excursion back to hell figured out. How it come to me was I was thinking what to wear to church to hear Hezekiah preach on Sunday.

"Oh," I says to me, real casual like, "oh, well, I brung my teal blue dress and the lace collar." As if I had ever wore that dress and that collar. I had stood there over my ironing board, peeling back and ironing that collar a pinch at a time without realizing why.

Cheryl sent it years back, the Christmas it snowed. I unwrapped it and I thought to myself, "Well, good. Something decent for them to bury me in."

I'm going to Alabama to die. It relaxes me to know it. There is nothing I hate worse than to be doing a thing and asking myself all the while, "Why am I doing this?"

I was made from Alabama clay. It's only natural I'd go back to it. Like our old preacher man used to say at them country funerals when he'd drop a fistful of orange dirt down onto the coffin. It's what we come from and what we become.

48

Hezekiah

He lay on the ratty Leatherette sofa in his office and glanced over the morning paper. He was nearly out for the count when his eyes landed on something that made him sit forward and shake so hard with laughter that Marcia, his secretary, peeped her head in to see if he was all right.

"All races, creeds and religions are invited to a Harmony Festival in *Prince George*!" He could barely get the words out before his sneezing laughter overtook him. He laughed until his chest hurt so bad that he thought he was having heart failure. That scared him a minute, but then he realized the pain was from the right side and his heart was on the left.

He culled the man's name from the paper and dialed his number. But there was no answer. He drummed his fingers on his desk and then he called Watnell Pegues looking for his daddy and was sad to hear that Watnell senior had passed over. "Watnell was a mighty soldier," Hezekiah said. "Stood right next to the King all the way through Cicero. Refused to bow down to Bull Connor's dogs too." Young Watnell allowed that he was teaching public school days and working on his MBA at night. Hezekiah told him he was one in a million and fumbled around his drawers in search of his old address book. Willie O'Neill. Willie had come out of jail down in St. Augustine about a week before the King's funeral. Said he was going to try to get his daddy's carpet business back on its feet.

"Willie?"

"Who is this?"

"Hez!"

"Naw . . ."

"Brother, dig out your marching boots, we're going to Prince George."

Prince George was a joke. The King himself hadn't been to Prince George. Even the most staunch member of the Movement conceded that Prince George would be Prince George until by some miracle it got swallowed up or plowed under or blown away. Willie got a great big chuckle out of that. But when Hez pressed on with it, Willie said he'd go gladly, seeing how little the average man had to hope for with the cream of the old leadership sold out to Carter and now Reagan, and he went on lamenting until he was in enough lather to promise he'd round up a few more of the old militia. Hez was lathered too.

"Pull 'em off of barstools, buy 'em out of jail, haul 'em away from their tractors and their flea-bitten mules and have 'em down by the King's monument at seven o'clock Saturday morning." He passed several hours like that. Then he went home.

Frances, the family housekeeper for fifteen years, was threatening to quit. Moena was back there in the kitchen determined to earn her keep by making supper. So far she had ruined a French porcelain skillet trying to bake corn bread in it and shorted out the microwave oven. Cheryl was in the breakfast room cooling Frances out when Hez got home. He made himself a good stiff drink and went to inspect the damage. Moena was frying okra.

"Mama, Frances does the cooking."

Moena was almost fit from trying to make sense of the electric stove anyway. She'd burned up the first batch and now the second was turning to greasy green cornmeal covered mush.

"Quickest way on earth to make somebody mad is try to do them a favor," she muttered, dumping sizzling green slime into the sink.

In seconds the room was filled with steam and the smoke alarm was screaming.

"If this is what money buys, I don't want none." Hez fanned down the alarm with a newspaper and switched on the vent fan. The cloud thinned.

"Come on back here and visit with me."

Hez settled Moena into his recliner and poured her three sips of peach brandy.

Moena sat down in the breakfast room with him. She immediately started complaining because Cheryl had wallpaper hung in the kitchen. Moena had never seen such foolishness. When she had swallowed her brandy, Hez poured her another two fingers.

"Get you a good slow sip, Mama. I got something to tell you."

Moena drank. A little amber liquid dropped down one side of her mouth. "Dereesa dead?" she asked.

"No, ma'am. Dereesa will be on in a day or two."

"What you got to steady me with brandy to say?"

"Saturday . . . on Saturday . . . I'm going to *Prince George.*"

"Prince George County, Alabama?"

"Yes, ma'am."

"What for?"

"A march."

Moena let out a gasp that pulled all the air out of her. She drew in a breath. She laid her head down on the table and said, "Lord, come for Thy world!" She shook with laughter from her head to her feet. That started Hez laughing.

"Prince George County, Alabama, on a march?"

Hez was laughing so hard that he could only nod. Moena was slapping the wall.

"Not scared of nothin', are you?"

"Too stupid," he giggled. Their laughter subsided. The old woman pursed her lips.

"You're doing a right thing," she said. "It's a fool thing, but it's a right thing." Then she drained her glass and handed it back to him for a refill.

"Don't be so stingy this time."

49
Heath

The panels of café curtain over the sink were frozen as stiff as wood when I pulled them back to see if I'd left the truck lights on. I slammed the thermostat in the hall with my fist and the furnace screamed. I spread the county newspapers on the kitchen linoleum and brought James Edward in. He's a stupid dog and he's old and he doesn't much care for me. His nose was wet, and he tried to run back outside six or eight times, so I figured he had been all right in his nest of rags under the steps. I trudged through muddy ice to the mailbox. There was an unsigned postcard of the Prince George County courthouse. *Die, Nigger Lover!* That warmed me up. The phone was ringing when I get back inside the trailer.

"You Lawler?"

"Yes, sir."

"Hezekiah Thomas down in Birmingham."

"What can I do for you?"

"I was hoping we could do a little something for each other."

Silence.

"It says here in my evening paper you're planning a demonstration up there in Prince George."

"Yeah."

"Highly commendable."

"Thanks."

"Idiotic. You know it's idiotic, don't you, boy?"

"Why?"

Hezekiah laughed out loud at that. He told me later it was because he took me for a naive kid. He wondered if I might even be up to something. No question there were many white people of goodwill out there. But he'd been tricked before. Accepted an invitation to a barbecue once and then found himself in the middle of nowhere at a Klan rally. Ran ten miles through fields with dogs after him that time.

"Are you a *native* of Prince George?"

"Yes, sir."

Silence.

"Well, if you're a native of Prince George, then you don't have to ask why it's idiotic—if commendable."

"Yes, sir, I have to ask why it's idiotic. The whole problem is everybody else is scared to ask why. But then I'm not afraid of anyone, especially these fools up here."

"You're braggadocious too. Look here. There's a Ramada Inn at the I-20 Sherman exit about halfway between White Oak and Birmingham."

"I know it."

"Suppose you meet me there tomorrow night at eight."

"Why?"

"How many of your friends and neighbors do you expect at your Harmony Festival?"

"Couldn't say." I could very easily say. I was expecting me. Period.

"Well, son, I'm working on a busload. You be there."

The minute I heard Hezekiah's voice, I knew who he was. Hezekiah Thomas was on Birmingham TV News ten times a year. Mostly because he was mad about something the city council or the mayor had done. I remembered last summer during the drought Hezekiah was out in the ghetto streets with wrenches turning on fire hydrants for the kids to splash in because the mayor had ordered the public swimming pools drained as a water saving measure. I remembered Hezekiah yelling that the mayor should order his rich friends to empty their pools if he was serious about conserving water.

It was a thrill to talk to a famous person like that. I'll be honest. I didn't much care for his patronizing, take-over attitude. This was my battle. It belonged to me, not some preacher who'd been on *60 Minutes*. I couldn't see losing several hours' pay just to drive down to the Ramada Inn and tell the man to butt out. I slapped the dog on the back a couple times and then he walked out into the cold. Just before I climbed into the truck, I had a shuddering sensation.

Vaguely the idea rose like an old locomotive beam burning through fog or a swirling star that stops suddenly and crystallizes into a sapphire. *Hezekiah had said he was working on a busload.* The thing was happening. People all the way down in Birmingham were reading about it. I flew down to the 7-Eleven and picked up a paper and there I was under "News of Local Interest." It was my high school graduation picture, the same one they had used when I was sent to Folsom for robbing that bowling alley. It told where to meet and what time and said the purpose of the walk was to demonstrate that all people are welcome in Prince George County. I stood there reading it over and over, more thrilled than I've ever been in my life. I was still standing there by the news rack ten minutes later when the district supervisor phoned to tell me I was out of a job.

50
Rose of Sharon

I thought surely the highway patrol deputies would have so many accidents to tend to with the snow and the ice on the roads that they wouldn't come. I gave myself the day off from worrying about it and hauled the library table up to the attic to begin stripping it. Then here they came, stomping snow and slush off their rubber boots outside the door.

They had me come back over the night the men planned it. I'd been over it so many times in my mind it was easy to recall in perfect detail everything that was said. What they didn't expect, and I hadn't fully realized until I told them about it, was Marjean's confirmation that it was Dashnell who pulled the trigger of Jake's gun. Apparently the officers had something that went with that because they asked me to repeat it several times.

They asked if I was mad at Dashnell and trying to get back at him for something—beating me, another woman, anything like that? I said I felt sorry for Dashnell because he was too thick to understand that pack he ran with had no regard for him. Easily led is easy prey. I said I had no deep-seated feelings about him one way or the other. My living with him had been mostly out of habit. My leaving had been inevitable. I guessed this thing with the man on the lake had been the last straw.

They were all nice fellows. One of them, the oldest, was a black man. I had to chuckle a little when I thought of Marjean having to answer his questions, but only a little, because he had a military bearing. For all I knew he could make things hard on me or threaten me, thinking I had more information. I can't imagine he felt too comfortable in the broad daylight up here in Prince George. Thinking back, he reminded me of a school principal we had here years back—unctuous was how Daddy described him.

Mama sat over in the corner by the pump organ listening, and I felt ashamed, not because of the events I was describing. I'd been over that with her. I felt ashamed of the things I was telling them about me and Dashnell, about his having been a habit and the way I saw him as ignorant and sad. Mother is well read. Daddy was an out and out educated man. Here I was admitting to these strangers that I had been untrue to my upbringing by marrying Dashnell. Mother didn't dance any jigs at our wedding. It wasn't her way to forbid you or predict doom, but she wasn't thrilled about it. I overheard Mother to say when my cousin Estelle married that it was a sin to push a woman out like Estelle's parents did. Mother saw nothing wrong with an old maid. I would rather have gone to hell in an oxcart than stayed single—back then. All the same, Mother put on a beautiful affair. You could say very fancy. She had a seven course supper afterwards in the Old Southern Hotel lobby. She let out her wedding dress for me and went through the motions of giving Dashnell my grandmother's emerald and diamond rings so he could give them to me.

I never came back to Mother once and admitted that I had made a mistake, not even when I moved up home. I never told her that I had married Dashnell out of fear that I might never otherwise marry. Now here I was, in her earshot, telling strange men how stupid I had been.

I tried to tell myself I had never been safer in my life than when I was with those three men from the Alabama Bureau of Investigation and their loaded guns in Mother's parlor. Another piece of me kept thinking they could decide I was their way into this killing on the lake. They could decide at some point to haul out their guns and take me in. I wondered who'd be there for me. Mother was too old.

Lily was gone. It confounded me that I had lived over half a century and accumulated so few friends. I imagined Marjean and the other women raising talk against me. I saw some desperate lawyer convincing Dashnell to say that I had gone off my nut and put them up to it or done it myself.

Of course that was only the fear in my heart raising its ugly head once again. I silently tried a little prayer that Michael England had taught us at discussion group. It calmed me considerably.

The ABI men hadn't been gone three minutes before Lily called. I will always feel kindly towards Lily. This morning I had my own consternation and Mother was low. I wanted to get back to stripping my library table, but Lily went on and on. Michael had taken her to some church or place down there close to Houston, Texas. She said it was like being married to a monk. They have to sleep in a little tiny room on a mattress on the floor, and they're both supposed to go off apart all day, her with the women, him with the men to work. She has to take a bath at a certain time, and then he gets his, and they eat supper in silence, and then they all gather together to chant.

She's miserable all over again.

She was all in a spin about Glen. Would I please go by to see him? He sounded bad to her. I didn't care how Glen sounded. I had this house and Mother and the ABI to think about. She didn't get much of what she wanted from me.

"Lily," I said, "I can't give you what you want. I don't have it."

"Have what?" She sounded startled.

"You're like some kid looking to its mama for happiness." She didn't like that. She got off the phone pretty quickly after I said that. I hung up the receiver and sat there a minute wondering, as I always do when I express the truth, if I should have kept my big mouth shut.

51
Dashnell

I didn't worry too deep about Marjean going cagey. She had always switched off like a light whenever Jake left the room. It was turning off cold. There's not too many nights of the year where I don't like to sit out at least awhile after dark. I'm generally a furnace, but not that night. I could see a shell of ice forming on the lake as I walked across the yards. I wasn't worried about Jake at all. One thing I knew was Jake would never turn woman and run off and leave me holding no bag. Hell, I *knew* that. However, it did seem peculiar that he hadn't come right on over and given me an update after the Alabama Bureau of Investigation boys left.

It started raining. There were holes of water in the ice on the lake and steam was rising from them. Now, believe this if you can, and if you can't, then know it's being told by a Christian. I got back up to my place and I sat a minute on the back steps, just long enough for me to feel that they were caked in ice. I was just fixing to get up and go in the house and get my keys and head on down to the café for some steak and eggs, and *this is the truth when a lie would work so much better,* I seen that nigger I shot, clean as daylight, that nigger in his boat gliding past, seen it so well I had to laugh because it was so real, I honestly figured it was Jake or one of them got up just like him and going past in a boat!

He found a hole in the floor of nigger heaven and slipped back down through or he rose up out of nigger hell. No, I'm not mistaken about this. He was skirting the edge of the lake and I followed him down around to where the yards run out and the land turns to swamp, followed him, my goddamn shoes cracking through ice into three inches of water, and he disappeared into the mist.

I don't remember nothing else after that, who called an ambulance or why. I woke up here in this damned hospital bed with the shakes. Nothing a couple boilermakers won't fix if that damned doctor will ever show up and let me out of here. I tried to leave of my own accord and discovered that my room is locked. You think you live in America and then something like this happens to you.

52

Glen

You pick up I-55 South close to Jackson, Mississippi, and you're in New Orleans before you know it. It was foggy crossing Lake Ponchartrain, eerie knowing there was black water all around beyond the concrete railing. I stayed behind a truck all the way through Metairie, so it wasn't bad.

New Orleans, as they say, is an old whore of a city. I first heard about it on a Boy Scout camp out when I was twelve. We sat around the fire in the woods, and the leader told us about the French Quarter and Cajun children dancing for coins and things that went on in upstairs rooms when the bars closed down that made a boy a man. That made me always love New Orleans despite the fact that I had never been there. You just say New Orleans, and I'm twelve, hanging out by a campfire with some guys and there's an older fellow's voice lulling you to sleep with vaguely sexual promises awaiting you way down yonder.

Watching New Orleans start to glow up out of the fog on the bridge after driving through snow and rain and ice all day was an oasis for my mind. I had already waked up snowbound in that motel east of Jackson, Mississippi, before I came to the full consciousness that I was seriously going after her. Last night, heading out of Alabama, I only had one electrified sensation. I was bringing her home. I was hell bent, fighting blowing snow, and my determination would be stronger in the end than all her objections. This trip was one pulsing round-trip Alabama–Texas–Alabama and my indisputable destination was my own driveway with Lily on the seat beside me. This morning in that Mississippi motel room I had time to consider my mission in greater detail.

I get uneasy in motel rooms anyway. No matter how decent, and this one was average, I can't shake the feeling that hundreds of people have laid on my bed, maybe thousands—dying old people, married people screwing away their road boredom, salesmen and hookers and crummy little affairs and families with kids leaving their scents and their germs and God knows what else behind. There's not a motel maid in the world who can sanitize all that, not at least to my satisfaction.

I felt trapped in that room watching the falling snow. It was a trap of my own design. Going after Lily had made one thing clear. Underneath all my crazy love for her, my twisted need to imprison and make love to a woman who found my touch unbearable, was a little cold fact.

I saw life as pointless long before I met Lily, and I sometimes wished to die beyond all moral and rational belief to the contrary. I chose Lily because she was bigger than all that. Lily was the only shield I ever had that worked, the only protecting thing I ever knew that could hold back that terrible, cold truth that life has no bearable purpose or reason. So what had started as an impulsive leap of faith had winnowed itself down into a matter of my life and death.

Then New Orleans was all around me like a sudden fortress or a wall against the dark thoughts of the day I had left behind me in Mississippi, and farther still, Alabama, the sad night wind by the empty lake, the getting up and going to work, the cold morning coffee sitting on the kitchen table in the quiet house when I came in at night, the same sock on the bathroom floor ten days in a row.

New Orleans drifted past like an accommodating hussy with a name like Harmonia—impervious and inviting and French and lovely and staid and humid and away. It drew me in. It asked nothing, offered everything. Or so it seemed when I had left the car at the Royal Orleans and let Bourbon Street pull me where it would.

Every face behind every bar, every beckoning iron stairway beside every facade, every blue note that drifted out of every joint along the strip, seemed to know me better than I knew myself. The Quarter was a town inside a city, a broken kingdom of shadows and tourists and torn dreams.

It was a place where the thick walls of stone churches kept God safe and deep inside away from its forbidden streets. It woke a thousand longings, all of them Lily. Or so it seemed to me that night as it pulled me and I let it, because the ache in my chest had diminished.

I sat in a filthy basement bar and made mindless conversation with men from New York and Russian sailors and one affable guy whose hand rested on my knee as we talked. You could actually peel the seconds off a minute in that town. I walked up and down a dark narrow street of old French houses jammed one on top of another and turned back up another when I hit the boulevard. I'm not a drinker, but I'd had a few that night. I was flying. I was ready.

She was standing on the corner of Dauphine and St. Louis streets in front of a jumbled-up little grocery store with giant boxes of cheap detergent piled so high you couldn't see inside it. Her hair was long and thick and brilliant yellow orange. The blue streetlight made a corona of green around it. Her skirt was short and her long mahogany legs rose like a narrow fountain out of her silver high heels. Her eyes took possession of me across the street a half a block away.

"Baby, run around the corner and get me a pack of Kools, will you, baby?" Her voice was like a feathered lasso dropping over my head and tugging at my torso.

"Which corner?"

She pointed, and I walked past a large red brick five-story house and down some steps into another crummy basement bar.

"They were all out of Kools," I said. She had a wide face, a broad little nose. Her pink lips parted revealing perfect white teeth that added up to a smile that didn't give a shit. I'm neither a smoker nor a man of the Word, but I followed the urge to open the Marlboros and place one between her lips, and then I was fumbling because I didn't have any matches, but she opened a tiny shoulder bag on a chain and handed me her rhinestone encrusted lighter. I lit one for myself, I suppose, because that's what a twelve-year-old Boy Scout on his first excursion to the Quarter would do. She exhaled, tweezing a shred of tobacco off her lower lip with two long neon pink fake fingernails.

"Willie got the van parked in the alley over here. Let's get this shits over with. Verline wants me to tell her fortune, wants me to say it ain't so, but she ain't bled in two months. She half crazy like it some big deal because she's afraid it'll turn out half black and her old man will kill her."

"It's forty," she said as Willie climbed out of the back of the van. Nice looking man, tall and thin and solid. Expensive leather jacket, creased jeans, nice shoes. I handed him two twenties. I thought he'd be a whole lot more menacing. We did it half-dressed. Then I was standing back outside the van.

"Willie, I'm going on up to Verline's."

"We need two more, Shasta."

"Aw, fuck that shit," she said, and then she asked me what I was looking at and told me to get the fuck out of there. There was something low and mean about the way she said it that gave me a funny twinge. I had an inkling that I wasn't done with her.

When you live with Lily, you live prepared. I'd been salting twenties and fifties in a hollow bedpost ever since we came to Alabama. So when I lit out from there, I had over five thousand cash. I left half of it in the hotel safe. I hid another thousand in the room. I put the rest in my front pockets in case somebody got my billfold. I sunk my hand down in my pants and dug out a wad and handed Willie five hundred dollars.

"That make it right?" Willie told me I was beautiful. Nobody ever told me I was beautiful before. I told him I'd take her back to the Royal Orleans with me for the night.

"You screw-faced honky shit! Them motherfuckers ain't going to let *me* in no fucking Royal fucking shit Orleeeen!

"Mother fuck, man"—she was talking to Willie—"I'm tired. Verline waitin' on me. What kind of shit are you pulling? He's a sicko. I ain't stayin' out here all night with this shits!"

Willie told her she was and told her to take a cab back—wherever back was—and then he took off in the van, but not before he told me I was beautiful again.

Shasta sat on the curb and lit a Marlboro, took a puff, then stomped it out. "What's this dried shit you got me smoking?"

I asked her if she was hungry. "No, man, I ain't hungry." She was mine. She belonged to me.

"It's cold out here," I said.

"It's wintertime."

"I didn't think it would be this cold in New Orleans."

"That's because you one ignorant motherfucker." I took no offense at her rage. I liked the way she talked.

"I like your hair," I said.

"Thirty-nine ninety-nine, and you get to keep the stand, but it ain't shit."

"Seriously. Are you hungry?" I was figuring to order room service.

"If you serious, then you take me to Antoine's." Everybody from up home came back from New Orleans talking about Antoine's like it was the Garden of Eden. It felt close to midnight. I doubted they'd still be serving. I was sure they wouldn't serve her.

"Probably closed."

"You probably give that junkie your last dime and you fixin' to shoot me. Show me your piece."

"I don't have one. I don't even like to go deer hunting." That was true about hunting. But I had a gun packed in my suitcase.

"Well, you one messed-up something."

She said Antoine's served until two. I couldn't figure her eating at a place like that. How did she know? She picked that up right away.

"I catch my last trick out of Antoine's when they close the bar. This pussy has rubbed the seat of every limousine in town." She said it with so much pride, I felt kind of impressed. She caught that too. It softened her a little.

"You go around to the back, show 'em your money, they'll slip us into a private room." She knew a couple semi-high-class hookers who had been in that way.

When we passed back by the St. Louis Grocery Store, there was a cluster of drag queens in gowns. Two of them were screaming and waving long, frosted fingernails at each other. A couple of them called Shasta by name and one called me a cute number. That really made me feel like a twelve-year-old Boy Scout. My right hand drew instinctively into a fist, but Shasta slapped it open before any of them saw.

"They'll pluck out your eyes and roll 'em down the gutter before you can say, 'Mother.' "

She got the time from a cop on the next corner and that's when I learned about New Orleans and time because he said, "Ten-fifteen." I had been in town less than four hours, checked into a hotel, showered and shaved and changed, walked at least five miles, talked to at least twenty people in ten different bars, taken some sorely needed relief from a whore in a van, and now I was taking her to dinner at world renowned Antoine's.

I tested my head, but Lily wasn't there. Lily was a name, and when I closed my eyes I couldn't visualize her or the house on the lake. I was betweentimes.

I spied a ten dollar bill on the pavement along Bourbon and my hand went for it, but Shasta's foot came down on my wrist and she swooped it up and crossed the street and handed it to a Cajun woman she called "Millie" who stood beside a limbless man in a large wicker basket.

She had it right about Antoine's. They took us into a little dining room like it was no big deal. It had a couch along one end and the door locked every time the waiter went out, and we had to unlock it with a buzzer under our feet.

She got pissed when they didn't have Champale and, MBA or not, I couldn't make a lot of sense out of the menu. We let the waiter choose for us. He brought us a bottle of wine in a silver bucket and she drained the bottle before I could down my first glass, so we ordered another one.

"What's the story?" She was much more animated now. She was younger than I thought by about five years. Prettier. I wished I'd paid more attention to that back in the van. It might have been better.

"Beg your pardon?"

"You ain't no Romeo. We done did our thing. You got some kind of trip to lay on me and I'd appreciate it if you'd get started. I'm tired." The way she said "tired" it sounded like "tie-yud."

"I bother you, don't I?"

"Shit," she said, and rolled her eyes. She was eating ribs. Mine was chicken. Obviously the waiter wasn't about to waste their gourmet stuff on us. She was looking me over, studying me, reaching back into that vast encyclopedia of human experience she had written with her line of work, trying to find me.

"What do you see?"

"Trouble."

"How so?"

"Let me see your hand."

"You charge extra for fortunes?" Even I knew it was a bad joke.

"I don't know fortunes. I read people."

"What am I? A novel or a short story?"

She dropped my hand. "Honey, they wouldn't put you on late night cable access."

We stopped at a store on the way back to the hotel and bought her a six-pack of Champale and three packs of Kools. She put a scarf over her head and put my jacket over her shoulders and stood close next to me as we crossed the lobby. It was after eleven, but the lobby was crowded and nobody said a word.

As quick as we got into the room, she flipped on the TV to catch the last ten minutes of *The Tonight Show.* She kept glancing back at me on the other bed to see what I was doing. She switched off the TV and opened a bottle of Champale.

"Tell me about her."

"Who?"

"Don't fuck with me, man. Tell me about her."

"It's private."

"It's fucked up."

"That too."

"You fucked up, screwed on backwards, missing a transistor, and I could blow your face off, call two friends down and it wouldn't nobody find you till you was bones. Not that nobody would care enough to look that hard."

A thrill like the one I had back on the street when she told me to beat it ran through me.

"Tell me about the bitch."

"She ran away with another man to Texas. I'm going to go get her and bring her back."

Shasta bent double laughing. "You ain't worth the hair on my ass!" Then she bent over me and gave my cheeks six or eight fast, hard little slaps. I smiled. There was shame in it, but I smiled.

"You're getting warm," I said, pretending I knew what I meant. I was having little spasms in my lower back.

"Willie take you five hundred. If I'm lucky, I see a buck and a quarter out of it. You splashing your money around. I see a shot at a couple hundred on the side. Do I?"

She saw more than I had ever seen. She scared me witless, but she was dead on target.

"Roll over."

She slapped my ass until it must have been red. I couldn't keep my buttocks from loosening and tightening. I was wriggling like a maniac.

"Hold on a minute."

She was on the phone. "Earlie?" Her voice was higher, softer, sweet as butter. "I'm up here to the Royal Orlean with some sick piece of shit, baby. I can't play house with you tonight, honey. You be all right, baby. It'll come on down in a day or two. You just nervous."

I took the opportunity to slip into the bathroom and take my clothes off. I unfastened one end of the spring rod that held the shower curtain and poked all the rest of my money except two hundred dollars into it and replaced it. I stood in front of the mirror. I was right. My ass was beet red. My eyes were a little bloodshot. I crawled back under the covers.

"Earlie, I'll take you to Planned Parenthood myself, Angel. You ain't got nothing to fear. You be back on the street in a day." Then she was whispering, giggling low and smacking the phone with her lips and making slurping sounds. "All right, honey."

"What the mother fuck you looking at, cow face?" Her growl was back. She jerked the sheet off me. "Skinny little piece of shit." I laid two hundred-dollar bills on the bedside table. She slapped me across the face. I was hard instantly. She jerked the lamp cord out of the wall and wrapped it around my neck, squeezing me. She slugged my stomach until I had to puke and she bloodied my nose. Then she turned me back over and pounded my ass with her purse. I couldn't feel anything but happiness. She drew blood from my shoulders with her nails and slugged my face and I was crazy for her, begging her for more. She spread a rubber over her index finger and rammed it up my ass and she unrolled another one down my shaft and she sucked me until pleasure was shooting out of my fingers and toes, and then she bit me and she stopped, and I was ripping at her clothes and she was slapping me back, and I could taste my blood when I kissed her breasts, and I had her down on the floor now, I was inside her now, pounding her. I'm big, too big for Lily, and she was pulling my hair, calling me names, telling me to stop or she'd kill me, but I didn't stop, I kept pounding and pounding and then I felt the rubber break, the thrill intensified and I was riding waves of bliss, higher and higher and fast and her fingernails were digging into my face when I shuddered and pure hot hell shot up and out of me, spurt after spurt of pleasure drew me on and I slowed down for a while, but I kept at it, kept at it, my insides tingling, my cheeks bleeding, her screaming and moaning calling me "motherfucker" because it had waked something in her too. She was giving it back to me now, squeezing down, hating me because she had started loving it, and she was Lily and I was Michael, and the first blue light of morning glowed outside the blinds when I rolled off of her and fell sound asleep on the floor.

53
Rose of Sharon

Edwina Johnston called over here around eleven clock that night and told me Dashnell had passed out drunk in her backyard. She asked me if she should call an ambulance and I told her yes. She said his hands were swollen and red and there was a bump on his forehead. I told her to send Jake up to the hospital with him. She said Jake and Marjean were in Chattanooga visiting their daughter. I knew that for a lie, because their daughter hadn't spoken to them in three years over her living unmarried with a man and not holding down a job and owing them money. Jake and Marjean were off hiding someplace. Edwina said her husband, Kenneth, was working that night. He might've been. I know they needed the money, but something told me he was sitting there telling her what to say. Kenneth was in on the dark business. He had surely heard Dashnell was the main suspect and didn't want any part of him.

It was almost midnight by the time I got to the hospital. The night receptionist told me that he'd suffered a slight concussion and that he was in a room asleep. She said he'd be out of there in the morning.

"Over my dead body," I says. "He's on a bender and he needs drying out." That's our hospital. Stick a Band-Aid on his head and send him home having DTs. I hadn't gone traipsing halfway across the county at that hour of the night for my health. I wanted him locked up someplace. I was scared to death of what he might do to me if he knew that I'd talked to the Alabama Bureau of Investigation. I also figured that Jake and his bunch would have an easier time of laying the whole thing on Dashnell if he was on a drunk. Sober he might not be so stupid.

"We don't dry nobody out here," the receptionist says, swaying her tiny shoulders as she talked. "You have to sign him in at the clinic over in Yellow." That made me tired. It had to be done right away. There were a lot of forms to fill out. We had to pull a doctor out of bed to have the arrangements made. Everyone kept telling me it could wait until morning. I knew if Dashnell woke up sober and hung over it would take a team of bears to get him into that clinic in Yellow. Luckily he was out cold. They moved him from his room, put him into an ambulance, drove him twenty miles and placed him in another bed with him snoring the whole time.

I realized driving home from Yellow at two in the morning that what I hated about it the most was facing the facts square. I had to do something about ending my marriage to him. I had to pack up the lake house and move my things out. I had to see a lawyer and go through the divorce. I had to organize and formalize and publicly declare that most of my adult life had been a waste.

I wanted to feel sorry for myself or angry at him. All I could muster was a general and vague regret at my own lack of courage because I had accepted such an abominable existence. For that I fully intend to apologize to myself if I ever get the strength to stare into a mirror long enough.

I didn't drive back to Mother's. I turned off left by the courthouse and rode up to the lake. I knew I'd find a mess, but what he was living in ought to qualify for federal disaster relief. I started cleaning and I worked through the rest of the night, running laundry between everything else. I found five dozen empty bourbon bottles and untold beer cans. He'd used every plate in the house for ashtrays. I had it fairly straight by sunrise, but it would take a week to make it right.

At the very least, I figured I'd get him sobered up long enough for me to set him straight on a few things. I'd have time to sort through and take what I wanted out of the house while I gave it a thorough going-over.

I went over home and saw about Mother and told her what was what, and then packed a few things and drove on back up to the lake. I wasn't sleepy. I opened the kitchen door and set to work cleaning the oven, and that made such a mess of the floor that I went on and stripped the wax and recoated it. The day passed. It was dark again. It was fine to be back up there with the moon on the lake. It was wonderful to know that Dashnell was locked up and that Jake and Marjean were away.

I had been with Dashnell and I had been with Mother, but I hadn't really been alone for more than a few hours in my entire life. It was a holy time.

I was there a week, packing and making things right. I made my runs for cleaning supplies early so I wouldn't have to talk to people in Winn Dixie. I figured I'd sell the lake house. I wanted my money out of it before Dashnell burned it down or lost it in a card game.

Nadine's oldest boy came on Saturday and helped me load the boxes onto Dashnell's pickup, and we put them in Mother's garage. Lily called me from Texas to find out if I'd seen or heard from Glen. She had called his office and found out he was missing.

A week after I signed Dashnell in for detoxification I went to see him. I was ready to talk to him about the divorce. I also wanted to find out if he knew I'd talked to those lawmen. I expected him to look and sound a whole lot better than he did. His face wasn't bloated and I could see he'd lost some weight. But he was pale and lethargic and spoke very little. The nurse said he was near death when he got there and, all things considered, he was doing fine.

Of course legally he wasn't fine. Dashnell was in more trouble than even he could imagine. Word was out all over town by now. Nadine had been calling with updates all through the week. His good Christian friends were lined up at the Alabama Bureau of Investigation telling the same story against him to a person. Jake had pulled them all together and rehearsed them to perfection.

Nadine stopped by the other morning. It was clear that she wanted more information than she gave. That husband of hers had obviously sent her over. Across the years I had gathered from Dashnell's end of telephone conversations that he was some kind of keeper of the keys within the Order. Sidney had heard that I'd been talking with the ABI. He wanted to know what I knew.

"Rose of Sharon, at first I couldn't imagine why a woman your age would leave a hardworking man like Dashnell Lawler," she started. I just looked at her. I had an idea where she was going with that. I was right.

"Well, of course, now that I know the straight of things, I understand it perfectly well."

"That's a private matter," Mother interjected from the dining room where she was rummaging through drawers. I had cleaned silver all the day before and she was having a ball arranging knives and iced tea spoons.

"Well, the fool went off on a drunk and killed that black." When Nadine says "black," it comes out "blayuuuck" in a silly singsong. "Sidney says Dashnell is apt to lose all he has over this." She was way out on thin ice and she knew it.

"What makes Sidney think Dashnell had anything to do with it?" I tried to sound as shocked as possible.

"Dashnell's been bragging about it since the night it happened."

Sidney is thick with Jake. He was up at my house the night they did it. So was Nadine for that matter.

"Not to me he hasn't," I says calmly. Mother kept trying to catch my eye, but I wouldn't let her.

"Well, poor Sidney and Jake and them are just sick over it."

"Sick over what, honey?"

"Well, the Alabama Bureau of Investigation, of course."

"The Alabama Bureau of Investigation?" I tried to sound light.

"As decent, law-abiding Christian men, Jake and Sidney and them had no choice but to say what they knew when the ABI called them in."

Mother slammed a drawer in the dining room. "There's nothing decent about a single one of that brood of vipers," she hissed. Nadine went as pale as rice.

It thrilled me when Mother said that. It wasn't the obvious truth of her words. Across the years even Nadine had allowed enough honesty out to betray the fact that she was hiding her brains in an effort to survive. It wasn't any revelation to Nadine. Mother's words revealed to me just how alive she really was. I felt obligated to stand tall with Mother, to turn her words into some kind of family statement.

"There comes a moment, Nadine, when the lies wear themselves thin and the facts shine through. So let's quit playacting and admit how scared we all are."

"Scared of what?" She wasn't going to surrender a lifetime of willful ignorance without a fight.

"Living," Mother purred, her eyes bathing me with pride as she entered the room.

Nadine made her excuses. She pushed that tired giggle and bobbed her head as always. But she was ruffled. At first I thought it was humiliation. Then I saw that it was dread. She had to go home and face Sidney. We hadn't given her a thing he could use against us. He was sure to give her perfect hell for that.

I let three days pass and then I went back to see Dashnell. If he was ever going to listen to reason, that was the time. If he didn't, I could go on my way knowing I'd done all I could for him. He still had a long way to go, but he looked better. The circles under his eyes had lightened some.

"You're looking better, Dashnell."

"Sign me out of here."

"I said 'better,' not well."

"You wanted me in hell. You got me here."

"You're turning into a nice looking man, Dashnell. You'll have women chasing you in no time."

"Bull crap."

I told him about my plans for the divorce and what I wanted. He didn't comment. When I told him how Jake and Sidney and the others had informed on him, he tried to make like he thought I was lying.

"What evidence has the ABI got?" he asked.

"Your print on Jake's gun," I said.

He didn't say a word for five minutes. He couldn't allow himself to conceive that they had all turned against him. At least not in front of me.

"Who brought the ABI in on this thing? You?"

"No."

"Who?"

"I don't know."

"Glen Pembroke brought the ABI in on this, and we both know it."

"I was led to believe it was a preacher up in Birmingham."

"What do you want from me?"

"I want you to listen to reason."

He told me to get the hell out of his room. He said he'd tell the ABI I put him up to it if I didn't get out. But I stayed.

"You have one chance," I said. "You let me get you a good lawyer. I know a good one. You tell him everything you and that pack of sorry sons of bitches ever did. Not just about the man on the lake, but all the other badness you've pulled against people—like setting that Jewish couple's house trailer on fire and threatening that Catholic priest and a hundred other things. *Tell* him, and then go to the police and offer yourself as a witness in exchange for a lesser charge than murder."

"You finished vomiting?"

"This is your only way out, Dashnell."

"What the hell do you care?"

"I want that pack of cowards stopped."

"Don't come here no more. Don't come, or I'll break your neck with my bare hands."

All the way home I wondered if it was because I'd moved out. Or did he have some hidden plan? Was it just the hurt that came with facing all those things the liquor had helped him avoid? Or was there something beneath my understanding of things? It was very strange. I had gone to help him. From my side that wiped the slate clean. Still I left with the uneasy feeling that I had somehow been duped. He was holding something up his sleeve. I prayed to God that he wasn't holding it against me.

54
Lily

This place is getting on my nerves major big time. I'm not one to be told what to do. These people here are like robots. I have no problem with all for one and one for all, but a person ceases to exist in a situation like this.

Michael likes it. They're thrilled to have him because of his Ph.D. He's leading seminars all day long, lying around on pillows discussing great ideas.

They call it the Center for the New World Order, but underneath those puffy white Indian cotton shirts I'm down there in the kitchen ironing, it smells like a pack of chauvinists to me. I earned my ironing privileges by being twenty minutes late for the women's morning meditation group. The women are expected to be down there in the main room on their knees chanting by 6:00 A.M. That's so we can have the men's breakfast for them when they come down at eight-thirty. They don't meet until after nine. Sounds like the same damned old world order to me.

Michael woke up that particular morning around five forty-five feeling his oats. I told him I was too sleepy, but he laughed that off, and I won't say I didn't enjoy it, but long hair and a head filled with New Age ideas aside, he's just one more man looking for a quickie and another half hour of sleep. So, of course I was late.

I dreamed about Alabama last night. It was one of those sunny late March afternoons with the windows open and a light breeze in the new leaves and the water dancing out beyond the porch. I had taken down the curtains and washed and ironed them, and they were billowing slightly. Mary Lea, the cleaning woman, had been over the floor with paste wax. The house felt clean and new and good—the way it was always told to me that I would feel after I was baptized. Maybe the dream means the house has been purified now that I'm away from it.

I tried to reach Glen three days ago at his office. We'd had a disconcerting telephone conversation a day or two before. It turns me inside out the way he still tells himself that he loves me. I finally called his mother. She claims to have no idea where he is. She wouldn't let me speak to the children either. There's something underneath this. If he doesn't call me back in a few days, I'm going back to Alabama to see about the children. I thought they were better off with Glen. I thought he'd put them first. That's a damned lie. The truth is I let Michael convince me that they would be better off with Glen because I wanted to believe that. I tell myself I'm no good for them. It's not true. It doesn't help. What am I going to do about my children?

I will always be grateful to Glen for certain things. I hate what I did to him a little more each day. Or maybe it's that I know my days with Michael are numbered unless he gets sick of this place pretty quick. It probably has something to do with this afternoon when I peeked on his seminar. He was massaging a little nineteen-year-old girl in the shoulders, and from the sanctified look on her face, I smell trouble. I wonder which Universal Principle he'll use to justify it to me, if he bothers. It doesn't fill me with dread, though. You climb as far out on a limb as I have and your survival starts to depend on shedding as much deadweight as possible, like all the lies I tell myself.

We meditate here. It's not much more than quiet time. We sit in silence alone with our thoughts. It's peaceful. I sit and wonder why I've never been happy, why I chase strangers and fantasies, why I feel alone. A little voice came back to answer that this morning. It said you have to love in order to be loved. I've never loved. I've only needed. It's not the same thing.

It's time for me to love my children. I don't know what that means specifically. I don't know what action to take. On another level it means that I've withheld my love from them because that's what my mama did. I realize now that will never make it right. I look back on my life with Glen in that house and I realize the one thing we had in common. We put our twisted needs ahead of the children's. I may spend the rest of my life trying to do something about that.

55
Glen

Both my lips were cut and my right eye was purple, and I could see a couple scabs in patches where Shasta had pulled out clumps of my hair. I had a shooting pain down my right front side when I took a deep breath, probably a cracked rib. I had scratches all over my back and shoulders. My head hurt. She had gotten out of there so fast she left the two hundred dollars on the bedside table. *Evil Motherfucker!* was written in red lipstick on the bathroom mirror. I found whiskey and Diet Coke in the minibar, and I downed half a pint. It helped. I finished it off and lay on the bed and slept until about three in the afternoon. I was fuzzy with too much sleep and liquor and pain when I woke. But the scratches on my back had scabbed over and the pain in my head had dulled considerably. I called room service, hoping food would help, and it did. Later I stood in a steaming hot shower so long it set off the smoke alarm in the room. It was night by then.

I had put on fresh clothes, and I was combing my hair down a little in front to cover the place Shasta took a plug when Lily came over me again. It pulled me to the floor and I sat there trying not to cry, but I gave in to it. I let the tears drop until it was like riding a waterfall down lower than I have ever been in my life. There are good cries and bad ones, and this was definitely bad. It brought me to the full depths of my sadness and it covered me. I wasn't crying. I was drowning alone in a black ocean on a dead planet with no hope of rescue or faith in the process. I was dying on that floor, a slow, terrible agonizing death.

The full memory of my night with Shasta towed me under and sucked me along as I saw myself there on the floor with Shasta ecstatic in the pain and the underlying hope that she would kill me and save me the trouble. I saw the true nature of my sickness. The only comfort in this world for me was unbearable torment. The only prayer I ever had was Lily, and she had deliberately abandoned me to this. She knew that I would have to hurt myself in order to feel anything after she dumped me. She knew that I would have to find a way to make it quit.

It almost ended there in that hotel room. I almost did it with my razor. Then I found the picture of Lily I keep in my wallet, and the purpose, the meaning of it all washed over me, baptizing me with pure intent. Besides, I was racked with pain and that woke desire. The more I hurt, the more I wanted a woman to hurt me, the more I desired the thrill of what Shasta and I had had the night before. It scared the hell out of me, but it governed all other reason. No shame or self-depreciation of guilt or silent prayer could quench my thirst. Only Lily would ever do that. I had to get to Lily. I had to find Lily. I had to touch her and be touched by her.

I saw them in my mind, Michael riding her, slow and easy and gentle and so good for her, all the way down deep good for her and Lily bucking a little, tossing her head from side to side, smiling and crying and *loving him back, the bastard, loving his heart and his prick, and now she was down on him and he was moaning that he loved her, and I begged them, I begged them to let me in. But they pretended they couldn't hear me. I kept telling them how it would be, I warned them, but they wouldn't look at me. They didn't know I would do it.* Didn't they know I would *have* to?

56
Dashnell

You could fill the Grand Canyon with what that stupid bitch don't know. Beginning with the Order. We didn't all move up there on that lake for the fishing. That lake is our sacred ground. Every one of us took a vow of silence at our Solstice Meeting at the Grand Encampment near Valdosta, Georgia. Every one of us signed a pledge that the secrecy of the Order is the most sacrosanct of all its commands. She don't know nothing about that. None of the women do. Only a faggot would tell a woman his secrets.

If Jake and Marjean have disappeared, it's because they're meeting with the Imperial Siren over in Louisiana. Jake is Chieftain of the Realm, the third highest official in the United States. If them boys told the ABI that I done it by myself, then it was to protect the secrecy and the sanctity of the Order. Any one of us can be called upon to accept such a sacrifice. It's part of our initiation vows.

The other thing Rose don't know is I didn't use Jake's gun. I used a weapon that's kept in the arsenal. It was put back in the arsenal that night. There's not a law enforcement official in Alabama who knows its whereabouts. The ABI don't have the weapon or my fingerprints. That's their bluff. Beyond all that, I met fifty ABI officers at the Solstice Meeting at Grand Encampment last summer. Any one of them would be honor bound to obliterate any evidence from the inside out.

Any legal attempt on the part of the State of Alabama to make a sacrifice of me would take place in Prince George County. There has never been a jury in Prince George that didn't contain at least six members of the Order. It don't take but one to hang a jury.

All that's just for starters, because Marjean has a cousin who works in this hole, and she brought me a message from Jake, "Stand by for a Seven." That means the Order has an operation planned. It is going to involve all members from the seven state southeast region. We ain't had a Level Seven operation since they shot Martin Luther Coon. It's Heath Lawler's nigger walk.

It makes my blood shout—my own kin, my Christian name abetting these Goddamn Watusi savage pucker-lipped apes. How it's going to gladden my heart to watch his eyes bulge as he swings from a tree on the courthouse lawn with his dick in his mouth.

Level Seven. It's D-day, the long sleeping dream will wake. Prince George will be the Fort Sumter, the shot heard round the world.

Seven. For seven angels. You got to laugh. Read your damned Book of Revelations, all you niggers and bitches! Man, oh, man, it tickles the hell out of me! Wrote down in plain English by God's angel baby, fairest Lord Jesus! Fair! Not nappy-haired, not triple-lipped—fair and pure! Goddamn people. God is telling you fools.

Is millennium just too damned big a word for your pea brains? You're looking straight into the sky-blue eyes of the year 2000!

Hell, Revelations 15, first verse:

"Seven angels with seven plagues, which are the last, for with them the wrath of God is ended." Read it. Seven angels pouring seven bowls of plagues on the earth. The right thinkers rising up, the angels joining them in battle, the descent of the New Jerusalem and the restoration of God's Kingdom on earth.

My only regret, my one failure, is Rose of Sharon. She was fast becoming a dried old prune when I married her. I don't mind telling you these babes around Prince George was wild about me. I could get stuff twenty-four hours a day. I took pity on Rose. Doing her was Christian charity. You don't know the times I stopped off with the boys for a beer on a Friday out at the Durango Lounge. Hell, I had bitches follow me into the rest room. I took one little waitress against the wall in there, and an hour later she was naked and whimpering for more on the seat of my truck, in the goddamned parking lot. There's a minister's wife in this town with six kids. She'd slip up under the bleachers at high school football games. I'd cover myself up with a blanket. She had a secret store of tricks that taught me a whole new regard for the clergy.

No. The blight was on the Rose when I took her. She tried to break my manliness. When she failed, she went to work on my boy. She done her damnedest to turn him yellow and queer. I'm proud to say his Lawler blood held true.

It's not pretty. I might have settled it with Rose in private. It was one thing her taking off and humiliating me. That part was mine to avenge. I would've made one more stab at breaking her satanic will.

Not now. Not a chance. She pulled the law into it. She turned the full force of her evil against the Army of God. It's out of my hands now. The code is clearly written. She'll be held and starved seven days and nights. She knows it. She'll be tied to a cross. The women will be assembled in a circle. The men will form an outer wall. The Eleventh Commandment will be read. (God, people's ignorance astounds me. It's well known there were Eleven Commandments. The Bible as we know it is not perfect. It was rewritten and perverted by the Jews during the Dark Ages.

The Eleventh Commandment says:

"Thou shalt not obey the serpent's daughter; nor seek the counsel of women; for theirs is the curse of Eve and the way of eternal destruction."

Then, it's written, she must be burned and any woman who shows pity, tormented.

But first, the nigger parade. They say a throng is expected. Let the damned come walking. The more fools, the more blood. The more blood, the more the real chosen of this earth will rally.

Oh, hell, yeah. I'm telling these faggot doctors every damn thing they want to hear. I have to be out of this AMA-sanctioned penitentiary in time to stand proudly among my ranks. It humbles me to think I had the honor to live and participate in history's highest event—the Battle of the Angels!

57
Hezekiah

The George Wallace Inn restaurant was crowded. It was close enough to Birmingham and frequented by enough northern business types to make the sight of a black man and a white one having lunch together no matter worthy of mention. But Hezekiah had another reason for meeting the boy here. He could tell by Heath's manner of speaking that he was a born and bred Prince George County cracker. He could easily be some Klucker nut who wanted a chance to shoot him. Hez figured at the very least if the boy was going to shoot him, there would be plenty of out-of-county witnesses.

The first thing Hezekiah noticed about the boy was his physical attitude. Heath was possessed of that arrogance men who have no foothold on this earth will adopt. It reminded Hez of himself years ago. When Heath leapt to his feet, the boy's height took Hez back a minute. He was over six feet with a wrestler's shoulders. His white shirt was worn, but it was clean and ironed. A scorch mark along the right wrist said that he had ironed it himself. It promised sincerity. Heath pumped his hand and smiled like a priest or a banker or a big time deal maker with an agenda. His teeth looked good, no small accomplishment for a Prince George County boy. His hands were broad and calloused.

Hez slid into the booth and lifted his menu and studied it. He laid it aside to study Heath. He thought he could descry some intellect behind the freckles and the dark yellow hair that almost hid his face, especially since he kept his head low.

"So you're putting on a Harmony Festival, are you?"

"That's right."

"What time Saturday?"

"Nine A.M."

"What's the plan?"

"A walk from the edge of the town to the square."

"Have you petitioned for a parade?"

"It's not a parade."

"What sort of protective arrangements have you made with local law enforcement officials?"

Heath smiled. "Man, you talk just like a preacher."

Hez made no response. He was waiting for an answer. Heath's smile faded.

"They won't give me no protection."

"Ask for it—in writing. In case you wind up in court."

Heath quickly pointed out that this was his festival. He was leading it, and Hezekiah and whoever else he wanted to bring along were welcome to participate, but the organization of the actual event was Heath's job. Hezekiah, who had organized hundreds of demonstrations and marches, large and small, was used to the inevitable local leader who felt his territorial rights were being violated.

"Don't want to steal your thunder."

Heath looked guilty. He had a conscience. That was good.

"What's the exact route?"

"It don't much matter."

"Young man, if I'm bringing a busload of black faces into Prince George County next Saturday morning at nine A.M., it matters to me and them enormously where they get off the bus and where they get back on it. You can be damned sure we want local law enforcement there in case of trouble."

"What kind of trouble?"

"The Ku Klux Klan kind."

"Oh, man, you're talking about six, maybe seven old farts."

"One man with one bullet shot the King dead in his tracks, and the Civil Rights Movement died with him. That, I might add, was in a city of a million people in a predominantly black neighborhood with security guards stationed close around him. We're going to be in a little all-white town in the middle of a county that prides itself on its all white population."

"Look, if them ol' boys give us any trouble and we got a busload of people, we can beat the hell out of them. Frankly, I'm looking forward to the opportunity."

Hezekiah smiled at that. Hezekiah laughed until he had to blow his nose and ask for water over that. His shoulders shook so hard three fat women with short haircuts in the next booth turned to look at him. Heath went beet red. He looked like he was about to pull out a gun and blow Hez to Georgia. Then he spoke.

"We won't perpetrate violence of any kind regardless of what opposition we face." Heath eyed him with dull incredulity. "You think that sounds cowardly or naive or preachy, don't you?"

"You don't know Prince George."

Hez sat up straight. His eyes narrowed. He flipped the back of one fist against his upper lip nervously. He cleared his throat.

"I may not know Prince George County, Alabama," he conceded, "but I knew a King."

Heath drew a waft of hair nervously off his forehead.

"I learned nonviolence from a King. I learned it walking beside him through fiery hordes of lost white faces in cities you'll never see. I learned it taking beatings in a hundred thirty-seven jails in twenty-seven states. There are no weapons in God's army. Now let's order some food."

Hez was sure now that it was folly to go to Prince George. It was utter foolishness to march into that hateful country behind this ignorant boy. Hez was thinking about all those he had recruited for the march, good people who trusted him, people who expected him to skulk out a neighborhood or a town or a county *before* a march and ensure all the basics like where the bus parked, who would be standing by with station wagons and a quick route to the nearest friendly emergency room if needed, and who on the local police force could make the chief understand that his force would be barbecued on the six o'clock news if it went bad for the marchers.

Hez was face-to-face with a pissed off local redneck who had taken on some *Harmony Festival* because he hoped it would catapult him to local prominence. This kid didn't know *jack*. This kid was living proof that a poor white man has no place to turn in this country.

Hez also knew he was already knee deep into this thing. He'd spent half the night praying over it. It was as if some ancestral angel had visited him in his sleep and given him the charge. Hezekiah was going to Prince George if every cracker in the county nailed him to the courthouse doors. The notion had worked its way down between his bones and filled him with an ache that could only be alleviated one way.

"Well, I hope you don't think the mayor is going to meet us at the edge of town with lemonade and keys to the city."

"Young man, I think you better examine your motivation here. Because it would appear to me that you're looking for a fight."

"Hell yes, I am."

Hez shook his head and removed his glasses and rubbed his eyes. "The whole point of this Harmony thing is to demonstrate the indomitable majesty of the human spirit."

"Man, if we don't stand up to them, they'll mow us down."

"If that's God's will, then so be it." Hez was taking the march away from Heath. He wondered how long it would be before Heath realized it. "Go on," said Heath, "I'm listening." The more Hezekiah spoke, the less the boy seemed to understand about the nonviolent nature of freedom, about the Living Hand of God lighting fires in the hearts of men and the oneness of the human spirit. But it didn't matter so much in the end. Because after an hour, Heath understood one thing very clearly. Hezekiah was in command of his Harmony Festival.

58
Rose of Sharon

Times get troubled and the night reveals its teeth. A hospital volunteer woman called here this evening from Galveston, Texas, to say Lily is in intensive care. She had found my phone number in Lily's billfold. She needed to notify her next of kin. I asked her if Glen knew, and she told me that Glen is dead. He shot himself after he blew Michael's head off and put four bullets in Lily's chest.

I did what I have always done when receiving the news that the world will never again be as I have known it. I disconnected from all sensation except facts and what actions were required. Mother was sitting three feet away from me when I took the call. She understood without a word that something had been torn asunder and action was required. She kept perfectly still.

I wrote down the woman's telephone number. I walked into the kitchen and took a screwdriver out of the drawer next to the sink. I picked up my car keys and threw a sweater over my shoulders. I remember thinking as I waited for the ice on the windshield to melt that southern people never dress for the weather. I had pried open Lily's kitchen window on two other occasions when she had been locked out. It's an easy thing to reach through and turn the door lock from the inside.

The house smelled of new paint and carpet. I found the address book where I knew she kept it in the desk by the telephone. I smiled remembering how Lily and I had laughed at the stupid man who had designed that kitchen to include a desk. She had a little brass desk plate made for it. "EXECUTIVE-IN-CHARGE-OF-MEAT-LOAF." It was still sitting there, still gleaming. Glen had left everything in that house gleaming. I drove back home and called the woman with the phone numbers. She told me that Lily wasn't expected to live through the night. Mother was still sitting there where I had left her an hour before. I hung up the telephone and explained things to her.

Mother told me to come sit by her on the sofa. She laid an arm on my shoulder and stroked my hair while I cried. Neither one of us said a word for a long time. Then Mother spoke.

"Did you ever notice how all great sadness is the same?" That took me back a minute. Then I realized what she was saying. I was sad over Lily. But I was reliving Carmen. That's when I noticed that her eyes were wet and red.

"What are you crying for, Mother?"

"My child is sad," she said.

Lily and Michael and Glen were splashed all over the Birmingham TV news this morning. Lily's mama and Glen's mama and the two kids. They're calling Lily everything but the Whore of Babylon and Michael a New Age guru, and Glen distraught and mentally unbalanced. I had three calls from two different channels wanting a comment. They had a lady reporter walking through Glen and Lily's house talking about a dream that was shattered by bullets and on and on like that. Lily's mama was on the noon news saying, "She was born thankless."

She made it through the night. I've called that hospital ten times, but "Extremely grave" is all I get. Mother, who's never flown in her life, came into my room and offered to get on a plane with me and go down there.

Lily doesn't have anyone now that her mama is a TV personality. Though it's her children I'm considering. It might mean something to them later to know their mother didn't die alone. I know Lily is going to die. All the same I called down there to intensive care and I asked the nurse to tell her that her friend Rose is coming. She said she would.

It might be she has enough consciousness left. It might be she understood when the nurse told her that I'm on my way. I don't know what that is to her if she does. It might ease her passing to know that someone is on the way. Mother repeated her offer to go with me. I wouldn't know what to do with her in a hotel in Galveston, Texas. I have tried to accept Lily's dying, but I can't stop begging God to let her live.

I wish life would make sense for five minutes running. I wish something dazzling would roll up out of the woods and swallow me. It seems ridiculous to say, but the truth is, outside of my child, I was never involved in life before. I was never pulled into that great big chain of events all around me. I never wanted to be. I was afraid it would swallow or diminish or defeat me. Now I'm afraid I was right. But it's not the dread of what I have to face alone down in Galveston, Texas, that pulls at my shoulders. It's the terrible sadness.

Oh, God, I don't want any more sadness. I want to sit in a room filled with pleasant, laughing people. I want to see Mother's forsythia bloom yellow against a clean April blue afternoon. I want to go shopping. I want a cousin I haven't seen in years to call me and say that she's pregnant and ask me to be the godmother. I want Lily to live. I got off the plane in Shreveport long enough to call the hospital. I spoke with the head nurse in critical care. She said she's weaker. If by grace she lasts until I get there, it's only so that I can help her die.

59
Heath

My daddy is a man of few words. He keeps his voice low. You have to listen hard to hear him. He was sitting there on the trailer steps when I got back from the 7-Eleven. He had the newspaper in his hand.

"Hey."

"Boy, I can't believe I been reading some of the things I been reading."

"This is a thing I got to do, Daddy."

"Why?"

As I stood there, it stunned me to realize that I have always been a little afraid of my father. It made me feel like a naked little boy caught pissing where I wasn't supposed to in the broad daylight.

"I won't be ruled by fear."

Daddy only knew one way of living. It had been beaten into him decades ago. Fear wasn't a subject he ever discussed. I thought he was going to punch me and I knew I couldn't punch him back.

"They should have kept you in Folsom Prison."

"I'm not trying to make trouble, Daddy. If others do—"

"You know damned good and well that they will."

"That's their doing."

"You're egging them on. It's not right."

"What's right about bullying and killing and running people

off?" I might just as well have punched him. I knew he'd take any defense I offered as a personal affront.

"I'm trying to be something, Daddy. I'm trying to stand for something."

"Your mama is at home on her knees praying for you."

The things that matter most in this world are simple. What I had wanted most in my life was to think that I was something more to my daddy than the booby prize for five forgettable minutes he spent with my mama in the dark. To that vain end I made a thousand mistakes in my life. Standing there in the cold with his eyes looking through me I finally understood I wanted something he had no capacity to give me. I felt worse than I did when that judge told me I was going to Folsom Prison for a year. If I hollered, he'd call me disrespectful. If I cried, he'd say I was weak. If I tried logic, we'd both be found frozen to death before he gave a millimeter.

"This affects more than you, boy. You go make a public jackass out of yourself and pretty quick people want to know where the rest of your family stands. If they burn your mama and I out over this, we have no place to go. We have nothing."

I wanted to holler. I wanted to pound it into his thick head.

Burn you out and leave you and Mama with nothing, the same way your grandparents did those black people they ran out of Prince George years back?

I kept still. That would have unleashed ancestral rage. That would have justified drawing a knife and trying to kill his own son. I'd have to kill my own father to survive.

"You leave me no choice but to disclaim you."

Daddy got back into his truck and drove off.

I stood there a minute drawing the cold air deep into my lungs. When Mama talked the way Daddy had, it was generally a mood that passed. But I knew Daddy would hold to those words. Daddy would go home now and pull out a bottle of bourbon and sip it until he was red eyed and fighting with Mama.

I went on into the trailer and scratched down some plans for the festival. I got sixteen calls that evening. Most of them were the same tired, breathy threats. I lay down on the couch in front of the television and drifted off to sleep. The room was filled with smoke and James Edward was barking when I opened my eyes. I dove for the door. I ran across the road and called the fire department.

I sat in the cold on the truck bed with James Edward and watched the trailer burn. Half the volunteer firemen in Prince George County belong to the Klavern. I wasn't really expecting the engine company. I just figured it might have some effect on my landlady's insurance. Luckily I had fallen asleep with my jacket and my boots on. I had to laugh when I considered how little I had lost. It was a big fire. The trailer sat up on a little ridge. I knew the flames were visible for miles. A blaze like that would normally bring everyone out. But no one came.

I don't know who spread the gasoline and pitched the first match. But I'll always believe they had my father's permission. It burned through the night and it kept that old dog and me warmer than we had ever been a single night with the furnace working double time. It burned clean, the white tipped flames hurling devil's fists into the sky. Then it was morning and I could hear starlings from the pink mist that hung in the wet gray trees across the road. I climbed into the truck. The seat was cold on my legs. There was frost on the windshield. The engine fought me a minute. The icy steering wheel stung my fingers. Then it turned over with a snarl that split the quiet. I was halfway to Birmingham before I remembered James Edward huddled up on a corner of the truck bed. I pulled over and brought him up on the seat beside me. He was shivering and probably hungry. I stopped at a café and asked for a bowl of warm milk. I was sitting on a stool at the counter looking at the morning news on an old black and white TV shoved up between a toaster oven and a coffeemaker. I saw Lily's picture flash on the screen. Glen Pembroke and Michael England were dead. Galveston, Texas, doctors offered little hope for Lily. I heard a distant voice say, "Lord, come for Thy world!" It was the waitress. James Edward had spilled his bowl of milk and she'd stepped in it.

60

Lily

I had always believed the mind is the first thing to go. It's not. It's the last. For no reason I'll ever know, I've been given these hours with the stitches burning in my chest and the cold and the memory of it. I don't think I can move. I know I'm getting weaker and colder, and there's a clock on the wall so I can watch the seconds. I had no idea just how long a second can be. I keep asking them if Michael died, if Glen died, if he killed anyone else. But I have to ask with my eyes, and this is a busy place. No one has time to interpret the twitches of my eyelashes. I try to think about God and heaven and eternal peace, but all I see is Glen standing in that doorway and Michael sitting straight up, pulling the sheet to his chest, his eyes pressing shut. Pitiful. Glen was calm, and that made me calm. There was nowhere to run, and the end had come.

Yeah, it's the most awful moment I ever lived through. Except that moment to this has been all the same. I'm still traversing that moment. I miss the kids. It would have been nice to tell them good-bye.

I don't think Glen intended that I should lie here, my mind wading through the hours, as I drift towards the dark. This is it. I can see. I can think. I can sense the end moving in. I bet Mama is having a field day with this. I'll say it to God's face, "I deserved to be loved." I think Rosie's coming. Or maybe I dreamed that. I hope not. I won't last long enough to see her. At this moment I want to believe I dreamed my whole life. Regrets? One. I was a bad mother. Two. I was afraid to be loved the way Heath Lawler loved me. Three. I never reported my daddy for what he did to me.

One more regret. One I've tried to hold out of my mind ever since this happened because it's bigger than the first three put together. They're both dead. I know they're both dead. I was just able to ask when they put me on the stretcher. The attendant was a burly man with a red beard and beer on his breath. The way his eyes twitched and he shrugged like he didn't know. That told me. I knew Michael was dead in my arms. I just wouldn't let myself know it. Glen Pembroke is dead because he had the bad fortune to meet me. Michael England is dead for the same reason. I don't have the nerve to ask God to spare my life. I exit this world sadly, against my will and before my time. But there is a dull relief knowing that I won't live to cause any more suffering. It took dying to understand that I gave twice the amount of pain that I took. I want somebody to know that. But dying is a thing over which I have no control. The time has come to embrace it.

61
Eula Pearl

Sidney forbade Nadine to leave the house that day on account of the trouble expected. She slipped out and run over here after he left. I had no idea what all that meant, but I was glad for her company with Rose of Sharon away in Texas. I asked her what trouble was expected. She said she didn't rightly know. So I asked her what trouble Sidney expected that would cause him to forbid her to leave the house on a Saturday. She generally hauls in a big load of groceries on Saturdays, stays gone all afternoon. She claimed she had no idea to what Sidney was referring, and we got to talking about my hooked rug. It's an Oriental pattern, and Nadine has drooled over every stitch for five years. At least I think I've been at it five years. I keep it there by the sofa where it's handy and it covers the cigarette burns in the rug from back when I used to smoke Kents. In those days, we all believed we smoked cigarettes for our nerves. Searle stayed after me about smoking for thirty-seven years. I quit smoking when I quit driving a car. I hated to have to depend on other people to pick up things for me, and I tried to reduce my needs down to necessities. Rose of Sharon and me was watching the floor finishers pulling up linoleum in the upstairs rooms. There was newspaper dated 1947 underneath it. We seen this old cigarette ad, "More doctors smoke Camels than any other brand." We laughed out loud at that.

Anyhow, me and Nadine had the Oriental spread on the floor. It's about four feet by five, and all I lack is the fringe. Nadine has the eyes of God. She jumped up and walked back into the dining room and looked out the window and said it was two boys creeping around the orchard. So? Two boys creeping around is half the reason for an orchard, and two girls would make the other. I ain't seen an apple off one of them trees in forty years. But then Nadine says she don't mean boy boys, she means young men. I could hear the voices by then, the men running up and down the road in little groups, parking their trucks, dropping their beer cans on the pavement, hollering at their women. I knew I was right to send Rose of Sharon away. I knew the thing I'd waited for had begun. Though God help me I didn't know what, and I wouldn't say nothing about it to another soul. It's pride, but I can't stand it when people smile at me and their eyes tell me I'm old and crazy.

You'd have to know the South to know the thing I'm trying to tell. Father used to say if you don't know the South, you don't know jack, but if you don't know jack you ain't born of the South. By that he meant it was a beaten place. By that, he meant southern blood and southern bone hammered into dust—thousands and thousands of fathers, husbands, sons, brothers, nephews and cousins put back into the earth. The hot August wind drew the dust off their graves and scattered it about the intervening years until every field and wooded acre, every backyard and dirt road alley, had been washed in that sacred ancestral dust.

Those who lived to surrender to hideous defeat lived to suffer the unconscionable vengeance of the victor. The righteous Union drowned the South in its own blood to prove our holy, inextricable bond. But when the war was over, what had not already been burned or looted was systematically stolen by a Congress of drunken thieves who hid their crimes behind a pretty word called Reconstruction. The southern survivor taught his child before the Word of God how to carry on, how to live in defeat, because as long ago as it seems to the victor, the loser bears the conqueror's vengeance a hundred generations, maybe more. You'd have to be of this place, you'd have to learn that at your mother's knee or experience the sanctity when you cut your hoe lightly through dry southern earth.

As long as I could, when trouble surrounded me, I'd get myself out to the orchard and find a tall crook in a peach or a plum tree in which to rest my weary haunches. Get your hands around the limbs of a good tree when hard times fall, and you will feel the sense of things, the motion and the gnarled eternity of life clutching and engendering life. You surrender to the vastness and strength comes.

Now I find myself drawing strength from my child, my little Rose, and it brings tears to me. So help me God, I don't think she minds it. In her way, I think she takes strength from that. I fight the old compunction to drift out there among the stars now that she's here and needing me. Nadine wails on and on about how Rose of Sharon moved home and rescued me from the grave, how I have color, how I've taken on some weight, how I started looking at the evening news again. I've fought my way back this far into living because Rose of Sharon needs me. Yet I've drawn the strength for that battle from Rose.

Anyhow Nadine was all atremble because two young men were climbing trees in the orchard, and I told her I didn't much mind and she turned white as heaven and says, "They're wanting a good shot." For the most part, Nadine is one of the most foolish people to rise up out of southern soil, but she has a grace, and that's her tendency to talk before she thinks. Nadine wouldn't have the sense of being to say she was against them—if she thought about it first. But by blurting it out, she revealed her true nature. Never mind what she says at church or when Inez and the boys are around or at the grocery store. You get the truth out of anybody when they're caught off guard, and you can triple that in Nadine's instance.

"What's going on?"

Once again, she claimed not to know. She was as flighty as a cat with tissue paper stuck to its tail. I figured Sidney was some part of the troubles coming. You could cut the air in that room with a slice of toast.

She give me what particulars I could drag out of her. One of the

Lawler boys was raising big sand. A busload of colored communists from Birmingham was expected.

With Nadine protesting every step, I went out on the porch. I could see who they were. You know them by their creased boots and their half-junked cars and their dollar store jackets. A lot of them didn't even have jackets. Skunks, godforsaken lost people who can't think of no other way to hold themselves over nothing than to make misery for a busload of Birmingham colored people. You ought to hear Rose of Sharon take on when I say "colored people."

Two young monkeys were in my orchard trying to get a better shot. I told Nadine to go on out there and run them off. But she wouldn't. I says, "Nadine, I can't hardly make it down the back steps and it would take me three forevers to walk down to the orchard. You could be back in a snap." But she refused. She was scared. For a second, I thought she meant of them shooting her. That's how she tried to paint it. She was scared word would get out that she had stood against them. She assumed that standing against that kind of criminal behavior makes a person president over whatever they stand against.

I was drifting into focus by then. I know these sons of bitches around these parts. They disgrace all the South stood for. At least the South as I have loved it all these years.

The North took slavery as their flag when they went to war against us. They didn't call it slavery when they sent eight-year-old Irish and English boys into mines and children to die in their factories. They called that their manifest destiny. How long since I watched the good people of Yankee Doodle Boston, Massachusetts, riot over school bussing? They call us hateful down here. Would the signers of the Declaration have had the time away from home if their well-educated slaves hadn't known how to keep things running? Or so my daddy taught me. The answer will come, and when it comes, it will come from the South. No one ever taught me that. It's just a common thing, known among all southern people of self-respect.

I should have been in my grave years ago. But, see, I'm waiting for something. I reckon that's how I got to the orchard, that knowing I had to. I reckon that's why I chased them two boys and their shotguns off my property.

I don't rightly know what passed this house. A bus. Two state police cars and a gangly mob of the worst dressed, least cared for, stringy headed human trash God ever forsook. Nadine wouldn't watch out the window. That's on account of Sidney was out there with them. I could stand in the high court and testify that Sidney was tossing bricks at those marchers because I saw him. Dashnell too. He's taken off a lot of weight. But it was him.

I couldn't eat and I couldn't sleep. There were footsteps and stair creaks and doors slamming shut. I caught snatches of conversation and just as I finally drifted into light sleep before dawn, I heard the ghost of a thousand horse hooves on the road.

62

Lily

It was my death dream. It was the end of my time and I surrendered to it. I was standing on the end of the pier watching the sun rise over the trees on the far side of the lake where the flat water shone black under thick gray skies. It was chilly. There was some wind. I was wearing an old green cardigan of Randy's. Glen stormed out of the house. He was naked. He walked out onto the pier with a stupid grin on his face. "Let's go swimming," he said. But he didn't mean swimming. I didn't want to. "Well, I do," he says. He dove into the lake and swam out about fifty yards. I said, "You better get back over here, fool. That water's cold and you're no swimmer." But he stayed out there treading water a long time. Then he says, "Help me, Lil, I'm drowning." One of his stupid jokes. I turned around and walked back up on the porch out of the wind, him screaming for help the whole time. Rosie was sitting there. "Is he serious?" she says.

"Hell if I know" was all I'd say. You know dreams. We were both eating chocolate dipped doughnuts from the bakery in Whitville, Alabama, where I finished high school. Rosie started down to the pier. I says, "Rosie you can't swim." She says, "Lily, we can't let him drown." She was fixing to jump into the water. I ran after her. Glen was bobbing up and down, gulping air and screaming, "Help me." Rosie and I jumped in the boat and went out there close enough to where he easily grabbed hold of the side. That's when he stood up and showed that he'd swum to a shallows where the water was only about three deep. Rosie was at the motor. I told her to turn around and head for the pier. But Glen pulled me into the water and starting kissing me, and when I fought him, he pulled me under, letting me up for air every couple of minutes and growling, "Say you love me!" He had himself pushed up inside me and I could see Rose standing in the boat with the gun. "Shoot!" I gasped. Glen was hurting me something awful, ramming himself in and out. I could see he knew how bad it hurt me. I could see that my pain was driving him wild with happiness.

I kept begging Rosie to shoot. Instead, she pointed the barrel down her throat and fired. Glen pulled me back under, his arms and legs around me, pulling us off the shallows and into the deep where the water was colder and colder and black and my chest was breaking. I felt the bottom of the lake against my back and something cold and metal sticking out. It was the gun! The one they used to kill that man on the lake.

Somewhere above the surface of the water, I heard a voice whispering sweetly. "Lily," it sang and I felt a flower opening in my chest. "Lily. . . ." In a minute I became aware of my lips pressed lightly together. They were dry. Then a swirling sky of reddish purple and shadows behind them. Rose's face was above me in the sky. Then the purple faded and brightened into pink. Rose came closer and more real. Then I felt her sweet warm hand across my cheek. "You made it," she said. That took a moment to comprehend. It was her. She was there and so was I in that intensive care unit bed. Every cell in my body rejoiced, but I was too weak to tell her.

She told me that God had spared me for reasons that would be revealed. Then she stroked my forehead until I fell back into sleep and dreamed about Michael's blood. That face Glen made each time he pulled the trigger, that familiar, vacant, detached look. I dreamt and remembered. It was close to dawn. Michael was asleep.

I was almost. We'd been awake making plans. He was talking a schoolteacher's job in Wyoming. I said I'd go anyplace with him but hell or Alabama. In my heart I already knew I had to go back to Alabama. Not to Glen or safe ground, but to see about my children. Somewhere over the last few weeks I'd gotten that clear in my mind. I was afraid of love, afraid to love or be loved, afraid it would destroy me. But it was slowly beginning to dawn on me that innocent children had no place in my fears. It didn't matter that Michael wouldn't lose any sleep over me. All that mattered was I had been a bad mother. I lay there beside Michael wondering how much of that I would ever be able to change.

I heard a scuffling sound from downstairs. A sleepy voice said, "Burglar." Then the door was open and Glen was standing there. For one tenth of one second I felt glad to see him. It seemed momentarily that he was offering me a way out of my troubles, and I was going to take it. I had just realized I would never take it when he opened fire. The blood was spurting out of Michael's neck and then everything went squashy, and I thought my body had died and my mind was hanging on a little while.

If I look back on that terrible dream of being pulled underwater, I can halfway recall the sense that Rosie was standing there over me the whole time, stroking my cheek with those tender cool hands of hers and brushing my hair with her fingertips. I will always believe that Rosie pulled me out of it. Rosie rescued me. Rosie parted some curtain of fear and climbed over a wall of all her sadness. She got on an airplane and came to Houston so that I wouldn't have to die alone. She touched my sorrow. Life happens when one thing brushes up against another.

I don't want to die here and now. I refuse to die. I choose life and all the terror it brings. I choose to live, to amend as much as I can the damage I've done. I want time for that, for whatever good I can do my children. Why does it take dying to admit that all my troubles amount to the unattempted good I should have been doing a long time ago?

Rosie's face shifts in and out of focus and breaks into fragments, then comes back together like a kaleidoscope over me. But her words are constant and clear and I draw them in through every pore and gather them in my heart.

"Rest easy, Lil. You made it."

63
Hezekiah

Blacks round here know about Prince George. It's just a common thing, like the clay in the field or some grandmother's curse handed down. There's an old saying "You make damn sure you don't give out of gas in Prince George County." Blacks just know about it. It's almost an accepted South Africa: No blacks in Prince George. I heard about this years ago.

See, it was kind of knowledgeable, I get uptight, you know I found God in Doctor King. Doctor King was not my God, but until I met King, I was very violent. I depended on a gun for survival. I hated white people. I generally faulted them for all my conditions. But through Doctor King, I found God and stopped wearing my gun. I had been an ordained minister twenty-three years before I found God, before my hate turned into love.

I get very uptight around Doctor King's birthday every January. I get uptight around April the Fourth, the day he was murdered in Memphis. I wasn't more than two feet away from him on that balcony of that ugly little motel. I fell over my King and I kissed him and held his hand and promised him that as long as I lived his dream wouldn't die.

His birthday is being prostituted like the birthday of Christ. Probably the second most prostituted birthday of any that we celebrate.

So there we were. The New Year had rolled in and Doctor King's birthday was coming again. All the smiling prostitutes had come back out of the woodwork. By that, I mean people everywhere all over the country having fund raisers in the name of the King, raising money for poor people who would never benefit from it, when that was King's portfolio like Gandhi's, like Christ's.

I didn't see a damned thing in Jimmy Carter. Except he took care of his boys and his girls. What he did for the masses of the black people, or masses of poor people, in this country was nil. He took care of Jesse Jackson. Jesse got a four million dollar grant. He took care of Coretta Scott King, he took care of Andrew Young, a few more. He took care of his boys and his girls, but, see, Doctor King told us that the job of the Movement was to establish a minimum quality of life for every American. And to raise that minimum to its highest height.

When that young schoolmaster fellow announced he was going to have a march up there in Prince George County on Doctor King's birthday, I said, "Great Christ, this is good." Then I saw him on television a few days later, white as a sheet, shaking like a leaf, scared to death, this *martial arts* teacher—I said, "Well, Prince George hasn't changed."

I saw in the paper a few days later where Heath Lawler had come forward to lead the march. Then another couple days passed, and Lawler is all over the newspaper talking about his own daddy had turned against him. I'd sat there in my home and I watched the celebration of Doctor King's birthday being carried on at the Marriott Marquis. They was eating caviar and drinking expensive wine, all of 'em dressed to death. I felt so terrible. I looked at them and I felt like, gee whiz, look how they're prostituting his life. Look how they're spending the dream on themselves. King was not about that. It's very difficult to identify King's life with that. Then it came on these two white men being pressured up in Prince George County. I started thinking in every movement we ever been in at least some white folks always came to our aid. So here's this white fellow up in Prince George in trouble, and all the black leadership is downtown eating caviar, drinking expensive wine, prostituting Martin Luther

King's birthday. I sat there and I said to myself, "If Doctor King was living, what would he probably say about Prince George?" I thought, "You know darn good and well you would have received a call by now.

" 'Hez, get your bag packed. We're going to Prince George.' "

I said to myself, "I've got to go." So I picked up my phone and called young Mr. Lawler.

I called this man. I said, "I'm the Reverend Hezekiah Thomas. I'd like to offer my support. I'd like to help. I'd like to see that march go through." Heath said to me, "Uh, thank you, I'm glad to hear from you." I said, "Okay, you come on down—to the Ramada Inn Hotel—tomorrow and I'll meet you in the lobby." I say, if he shoot me, a damn lot of folk going to be able to see it, you know.

So he met me there. What he said to me was "Reverend Thomas, I know your reputation. I know you marched with Martin Luther King. I know you went up against Bull Connor in Birmingham and Jim Clark in Selma and lots of others. But you've never faced racism like it exists in Prince George. These people are taught from the cradle and they carry it to the grave. It's like a religion. It's like a cult. If you come to Prince George and march with me, I'm afraid you won't leave there alive."

To say that to me—I live out that creed that Doctor King taught us, "To fear is only human. But to allow fear to control you is inhuman." If I'm scared to do something, I swear to God I'm going to do it. Now, if I'm not afraid, I may be nonchalant about it. But if I'm afraid, I have to do it. *Prince George is like bundling up all the fear from all the marches and protests and jail cells I've seen and putting it on my shoulders.* I told the young man, I said, "Well, I've heard that song before. But I know God. If it's God's will, I'll make it through, and if it isn't God's will, I won't."

We have a little monument to Doctor King down here in Birmingham. Whenever I feel weak, whenever I feel alone and afraid, I go there. All I got to do is stand there and mean it and I gain strength. I went by the statue, and I walked away from there believing that Prince George held my destiny. It was as if the King had dropped down and said, "Hez, what you do in Prince George will be the culmination of all that we done did before."

I went on home and I said to myself I should give others the opportunity to make their witness with me. I shouldn't sneak off up there and be selfish and greedy. Another thing I said—a lot of people are going to say, "I'da went with ya if I'd have known." So the next morning, I called a press conference at Doctor King's monument and I had Heath up there with me. I had a little statement I read, I said that at last I was going to Prince George County, after seventy-five years, I was going there to face that brutal racism. I really didn't think nobody was going with me, except Willie O'Neill to be honest with you—knowing how black folks feel about Prince George. I got my older son and daughter to come and I really thought that would be all. We were planning to start out from the church that morning. We got there. A big old gentleman grabbed me by the hand. It felt kind of good. He said, "Hez, I've come to pray with you." I said, "Pray with me? Okay, but when we get through praying, we're going to Prince George." He said, "Oh, no. No. I'm not going to Prince George." I said, "Well, I don't need your prayers. You need *my* prayers." But then there were some others waiting for me at the monument. Downtrodden looking. One fellow in particular, he always showed up when there's a march. Strictly a street person like a bag lady. He started smiling, showing his teeth were out, and he says, "Hez, I'm here." A nice man. I hadn't seen him since the garbage strike in Memphis. It was about thirty others. They all got on that bus. We took off.

I talked nonviolence all the way up there. I kept saying, "If you can't take it, don't get off the bus. You've got to be willing to take the most brutal beating. That's how you show strength and evidence of your faith in God."

I talked about to hate is to be weak. Hate destroys the hater. I talked about Jesus bearing his pains on the cross and Gandhi of India and King. I had a premonition. I expected it to be bad. But honest to God I didn't expect it to be as bad as it was. We left here late. I had a suspicion that we was being set up. Because Heath had worked with the sheriff, and basically the sheriff decided on the logistics.

I reckon that's how the Klan come to schedule their rally on the very spot the sheriff had chosen for our march to commence. Any nut would have put one group on one side of town and the other group on the other. That sheriff must have figured we'd back down as quick as we got word that the Klan would be waiting for us. I reckon that's why he delivered me so many messages on my answering machine.

When the bus pulled off the interstate at the White Oak exit, it was only about ten or fifteen people waiting on us. They stood there waving signs and hollering as we rode past. That flooded me with hope. I thought maybe the Klan had finally lost its hold on Prince George. But when we arrived at the place where the march was to start, I quickly discarded that notion.

It was like a war zone. Now your eyes and ears, even your heart, can play tricks on you under such fearful conditions. But I'll swear to the Lord my God it was close to fifteen hundred of them jammed into that field alongside the road. I've been through a lot of these things before. I'm not a neophyte. I'm a veteran of mob violence. But the sight of these people threatened to drown me in dread. We stopped the bus where we'd been told to. Then here come the sheriff rushing up to me.

"Ain't you done heard they was rallying here today?" He told me not to let anybody off. "Wait a minute. Wait a minute, it's too dangerous."

"Hey, man, we getting off this bus. We're fixing to march in Prince George County today. I know it's been seventy-five years. We've come to make history. We've come to make our witness. We've come to honor Martin Luther King, Jr." That sheriff wasn't studying me. He was eyeing Heath like he'd brought the four Horsemen of the Apocalypse home.

We commenced to filing off that bus. Those people were so souped up, it looked like to me they was *gliding* across this four feet fence, screaming and hollering, "Kill the niggers" and "Fuck the niggers" and "Goddamn the niggers" and "Here come the niggers bringing their AIDS up here!" They just raged all kind of vulgarities.

Heath and I were trying to line everybody up. Our people acted real good. They responded very well to all I had said about keeping calm. We had a quick prayer. I said a quick prayer there. Quite a quick one too. Because I thought we could get away from the mob. That was a possibility. I know the sheriff must have had some plans of protecting us.

If he had any, I never knew them. As we went to march away, the crowd started badgering us with bricks and bottles and stones and pieces of iron. I kept trying to tell everybody, "Stay put. Keep praying. Keep marching. Keep your composure. Be nonviolent." Finally, it got so bad, I asked the guy to pull the bus up along beside us. Then they started throwing junk over the bus, from the front of the bus, from the rear of the bus. A brick hit me in the head. It just staggered me. But I tried to keep my composure, because I know if I ever lose my composure, I'm the leader, it's going to be a bloodbath right there if I ever start fighting. Because everybody really is watching me and I know that. I kept trying to sing these freedom songs. Because these freedom songs have pulled us through so many times even though it was deathly fear. When you start singing those freedom songs, a kind of oneness comes about, a kind of bond of mutuality, of love, respect and protection. So I start singing and I kept throwing in things like, "It's okay. It's going to be all right. God will protect us. Love, not hate." Things like that.

That's when I noticed this great big old white dude. He was trying to get a clear shot at me with a big brick. He would run up to the front of the bus and I'd kind of fade back and then he'd run to the back of the bus and I'd slip forward and finally I thought, "Well, I'm going to have to *try* him." This is a key point. I said, "I got to *try him*." So the next time he got within clear view of me, I looked at him and I smiled. He went berserk.

"Oh, goddamn! Got to kill that nigger! Them goddamn niggers' marching! Now that nigger done *smiled* at me!"

He started throwing bricks and rocks, and he couldn't contain his shouting and flouncing about because I *smiled* at him.

* * *

Heath was a soldier on duty that morning. I knew he must be dying inside. These were mad men to me. But they were his people, his family and friends. This was his place. He was standing alone and apart from his time.

The press kept running into me and saying, "Reverend, is this bad?" I kept telling to them, "No it's not so bad." *I was seeing it and I couldn't believe it. But once that fear gets a toehold on any part of you, you're done for.*

"Rev, you ever seen it this bad?"

"Yeah, we've seen it."

I was ducking and dodging and trying to walk and watch and hold myself back from going after those evil, ignorant people with both my fists. A great big old stone hit my right knee. It just busted my leg. Something hit me then. Then that old ratty fellah with the missing teeth came up to me. He'd showed up for every demonstration since 1965 on the Selma–Montgomery March.

He said, "Rev, it's bad. Ain't never seen it this bad before." I had no choice but to accept how bad it really was.

Then what appeared to be nothing less than a little miracle happened. I noticed we were marching out of range of those bricks and bottles and so forth. I said, "It's going to be better now. They done thrown out." We walked along a few more yards. Then my heart stopped. I looked up ahead a few yards and I seen them folks had another damned pile of them bricks and rocks.

That sheriff had set us up.

Here they come again, bricks and rocks. Oh, my God! By that time, a lot of them had gotten in front of us and some had gotten behind us. They'd crossed that road. They were throwing bottles and bricks and objects so hard that when we ducked they were hitting their own people on the other side and knocking them down. Somebody said, "Reverend, they're trying to incite a riot." I said, "Hey, man, you don't kill your friend *inciting*. Ungh-ungh. These people just ignorant"

We ain't never faced a mob like this before. All the other mobs were basically white males. At least a third of this mob was women. They had babies in their arms and little children beside them, children raging all kind of vulgarity, "Fuck the niggers. Kill the niggers." Then I noticed a good fourth of that mob was seventeen- and eighteen-year-olds. Ain't never seen a mob like this before. Except once before.

The only time we had ever faced a mob similar to the mob in Prince George was when we marched out in Cicero in Chicago in that Polish community. That was no mob in Birmingham with Bull Connor. Or with Jim Clark in Selma or Hoss Manucy and the Night Riders of St. Augustine or in Philadelphia, Mississippi, or Grenada, Mississippi. We didn't face no mob like this mob. I know this mob has the *will* to *kill*. I started thinking. I've been beaten. I've been jailed 137 times. I've been beaten in more states and bled in more states than maybe most people will even travel in. I can take that beating. I'm prepared. I know something is at stake much greater than me. Out there by myself, they'd have to kill me. I looked at the fear on the faces of those brave souls out there marching. I knew they was going to attack us. They was at a pitch. It was going to be a mass murder.

Just at that time, somebody threw one of those bricks and it did hit a state trooper and almost knocked him out. Heath must have known the man because he broke out laughing. That's when the police finally *tried to make an effort*. See, it was a big long van right in front of the bus. I didn't know what was in that van. The van doors flew open and these men come out dressed like soldiers fixing to fight a war. I thought they was coming after us! Those were the sheriff's deputies. Been in that van all along. The people raging now! Mob violence have set in. There is no way to stop these people short of killing them. I really started thinking evil, I says suppose they attacked us to kill us? Suppose one of these good people is killed and I survive? What kind of life would that be knowing I'd led somebody to their death? I said I really have a mess on my hands. By that time, they was closing in all around us and it was just a matter of time before they killed us.

Here come the sheriff hollering, "Get these people out of here. You going to get these people killed. Get them out now."

I said, "Sheriff, we can't run." So then he said, "Would you at least put your people back on the bus and pull the bus down and give us a chance to try to contain them?" I just knowed they was not containable at that point. Nothing but my blood—would quench their evil thirst. I said, "Okay, I'll put them on the bus and we'll pull down. But you got to understand we're going to get off and finish this march in this county today."

"You going to get these people killed."

"Well, I don't want to get nobody killed. But we can't run."

So we got on the bus and pulled the bus down about half a mile. I felt certain the sheriff was back there trying to contain the rioters. We open the door and the sheriff standing there. Now that sheriff was *serious* then. He was not jiving. That man was shaking like a leaf on a tree if he'll ever admit it. I believe they had set us up to keep us out of that county. I'm convinced just as sure as hell the majority of people that beat us up in Prince George were *articulated,* many brought and paid by a little small white power structure clique to make sure blacks don't get enough nerve to come back to that county. Keep that land. It has an unusual *absorbent* value. Anyway, here's the sheriff.

"Don't get off this bus, you going to git this people killed. They coming! They coming!"

"That's *your* problem!"

You know, I figured if Doctor King could die and Malcolm X and many others, at least we could march in Prince George! If we have to take a beating, then take it.

"Don't get them off the bus!"

That fool sheriff thought he had somehow tricked us back onto the bus. He thought we was going to ride away with our tails between our legs. I could see the mob was get closer. We got off that bus. Honest and truth, the sheriff said, "Come on!" He begun to leading the march, hot-footing it up the highway!

"Sheriff, you can *jog* if you want to, but we're going to walk *in Prince George County today*!"

I started everybody to singing and we made it to the place where the sheriff had chosen for us to terminate our march. By this time, several of the protesters had jumped in their cars and made it down where we was. The sheriff says, "All right, you done had your march, then get them back onto the bus and get out of here." I says, "No, no. No, Sheriff. We're not running." I started to say like "Gimme liberty or gimme death and I'm American and this is America." He was just screaming and flagellating and waving his arms. I said, "No, but I got a speech all prepared." The sheriff said, "A speech!? A speech!?" I said, "I know a black man have not spoken in this county in seventy-five years. But this one black man is going to speak in this county today. If it costs me my life, I'm making my speech."

Well, the speech wasn't no more than ten or fifteen minutes. The hoodlums was swarming around us. I could see the local fire chief giving us the nasty sign. But it looked like some of the blaze had went out of them. They hadn't run us off. They couldn't kill us in the broad daylight with the press watching.

We got on the bus and we started back. We all sat there for a long time in a kind of silent shock. We had to contemplate what we'd just come through. We had to absorb what we'd just done. I set there, my head aching and my knee busted all up and I started laughing and some of them says, "Reverend, what's the matter?" I said, "Them's some *bad white folks.* They're bad."

I started thinking as the bus drove along, I had such a glorious feeling to come over me. Such a wonderful feeling, such a rewarding feeling. I started laughing again. I mean I was cracking up.

"You know, I can just see old Doctor King up there in heaven. I bet he's just tickled to death. I could see him nudging Gandhi saying, "Look down there in Prince George County. It's not all over! They're still on the march to freedom; they're still waging the holy war to make the dream come true." I just could see him laughing. I said he probably told Gandhi to ask Jesus would he get off the throne for just a little while and observe what's going on in Prince George County. I said to myself, "We can be pleased now because we have adequately celebrated the birthday of the King."

We came on back home, leg aching, head aching, and I was watching television and we have that old song, "I Ain't Going to Let Nobody Turn Me Around." The news came on and it said that Reverend Hezekiah Thomas and his contingent was run out of Prince George. Which we wasn't.

I caught Cheryl's eye. I said, "I got to go back. We didn't make it plain. I got to go back." Cheryl closed her eyes and said, "Lord, come for Thy world," and walked out of the room.

No, I got to go back. They can never feel that they frightened us into giving up our constitutional right. The United States Supreme Court ruled back in the late fifties that peaceful demonstration was a matter of free speech. One of the greatest freedoms we enjoy in this country. I said I got to go back. I said I got to go back to Prince George County. I began to try to call around and drum up some support. I'm like this. If I think I'm right I'm going to do it. If it costs me my life, then that was the price I was supposed to pay because I certainly couldn't live—that old saying, "Before I'll be your slave I'll be buried in my grave and go home to God and be free," I live that. Doctor King lived that. He taught me that. He'd preach like hell on Sunday morning. But unlike other preachers, come Monday he's out in the streets making that sermon become a living reality, blowing breath into that sermon. I'm just like that. I don't want to go back to Prince George. But every county in America is my home, and I have just as much right to march in Prince George County, Alabama, as I do in Washington, D.C., and I'm not going to let them take that right from me.

Well, now, my old mama, she was settin' across the den watching me rant and capitulate. And my pitiful excuse for a sister Dereesa setting on the couch eating cereal from a serving bowl with her dyed red hair on curlers the size of soup cans. The two of them looking at me crossways like they do when they think I lost my mind. Dereesa says, "Well, brother, you select your tombstone before you go." I admit it. I turned ugly. I said, "Sister, you got a nerve to sit up in my house, eating my food and talking to me like that."

I was wrong. Dereesa had every right. She's my sister and nobody ever became as trifling and poor boned as Dereesa without some help from life. She wasn't her fault and I knew it. She let my remark pass.

It got as quiet as a well bottom. Then Mama said, "He's going, Dee. If there's anything left in us, we're going with him."

64

Heath

I had rented a room from an old man down in Yellow who either didn't know who I was or needed my money so badly he didn't care. I was lying on the bed watching the news coverage. I had a cut on my chin and a bruise under my right eye. No use pretending otherwise, my head hurt. I felt dizzy when I got up or sat down too fast. I was shaky like I was coming down with a cold or the flu. But it wasn't the flu. It was the eyes of the crowd. It was the voices of people I'd known all my life, friends and cousins and former teachers, even that Pentecostal preacher who had befriended me the summer I got religion, condemning me, wishing me dead.

I had thought of myself a kind of David against Goliath. But my slingshot hadn't worked. The great ugly giant had proven his power over me. Prince George would never change. It would go on forever, an impenetrable fortress of ignorance and fear, a godless corner of creation to be shunned by all decent people.

What had overwhelmed me that afternoon was the size of the crowd. In spite of what I wanted to believe, the Klan was somehow rekindling strength. I had expected fifty, maybe seventy-five old diehards out there. I had believed until that afternoon that because *I* had changed the world had changed. It wasn't so.

I was stunned by some of the faces I saw in that crowd. Like my daddy. I didn't figure the man for a flaming liberal. But I thought he was above hurtling rocks and bottles at his own son.

Something whizzed by my head. Then I heard a thud. A bullet had made a perfect little round hole in the window. The pane didn't shatter, but the mirror on the opposite wall did. I dove for the floor and I waited. I peered out into the yard. Nobody. Nothing. Mist and blue streetlamp, my truck. No footsteps fading on gravel, no neighbor's dog barking, no engine starting. Nothing intruded on the quiet. I sat in the dark on the floor. I didn't know if I was awake or asleep, if some phantom was screaming in my head.

At last I understood Michael England's fear. Like me he must have lulled himself into the belief that if he stood against their ignorance, the light of truth would somehow dissolve it. Like me he had come face-to-face with their dark power. Like him, I finally accepted that I had to leave them their dominion over that cursed corner of God's earth. I had to grant a certain wisdom to his fear. Like Michael England I had followed my heart to the edge of a cliff. It was time to turn around, to surrender to the shadowed ignorance and superstition that had overpowered me.

I woke up around three A.M. It was raining hard. It was cold. Something swirled blue in the darkness. At first I thought it was the fear. Then it started to roll like maybe cigarette smoke. It was too sad to be an angel. It wasn't of this world. If I had to give it a name, I'd call it the sum of human failure. I was alone and afraid in the dark and the rain. I was afraid. The fear had won. There was no point in trying to sleep. So I rattled around pulling the sum of my worldly possessions into a pile. I had to wait out the rain before I could put my things into the back of the truck. I had no idea where I was going or how I'd get there. But that's my life in a nutshell. It quit raining around seven. I dried the truck bed as best I could with an old sheet. I was loading up the last of it when I heard the phone ringing.

"Lawler?" It was the reverend. "You alive?"

I said I was.

"Lawler, we got to do it again."

I thought he was kidding.

"We're going to let the grass work on this one. We're going to get organized. We're going to put the word out. We're going to go at it slowly and carefully. Then we're going back to Prince George with the Army of the Lord!"

Neither one of us said anything for a minute. Then he cleared his throat.

"Lawler, you're in, ain't you?" He sounded tired. He sounded old. "Lawler, I need you."

For the first time in my life I understood the terrible price of faith. The faithful do not work on with any surety or comfort. The faithful merely continue in darkness and fear and disillusionment. They continue on without hope, past reason. The burden they carry is their fear. Their belief is no more than the actions they carry out.

I heaved into a wave of nausea. I swallowed hard.

"Yeah, Rev, I'm in."

65

Rose of Sharon

She's different. I try to let her know she can talk about it. But I don't force the subject. She must not be ready. Something is broken in her. It's not just physical weakness. Those bullets went a long way. They exposed her heart and soul to the open air. She's gaining strength. Her voice is back. But the restlessness is gone out of it. She's calm. It's because she's living on past her worst fear.

A brother from California showed up to claim Michael's body. He didn't talk to either one of us. The clerk down in the morgue said he was the imperious type. He made fun of her Texas accent. He barked orders at everyone. He made it abundantly clear that Michael was the black sheep of that family. He acted like they had always expected Michael to come to no good end. That's a big cover over something. But what we'll never know.

I've given routine to my days. Very early in the morning I dawdle along the beach. The dark gray water turns pink and then slowly deepens into blue green as the sun rises. Eight o'clock I take my breakfast in the motel coffee shop. I've been here ten days now. I'm practically a regular. Helena knows just when to pull my toast. Nine-thirty, I'll call Mother.

I learned how to get to the hospital on the bus. But, if it's pretty, I walk. It takes about forty minutes. I generally stop off at the bookshop in the next block. Lily is one voracious reader.

It's all but over, though. She's walking up and down the corridors now. She's in the chair most of the day. Thursday or Friday at the latest, she'll be out of there. There was no question about where she'd go. I'm taking Lily home with me and Mother for the next while. She's got to sort out the rest of her life. She said she'd go straight on back to the lake house. She asked me to find her a live-in care giver for a few weeks. But I wouldn't hear of it.

In the first place, she doesn't need to be by herself with a strange care giver at a time like this. Sad to say I think Mother and I are all that stands between her and universal estrangement. Not that I have anybody except Mother and she's breaking.

66
Eula Pearl

It felt like Rose stayed down in Texas three forevers. I really thought she'd gone down there to bring a corpse home. But something wasn't ready to let go of Lillian. Dashnell's nephew called over here three or four nights ago. I thought it was Rosie checking in when the phone rang. He told me who he was. If I'm remembering straight, he's that little towheaded one we called "Spit-in-the-Pants" the time we went up to the state park for the Lawler Gathering. I had no earthly business out there eating their food. I never ran with any Lawlers and it was not my intention that my daughter would become one. There is a lot of whiskey put back in that family. Near about all of them have seen the inside of a jail one time or another. Anyhow, I remembered the boy because he and Carmen stayed out on the lake in a rowboat until after dark and some of the men had to go out to find them.

He asked about Lillian. I've begun to feel like Lillian Central out here. Half the town has called to ask about her. I'd like to say they called from charity, but she's a big topic in these parts and everybody is just trying to stay up on the latest. I believe Heath was the only one to ask for an address and a room number. I told him Rose was down there and he sounded genuinely glad. I don't know what the connections are. But it pleased me that any Lawler has a positive feeling towards Rose of Sharon. Them people stick together. They're Lawler right or wrong types.

I had talked to Rose of Sharon earlier that afternoon and she had said, barring unforeseen complications, Lily was going to be out of the hospital by the weekend. Like I say, I don't know what the connection is, but there must be one because I could feel Heath Lawler grin on the other end of the line when I told him that. Then I told him that Rose of Sharon is going to bring Lillian home to recuperate with us awhile. He mentioned that he's handy and he'd noticed we're doing things around the place. I told him I keep as far out of all that as I possibly can, but I'd sure mention it to Rose of Sharon when she come in.

I've been starching sheets all morning. I threw three blackberry pies. I tried my pound cake, but it wouldn't rise. It came out gooey. It's too humid. But the fact is I like it that way. I can make a good supper out of a bowl of Jell-O stirred up into fallen pound cake. It killed my soul, but with Rose and a guest expected here home, I had to let Nadine take me to the Winn Dixie. My cupboards are groaning.

I hear tell Lillian's so thin you could read the newspaper through her. I can get back there in my kitchen and cook my way with Rose gone. Though I can't find half my things and I'm not used to hers. So, me and Nadine was in the Winn Dixie, which takes me a year anyway. But Nadine had to talk to everybody in the place. She went to telling everybody that Rose of Sharon was bringing Lillian back. Two or three of the women came right up and said to my face they wouldn't allow such an immoral woman in their houses. One of them said Lillian was half the cause of the trouble coming and Heath Lawler was the other half. I had no earthly idea to what they were referring. But I haven't heard people speak of "the Trouble" in that way since the night this county nearly burned to the ground more than seventy years ago. I wouldn't ask neither. Not with Rose of Sharon being criticized for helping somebody out. As Searle used to say, that's Christianity Prince George County style. If you ever want to see evil, then you watch Nadine and that pack from her church running somebody down with their mealy jaws barely opening and their heads bobbing and their little hands waving with their fingers pressed together.

But it stirred things, them saying "the Trouble." I got up twice in the night thinking I'd heard my back door slam. Finally I went to peeling apples and I made a cobbler. Who in the New Jerusalem is going to eat all this food?

Those women up at the Winn Dixie was riled. They're working up to something evil and you can almost feel it spreading up and down the road here. Like a bad wind gathering before it blows. I thought Rose would be home by now. The paper said they had storms over Texas this morning. I warmed supper twice. The rolls went so hard I had to run a fresh batch in the oven. I'm so brittle with worry I feel like I'm going to snap in two. But I dare not show any effects of it when she walks in that door. You don't worry about Rose to her face. She's at that in between age where people think they can handle life all by themselves.

67

Heath

She was out in the yard taking some air and sunshine and talking to Aunt Rose, who was dividing monkey grass along the front sidewalk. She was wearing a gray cloth coat and her hair was covered in a scarf. It was sunny, but it was still right chilly. She looked different. For all she'd been through, she looked younger. At first I thought it was because I'd never seen her without her makeup. But the change ran much deeper than that. She cried when she saw me the way people who have been through a trauma or a death will cry when they see you the first time after. I held her for a long time. I cried too.

Hers were tears of remorse. Mine were tears of joy. I hadn't counted on being that close to her again. It was a passing moment, but it reminded me why I had made such an ass out of myself over her. I didn't want that to show. I didn't want it to add to her consternation. She needed my support more than she needed my love. The longer I stood there the more I knew that it had been a mistake to come. I would never stop loving her. Sooner or later it was bound to show.

"Are you trembling?"

I just shrugged and smiled nervously. Aunt Rose had managed to slip off around the side of the house without either one of us noticing. Aunt Rose can be the most weightless, practically invisible woman on earth when she chooses.

"Walk with me."

"Are you able?"

"Can't exactly lift weights yet. But I walked half a mile yesterday."

We had passed a hundred yards up the road. I didn't know what to say, so I told her all about plans for the march the Saturday after next. She had wrapped her fingers around mine and I was trying to keep from holding them too tightly. Every now and then she'd give mine a little squeeze. She thought I had come back to her with the love of a brother or a friend. I knew I could never love her that way alone. My heart couldn't bear it. I couldn't tell her. I wanted to run away. It started to sprinkle. We crossed the road and stood in Miss Eula Pearl's deserted peanut stand.

"Heath? Do you know why I came back here to White Oak?"

"No, Lily, I don't." I really didn't. Coming back here was deliberately slapping herself in the face with a lot of people and things she'd be better off to forget.

"I had to see you. I had to explain why I hurt you."

"Done is done, Lil."

"You're all over me?"

"In a manner."

"I see."

I didn't have a clue what I was saying. I was just trying to crawl my way from moment to moment. I couldn't help it. I had to ask her.

"Why, then? Why did you hurt me?"

"I was afraid of you."

"You mean you thought I might do something crazy, pick a fight with Glen or tell the wrong person about us or . . . ?

"I was afraid if you knew how much I loved you, how much I was really beginning to want to be with you, I was afraid you'd use that against me."

A thrill went through me when I heard those words but I didn't trust myself to say more than "Why would I do that?"

"I didn't say you would. I said I was afraid you would."

"But why?"

"You weren't like other men I've known, Heath. You talked to me. I mean way down inside me. When you made love to me, I could tell you wanted to please me as much as yourself. You thought you loved me."

"I did love you."

"But you got over me. If I hadn't pulled back when I did, I would have lost my mind over you."

"I don't understand!" I was practically yelling. It was like sirens wailing in my ears. I couldn't stand much more of it. I was going to have to take off running and leave her there. Or I was going to turn into a sobbing pile of jelly.

"You're a prince and you don't know it. Your nails could use a trim and your grammar isn't always the best. You haven't found yourself. But you're a prince."

I don't think I could have guessed in a million years where she was heading with all that.

"I'm a stupid redneck who wears his heart on his sleeve. I'm a convicted thief and to this day I'm not positive which fork you use for the salad."

"No! No!"

It was a scene. I was bawling. She was shaking me.

"You wanted more than my body, Heath. You wanted more than a prop for your ego. You listened when I talked. You made me feel worthwhile."

"Michael England didn't?"

"Michael England pretended he did long enough to teach me what he liked in bed." Now she was crying. "Michael England and Glen in his way and every other man who ever touched me all the way back to my daddy."

Oh, man. I'll never forget it. The rain was slicing across in front of us like sheets of tin. The words would slide up my neck and then stick at the back of my mouth. I was fighting for breath. I hope I never experience that kind of helpless panic again.

"Lily . . ." I was all hoarse. I was seeing swirling things. "Oh, God, Lily, I love you."

She went so pale it scared me. Her mouth froze half open. I thought she was dying for a second. She started crying again. She was covering me with kisses, pulling on my hair, weeping and smiling and telling me she loved me. It may have been a flash of lightning. But it was like some celestial switch was sudden thrown open and a beacon shone on the world. We just stood there until the rain was gone and it was fully dark, holding each other, stunned and stupefied by the miracle.

68

Lily

This was late on a Thursday afternoon. It was going to rain again. You could cut the air with a knife. It was a patch of weird, warm weather that had strayed off the Caribbean and drifted up over Alabama, making it feel like summer on another planet. Rosie was inside dressing quail. I was out on the porch with Miss Eula. I was sitting close to the door half-listening for the phone. Heath was in Birmingham working with the reverend on plans for the second march. I was expecting him to call. Rosie had turned the dirt around the shrubs by the porch after lunch. The wet earth made the world smell new.

It had been a February afternoon with the false promise of spring in the thick buds. The closer it came to dusk, the warmer it got. It gave everything an end of the world feeling. Now there were purple clouds threatening. Several flocks of starlings had passed over. Miss Eula was sewing fringe on the most beautiful hand hooked rug you ever saw. She called it her "Oriental," but in truth it displayed a story from her childhood. An accomplished woman like Miss Eula always makes me feel like hell. I couldn't knit a pair of booties. No patience with it. Rosie told me Miss Eula started that rug the week Eisenhower was inaugurated the first time. But her greatest gift is her ability to disappear and listen in a way that invites the speaker to go on. I was running back over things half to myself.

"I'll see blood in my dreams for a long time to come. I'll see Glen and his gun when he isn't there. I'll walk into a department store and catch the scent of jasmine soap and think of Michael. They can't stitch your soul back together."

"You have to do that for yourself," Miss Eula said, drawing and twisting the silk cord.

"You get stuck on the way life can splinter in a second. You can forget it falls back in place almost as quick if you let it. If you love it. If you're grateful for it. She's a hateful old witch, my mama, but she was right when she said I was born thankless. I've started to learn a little about gratitude in recent days." I was spinning between hope and regret, trying to put a placid face on things.

A car pulled into the driveway. Rose stepped into the parlor and peered through the glass curtains to see who it was. Rosie stepped in from the kitchen. She and Miss Eula shared a look. It might have only been a second. But I'd swear their eyes were locked for an hour. It was like they were stuck on electricity. I could only assume it meant something bad. Rosie raised her arms and pulled her fingers back in a way that said it's all right. She walked out on the porch.

Something was passing before us. I glanced at Miss Eula, and for half a second I imagined she was young, no more than a girl. There was a distant streak of lightning. Rosie and her mama are charmed. Something invisible and silent had suddenly begun to swirl around us. (When I told Heath later he said it was probably electricity in the air. Oh, I says, rolling my eyes, is that all?) Rosie moved down the front steps.

The driver's door of the car swung open. It was getting dark. You couldn't see inside the car. You couldn't tell who it was. But as that door opened, a circle or a cloud or a big spot of clear purple like a blob in front of your eye from a sudden bright light, hung suspended over the two women as they stood there conversing. I blinked, but it was still there. Miss Eula stood up and pointed at it. Rosie turned back to her mama for half a second, silently acknowledging that she saw it too.

She was a tall, thin dignified looking black woman in a tailored suit. Her hair was silver and she wore it in a page boy. She handed Rose a folded piece of paper. It was the round watermelon colored stationery that Rose had kept by her stove up on the lake for grocery lists and phone messages.

Rose threw her arms around the woman and the two of them stood there crying. I looked to Miss Eula for an interpretation or sign of what appropriate action should be taken. She was cutting a bundle of silk threads for next installment of fringe.

The lady got into her car and drove off. Rose walked back up the steps and into the house. I waited a long time for Miss Eula to say something. She looked to be traveling time as Rosie calls that expression she wears before she starts one of her stories from the dim, dark past. Finally, when I couldn't stand it any longer, I broke the silence, "Miss Eula, is everything all right?"

"The Trouble is back," she said, using her eyeteeth to cut a strand of thread.

69
Rose of Sharon

Mother took to Lily right off. I knew she would. Mother likes frank people. I admit I spent the first day or two trying to make everything smooth between them, monitoring their conversations at the breakfast table when I had other things to do. They caught on to what I was doing and shut me out. I had no call to hover around them waiting for one of them to snap or bark. There's a good deal of conversation and a lot of laughter between those two. Lily reminds Mother that she had her day. Mother even dug out an ancient picture of herself from one summer when she had peroxided her hair. I had never seen it or known that my mother went through some blond years. Mother reminds Lily that she's a good person. She understands how deeply Lily longs to believe that about herself.

Late Thursday afternoon I was in the kitchen dressing two quail that Nadine had brought to us. Sidney likes to shoot them, but he doesn't eat them. Nadine can't bring herself to touch their carcasses. They don't thrill me, but the only thing more senseless to me than hunting is letting the game go to waste. It was ponderously warm for February. It's weather you can't trust. Invariably a sudden rush of cold wind will drop the thermometer thirty degrees in ten minutes and the sky will drop and, apt as not, you'll have ice and snow by morning.

I was looking out the window over the sink. The sun had dropped behind the trees and the sky was orange. *I heard the undertaker's wagon pull into the front yard.* I didn't pause to ponder what specific sounds a funeral wagon makes. I didn't hold myself back a minute to realize that I had never seen or heard a funeral wagon. I wasted no time considering that even if I had ever seen one, it wouldn't make a sound that would identify it. Nor did I bother to remember that the last horse drawn wagon of any type had disappeared from these parts twenty-five years ago. I untied my apron and walked into the parlor and peered out the window to see who was dead. Mother and Lily were looking too.

There was a red Buick on the driveway. I didn't remember it at first. I looked at Mother and she looked at me. We were silently asking each other who it was, but neither of us knew. I went on outside and down the steps and approached the car. I figured it was someone asking directions.

Mrs. Smith got out of her Buick. She had changed her hair since then. She was also dressed for an occasion. It didn't dawn on me until weeks later that she had dressed for this specific occasion. Mrs. Smith was taking a monumental step. She reached into her purse and took out a folded piece of paper. It looked oddly familiar. Then I realized it was just like paper I used to keep beside my stove.

The note was written in Dashnell's left handed scratch. *Next time you show your black ass up here on this lake—you die.* She said her husband had brought it home from his next to last fishing trip up on the lake. It was written proof of Dashnell's intent to kill that man, the missing piece of evidence the law needed to charge and convict him.

"Why have you brought this to me?"

I knew why. She knew I knew why. The only other place to take it was the Alabama Bureau of Investigation. If Mrs. Smith placed it there in the wrong hands, it would dissolve like mist into the sunrise.

"Are you planning to play the fool your entire life?" It was a true, clean voice, but it wasn't hers and it wasn't inside my head. I glanced around at Mother and she looked at me as if she'd heard it too. Lily looked scared.

I asked Mrs. Smith to come inside. She cocked her head towards the fading sun and said she'd best get out of Prince George. She got back into her car and started the motor. I watched her back out. I walked back inside the house. I went back into the kitchen and finished dressing those quail.

70
Eula Pearl

If it moves at all, time travels in circles. More likely it just hovers, tucking itself between the attic eaves or hiding in the woods. It doesn't march straight on and on and on unbending like they showed it in that historical chart that sat above the blackboard when I was in school.

You live a day in a certain spot, and you wait in that spot long enough, and you'll find yourself back in that day. All the weeks separating then and now pile up in that place until the present whirls and whirs into a spear that breaks it open.

Like Thursday last.

Last Thursday I opened my eyes and the bed was still warm where Hattie had lain beside me seventy years ago. No matter that Searle had slept there several decades in between. It was Hattie. It wasn't just the general warmth of Hattie long ago. It was the day we buried Wee Mother, the morning after the horses ran the road all night and smoke hung thick in the trees. *I could just make out her lavender scent and the soft roar of the crowd downstairs in the parlor. A giant odor of tuber roses met me at the top of the stairs. The sky was a deep gray veil through the front door glass. Underneath there was a green copper cast that bore watching. Across the road I could see the charred ruins of Moena's house. There was an angel in the tall grass by the ditch. She had come to bring Wee Mother her wings and lead her to Pastures of Glory.*

Thursday last, as clean as the eye of God, while Rose of Sharon and Lily was still in bed asleep, I dropped back to that terrible day. I was in it. I have outlived all use for my religion. I was never a deep believer and never one for spells or enchantments. I never visited a fortune-teller or took a thing for a celestial sign the way so many of these blind fools around here do. But this is no illusion. *I was alone in the parlor with Wee Mother, telling her good-bye.*

I have revisited that day a thousand times since I first passed through it. It was the morning after the end of a world. The Trouble had erupted full blown across the land. I return and I study that day while I relive it. It has more dimension than ordinary memory. The odor of death and tuber roses, the fear in Moena's eyes. I would rather think that it's only a burdensome memory like sitting in that stifling Baptist church crammed with oily haired Lawler men and puffy Lawler women in cheap dresses with babies on their laps watching Rose of Sharon marry into a life of regret.

Now that stops me because the impossible came to pass there the day Rose of Sharon slammed the door on that remorseful existence and came home and made me ashamed that I gave up on her. Time, that undefined thing that moves us around and back, made an exception and crept perceptibly forward when she did that.

But the terrible day I experience is neither imagined nor remembered. It rattles there like one of Wee Mother's Dresden cups when a semi lumbers past trying to avoid the weigh station on the other side of town. It's a confounding experience as mysterious to me as life itself. In my younger days I considered discussing it with someone. I thought maybe a minister or a doctor of some kind. I still held some hope the thing could be explained away. But then one time maybe five years ago I slipped back to the day. *The roses on the parlor walls were dripping, oozing purple and red spots that rolled into nothing on the carpet. There was a lake where the road had been and the branches of the trees melted into fountains. Across the road smoke billowed from the ashes of Moena's house. Behind it in the fields there were clusters of the unhappy dead driven by the shame of blood on the land. The dead were moaning beneath the curse that come in the night and unhallowed their ground. They were abandoning us, severing us from the rightful order of time and place, dropping us here to live out the blight that had come in the darkness. I turned away from the window and looked through the long skirts and the muddy shoes towards Wee Mother in her casket and I saw the lady smile. This that I'm about to tell is a sacred truth. The lady was the Angel on the Road and the Angel was Rose of Sharon. Her smile drove a beam of light into my heart and it drew up tight like a fist of hope that became the will that keeps me clinging to this life.*

It was a day of great sadness and shame. It was a day that tilted all the days that came after in a darker direction. But it brought me the hope of illumination through the light of my Angel Rose. It promised healing and redemption through the child who would replace me on this earth.

Listen to me. Listen! I am not godly or sworn to Jesus. But this is real and has to be told, especially now with the Trouble returning, the threat of more blood and darkness looming. The angels are gathering for the battle. I hear myself telling you this and think, "Gibbering Fool, hush! Fall into your trance and die." O God, I have come through this life the longest and the deepest way, let me rest!

Rose of Sharon had told me that Lily is wild about country ham. I had one desalting in a washtub by the back door. Last Thursday. I have to concentrate or I'll be off again. Or was it Florence who loved country ham? *Florence's wedding day! We had copper skies then too. Red purple swirls over the front yard. Some of the Birmingham cousins called us country because we served country ham. If that insulted Mother, she never let on. Or maybe she was too upset to notice. Florence was marrying a Republican, no small grief in our house at that time.*

But this ham was Thursday. It was too warm and close and a violent sky threatened. I'd been soaking the ham in a washtub two days. I stepped out into the yard to run the hose into the tub and cleanse the water of the salt. Then Nadine showed up with fresh killed quail. Rosie took them inside to dress them. I was set on cooking that ham, but I've learned to go with a day when it does me like that. The ham would wait. The quail wouldn't unless we froze it. I've had iris bulbs in the freezer forty years waiting for me to plant them.

The ham water was still drawing brine. That ham needed another day's soak and two or three more hard rinses. I let it be and pulled my Oriental out and went to stringing fringe. Lily watched me fascinated like I was turning straw to gold.

It was drawing up on suppertime. Lily was beside me. She's a fine girl and my only regret is that it took so much sorrow to bring her to our house. Time was dripping down over us, beading up silently like an ice storm in the night.

Mother stood by the door watching for the funeral wagon to carry Wee Mother down to the church. She was real held together. I think it was part relief that Wee Mother's suffering was over and part exhaustion from being with Mrs. Brown all night.

"Ya'll want me to cook this quail?" That was Rose of Sharon in the kitchen. She forgets I can't wait that long to eat. If it gets past five o'clock, I get over being hungry. A car pulled into the driveway. Rose of Sharon came into the parlor to peer out at it. I glanced around from my chair on the porch to look at her, long enough for her to catch the faraway look on my face. Rose knew I was experiencing back time. *Mother was fussing because it looked like rain and the undertaker had been so long bringing the wagon.* Rose of Sharon stepped towards the door *where Mother was standing* and I saw her step back a little so as not to walk directly into Mother as she walked out onto the porch. Her eyes froze on mine, asking me for confirmation. I nodded. She'll get it a little along—same as I drew it out of my mother as she aged. The dead and the past are always with us. The past has unfinished business which some in the living present are chosen to complete. This I have come to accept without formal indoctrination. The past is as inescapable as death. It presents itself to us and our salvation comes when we endeavor set it to rights. This was told to me by my mother. This I hold sacred above all other tenets. As Rose of Sharon moved past me and descended the porch steps, I saw that she was crossing over to receive her duty out of time.

A Buick had just pulled into the driveway. I don't know cars, but I can always tell a Buick. A black woman, well dressed and quietly determined, got out of the car. There had not been a black human being on this property in seventy years. I saw its meaning at once. The Day of the Trouble was coming back. Lily looked at me as if she was seeing a ghost. Rose took a folded sheet of paper from the woman. In a minute the woman got back into her car and drove off. Rose went on back inside. Lily asked me if anything was wrong. I don't know what I said. I was perspiring like the Fourth of July.

Rose did what she always does when a thing passes before her, changing everything. She went on as if nothing had happened, dressing quail, folding a load of dish towels and starting supper. It seemed best to give her berth, so I went on into my bedroom and switched on the news. It was close, almost hot, so I opened a window. When I looked out into the backyard I saw Lily standing at the very edge, staring down through the orchard into the pasture. I stood there a minute, watching the orange sky darken through the apple trees. It wasn't just my room. A wall of warm air nearly knocked me down when I opened that window. Through the door that leads to the hall there came the sound of the kitchen window fan starting up. Lily heard it too. She turned around and eyed the house. She had removed her sweater. She held it in her hand. In a minute she saw me and approached my bedroom window.

"Weird," she said referring to the sudden warmth and eyeing me the way the young will look to the old for an explanation or an accounting.

"Mother?" Rose had entered my room. She was standing behind me. Sweat was dripping off her forehead. "What's going on?"

I told her I didn't know. It felt like August before a storm.

"Y'all!" Lily shouted. Behind her the tall dead pasture grass had begun to bend and a hot wind was blowing up out of the woods, shaking the bramble and the weeds in the consecrated patch that had once been a cemetery. Lily took out for the house and as she did a streak of pure white lightning split an apple tree fifty yards behind her. The wind was so warm and dry that it lifted patches of wet earth and spun them into little cyclones. Dust was beginning to fly.

"It's like January in hell," Rose said as the windows started to rattle and the curtains flew up in my face. There wasn't a cloud of any mentionable size anyplace. The air was screaming now. It choked us. A sudden hail slammed against the house, cracking windows and hissing like a thousand serpents on the roof. Then in a minute, like we had imagined the whole incident, all was stillness and the air was cool.

Lily came into my room.

"What the hell . . . ?"

"Weather pocket," Rose said as if she had seen one before. It was feeble, but it was more explanation than I could offer.

"I thought it was the end of time," Lily said. Then she giggled, sinking onto the bed.

"Miss Eula," she says, "your eyes were as big as teacups," and then she laughed proper. Rose either thought that was hilarious or she needed an excuse to laugh, because she squealed, bending double. That set me tittering. The three of us sat on the edge of my bed and laughed and laughed until it was pitch dark and the melted hail on the yard was working itself back up into a light frost.

Later Rose made us toasted cheese sandwiches and popcorn. We ate off our laps in the parlor which had gotten so chilly that we lit the new gas logs. I generally want the lamps bright, but that night we kept them low and the light reminded me of how it felt when I was a child. Or maybe it was that Rose and Lily were like children that night. They wanted stories. So I told them about the Trouble, some of which Rose had heard and some I only remembered as I spoke. It was late when we went to bed. I closed my eyes thinking something had shifted, something was better or accepted or completing itself. Something had slipped back into the house after a long, bleak absence. Maybe it was love or laughter or my imagination. It seemed to me that a good life was being lived there again. Or that it would be. Or that things would be as mysterious and troublesome as ever, but all right. Just before I nodded off, I heard

Rose slip down the hall and into the living room to turn off the gas logs.

Rose stuck her head in my room to say good-night. I asked her what that woman on the driveway had given her.

"The keys to the kingdom," she says. Even later when I knew what the note meant, I didn't really understand her words. Some time after it dawned on me. She hadn't meant those words as some mean personal triumph over Dashnell. That woman had given Rose the means to end the spell of evil that had laid on this land since that Sunday my grandmother lay a corpse in the parlor. Thursday last and that evil Sunday more than seventy-five years ago had blended into one.

71
Hezekiah

It raveled. The thing just raveled. The news story helped. As quick as Hez put out the word he was going back to Prince George, he had several dozen calls—half of them white people—all them declaring themselves ready, willing and able to march in Prince George County with him. That was Monday morning. Monday afternoon the wire services grabbed hold of it. CBS News ran footage of the Klanspeople tossing bricks and bottles at the first marchers. The next day there were pictures on the front page of every major paper in the country. *The Atlanta Constitution* ran a headline: "American Apartheid!" If Doctor King had descended from heaven, stood on a mountaintop and proclaimed this march a new covenant, there would not have been a bigger reaction.

Tuesday morning rained phone calls. Hez and Heath had three churchwomen helping out the receptionist. They gave five interviews Tuesday afternoon. By that evening, Heath called the phone company and had five extra lines installed.

The governor called around one o'clock. He flew up from Montgomery to meet with Hez and Heath the next morning. They were expecting five thousand marchers by now. They wanted state patrol protection. They wanted the head of the Prince George County sheriff turned around and inside out. They wanted the Klan out of the state on Saturday morning. The governor, who had just fielded a phone call from the White House about the upcoming march, was more than willing to comply with their requests.

It raveled and it raveled and it raveled. Money started pouring in on Wednesday morning, one, two, ten thousand dollars to pay for buses and banners and everything else they were going to need. Hez took phone calls from movie stars and senators and UN delegates. Area hotels were booking up. Rental car desks were selling out. Suddenly, it was as if the whole damned world had put their heads together and said it was time to whip Prince George County's butt. They were expecting a special train from New York City. A group was flying in from Sweden.

Thursday morning, Hez called back over to the governor's office and advised him to prepare for enough troops to protect twenty thousand marchers. The Guardian Angels wired from New York to say they were coming. By Thursday afternoon, the giddiness was wearing thin. Hez and Heath were trying to plan portable johns and bus service to Prince George and meeting with crowd control experts. They called the governor and secured advance National Guard troops to flush through the area in case of snipers. They arranged food vendors and emergency medical services until late Friday night.

He got home around one A.M. Moena was sitting at the kitchen table. He pulled a hot plate of ribs out of the microwave and sat across from her. She asked him why he was so late. It made him feel sixteen.

"Plans for the march."

Moena knew all about it. She had seen it on the news.

"We're all going," she said, stuffing a wad of corn bread into her mouth.

"Who all?"

"Cheryl, the kids, Dereesa, me . . ."

"Mama, you can't march five miles."

"I got a chair. They'll push me."

It didn't make sense. She had never marched before, not even in the big one to D.C. in '63. He'd even begged her that time.

"Why this march?"

" 'Cause we'll be marching home this time."

Hadn't Beauty B., his grandmother dead and gone fifty years, held him as a boy under a pump drawing icy spring water and baptized him in the knowledge of that? Wasn't that the thing she had burned into his mind above all other things? *We was run out of Alabama.* Could Hez name another county in America where a black man in this day and time was so afraid to tread?

Moena had only talked to him about it once before, on that sticky Sunday afternoon they had laid Grandfather in that South Carolina pine grove. She had been a lost and bitter young blind woman then. She was tender as she called it up now.

"Hell come that night," she began. "Hell ascended from the deep and spread around us. I've been in that hell ever since." There were tears in her eyes. They weren't just the overflowing feelings of an old woman whose body had grown too brittle to contain them. They were the aggregate sorrows of one whose entire existence had been twisted into a daily battle to endure sudden, meaningless and cataclysmic loss. It was a grief made more profound by the small well of clear memories of the innocent years that had preceded it.

"You were born into that hell and raised up in it. I knew another time, another way. I came from a place before it. I'm going back to that place in the morning."

This was a woman Hez had never known. This was a child who had lain in the shining yellow grass and given her heart to the wind.

"Tell me about it," he asked. Never had he seen then and now so tightly drawn together. Never had he so clearly understood his private stake in the march they would take in the morning.

She took him back there. She painted shadowed places where children played barefoot in warm silt on August afternoons. Her face glowed as she told him how the newly furrowed land would turn purple and ochre before the March sun sank behind the woods. She taught him the balm of the big people's voices wafting through the screen door washing her drowsy eyes with safe sleep. She told him how you knew which neighbor was passing by the individual rattle of his wagon. She told him where honey was hidden in what tree and how Beauty B. had turned thread into lace and sewn it on sheets and pillowcases and used them to make up her bed the Christmas Eve before the Night of Evil.

She went on like that until she was too tired to talk. She pulled herself up slowly from the table, said good-night and started out of the room.

"Mama?"

"Yes."

"You ever hear Beauty B. now?"

"Beauty B. is the one who brought me back to Alabama. And you're the reason why."

72
Dashnell

Get this, America. I was at home in my own bed sound asleep when two carloads of Alabama State Policemen trespassed on my property, destroyed my personal property in the form of bashing in my front door, stormed into my room and violated my civil rights by forcing me out of bed and handcuffing me and hauling me away without that first Miranda right!

I was held in a cell at the county jail for eleven hours waiting on some goddamned faggot piece of a public defender to get me bailed. Finally, he gets that took care of and I'm released and the son of a bitch wants me to come right over to his office with him so's we can discuss the case. I don't know this guy. He isn't true Prince George. He moved up here from Mobile a few years back on account of his wife is from here and her daddy has money and influence and other vulgarities.

"It looks pretty bad," he says. "Let's start with you telling me everything you did, how you planned it, how it was carried out." I asked him was he working for me or them.

"You mean the prosecution?"

"I mean the antichristian communistic organizations which have chosen Prince George County for the site of a race war."

"Just tell me everything that relates to your specific crime," he says dryly. That told me everything I needed to know about him.

"Man," I says, "man, we got a nigger war headed our way tomorrow and you want me to set up in your office and talk a whole lot of bull crap."

"I have to know everything, Dashnell, including who else is involved."

I says, "Look. Let's us go on up to the Landing and eat some catfish, pass a bottle back and forth between us and I'll illuminate the situation for you." He didn't cotton to the notion, but he come along behind me in his precious fairy faggot BMW. So, we're setting there and I'm getting some nicely peppered purple onion and a hush puppy or two between my teeth and he starts in.

"Let's plead it out," he says. "You agree to tell the DA about the others involved. I explain to the judge that you've requested treatment for advanced alcoholism. With any luck, you won't do more than five years." If I hadn't been so damned hungry, I would've broke my plate over his pointed head. "You just enjoy your meal," I says, "I'll worry about the law."

"This thing is a lot bigger than you think it is, Dashnell. The media has already linked this big march they have planned to the murder of that black man on the lake. The district attorney's office has already received over a hundred letters demanding that justice be carried out."

I figured I'd have some fun with him before I fired him. "Sweetheart," I says, "I didn't kill no black man on no lake."

"You didn't?"

"No, sir. I cleansed the area."

He laid his knife across the top of his plate like a little fairy fay. Then he pulled out his wallet and laid a twenty-dollar bill on the table. He cleaned his teeth with his tongue, wiped his mouth real dainty-fied like and stood up.

"Haven't seen my wife and kids all day. I'll just head home and leave you to seek other representation."

That flew all over me. I jumped to my feet. "Set your pink ass down in that chair and let me give it to you plain."

He remained standing.

"Your father-in-law maintained extremely close ties to the

klavern and supported our activities with generous donations. Obviously you was handpicked by the klavern to represent me. You was assigned to represent a whole hell of a lot more than me. You was assigned to represent the last best hope of the white Christian race of which I am but a symbol and a standard bearer. I ain't pleading out nothing and I sure as hell ain't naming names. I plead innocent. We own that motherfucking courthouse, judge and jury."

He smiled and give off a laugh that wasn't much more than pressed air.

"My father-in-law has been dead for five years. So far the prosecution has in their possession a note in your handwriting threatening to kill the man. This morning I was privileged to read six separate signed statements by members of your almighty damned klavern stating unequivocally that despite their best efforts to stop you, you went out and shot that man in the back. One of that holy bunch of fools handed over the murder weapon with your fingerprints on it. That's premeditated murder, Mr. Lawler, punishable in this state by the electric chair."

Well, I had me a big laugh over that. Because under the front seat of my pickup truck in a plastic bag I keep *The Book of the Order* give to me by my daddy who got it from his daddy who helped to write it in 1911, the year of the First Holy Purgation. If you will read that book, it says quite clear that towards the end of this century Satan will raise up an army of niggers and they will swoop over the land. It further states that "one of our own, little thought of or believed and often mocked and derided, will suffer betrayal. In that dark hour, he will become veiled in purity, possessed of a light and a shield of honor, and he will deliver the white man from the pestilence." That one is me, America!

I let that namby pamby fool walk away. I enjoyed my catfish and hush puppies and ordered an extra bowl of that Landing slaw which has no equal on this earth. I washed it down with good clean bourbon and left my former attorney's twenty on the table to pay for it. I run by the liquor store on the edge of town for some fortification. I had one hell of a night ahead of me.

I swung by the lake to see if there was any lights on in Jake's house, but it was dark as a tomb. I pulled into the Billups station there by the interstate ramp and called Sidney. Nadine, his dried-up witch wife, answered the telephone.

"Sidney there?"

"Who wants to know?"

"Let me talk to Sidney."

"Dashnell?"

"Yeah."

"I heard you was in jail."

"Get Sidney."

"He's not here."

"If he's telling you to say that, Nadine, he better be smiling." I had passed their place on the way out to the lake and seen his truck on the carport. I'll admit it. I broke code there. I threatened a member of the Order. I lost myself and I'm not proud of it. "You tell him I need to talk to him now and if he don't see fit to do so, I'll sing pretty for the ABI." Of course I wouldn't, not in one million years. I have too much character for that.

"Yo, Dashnell." That was Sidney. He's one of the Chosen, but one of the least of the Chosen in my estimation.

"Look here. I need the combination to the arsenal." I didn't have him on the line to talk about the weather.

"Can't do it."

"We got a Code Seven working."

"All activities have been temporarily suspended."

"Why?"

"My supper's getting cold."

Like I believed that at nine-thirty at night. But he hung up. I got a busy signal when I dialed back. A man has to do what a man has to do. I drove back to my house and went into the garage. The electricity had been cut off. It was hard to see, but I found that hacksaw.

I could take you to the arsenal, but I doubt I could direct you there. You go out past the covered bridge on the Indian Road and then you follow three more dirt roads until you run out of houses. It's an uphill path from there, easy enough to find during the day, but next to impossible at night. It's a cabin sitting on what become government property when they went to damming up every stream in this part of Alabama. It took the better part of an hour to saw through that lock. It was four trips up and down that path before I had enough dynamite. I couldn't find a detonator. But I'd worked with a long fuse before.

There's a temporary wooden bridge in a low place surrounded by thick brush and evergreens about a mile outside of town. The old concrete bridge was cracked when a semi overturned on it in an ice storm. A couple floods last spring did the rest. This wood replacement isn't much more than a few dozen railroad ties nailed together. The marchers will be coming over it on their way to town.

Now get this. I got the news in my pickup truck driving over to the Landing to eat catfish with that nervous piece of a nelly-faced lawyer earlier this evening. They got every flaming liberal asshole in the United States coming to be seen in the nigger walk tomorrow. Kennedys and senators and representatives, earls of England, Japanese chinko royalty and movie stars. They'll all be in a pack at the head of the walk, carrying banners and posing for the cameras, showing their fake love of niggers for all the world to see.

I'm no fool. I got myself hid under spotted khaki cloth down here in the shadows. I waded a mile from upstream in my hip boots. It's a sheer thirty-foot drop from the river's edge here. You can't climb down here from the road unless you fling yourself into the water and you'd smash yourself into pieces on the rocks. They'll never find me—not that anybody's looking. That's the beauty of it. Nobody has a clue what I'm doing. There's nobody in this world to know or care of my whereabouts. No one to report me missing or come looking for me. I hid that pickup truck so well that even I might not be able to find it. I'm angled off here where I can see the patrol cars running the march route. But I'm out of the path of their beacons when they slow down to search the water and the banks.

One match, forty sticks of dynamite and all the world is going to see that the Order has been a sleeping giant, a great and mighty force waiting for its place in time. They'll be plenty of press in the vicinity to catch the show. I'm going to give them the finale of their dreams. Hundreds of thousands of decent white men and women the world over will see the work of the Order carried out here and their hope will be renewed. Their hearts will rejoice. They'll send their money and ask where to join. They'll volunteer and rally and unite. They'll take courage from it and pick up their own gauntlets and carry forth the holy work of taking white America back.

Then let's hear what that stupid cunt Rose has to say about me. Then let's see her dry haint skeleton of a mama look at me like I'm a dog turd on her living room rug! Let these turncoat, yellow-spined Brethren of the Local Order brush me off! Because I know what they claim to know. I see what they've blinded themselves to. The Savior of Humanity did not arrive on this earth in no Cadillac. The Savior of Us All hadn't never eat no lunch at no country club. He come into this world in a crummy little stable smelling of horse shit and cow manure. He made himself low down the way some people in these parts love to try to make us Lawlers feel.

But who will they say this time tomorrow lifted the hopes of the white race out of the cesspool of modern liberalism? Who will history record and remember as the one who spread his arms and turned back the tidal wave?

It's a damned pretty world out here tonight by this bridge. Man, I set here and look at the swirling stars and the moon reflecting off the ice in the stream and I see the Kingdom Coming. I know this if I have ever known anything, it's going to be a whole new world in the morning.

73
Heath

I got back up to Miss Eula Pearl's house about ten o'clock that Friday evening. There was nothing left to do. Hez had a hundred volunteer organizers tending to every detail. I figured to spend the night at Miss Eula Pearl's and then drive over to the start point with Rose and Lily in the morning. I had just taken a shower and I was sitting in Miss Eula's living room with Rose and Lily telling them about all the newspaper reporters I'd talked to that day and what all I'd said. Hez and I had made a big show of talking to the press together—him, an old civil rights war-horse and black as Moses, and me, pink faced with yellow wire blond hair and my Alabama red neck.

A Chrysler that was hurting for a new muffler pulled into the driveway and a tall, skinny woman came in the door without knocking. She was dripping in sweat and shaking like a leaf. Rose went out on the front porch with her. In a minute, Rose stuck her head in the door and asked Lily to join them. I went and sat on the porch side of the room to see if could determine what was eating her.

"You're not telling all you know, Nadine." That was Aunt Rose, though her voice had an edge I'd never heard before. "That is all I know," Nadine whined. "If Sidney knew I was over here . . ." I could tell she wasn't kidding. Lillian jumped in at that point to say it was too cold to stand out there on the porch.

In a minute the three of them were sitting in the living room, which Miss Eula calls the parlor.

"What's the trouble, ladies?"

"She says Dashnell called out to her house threatening to blow up the county."

"Why would he call her house?"

"She won't say," Lily cut in.

I knew why. I knew about the arsenal they kept hidden someplace in the woods. Kids in Prince George grow up dreaming about it. They spend whole summer afternoons on their bikes trying to find it. We had all heard that Nadine's husband, Sidney, was the official Keeper of the Arsenal Key. I remember one time when I was about ten. Me and three friends stood in the back of the hardware store not three feet behind Sidney trying to figure which key on his chain might unlock it and how we could snatch it without him catching us.

"I know nothing." She was lying. She was also too addled to maintain her veneer very long. She didn't really want to. Lily sat her down.

"Let me get this clear, Nadine. Dashnell is fixing to blow up the county. But you don't know anything about it?"

"That's right."

"Then how do you know Dashnell is fixing to blow up the county?" Rose chimed in.

"He called Sidney."

"Why?"

"I don't know." You could see by the way she set her jaw that she did. I figured I'd cut through some of her net.

"Dashnell thought Sidney had access to the arsenal?"

"Sidney don't know nothing about no arsenal."

"What's Dashnell planning to use to blow up the county?"

"I thought I heard him to tell Sidney dynamite."

"Where would Dashnell get dynamite?"

"I have no idea."

"What the *hell* do you want?" That was Miss Eula, waked by the commotion, still pulling her bathrobe over her slip as she came into the room. At that moment, in that light she looked maybe a hundred and nine and mad as hell.

"I just thought you should know."

"You obviously think you're talking to pack of damned fools, Nadine." Miss Eula was beet red with disgust.

"Never mind, then!" Nadine tried, starting for the front door as if she had been greatly aggrieved.

"Set down." It was turning into Miss Eula's show. It was something to see. "Set!" She said it with such force that all of us sat immediately. It was as if she had some private score to settle with Nadine. Everything got quiet. Then I spoke up.

"Let me get this straight. Dashnell Lawler called out to your house and spoke to Sidney. He wanted access to the arsenal, the collection of guns and such that the Order keeps hidden somewhere in these parts?"

"Is that what he was talking about?" Nadine tried to sound convincing. Miss Eula let loose a string of bile that we couldn't exactly follow, words to the effect that Nadine could leave off her cow eyed innocence, she wasn't running her mouth with that coven of hypocrite churchwomen up at Winn Dixie now. Whatever it meant, it worked. Nadine's face relaxed and her eyes returned to normal.

"Sidney is a good man. He's too easy led and sometimes gets pressured by some of the other men into doing things he doesn't want to do. . . ." She was coming down to it now. The upshot of what she said was that Dashnell had gotten into the arsenal and taken an undisclosed amount of dynamite. With the second largest civil rights demonstration in history only hours away, it wasn't hard to put a finger on his intent.

Nobody bothered asking the fool woman why she hadn't gone straight to the police. She was scared Sidney would be exposed for the Klucker garbage he truly is. Lily made Nadine a cup of tea and I called the sheriff's office. Then I called Hez, but he said with every able lawman in the state on patrol and the eyes of the world on Prince George, he didn't see where we had much to fear from a drunk redneck and a stick of dynamite. I had learned a lot from Hez in the preceding days. Most of it boiled down to thinking before I spoke. Still, I knew he was wrong about this. Like all vermin, these Kluckers are experts at hiding. You can't underestimate that. James Earl Ray had shot Martin Luther King and killed a whole movement. Dashnell held James Earl Ray up as a knighted saint, a hero who had offered himself as sacrifice to a noble cause. This was Dashnell's once in a lifetime chance to have the eyes of the world on him. He'd cheerfully blow himself up with a hundred innocent people to achieve that. He'd burrow into the ground or hole up in a hollow log or crawl into the trunk of a parked car and wait for his moment of evil and glory.

I called Hez back three times over the next hour. His office had shut down for the night. I tried his home, but the machine kicked in and the message tape was full. The sheriff's men showed up a few minutes later. I called their office every few minutes for the next two or three hours. No one knew anything. No one ever does in Prince George County. The night was racing past. I had to do something. I slipped on my jacket, got into my truck and went to join the hunt.

74
Rose of Sharon

Mother got short with Nadine that night. I felt sorry for her. I know what it is to live with a man like Sidney. I know what a painful thing it is to endure thoughts you can't express for fear of the back of his hand. I've been intimate with all those torments and I would still be if fate hadn't intervened. It went all through me to watch that poor woman quake as she talked to the highway patrolman. Sidney would break her arms if he found out.

Heath called the sheriff's office every fifteen minutes for the next hour. They claimed they were out looking for Dashnell. I just couldn't shake the feeling that the most terrible thing I ever experienced was about to take place. Mother pulled on some clothes and went back into the kitchen and started cutting biscuits. Lily and I half played a game of hearts.

Somewhere in there we got the information that Dashnell had been arrested and charged with murder that morning. All the Klavern members questioned had signed statements promising to testify against him. This was a whole lot more than evil Klan business as usual for Dashnell. This was him against the world. There was going to be blood on the road in the morning.

Lily threw her hand down in disgust, "Y'all, we ought to be out there looking for him." I failed to see the wisdom of that. Dashnell was armed and surely drunk. He'd have no qualms about shooting any one of us sober, much less in that condition. I said as much.

"They'll find him," Heath said, biting into his thumbnail. Lily fussed at him to quit that. Heath called the sheriff's office again. This time they had news. Someone had tipped them off as to the whereabouts of that arsenal. The sheriff's deputies had found it broken into and guns and dynamite was missing. By now there was a steady stream of patrol cars and searchlights rolling up and down the road. In fact there were so many lights it created a kind of blue gray, false dawn. Now and then we'd hear a group of searchers passing quickly on foot. Mother had gone out onto the porch without her coat. I went to bring her back inside.

"Get on in this house before you catch your death, Mother."

"I've lived this night before," she says. Then she followed me back into the house. I'd really like to know what all was said at our house that night. There was all kind of strange sentiment expressed. Voices and faces blurred. I kept trying to pray. Lily and Heath kept snapping at each other. The only calm one was Mother and she kept saying it over and over: "I've lived this night before."

Lily said if they didn't find Dashnell, then Satan and an army of machine guns might as well meet those marchers. The results would be the same. Heath had his coat by then. Lily asked him where he was going. He said he was going to find Dashnell. Lily called him a damned fool. She was drowned out by the noisy passing of a National Guard convoy. I counted twenty trucks piled with soldiers. Before Lily could resume, Heath was standing in the door.

"Y'all keep away from that march unless you hear back from me." He was gone. Lily went half crazy cursing him. It was easier to let her rave on than to try to make her hush.

"Now see here," Mother cut into her ranting. "That reverend can't call off his march. That reverend knows if he calls off his march, the sheriff and them will call off their search for Dashnell and a lot will have passed for naught."

"Mother, that's for the want of sense! Saving people's lives isn't for naught." Everything I ever held on to was crumbling. It felt like the house was rolling back and forth. My mind would run off on tangents the length of a football field, but when I came back around and looked at the clock, sometimes only twenty or thirty seconds had passed.

After eternity I could see daylight running a low dark pink streak behind the trees across the road. I imagined that down in Birmingham marchers had already begun lining up for their bus ride up to Prince George. You could smell death. You could almost touch it. Lily caught a radio news report. There was a search for an armed terrorist in Prince George. So far march leader Reverend Hezekiah Thomas was not available for comment.

"Well, they must have a thousand men out there looking for him," Lily says, putting on the television to catch the early news. There wasn't a word about Dashnell. But they showed hundreds and hundreds of people gathering at a line of Greyhound buses that stretched as far as you could make out. There were a lot of children and mothers in that crowd. I felt like I had swallowed a bushel of scrap iron.

They switched to the front of the bus line where Scenicruisers were already beginning to pull out for Prince George. "I'm calling down there to that television station and warning them about Dashnell," I says.

"You'll do no such of a thing!" Mother laid her hand on the telephone. Lily came and laid her hand on Mother's shoulder. "These people have to be warned, Miss Eula," she says a little too kindly. Mother won't sit still for being talked to as if she's senile. Mother pulled that cord around her hand a half dozen times and jerked it from the wall.

"You'll bide and you'll let destiny take its course," she growled. "Nothing you say or do will make the slightest difference."

Suddenly it was as if the room had five corners. Nothing made sense. Heath had gone off to find Dashnell despite the fact that a thousand others were already searching. The reverend had refused to call off his march even though it meant untold numbers of innocent people might be killed. Mother was jerking the telephone out of the wall.

Lillian was staring out the living room window . . . I told her not worry about Heath. Then mother sighed.

"What is it, Mother?"

"I don't know, baby girl." I couldn't say when she last called me that.

Then we stopped; listening hard, and Mother said, "The angels are coming." It was faint and it was far away, but it was singing and it was sweet and you had to believe if only for a second, that the Kingdom was coming home.

75
Heath

It was drizzling. The rain came in strings that made slush piles on the hood when it dropped off the windshield wipers. I had to drive slowly. There were search parties carrying flashlights everywhere. A state chopper had landed in Miss Eula's lower pasture and three men were struggling to untangle the leashes of a half dozen bloodhounds. It felt like some devil's parade out there. I lost track of how many different local and state and military guys stopped me and searched the truck. I was beginning to think Hez had been right. If Dashnell was within fifty square miles, he was done for.

I kept thinking, he'd probably been planning this for some time. Those Kluckers are like rodents when it comes to burrowing themselves in. Like most cowards, Kluckers hide deep. I remember once when my grandfather's barn burned to the ground. The ashes were barely cool before the rats swarmed up out of the cool ground below to feast on the seared carcasses of the mules.

Still I was afraid that some commanding state police officer would decide that Dashnell wasn't in these parts and call off the hunt. I had visions of hundreds and hundreds of innocent people walking arm-in-arm into sudden hellfire. I saw heads ripped off shoulders and bloody arms flying. After a while it became clear that it was useless to search from the truck. The other vehicles and the searchers were in my way. I pulled over and felt the left side of the truck mire down in the muddy shoulder. I started searching the low brush that sloped down into the woods at the side of the road. I knew I was covering ground that had been examined by hundreds of other eyes in the last few hours. I'd work a quarter mile of undergrowth on one side of the road, then I'd work my way back on the opposite side. I'd get back into my truck and fight mud until I moved forward to a new starting point and began the process all over again. After about forty-five minutes I left my flashlight in the truck. The sky was dark purple gray and there was pink mist in the woods. The tree limbs were already beginning to glisten with ice. There would be half an inch on them by noon. It was dreary, hopeless work. My hands and feet burned with wet cold.

Hell is a damp Alabama February night. I worked my way around a curve to where the road inclined sharply down towards Potts River Bridge.

At first I thought the singing was the cold or my tired mind inventing comfort. My eyes were bleary and every shadow, every voice in the distance, seemed like an echo from the dark and troubled past. There were no words yet, only voices far and dim. It was spitting snow. The sun in the east was still below the clouds and it gave an intolerable luminescence to the wet, leafless trees and the red mud and cracked asphalt. It illumined all the ugliness.

I stopped a trooper to ask if there was any word. No sign of him, he told me. He was someplace close and hidden. He was waiting for his moment. It seemed to me as my eyes searched the stinging damp that Dashnell Lawler and his kind would eventually inherit the earth, that evil was indefatigable, more tenacious than good.

Dashnell Lawler was out there someplace, an invisible and unconquerable force of evil. Innocent people were about to die. I was powerless to do anything to stop it.

I could make out the words now. "Mine eyes have seen the glory . . ." All righteousness, all hearts aglow, and marching into danger, into torment, into hell because Dashnell Lawler waited like an eternal blight on a godless land. I could see the first wave of marchers topping the hill at the Prince George County about a half mile ahead. There was no time to make Hez listen to reason. We had to stop them.

My feet hit the ice covered bridge and I was spinning, fighting for balance, as the voices grew louder and my head hit the frozen wood. Then blackness and stars as the bridge began to shake from their approaching cadence. Then my eyes were open and I saw the brown and green blurring motion below. It wasn't water. It was rocks moving. No. It was a rippling sheet of khaki. Then I saw a hand. Now an arm as the singing threatened to deafen me and the pain of my fall exploded. Now it was a figure, leaning forward, holding a lighted match. Him. It was Dashnell and the match was touching a fuse. I waved my arms and I hollered, but there was no sound save the hymn of approaching death. Then a bullet sang louder than the throng and Dashnell slumped forward, his arm, his hand and the burning fuse slipped into the water.

Two pairs of arms were pulling me up to my feet. I was moving away from where men in uniforms were leaping over the side of the bridge. The next thing I remember is drifting free above a thousand singing heads. When I came to I was lying on a stretcher in the hospital emergency room and my head burned like pine tar. I'm told I slept two days. My picture had been in *The Birmingham News*. The President had sent me a telegram. People were calling from Los Angeles to see if I wanted them to make a television movie about me. Lily and I laughed a long time about that.

76
Eula Pearl

Life will devil and vex you. It'll slap you back down onto the very soil out of which you have struggled a lifetime to rise. It'll lay more torment on your soul than you can bear. Some take strength from their pains and rise above them. Others bend to them and fall away forever. I keep trudging forward, if there's any such thing as forward.

It isn't what you know. Life is what you touch. It's what to hold dear even when holding is no more than dreaming or remembering. I chose Moena. I held and let go of many others. But I kept Moena close.

I had an unusually deep sleep after lunch on the Friday afternoon before the big march. When I woke up around three o'clock, there were highway patrolmen combing the yard. Lily said they were looking for possible sniper hideouts.

I was shaking off a dream and it didn't register what she meant. I had awakened with a sudden thing to be done that moment. The dream had flown off and left it for me.

I will need to do a thing three forevers, put it off over and over again for no reason and then suddenly find myself in the middle of doing it. Searle used to call that doing things on God's time. But often as not these things will fall out of an afternoon nap. That's how it was with me and those iris bulbs that afternoon.

As quick as I was as awake as I get these days, I dragged a sack of frozen iris bulbs out from the deep freeze. They're easy planted. You don't even have to dig a hole. Just toss them where you want them to grow and sprinkle some silt on the rhizome. Rose, who hates my irises, asked me what in thunder I was doing. I get worn with people waiting for me to go crazy. I just muttered, "None a ya . . ." and went on out the back door. It was already spitting drizzle. It was right windy, too, especially for February. There was water in that sharp breeze and I knew, if it kept up, it would be blowing ice by sundown. I found a calm, sheltered spot on the south side of the house and I set to work. The topsoil was frozen, but the ground beneath was soft. Rose of Sharon had worked all the dirt around the foundation. I didn't have but maybe a dozen to plant.

Sometimes you get to thinking your time is hanging over you. You see yourself all laid out pretty. You hear the talk. You imagine people running their hands over your things after you're in the ground. Imagining all that isn't really dying or how it is. That's trying to live forever.

Other times, you measure the resistance in your shoulders to the weight of the day ahead to calculate how much strength you have left and you know it's coming and the only sense you can make is bending into it. Sometimes you don't do an important thing because you think you're only living to see it finished. But its realness sneaks up on you. Its realness catches you quiet, alone, fluffing your pillow some interminable night. You stay awake and wait for it hoping you can scare it away. Or maybe it doesn't sit right, the notion of dying while you're asleep, because if you have to die, then you ought to know when it's happening. You ought to experience it. Maybe you do anyway.

It was nineteen hundred and forty-seven when Searle took it in his head to plow the pasture where the graves were. The stones had long since fallen and crumbled. To the casual eye it was no more than a wide snarl of Johnsongrass. But it was holy ground to me. They had built a church to go with it. It had burned in the Trouble. I forbade him to disturb it.

Searle was planting everything but the front yard in cotton that year of '47. The price of cotton had jumped over the moon. He saw it as a snarl of weed that he could turn into another bale. But I remembered when Moena's granny had been buried there. That had been well over fifty years back even then. I believe to my soul Moena's granny was the last to be laid to rest in that cemetery. I just couldn't think of a tractor disturbing her bones, if it was even any bones left by then. Searle argued strenuously with me that those dead had long been dust; they was gone back to dirt. The purpose of dirt was to resurrect life, to return it another form. I says, "Fine. Go plant cotton on your mama's grave!" That stopped him.

So back then in '47 I went down there to the graves on the pasture's edge with two hired men. The three of us dug post holes and strung barbed wire to save it from Searle's ambitions. It was the thick of June. There was heavy Johnsongrass and thistle and crumbled and cracked cement from the tombstones and I don't know what all. It was hot work. One of them found the clump of irises. They weren't more than little spears choked back and shaded by grasses. It made no sense to weed them. Field grass will take a patch of irises in three days. So I dug them out as careful as I could. I remembered it like yesterday. The year before her long illness and the Trouble, my grandmother had given those irises to Moena so she could plant them on her granny's grave. I had gone there with Moena when we were six years old. We had pressed them into the fresh mound of dirt. It had given us both a lovely comfort.

That was worth more to me than an extra bale of cotton. Searle had come up poor. He had watched his daddy lose everything to the bank while he was off fighting the First War. Searle had a regard for money in the bank that I never completely learned. Nadine's curiosity about my savings isn't totally unfounded. Searle left me well beyond a million when he passed. I had nearly another million he never knew about. That was from mother's aunts dying off one by one. With leasing out the land and putting back a little from my Social Security, I've near about doubled it all over the last twenty years. I don't think Rosie knows, but she'll have a wad to spend as she sees fit when I'm finished dancing on this tired earth. Though to hear her tell it, she's put by plenty of her own down the years. Thrift has always run through the women in our family.

I had intended to set out those irises the day we took them up in '47. But Mother, whose health broke fast that year, had a spell that afternoon and I had to carry her into White Oak to see the doctor. I had little enough time to string fence in a pasture and less for setting out irises. I set them by the back step and there they lay one whole summer. Then one fall afternoon I swooped them up and dumped them into the deep freeze on the back porch to prevent them from sprouting.

A thing stays in a place for a time and we forget how it got there or why. It just sits there and little by little it becomes its own reason for being there. It takes a certain power over us that way. I moved that sack of bulbs twice when I bought new freezers. The last time was about fifteen years ago. Even then, I wasn't freezing sides of meat and garden truck like I once did. A few weeks back Rose of Sharon bought the new side-by-side refrigerator-freezer saying we had no use for the deep freeze anymore. We gave it to the Goodwill. Last thing I did before they hauled it away was reach inside it and pull out that sack of iris bulbs. I pitched them right back where they had spent that summer forty years ago beside the back steps.

I finally put those bulbs in the ground that Friday afternoon late with Rose of Sharon fussing over my shoulder and the frozen wind burning my neck.

"Mother, why are you out here in this cold and wet planting irises?"

Rose of Sharon kept moaning about the cold and I kept telling her to go into the house. She tried to take the shovel from me once, but I jerked it away with a velocity that confirmed for me that this was my thing to do, my pardon to finish.

"Mother, what in thunder are you doing?"

"Doing?" I says, sprinkling the last rhizome with frozen, powdered leaves, "I'm done, child." We were back in the kitchen two minutes later, me at the table and Rose hovering over the teakettle. "Mother, I really wonder about you sometimes."

"I wonder about you too, Rose." That quieted her. Not my

words, but the weight of their intent. It was a day for turning more things over than tired ground and iris bulbs.

"What do you wonder about me, Mother?"

"I wonder how with all your nurturing goodness you have come this far without fixing your heart completely on something and loving it beyond all cost." I thought she'd come back at me with Carmen, because a mother will love her child beyond cost. But that's a given thing. I meant something different and I was gratified to see she knew it.

"I don't know." She was hurt. She looked like she might crack in two. I almost wished she would just so I could see down into the middle inside of her and understand her insides. I should have been sorry I had opened my mouth; but I felt the time slipping beneath me and I wanted to know if it was something I had held back. I wanted to hand it over to her now while I was still drawing breath.

"I've always been a disappointment to you, haven't I?"

I listened hard, but I couldn't discern even a trace of self-pity. She sincerely wanted my answer.

"Yes."

"Why?"

I wanted to box her ears and shout that she tried to put a frame around everything and an engraved brass explanation underneath it.

"Because you are a fearful person, Rose of Sharon. You live in fear. You married in fear. You run home in fear. After I'm gone, you'll cower around this house in fear like your own ghost!"

It was as if I had sheared a layer of her skin. I have no word for the expression on her face just then. That's because she wasn't feeling as much as she was thinking through what I had just said. But she came right back in a split second with a retort.

"Well, at least I have been to Texas!" She said it so straight and flat and fully that there was nothing either of us could do but fall out laughing.

"Rose," I cackled, "that's the most ridiculous thing I ever heard.

"Mother," she spit out between giggles, "it's the most ridiculous thing I ever heard and I'm the one who said it." We must have been loud because Lillian peeked in to see what the noise was. But she sensed a communion that couldn't include her at the moment and she quickly vanished.

"Why don't you, Mother?"

"What?"

"Live in fear."

"Because there's nothing to fear in this world, child." Rose of Sharon drank my words. I could see by the wry turn of her bottom lip that they had taken.

"Mother, you know things." It comforts the young to believe that about the old. "Why didn't you teach me that forty years ago, Mother?"

"It can't be taught," I says, "any more than you can learn to pray until you let God steal into your heart. You have to live your way to it. Rose, there's no pain in this world like fear."

"No, ma'am, there isn't," she said, and a veil that had separated us was lifted. Though neither one of us made an immediate comment. We sat in living silence for a good while. Rose cleared her throat.

"I want to get to know you more before you die, Mother."

"You will," I said, wondering as I always do if I was taking my last breath.

"Mother, what were you doing out there in the cold planting irises?"

The warm tea had steadied me. "It's just something I've been meaning to do." That pacified her. I was glad. Rose went back upstairs. I poured more tea and I sat a good while. I was trying to remember my dream, but it wouldn't come back to me. It was enough that I had finally thrown a little piece of Moena to grow against the back of the house. But there was more to it. A good deal more was turning that day than tired leaves and irises. A little ball of eternity was gathering that Friday afternoon, drawing up fragments of time and event. In less than twenty-four hours, all the days of my life would show me their accumulated meaning.

It would make a better story to say that I sensed it sitting there in the kitchen watching the gray sky glow pink through the wet branches of leafless trees. But the longer I sat there, the more my thoughts turned to pie. I pulled the flour canister from the cupboard. I dug out my sifter and I set to work peeling apples.

77
Hezekiah

Hez went to laughing so hard when he saw the multitudes, he thought his head would split in two. There wasn't an available bus between Birmingham and the Gulf Coast, or any other coast for that matter. He had rented every one. As close as he could tell, he was going to be about forty-five coaches shy. Forty-three chartered airplanes were scheduled to land, one all the way from Stockholm. There was so much traffic backed up out of the airport, they said it was taking people three hours to make the two-mile trip to downtown Birmingham.

The first demonstrators would arrive at the Prince George County Courthouse two hours before the last left the King memorial site thirty-two miles to the south. Just before the march commenced, Hez tried to reach Heath at the number he had given him up in White Oak. He wanted an update on that Klucker who was apparently planning to blow them all to kingdom come. It didn't matter. It wasn't that Hez was Oblivious of the danger. Hez had every intention of making damned sure the man had been apprehended before they crossed into Prince George County. He couldn't let Heath know that. Things were sounding pretty hysterical from up at Prince George. Hez was afraid if he delayed the march as much as an hour, the lawmen up there would let up their search. Or word would get out and the Klan in general would get inspired. He could halt the march at the county line if it became necessary. He had prayed fervently through the night that it wouldn't.

As nearly as anybody could estimate, they were expecting forty thousand. They were coming from New York and they were coming from old York, England. They were flying in from Nome, Alaska, and Calcutta, India, and Buenos Aires, Argentina. They were rolling down the highways so fast and thick, you couldn't get a hotel room anyplace in central Alabama. It was all because a national news broadcast had run a thirty second videotape of the Kluckers hurling bricks and bottles at them during the last march.

So far, his office had handled seven hundred thousand dollars in contributions. Hez had spoken with the President as well as the heads of a dozen foreign countries. Every politician who was running for office within five thousand miles had agreed to walk at the front of the march along with Mrs. King, mayors, senators, representatives and several dozen college and church choirs.

The phone rang and Hez started laughing all over again. This time he was laughing at his addled sister Dereesa. She was fit because their mama was insisting on marching. That meant Dereesa would be stuck with the task of pushing her wheelchair up and down hills the full five mile route. Dereesa was claiming lumbago and insomnia and nerves and every other ailment she could manufacture. Moena was set like three-week-old cement. Dereesa was going to have to roll her mama home. The notion rested like a benediction or a blessing on Hez's shoulders. His mama would touch the sacred soil of her ancestry and close the troubled circle of her life's journey.

78
Rose of Sharon

A little before eight that Saturday morning, a highway patrolman came to the door and told us that Heath had suffered a concussion from a fall. He said that Heath would be all right, that it wouldn't amount to much more than a bad headache for a few days. The man wasn't down the front steps before Nadine came running. It was from her that I learned I had become a widow and Heath Lawler was a hero on the national news.

The marchers were getting closer. We had heard their singing gradually grow louder for the last half hour or so. Nadine was feeling like a heroine because, after all, she had tipped us off about Dashnell. She wouldn't join the marchers with me for fear of what Sidney might do. But she was feeling celebratory enough to offer to drive Lily up to the hospital to see about Heath. In a woman like Nadine that amounts to largesse.

When the first line of them streamed over the crest, the ground began to tremble. Soon wave over wave streamed past, singing and carrying signs and laughing and talking. This was pure celebration, a parade of hearts, a healing stream gushing over a broken land.

It was bitter cold. Now and again the wind gusted. They had walked a long way in winter coats and they looked hot and tired. I took the garden hose down by the fence and let those who wanted pause to drink from it. A lady from Detroit stopped to fill her thermos. We chatted a minute. I asked her did she mind if I walked beside her. We talked needlepoint and hooked rugs all the way to the courthouse steps where the speeches were beginning.

The minister from Birmingham opened his Bible. He said he was about to read us all he knew and ever hoped to know. He said the words contained his whole life. His voice just cascaded. It washed over this forlorn place like a lost river flowing home.

"And the ransomed of the Lord
shall return . . . with singing;
Everlasting joy shall be upon them;
And sorrow and sighing shall
flee away."

79

Eula Pearl

Lord, come for Thy world! All that can be seen, has been seen. Lord, come! It was an ocean, a giant sea of heads and arms swaying down the hill. You have never heard the likes of their singing. It was perfection. It was beautiful. It shone like the Rapture. I stood on my front porch trembling before the majesty of it. They raised such a joyful noise the windows were rattling.

Nadine had run Lillian up to town. Rose had joined the throng. I had a mind to do the same, but I honestly didn't know if I was able.

There were women with dots on their foreheads wrapped in bright silk. There were bearded men in dark suits and stovepipe hats. Now and then there would be young men with long hair strumming guitars and young ladies in striped shawls. They called to mind some of Carmen's friends from his college days. They passed like a river of happiness. My arms grew weary from waving at them. Everything was whirling and glistening and echoing sweet. I thought the happy energy was going to bear me aloft.

I had to sit down for a while and remind myself that I was still of this realm. It was as if I had suddenly encountered the Face of Heaven and it was more alive, more beautiful and living, than I had ever dared imagine. It pleased me to know that Rose was a part of this breathing miracle. For all this, I still had Dashnell heavy on my mind. It come to me all of a flash that this was pure and holy joy, that Dashnell must have intuited that it would be, that he lived in utter terror of so much shining sensation.

After an eternity of bliss I noticed the crowd was beginning to thin out a little. There were several people in wheelchairs now, young men with withered, useless legs and muscled arms and healthy faces rolling themselves along in God's Army. My arms and legs were getting stiff from sitting in the cold. I stood to move inside the house. I took one last look, letting my eyes wander over the moving heads and up the hill where an arrow of sunlight had broken through. I saw a shining thing appear at the very top and soon realized it was another wheelchair. Something round and purple and swirling seemed to hover over it. But as they moved down the hill and out of the sun towards me, I saw it was a woman in a purple coat pushing an old lady in a wheelchair. I couldn't help but think that poor old thing must be shaking with cold. The wind had picked up and the temperature was dropping. She was tucked in under a blanket, but she had to be freezing to death. I stepped down off the porch and approached the road and to ask if she wanted to come inside to warm up a spell. As they moved closer I could see that the lady pushing the chair was miserable and exhausted. I knew they couldn't hear me for all the singing, so I waved to get their attention. The woman guided the chair towards where I stood at the side of the road. As she did, my eyes locked into those of the old woman in the chair.

I knew those eyes. I had always known those eyes. I had felt them watching me a thousand summer afternoons. I had remembered them in countless troubled dreams. I had waited for them, watched them leaving, prayed for their return.

"Moena!?" I gasped, my chest pounding, my hands shaking, the ground beneath me beginning to soften.

"Eula!" That tired old face drew back into a grin and she stood up and threw her arms around me. I held her with all I had left in me, held everything that mattered, and I prayed, "Take me *now,* God, take me in this sunburst with the singing in my ears and her trembling arms around me."

My legs began to buckle and someone righted me. Moena sank back into the wheelchair.

"Eula," she moaned, the accrued sadness of her years swelling up over her and swirling around and around. "Oh, God!" we cried in unison, weeping and trembling and I pulled her right out of that chair and clung to her neck all over again like a twig in a torrent.

I caught my breath a moment to be sure I wasn't dying—that this wasn't a tender illusion fate had provided to ease me out of this world. Then Moena giggled and I knew she was real.

Everything after that blurs until somehow I was sitting in the parlor and Moena was opposite me and no one knew what to say or how to begin. Rose came home eventually and I cried so hard I couldn't explain it so Dereesa, Moena's daughter, did. Others came later. Lily. Moena's son Hezekiah, the reverend. It was like when Searle died. I was home amid a houseful. People were doing all around me and I let them because I had no will of my own. I do recall much later that evening, the reverend and Dereesa said that it was time to fetch Moena home. I did rise to that occasion. "Moena is home," I says. "Now, no more about it." Moena snorted a giant laugh when I said that. I must have been direct and forceful and true when I spoke, because it wasn't long before the reverend and Dereesa said their good-byes and went on back to Birmingham.

The next day turned warmer towards midafternoon. Moena and I walked across the road and stood about where Jake and Beauty B.'s house had been. Moena said she got a feeling for the place by looking back across the road at our house. She said it hadn't changed a lick. I reckon Rosie has near about put it back to rights. Moena probably wouldn't have said that a year ago.

By the by we wandered on down to the old cemetery spot. I told her about taking up the iris bulbs and she told me I had no call to take them and I had to put them back. I offered the best explanation I could for my actions, but she wasn't interested. We liked to have gotten into it right there, except Lily came over to say that a reporter from *The New York Times* was at the house and wanted to take our picture.

80

Hezekiah

We drove back up to Prince George several times that spring to visit Mama. She grew increasingly frail as the weeks passed. Finally, when she could no longer stand of her own accord, Rose of Sharon set up a bed in the parlor. Ironically, the ancient blindness revisited her in those last weeks. Miss Eula, who was herself noticeably weaker, rarely left Mama's side day or night. She hovered over her, whispering in her ear, plaiting and replaiting her hair or wiping her cheeks with damp towels. In the end my mama died in her sleep on the land where she was born.

Heath raised a crew and cleared the old cemetery at the edge of the pasture behind Miss Eula's house. We buried her there on a gray Sunday morning towards the end of June. *The Washington Post* told her story, how she had been driven out and how she came home, a native of Prince George County, its first black citizen in almost eighty years and the only one of the thousands who fled to actually return.

Three months later Heath phoned to say that they would lay Miss Eula beside her the following morning.

It was a dry September afternoon. After the service we sat on the porch: Heath and Lily, Rose of Sharon and me. We talked until after the sun had gone down and a new moon hung tender over the trees in the east. We shared pieces of the story, patching and weaving it together by turns until we understood how it had brought us to that place and bound us to each other. Returning late on the road back to Birmingham, I understood too how the past is a work in progress, one generation handing down to the next its unfinished toils, adding onto an eternal chain of human endeavor, struggling and straining and stretching beyond the bounds of our own time into eternity.